Hospityable

Part One
of
The Donald Diaries

Also by David Halpin:

The Nobody Saga:
Poetry and Random Thoughts from a Depressed Mind
(Autobiography of a Nobody)

More of the Same
(Continued Saga of a Nobody)

Some More of the Same but Better
(Episode Three of the Nobody Saga)

Even More of the Same and Even Better
(Chapter 4 of the Nobody Saga)

Yet More of the Same ... Still Better
(Book V of the Nobody Saga)

Much More of the Same ... Gratuitously Better
(Book 卌 / of the Nobody Saga)

Bigger and Better ... Sameness
(Lucky #7 of the Nobody Saga)

Other:
Numpty-Rhymes, Numpty-Bys and Numpty-Songs
(Poetry from Numpty's Doctor's Brother's Goose)

Hospityable

Part One
of
The Donald Diaries

David Halpin

This is purely a work of fiction. (Mostly, at least, but I didn't say that. ☺)

Names of characters and places have been altered, events have been grossly exaggerated, and reality has taken a veritable beating, all in the name of having some good clean fun. (And making money, obviously; unless you stole this from your local Oil Rig, which makes you bad and naughty!) Any resemblance to actual persons (Breathing or Not) or events (Real, Unreal, or Not Real) is coincidental. (If it protects me from some, any, or all litigation, it is a huge bonus).

Any breaking out of character, bursting out in laughter, or sides being split (or even someone looking at you funny) is *Your Problem* now, as you have just read this warning. I think it is a little bit fiendish to have this *In the Beginning* before any of the documented hilarious, but fictional events have had a chance to ensue. That is unless I came up with an extra-large helping of amusing for the back page, as you probably haven't read this warning yet.

This book is not intended to be a substitute for medical advice from anyone. You should regularly consult with any number of Psychiatrists, Psychologists, Psychics or Psychopaths until you are convinced your almost-funny-bone is still intact. But seriously, this book is meant to make you laugh. Don't try and think too much about any of it. It should come as no surprise to learn I didn't. Like any dangerous activity, projectile *blurtation* of a mouthful of liquid may occur. Be mindful of this if you are drinking a hot coffee or a nice Chianti.

ISBN: 9781922751201

Dedicated to:

Everyone who has ever had a disability - of any kind
Everyone who has ever cared for these people
And all of the wonderful people at SJOG!
Re: SJOG (Inspired by the St. John of God, North Richmond legends) p268.
* Extract from The Donald Diaries.

My GP (Dr T)
My Psychiatrist (Dr J)
and My Psychologist (Mrs A)
In order of my appearance to them.

My crazy friend Charles Wiseman.

And introducing Chuck Norris as Chunky Poopy

Comments:

"OMG Just read the **<spoiler>** chapter. Hilarious! Laughed out loud."
Lady M

"Sorry… I like to think I am NOT laughing *at Mental* people… I'm using these *severely exaggerated* personal experiences to try and get people to laugh. If this provides even a touch of education or understanding to the stereotypical *Normal* population, then I feel my project may have been worthwhile. If it also provides me with some money, then more's the better! (Much more, please).

A fat man can talk about the idiosyncrasies of fat men (and race isn't an issue), a short woman can talk about the peculiarities of short women (and age isn't an issue), and a mentally different person can talk about the eccentricities of mentally different people (and the flavour of issue, ironically, isn't an issue).

I am not meaning to trivialise any disability (of any kind), anyone, or anything. I believe this story is not laughing *at* us; it is laughing *with* us. However, this is a slight distinction, and if anyone is offended, even slightly, I am truly sorry…."
Extract from The Donald Diaries.

Table of Contents

Tables of Dis-Content

Introduction

Enter the protagonist, the hero,[1] the star... Donald.

Donald Halfbrain is a quiet, unassuming and intelligent character who is simply perfect for the narrative of this comedic, semi-autobiographical and semi-fantastical but oh-so-very-close-to-reality semi-whimsical yarn.

Just by reading a short way into this story, you will come to understand Donald is also completely, absolutely and undeniably bonkers. Throughout his whole life of 50^2 years, he has surrounded himself with activity but has never actively participated in any of the activities. He has been there to cheer on, to console, to applaud and to be extremely proud of... But he has never been on the receiving end of any sort of favourable scrutiny.

Until now...

Donald has lived most of his relatively ordinary life doing a lot of nothing exceptional, some nothing creative and a bit less than nothing noteworthy. He is just your average, everyday, *normal* man. He struggled through his early formative growing up years, as everyone did; he struggles with his friendships, as everyone does; and he struggles to make sure he fits in, as everyone should. This is how Donald tries to project and thus protect himself. He puts on a very brave face for the outside world, and as it is such a good mask, most people don't have a single clue of what is so substantially wrong with him.

---

[1]   If you could be convinced to call a single fluorescent orange witch's hat, directing you around a piece of maintenance to the road of life, a *hero*.

[2]   Or maybe *fifty* years? I should probably figure out these figures before I go too much further. The number two footnote reference makes it look like 50 squared... Donald isn't 2500 (or two thousand five hundred) years old, just in case you are thinking, erroneously, that he is absurdly ancient.

Waking up one day, and that *one day* for Donald is today, to find himself surrounded by a euphemistic *hospital* aura was quite a shock to his system. This was the very same system to have never failed him before. He didn't really think his life had been going so badly. He had, however, never in his entire life been quite so completely, absolutely and undeniably wrong... Granted, this situation would be a particularly unusual situation for many people, and it is also, probably, a seriously clichéd one for a comedic, semi-autobiographical and semi-fantastical but oh-so-very-close-to-reality semi-whimsical yarn...

For this lone man, Donald Halfbrain, it was going to be:

Story Defining...

Life-Changing...

Legend Creating...

Cue the drums da-da-da-dum...
Camera pulling back into a wide heroic shot...
Wind blowing through his hair...

Pulling up his not necessarily so metaphorical Happy Socks, his favourites were the reddish Where's Wally?-esque ones; Donald, our intrepid Hero, set out to explore this wild new environment, the small microcosm he would be calling his home... For at least the next few weeks anyway...

Welcome to: Saint Rita's Sanatorium for the Clinically Mental[3] and
Hospityable: Part One
In the series of
The Donald Diaries.

---

[3]   Saint Rita is known as the "Patron Saint of the Impossible." Seriously! You couldn't get a better name for an institution if you were trying to write a fictional comedy novel... Err, um, cough... Continue reading please...

Chapter 1:
Monday Morning
(Bedroom)

Waking up slowly, Donald reached over to turn his as-yet-silent alarm clock off and to grab his glasses from his nightstand, only to find there was a wall where there shouldn't have been one. This created much confusion in his morning stupor. Why would he have moved his bedroom furniture while he was sleeping? He opened his eyes…

Ahhhhh…!

Sitting up on what he could only assume was Baby Bear's bed, Donald fumbled around in the semi-darkness of early morning and completely failed to find his bedside table lamp, his CPAP machine, his emergency medication, or any of a million other of his things that could have been there. He looked for something familiar to provide him with a small degree of understanding about his current situation. His hand found what felt like a panel of switches on the wall, and not caring about the result, Donald started switching with gay abandon. Three clicks later, a tiny far, far away light, situated surprisingly directly above his head, turned on. When this light was added to the, also very tiny, but not so far away, light coming in from the window, Donald was able to deduce, "Puppy, I've a feeling we're not at home anymore."

Putting on his confused face, Donald jump-started his mind, unfocussed his eyes, cocked his head to a thinking stance and became slightly nostalgic. Donald has always been infatuated with time. He has been punctual to every place he has ever needed to be; he has always been behind the times with his electronic gadgetry, and he firmly believes the trite *Time Will Heal All Wounds* comforting cliché is complete bunkum.

Furthermore, he has read *A Brief History of Time* and understood some of it; *The Wheel of Time* books and persevered to the very end; and the *What's the Time, Mr Wolf?* book without being eaten. Knowing *The Time* for Donald was not optional; it was an ordered obsessive compulsion. His internal clock was uncanny with its accuracy, and it was telling him, "Oh, I guess it's about half, or a little bit more, or less maybe, past nine o'clock.[4]"

The first, but by no means the greatest, obstacle Donald noticed[5] was his complete and utter[6] lack of clothing. None! Zero! Zip! Being unaccustomed to exposing himself, even in front of a dirty mirror with most of the lights turned off, his stark nakedness made him very uncomfortable. This, however, was to become a second-tier issue when he finally realised he was not just naked; he was naked *and* away from the vicinity of his own comfy bed! It slowly dawned on him; there were none of his prized stuffed animals on the table beside this unidentified bed. There were no remote controls within-easy-reach-without-getting-up, and most importantly to Donald, at this point, there were none of his clothes meticulously strewn about the floor.

"Where am I?"

Unfortunately, "where am I?" was becoming an all too frequent question coming from Donald's mind. Generally, Donald could recognise his location after only a short while and just a bit of a look around. He could then inform his mind where they both were. But this time, his current location recollection was not so much. His mind could also add the following three questions for even more confusion:

"Where was his afore-thought-about much-beloved Puppy?" Puppy is the small stuffed toy Donald has had forever.[7] It could be relied on to create such a level of comfort in Donald his stresses would simply float away. To Donald, Puppy was one day going to grow up to be an unreal, really real puppy.

---

[4]   His internal clock ran on "approximately 24-hours-a-day" time.

[5]   Mindfully "noticing his thoughts and then letting them go without any judgement," was to become the most reviled, sceptical and unachievable lesson Donald would(n't) learn during his stay at Saint Rita's.

[6]   Don't these two terms, complete and utter, mean exactly, totally and fully the same thing? Built in existing inherent redundancy in common, usual and every-day sayings, is unfathomable, confusing and perplexing to me.

[7]   Forever, according to Donald, was since 14/02/1968, the date of his auspicious (or maybe it should be his conspicuous, or suspicious) birth.

Secondly... "Where was his afore-slept-upon much-beloved bed?" It had taken Donald forever[8] to select the perfect yet still affordable receptacle for his unusually long slumbers and slightly rotund[9] dimensions.

And finally... "Where was his afore-worn-a-bit much-beloved wardrobe?" To the untrained eye, Donald's wardrobe might have seemed to be little more than a slightly random placement of his lightly worn clothes about the floor in a sightly colour coded fashion.

Donald's placement of his clothes was by no means random. Even though their randomness was forever[10] being altered on their flight across the room during his daily bouts of undressing, he knew where every piece of clothing was, where every piece of clothing belonged; and how many wears were left for every piece of clothing until it theoretically needed washing.

There were always three of everything in, on, or from Donald's mind:
- One to set the scene;
- One to emphasise the seriousness of everything; and
- One to deliver the final mortal blow.

He also likes to drastically exaggerate everything!

After this initial shock, which had registered a twelve on the *Donald-Oh-Goody-Not Meter (DOGoN)*,[11] Donald gave himself a moment to acclimatise to his surroundings... Deep breath in... And hold for one thousand, two thousand, three thousand... And long slow breath out... Deep breath in... And hold for one thousand, two thousand, three thousand... And long slow breath out...[12]

---

[8]   This *forever* was a two-hour long excursion to a local bedroom furniture factory outlet, half of which was a very personal interface with a *smart bed*. A smart bed is a bed (duh, obviously), with many physical sensors and is connected to a computer. You answer a few standard questions and then lie on the bed with an appropriate pillow in your preferred sleeping position. The smartness then whirls and clicks for a bit to determine the best bed for you. Interestingly, the resultant bed is always, conveniently, in stock.

[9]   Yes, *slightly*! Bite me and see... Or just Bite Me!

[10]   This, third and final, *forever* is ongoing.

[11]   Donald's DOGoN scale went from a layman's one-Unstressed, to a dead man's thirteen-Too Late. He was also slightly smug to be able to add to the plethora of acronyms available in the psychological arena.

[12]   How many of you were breathing in and out in time with Donald?

What was missing from Donald's mind at the moment, showing it was still trying to hold on to an infinitesimally small amount of control over Donald's subconscious, was any memory of a bright white light being shone directly into his closed eyes, seemingly, every hour. This light was usually followed by a sad sounding voice, "Sorry, Donald. Go back to sleep." Then the only thing left after each shining was a single reverberation, of an echo, of a memory.

Once Donald's twelve DOGoNs had been reduced to a much more socially acceptable number of nine, he performed a complete scan of the room to try and determine the answers to some of the rapidly mounting, very perturbing and as-yet unanswered questions from his mind.

There was a window, a washbasin and a mirror. Three items were a start.

The window was facing, presumably, to the outside. It was looking like a normal window should: clear enough to see out of if you can press your eyeball up against the glass; allowing in a very small amount of vitamin-d deficient sunlight; but not clear enough to allow anyone a close inspection of the inside from the outside. To Donald's mind, it was oozing an air of, "Don't mess with me, and I maybe won't open one night to allow a masked deviant in to assault whoever[13] they might find asleep in the bed. Kapish?" Donald also noticed the window was in a *locked from the inside* state.

The washbasin looked like it might have come straight out of a demolished primary school washroom. Large, rectangular, close to the ground and made from the same white porcelain the equivalent toilets were usually made from. It had a swivel faucet with a lonely cold tap and a slow drip. Donald assumed this was a "safety measure," as you can trust hot water only so far before it requires a "Warning – This HOT water is HOT!" sign.

And thirdly, the mirror was very dull, very grubby and very, very not-glass. It could quite possibly have been made out of what might have been an old oil catch tray from a mechanic's workshop that had issues with cleaning and had been run over by an ancient steamroller (the tray, not the mechanic).

Donald did his mouth opening, jaw-dropping and sharp inhalation thing. Staring wordlessly at his own dull reflection, twenty-three heartbeats later, he was still struggling to reconcile the image he was seeing in the mirror. There were no words appropriate. He thought about going down the "You talkin' about me?" or the "Who is the craziest one of all?" routes but finally settled on the more confusing than accurate path of "Destroy the image in the mirror, and you will have destroyed your enemy."

---

[13] Or should this be *whomever?* Whom reallym knowms, orm caresm, whatm thism shouldm bem anymhow? Notm mem, that'sm whomever.

On a much closer inspection of the washbasin area, Donald noticed there was no plug, no soap and no towel hanging on the mostly attached to the wall unheated towel rack. But what was there, however, was a "Clean Hands are Glad Hands" sticker, which was halfway through its peeling off process from the top left of the safely round-cornered, sideways turned and rectangle-ish very-dull mirror. The insincerity of the whole scenario was as inappropriate as the *Blackface* image of Al Jolson[14] holding up his Glad Hands *Mammy* style…

SaRS Unofficial 1 – Clean Hands are Glad Hands

---

[14] For those who don't remember Al Jolson[14] (or The Goodies), he was billed as The World's Greatest Entertainer and The King of Blackface. He was also the highest-paid entertainer in the 1920s.

[14.14] Apparently, you can't insert a footnote, within a footnote, within a Word document, of a to-be book. So here I am doing it manually… Some interesting factoids about Al Jolson: he was Jewish; he was born in Russia; and he was an entertainer for The Troops during WWII. His death was partially attributed to the harsh schedule he kept while he was entertaining The Forces during The Korean War.[14]

[14.14.14] I'm surprised this didn't ever come up in M*A*S*H.[14]

[14.14.14.14] I have to stop big footnoting myself now. If I don't, I will run the risk of stepping over the line and end up walking onto the next page. (I just skipped ahead to make sure I didn't. I didn't).

The furniture littering the room was:

- ✗ A bedside cabinet, sans stuffed toys and remote controls. It did come complete with a lockable[15] drawer, though;
- ✗ A small table with two very swivelled looking chairs;
- ✗ A wardrobe that had participated in way too many wars; and
- ✗ A rubbish bin, lined with a red and brown stained plastic shopping bag, which did not beckon any closer investigation.

Finishing his inspection, Donald wasn't at all surprised to see there was a door to his cell which was, predictably, closed. The door, to Donald's lacklustre imagination, looked like the doors you would most often find in the restricted sections of magical world stories, which lead the suspiciously innocent hero to many unthinkable or ironical places. Doors like this will commonly invite you to turn around and never, never, ever, ever, come back.

This door had a *"Please keep this door Closed ALWAYS!"* non-hand-written sign sticky-taped at eye-level on its inner side. Donald thought this was very strange, "If the door was already open, you couldn't see the sign, and how are you able to go through the door without opening it first anyway?" It was doors and signs like these that were always causing some of Donald's unrest...

Please keep this door
Closed ALWAYS!

Also attached to the back-side of this door, slightly lower than the *Closed ALWAYS!* sign, by the far less conventional method of using the lower half of a syringe as a thumbtack, was a fairly lengthy note. Donald presumed the note was written by a previous shorter occupant of the room and was unsure of when it was, why it was and even what it was. The black colour of the text seemed to be instructions on how to treat mental patients, and the red part was full of the fuzzy feel-good sayings Life Coaches would drum into you, but none of it gave him any answers, and all of it, because it was hiding behind the door, had given Donald the overall feel of the creepy heebie-jeebies.

---

[15] *You had to supply your own padlock, some of which were conveniently offered for sale at the reception desk. "Cheap at half the price," apparently. They each came with three keys: one for you; one for the nurses; and one to lock inside the drawer just in case you lost the first one.*

Take me... Lead me... Help me... Show me...

Mantra ~ मन्त्र ॐ 唵

How should you treat a mental patient   if you want them to become well?
Remember, they might be impatient,   they want to get out of their Hell.

Every day, in every way, I'm getting better and better
I breathe in, and I breathe out, and I will choose if I matter

First, you must find out why they are there   Once you have an answer to that,
it's time to show them you really care,   take off your psychologist's hat.

I am bigger than my issues, and I choose to get through this
My values are important, then as always, this too shall pass

Don't show pity; show them empathy.   Tell them all who they are matters.
Do not be long-winded... Brevity...   Remember, a harsh word shatters.

Failure will lead to success, be not afraid to let it go
I am stronger than I think; this all won't matter tomorrow

Take notes; you should record what they say,   every one of them will forget.
Find their triggers, why they lost their way,   teach them to find a safety net.

Handle uncomfortable; all I can do is do my best
This is only for today; I am enough for any test

Do not let others answer for them;   this is not what it is they seek.
There must be no generalisations;   every person there is unique.

I am in control of me; this is but a moment of pain
I have been struck down before, and I can get back up again

If they run away, it's what they need.   Optional participation.
Therapy should help them to be freed   and not become anger causation.

My life is beneficial... I am not in any danger...
White, green, yellow, blue, red, black, let lunacy be a stranger

Take me from the unreal to the real;   Lead me from darkness into light;
Help me so once more I can feel;   Show me how I can win this fight.

SaRS Unofficial 2 ~ Mantra

Once Donald had a complete misunderstanding of his whereabouts, he tried to address his undressed situation. He gingerly opened the wardrobe door to have a look. The door was barely hanging on; both of its hinges were nearly unhinged, so much so, it looked like it would cry "enough" if a single oomph was applied in the wrong direction. On the backside of this door was a crayon drawing of a stick figure who had lost a game of Hangman...

"Not a good look," thought Donald.

Inside the wardrobe was a small shelf Donald assumed was for his shoes. The presence of a pair of his shoes and his thongs were a big hint. There was a small hanging space for his dressing-gown,[16] a single pair of jeans,[17] and his complete set of Hawaiian attire (a pair of shirts plus one). Lastly, there was a small set of drawers, presumably for his t-shirts, shorts, socks, underwear and other unmentionable[18] smalls. The questions lurking at the back of Donald's small mind trying to get out were, "Wha, whe, whi, who, whu? Arrrrrgh! Who put my stuff here? And why is everything so small?"

Overriding his mind's confusion, Donald selected one of the Hawaiian shirts (the one with a kookaburra sitting in an old palm tree and a map of the Hawaiian interstate… Yes, I know, right… Am I joking, or not?), his pair of faded blue jeans and a single pair of his, obviously re-mentionable, unmentionables. Donald was accustomed to walking everywhere barefoot, but this time he chose to wear his thongs just in case.

Dressed appropriately, maybe not so much, Donald turned the handle he thought would open his cell door. As it was turning, he didn't know if he was excited, apprehensive, or if he was just plain old scared. Again, there were the three competing options prompting his next thought, "Why are there always three options for every question?" Then Donald did what he nearly always did; he continued on without waiting to know what the answer was.

He opened the door ever so slightly. Having a very quick peek through the crack, Donald could see there was some sunlight streaming down from a dirty skylight trying to illuminate the gloom. After waiting a short while, to become accustomed to the slight light sight, Donald looked at what was on the other side of the door to his cell… It was the number 41.

"Damn, so close and typical," is what he thought next. Closing the door to quietly ponder his situation, Donald continued his thought, "this is exactly, and ironically, what I should have expected…except I didn't expect anything."

------

[16] Donald's dressing-gown was older than most at thirty plus years… It was so old… If it appeared on television the image would be in black and white.

[17] A pair of jeans means one trouser type garment, with two openings for your legs. A pair of shirts means two upper body garments, each with two openings for your arms. A pair of socks means one set of two matching socks, each with one opening for your feet… Just sayin'. How many would a pair mean if you wanted a pair of glasses' frames fixed?

[18] Ooooops, I guess they are mentionable after all.

Recovering some of his very limited composure, Donald opened the door again and was relieved to see the slight light sight outside his door was still the same as it was moments before. He opened the door further just enough so his taxi-door wide ears would fit through the opening. So far, so good. There were no traps, no additional hurdles and most importantly, no one.

Swivelling his head, Donald started to take in the complete view of the short corridor directly outside his room: stunningly benign cream-coloured walls; another door to the right just a short way down the corridor; the dirty skylight; and some blue tightly looped carpet on the floor… With what looked like an old stain of Blood.

Blood?

Blood!

Less than a second after this thought tried to appear in Donald's mind, his automatic *survival of the scaredest* instinct was kicked into action, and it was telling him to "Close the Door…

Blood,

Faster…

Blood,

More Closed!"

Donald had successfully retreated to the limited safety of his cell.

Flopping down on the bed with an unrelieved sigh, he started performing his default stage one internal monitoring checks:

- A heart rate of one-oh-four.[19]
  Within acceptable limits?   Check.
- No broken or cracked anything?   Check.
- No leaked, or leaking, fluid?   Check.

Moving on to the stage two checks, are all my senses functioning?

- Sniff, snort, sniff…   Check.
- Look, blink, look…   Check.
- Touch, ewwwww yuck, touch…   Check, and
- Listen, wiggle, listen…   Check.

Four out of five ain't bad, and just as well… Because he certainly wasn't going to lick anything today.

His next question was the obvious… "Where am I?"

---

[19]   Simply calling it one-oh-four raised it to one-zero-eight.

Donald decided he needed to have a more thorough inspection of his tiny *rectangularprismicle*.[20]

He went over to have a look at, and a look out of, the window. He fiddled with the locked lock for seven seconds but was unable to persuade it to unlock. Tugging lightly on the frame, there was no appreciable movement, so he put his feet against the sink, which he had politely referred to as washbasin earlier, and with both of his hands on the window frame, pulled with all of his might. Donald was unaware he was creating a cartoon-like clichéd situation, even with his mind screaming at him to "Stop all of this stupid foolishness right now!" and then...nothing. Releasing his grip and regaining his footing, he extracted himself from the flying across the room nearly comical situation.

Moving on to the bedside table, which was sitting in the place where his nightstand should have been... It was a two-drawer, flat top and smallish box. Opening the upper drawer, Donald saw it held his wallet, phone, paddle (iPad) and what looked like a homemade hotel Welcome Pack. Checking his phone, he found it was completely flat. The battery, not the actual phone, which was only mostly flat. "How flat was it?" you ask. It was so flat you couldn't turn it on even if you were the nicest, smartest, and prettiest Apple Genius Bar Lady to have ever poured a blushing pink-lady apple cider.

The next obvious thing to check was his paddle. It started to turn on and displayed the super bright bitten apple logo. This indicated it was not just off; it was off-off. "How off was it?" you ask. It was so very off any apple cider you made from it wouldn't require any additional fermenting to make it alcoholic. Groaning a sad laugh to himself, at himself, and by himself, for the last few abominable sentences, Donald waited remarkably patiently for his paddle to finish turning on. Once it had turned on completely, he was able to resume his morning ritual by checking the *Notes* application.

Donald would always stand his paddle on his nightstand overnight, on the off chance there might be some inspirational remarks waiting to leak out of his sleeping subconscious. Frequently he would wake up and read what he had written, but rarely would he remember writing what he read.

Today seemed like it was going to be one of those frequently rare days. In the mornings of those days, Donald usually wanted to get over, be done with and then forget it... In more ways than one.

____

[20]   Even though *cubicle* would have been a perfectly reasonable reference to his tiny room, Donald's mind would always go with the literal definition of everything. Paradoxically creating a new word to facilitate his *literalation*.

Because I'm Mental[21]

I'm writing of my mental stuff and giving it to you to read
Tell me if you have had enough, this is just something for my need
It might sound stupid, but it's serious
I am being totally traumatised, and now I'm becoming delirious...

    Listen to me! I'm a loser with no future; it's no humour cos I'm mental
    I'm no Super, just a tumour, an intruder, cos I'm mental. It sucks!

They all say I am fixable; I don't know if I believe that
It would be effort biblical! They are only there for the chat
The effort would be mine, and mine, alone
Or, I could be institutionalised; at least then, I could have oxycodone...

    Listen to me! I'm a loser with no future; it's no humour cos I'm mental
    I'm no Super, just a tumour, an intruder, cos I'm mental. It sucks!

So, I plan to write it all down; maybe some might pay attention
Or, I could move to a new town, live out my life on the pension
I can't get over this; I can't forget
My brain chemistry can't be normalised, but I haven't given up on me yet...

    Listen to me! I'm a loser with no future; it's no humour cos I'm mental
    I'm no Super, just a tumour, an intruder, cos I'm mental. It sucks!

Unfortunately, the instant Donald finished reading the last "It sucks!" the paddle's battery joined its smaller sibling and entered into the completely flat overnight zone. Returning it to the top drawer of the bedside table seemed to be as good an action to take as any, so he just did it. Then he investigated the second drawer, hoping to find a charger for his *iThings*...

Nothing.

His mind then glimpsed on, "Maybe, maybe, just maybe these iThings are only decoys designed to keep me quiet." It then followed this thought with, "How am I going to find out if keeping me quiet is indeed the case?" Finally, after synchronising with the fact he had just read what he allegedly wrote last night on his paddle, it trailed everything with the ever-present, "Ahhhhh...!"

Donald was starting to see through the common thread of misfortune, misunderstanding and misadventure. It was all unravelling at a far worse rate than slowly and gave no visible or audible signs of ending.

---

[21] Inspired by *Because I'm Awesome* - The Dollyrots.

With no battery, no charger and no other ideas, Donald sat down with the alleged Welcome Pack. The front sleeve of the folder held a badly photocopied page with the words, "DO NOT REMOVE," formed completely out of smiley faces... It wasn't nearly as welcoming as you might think. The other words on the page, "ALL ABOUT SARS," were written in up-side-down smiley faces.[22] Donald thought, "Someone seems to have gone to a lot of trouble formatting the Welcome Pack... I don't know if that bodes well for me or not."

DO NOT REMOVE
ALL ABOUT SARS

Reading past the happy cover page, Donald found out *SaRS* stood for Saint Rita's Sanatorium. There was also some possibly very interesting information about the history and development of the facility. "At least," Donald thought, "it may be interesting to someone whose interest was piqued by reading stuff like that." He then made himself a mental note to read it sometime, purely to see if it was something he might be interested in reading sometime.[23]

"Saint Rita's Sanatorium..." mused Donald, "I guess that is where this is." He leafed through the leaflets and made another mental note to stop talking aloud to himself, as someone might think that was a little crazy.

One of the pieces of information in the Welcome Pack was a convenient three-week rotating timetable for Group Sessions.[24] There was also a three-week sample menu of food to be served in the dining room and a three-week conjecture of extracurricular activities most likely to be offered, or at least to be available if you cared to go looking.

Discovering no real insights as to why he was where he was, Donald once again performed a metaphorical Happy Socks pull up[25] and mentally prepared himself to head on out... Into SaRS.

---

[22] Does this make them sad Picasso faces?

[23] **Note to Author:** Don't forget to write this bit. **Reply to Note:** I did.

[24] *Convenient,* because it just so happens most health funds will only ask questions after the first three weeks of hospitalisation. It is surprising how many different diagnoses can be cured in exactly three weeks.

[25] It's a little too tricky to do a real sock pull up if you aren't wearing socks.

He opened the door again, for an astonishing third time, repressed some of his fear and looked out past the door, past the cream walls and past the Blood stain. Summoning the energy required to exit his capsule, one short step for mankind later, he was standing in the corridor.

Donald knew his room was number 41, so it came as no great surprise to him the door he could see from inside his cell was… Door number 42.

Door number forty-two, four-two, XLII, 101010, 2A, 卌卌卌卌卌卌卌//.

Surely it will hold many answers.

Donald stood outside the door, numbered 42, deep in thought. He stayed standing there for what must have been minutes, wondering, "What do I do? Should I knock? Should I open the door? Or should I repress my curiosity, walk away from the door and find someone to help me… To tell me what to do?"

Again, there were three options; there were always three options. Donald, never having been accused of being a very bright spark, chose option number two to do, and then his mind automagically started humming the old Police song, "The do do-do, that you don't do do-do.[26]"

Soon, even Donald's do-do song was drowned out by the more eccentric dramatic drumming, which regularly filled in some of the usually quiet spaces residing somewhere in the far recesses of his mind. The cacophony inspired Donald to choose this time to wonder if anyone else's mind was supplied with some sort of musical accompaniment like his was. He also questioned, "If a movie was to, let's say, include some silent drumming of the da-da-da-dum dramatic drum-beat, inside one of the main character's head, is it infringing upon any copyright laws?" and also, "What about referencing a song with an incorrect reference?[27]"

Shaking his head, while he put these presumably absurd thoughts into his ignore bucket, without worrying what the answers might be and making no judgements about his sanity,[28] he opened the door after closing his eyes.

Slowly reopening his eyes, Donald started to see behind door number 42. There was no jackpot prize holding many of the answers he was hoping for. Disappointingly, for Donald, he was looking in at a clean bathroom. "So close," "typical," and "bugger me" were the three recurring thoughts coming to the mind of someone who never really gave an ironic euphemism.

---

[26] Yes, I know. It would have been fantastic if they did do-do though, right?

[27] Something to think about Mr. Spielberg. But seriously… The pause outside the door must have been more than just slightly pregnant, with the amount of drivel shown to have passed through Donald's mind.

[28] Unwittingly, this is where Donald didn't start to learn mindfulness.

Donald instantly became side-tracked from what he thought he was going to do next. Looking over the contents of the room, he saw: a shower with a "Warning – This HOT water is HOT!" sticker peeling off over the hot water tap; a sink without a plug; and a toilet looking like it would be right at home inside any caravan park. One small mercy, though, there was no mirror. He also noted there were protective guards over all of the *jutty-out-bits* less than a meter off the floor, presumably making it difficult for any seriously height-challenged inmate to use them as some makeshift gallows.

Without the sought-after quick answers, Donald turned and headed to the end of his corridor. Two steps later, he could see around the corners. To his left, there was a corridor with a series of doors, seemingly randomly placed; and to his right, there was another corridor, complete with another series of doors with the same seemingly random placement.

He could hear tell-tale sounds of activity up the right-hand side corridor, and as they were much louder than his heartbeat, he chose to venture into the left-hand one. Two short moments later, Donald saw a figure coming directly toward him with no shortness of purpose. When she swept right past him straight into his room, Donald didn't know if he should feel violated, insulted or concerned, so he went with his standard default state of confused.

Hearing a *click*, seeing a light *flash* off, feeling a cold *shiver* down his spine, tasting a *palpitating* fear and smelling his *humiliating* embarrassment, Donald finally realised one of the switches he turned on earlier must have been the emergency senses phenomime sensing button. Thoroughly unimpressed with the response time from the nurse, as it has taken her nearly thirteen pages of monologue to appear. Donald prepared himself for his first berating for issuing an emergency call for a non-emergency case of simple confusing darkness.

The resultant happening was to be silently ushered down the hallway into a room displaying the bemusing title of "Interrogation Room Too.[29]" Inside the room, every conceivable place, as well as more than a few inconceivable ones, was covered over with a "We are here to help U!" "This is a safe place for U!" or a "We can't spell ~~Qure~~ Cure without ~~you~~ U!" poster.

Donald sat down and waited, passing the time counting posters.

The momentary length of time it took you to read the previous sentence was how long Donald managed to sit still. Curiosity got the better of him, as it always did, and he looked around the room.

---

[29] Did this mean *as well?* If so, *as well* as what? Or did it simply mean the sign-writer wasn't edumacated very well? Or would that be too mean?

In a box marked "Sensory," he found some paper, a clipboard and some blunt crayons, so he sat down again and started a crude drawing of his room while he continued to wait again...

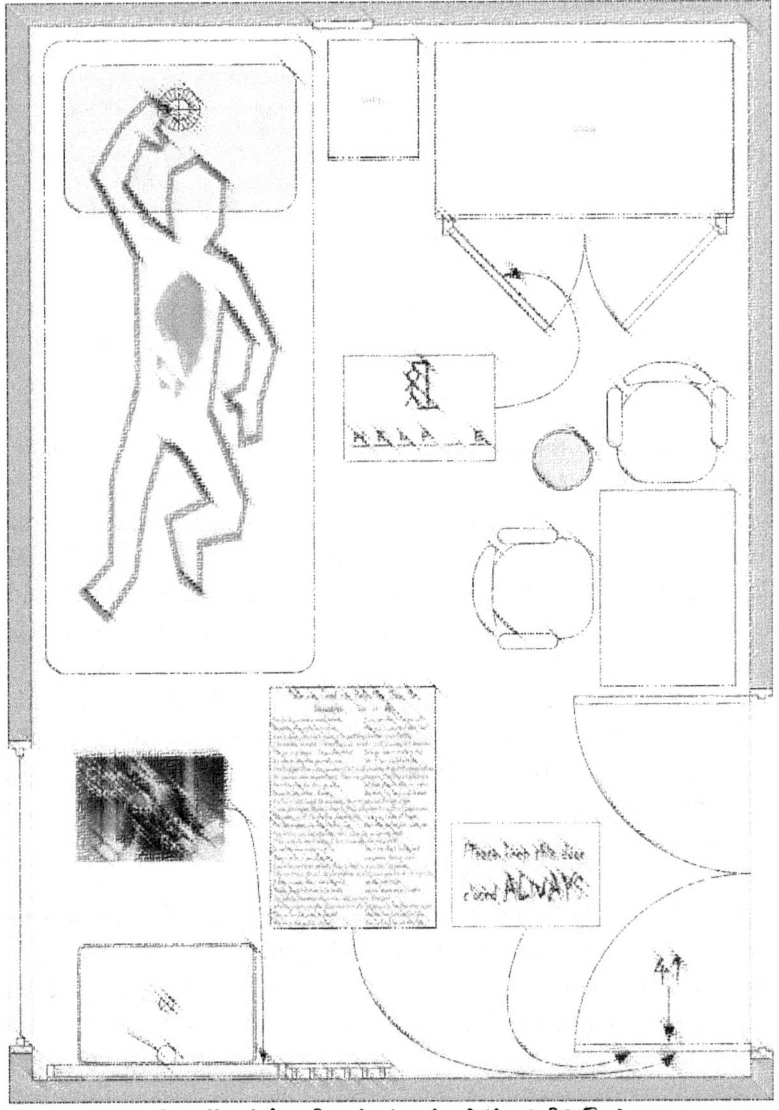

Donald Official 1 – Rough sketch of My SaRS Bedroom

Chapter 2:
Introductions
(Interrogation)

The nurse-like female person, who had just escorted Donald to the Interrogation Room Two, entered and closed the door behind her. Sitting herself down at the end of the table, she looked dramatically at Donald and his drawing. Straightening the documents on the clipboard she was holding, shaking her head sadly and letting out a pent-up disappointment sigh, she introduced herself as, "Nurse Dolly Dix, but you may call me DD."

Nurse Dix then went on to explain the situation of names to Donald. "OK, Donny… May I call you Donny? Donald is so… Formal and duck-like. I think we should start with using informal names, so I can be comfortable talking at you, and you can be comfortable listening to me. This will definitely assist with your becoming better, and I find… Blah, blah, blah, blah…"

Donald had already tuned out way before she finished this non-pausing, probably routine and seemingly never-ending question.[30] In fact, as soon as she called him *Donny* without first waiting for an acknowledgement saying this was acceptable, he pigeon-holed her as "one of *those annoying people* who assumes everything they find appropriate and comforting, everyone else must also find appropriate and comforting." For Donald, this was definitely not so.

Donald thought he already knew what she thought of him… "An old man who has: a tenuous grip on reality; very little life experience with living; and certainly, he had no business being out of bed, or bounds, in the middle of the night." None of this was either appropriate or comforting for Donald, even if it was probably accurate.

---

[30] Are questions like these just statements if you don't wait for an answer?

He was slightly thankful she hadn't called him "Don." Truncating his name to Don always, inevitably, leads people to taunt him with, "Is DON. Is GOOD." Donald never found any of this appropriate, comforting, or GOOD. Completing the near mandatory triumvirate of findings.

Tuning back into the dialogue, masquerading as a one-sided conversation, Nurse Dix was saying, "...but before any of this can happen, the first thing we must do is go through a short set of questions. We will use your answers to these questions to help us define a baseline of your physical health, mental stability and overall lucidity. When I eventually allow you to be discharged, we will ask you a similar set of questions, and then we will compare the results. By doing things this way, we can, hopefully, add yours to the many favourable statistics to show everyone just how good our **SaRS**[31] hospital really is."

Leaping forward into the basic attention and concentration section of the interrogation, with what was likely the shortest leap ever recorded, Nurse Dix began by instructing, "Now, I want you to try and remember the following four numbers: pi,[32] 666, thirteen and 24.96. Can you also try to remember these four words: car, apple, mouse and tree?[33]"

Donald stared at her dumbfounded, thinking, "Of course, I will be able to *try* and remember those numbers and words. It's not like I will start counting and go nine, ten, eleven, twelve, 14, 15... I won't forget the red/green, apple-shaped, generally crunchy fruit is an apple... I am not completely stupid.[34]"

Glazing over slightly, probably due to the highly repetitious nature of the questions, Nurse Dix continued the interrogation... "Let's begin again by you telling me all of your thoughts and feelings about your physical symptoms."

---

[31] When DD talked, you could just tell she was speaking in bold italics, even though it wasn't strictly necessary.

[32] What I find interesting about Pi is how it can be included in the lists of numbers, words, letters, charts and even foods.

[33] She didn't want the actual reply to these instructions, which would have been "Yes, and Hells Yes." She wanted him to remember, and then recite, the numbers and words. Obvious to everyone except Donald, obviously.

[34] This shows the literal mind at work inside Donald's head. What he would have much preferred her to say was, "I'm going to say four numbers and four words, and your task will be to recall them at the end of this interrogation." But this is not what she asked. It is never what they ask.

Donald, not really understanding the concept of a difference between his thoughts and feelings, started telling her his medical life story. He has told this same story to his GP, his psychiatrist and anyone else who would stand still long enough to listen. So, he felt dreadfully comfortable telling it again. The medical facts-of-Donald's-life was always a double-edged topic for Donald.

Note: This section of Donald's story has been removed because it wasn't very interesting. Donald always followed the rules, did exactly what he was told to do and was nearly as adventurous as a clod of moist dirt. He was, quite frankly, boring except, of course, for the actual gory medical bits. These were of such a highly sickeningly graphical nature I had to have them removed as well. Now you can still read the book while you are eating your lunch.[35]

Nurse Dix wrote the following on Donald's chart:
- *No history of alcohol or illicit drug abuse;*
- *No history of prescription drug abuse;*
- *No history of legal drug abuse; (not counting coffee)*
- *No history of self-harm;*
- *No history of prolonged eating disorders; and*
- *No history of… Anything…*

After Nurse Dix had unkindly but accurately summed up Donald's entire life with those six lines of "*No history of*," she asked him, "And how do you think you are coping with your mental issues currently?"

Flummoxed, Donald could only reply with a reluctantly broken and slowly questioning, "Obviously… I'm… Not…?" While saying these words, he was also thinking, "I have just described my complete doctor-full medical history, and you think I can cope, or have been coping? I have verbally illustrated, in way too much detail, my physical issues, and you think I can, or have been, coping? I'm in this freaking Mental Hospital, and you think I can, or have been, coping? Are you sure you're qualified to be a person, let alone a nurse?"

Nurse Dix ignored the bewildered looks on Donald's face and continued with the actual question part of the attention and concentration section of the interrogation… "Who is the current Prime Minister of Australia?"

Donald knew there *was* an Australian Prime Minister, but he didn't know their name or even their gender. This wasn't because he was living in his own little fantasy world; even though he was, it was because he just didn't care. He didn't think it was up to him to provide answers for any simple pub trivia type questions; let her go and find out for herself if she really wants to know.

---

[35] *Wasn't that nice of me? Why do rhetorical questions have a "?"?*

Donald also cynically knew that if he did answer any of her questions with his typical, "I don't care!" it would be transmogrified into, "I don't know." But, as he also didn't care about this, he answered her, "I don't care!"

"Hmmmmm... I see... Yes... Very interesting..." mumbled Nurse Dix while scratching away at something on the answer sheet. She looked up at Donald and asked, "And... Do you know what the day or the date is?"

Donald astounded her by replying, "Monday, the eleventh of the twelfth. I don't exactly know which year it is, somewhere in the late two thousand and tens, I think." Then he added as an afterthought, "Does it matter?[36]"

"Oh goodness gracious, Donny, no. No, of course, it doesn't *matter...*" more scratching, more looking, more scratching...

Donald was starting to think maybe Nurse Dix had a sheep, or seven, loose in her own top paddock. He took this opportunity to have a closer look at her SaRS identification tag while she was scratching away...

> Primary Nurse – SaRS
> Ms Dolly Dix (DD) MSN, MHRN
> Authorised for EVERYWHERE
> ANYWHERE and OVER THERE!

Apparently, Ms Dolly Dix (DD) was a bona fide nurse and not a sad mental inmate pretending to be a nurse... As Donald's clichéd imagination was trying to make him believe. This still didn't provide Donald with a great amount of comfort, so Primary Nurse Ms Dolly Dix (DD) was staying firmly entrenched in Donald's *those annoying people* pigeonhole.

Continuing with the questions, Nurse Dix asked, "What do you get when you multiply six by nine?"

Donald was clearly taken aback by this question. Did he give the obvious hitchhiker answer of "42;" did he give the mathematical answer of "54;" or did he give her his tried-and-true answer of "I don't care?" With all the confusion still floating around in his mind, Donald went with "54," as he didn't want to show her too much of his *those annoying people* self just yet.

---

[36] Where to place the actual question-mark (?) is confusing. If the entire sentence is a question it goes outside the quotation marks, if the question is only part of the sentence it goes inside the quotation marks.

To me, this just looks weird. After much investigation and soul searching, I went with *all question marks inside the quotes.* This isn't strictly correct, so, I guess the question on my fingertips is, "Do you care?" or, "Do you care"?

"Now, let's discuss your personal details..." was Nurse Dix's next foray into the uncomfortable, uncharted and mostly unacceptable territory of Donald. "What is the date of your birthday? And, how old are you?"

Donald thought, "If the last 37 minutes of conversation wasn't personal... I, personally, don't think you understand what the word *personal* describes." Striving to keep the conversation on a non-physical level, he replied, "The date of my birth was St Valentine's Day, 1968, and as discussed previously, I don't know what the year is, so I can't tell you with any accuracy what my age is, but I think it is somewhere on the wrong side of 50."

More scratching, turning over the page, more scratching, grumble-mutter scratch, "Can you approximate what your weight and height figures are?"

"These details should have been close-enough obvious," thought Donald, "I am, after all, sitting right here... Right in front of you. Right?" Starting to lose his bottle, just about ready to blow and becoming aggravated to the point of breaking, Donald replied to her question in his casual *bestest* smart arse, but still technically not telling a lie, fashion, "I am one fathom deep, I weigh 3,500 ounces and am a pear-shaped ambulatory biped."

This extra answer, on top of all the attitude he had been displaying, drove Primary Nurse – SaRS, Ms Dolly Dix (DD) MSN, MHRN all of the way up to the verge of throwing something painful at him. Gritting her teeth and swallowing her anger, Nurse Dix asked, "And finally, can you remember the four numbers and the four words, I asked you to try and remember at the beginning of our little question and (non)[37] answer session?"

"Yes."

"Would you care to elaborate?"

"No."

You can rest assured if the pen in DD's hand was a pencil, so tight was her grip, she would have left a set of right-hand finger-shaped indentations along the shaft before it gave up and crumbled into dust. "Please tell me what the four numbers, and the four words, I asked you to remember earlier were."

---

[37] The *(non)* was only implied in her tone of voice, but Donald heard it.

Although Donald complains bitterly that he can't understand subtle vocal inflections, the derision in her voice was so far beyond subtle it could have been understood seventeen streets away, by an unfocused lip-reader, who was participating in a crowded New Year's Day celebration.

Proudly and without hesitation, Donald replied, "π,[38] the Devil's number from Revelations, the generally accepted *triskaidekaphobia* unlucky number and the square root of six hundred and twenty-three (to two decimal places). Those are the four numbers, I believe; and Ford Edsel, Granny Smith, Optical and Scribbly Gum are specific examples of the four proffered words." Donald just sat there quietly, waiting for whatever was coming next.

Nurse Dix looked up from her pile of scratchings, she looked back down at the first of the question sheets and turned it upside-down to try and make sense of the answers. Her jaw dropped, and her eyes glazed over, even more than before. All this extended while Donald was casually trying to look like he didn't have a mischievous grin on his face, and he was failing dismally.

"Alllll riiiiight…" were the words stumbling to get out of Nurse Dix's mouth, which were accompanied by a level of glaze from her eyes never seen before. If Confucius had seen it, it would have confounded and confused even him!

Donald was pleased with this reaction. "I've still got it!" he congratulated himself in his tiny obtuse little mind. "I don't know what the *it* is, but I've still got some. Bring me the next victim."

Shaking seven-tenths of the glazed look off her face, Nurse Dix held onto the information making limited sense to her. She dived into[39] the information, introduction and instruction section of the hospital integration process.

"The daily schedule of activities is included in a folder you will find on your bedside table. Please make sure to read this and familiarise yourself with the appropriate activities for each day. This will be your only solid link to survival while you are being treated at SaRS. Trust in it well."

It didn't sound much like a mental redevelopment instruction to Donald.

Continuing along her *diatribal* route, "The weekly list of food, purporting to be available from/in the SaRS dining facility, is posted each Monday on the noticeboard located near the common area. Don't bother reading it, though, as it is generally posted sometime after the food has been served." This didn't matter to Donald as he usually ate everything placed in front of him anyway. Any food he didn't have to cook or catch[40] himself was good food.

---

[38] It beats me how Donald vocalised the pi symbol.
Oh, yeah, I guess you just say *pi*.

[39] Yeah, blah blah blah, shallowest dive ever recorded… Already done that.

[40] This comment relates to an unfortunate fishing incident from Donald's childhood that we won't try and delve into now. The psych*s will earn their money dealing with this issue much later.

"Smoking is prohibited unless you have a letter from your doctor stating, 'smoking is a required medical activity.' But, as none of the doctors here issue such letters, smoking is prohibited." Again, this didn't apply to, or faze, Donald in the slightest because he didn't smoke unless he was actually on fire.[41]

Nurse Dix went on to explain about the medication regimen Donald must adhere to and where he should go in the morning to have some of his Blood removed, just to be sure, and probably many other important things...

Donald phased out of the conversation at this point,[42] [43] so he missed: the introductions of the other staff members he will most likely interact with; the locations of all of the activity rooms; the locations that are most definitely out of bounds; where to go if he needed any additional help; where to go for his medication; where he could buy additional food and beverages; and where the common areas and patient facilities were.

Donald only became aware the interrogation had reached the end of the friendly conversational part when Nurse Dix shook him gently by the shoulder and indicated that he should follow her. In an after-interrogation haze, Donald stood up and started walking a few steps behind her. A few steps behind her later, he realised he was being led back up the corridor to his room. Once they reached his room, Nurse Dix informed/asked Donald, "Now, I need to remove any potentially dangerous items from your personal belongings. May I please have your permission to rummage through your things?"

It didn't sound much like a request to Donald.

Nurse Dix began her rifling process without waiting for the unnecessary response from Donald. Razorblades... Gone. Shoelaces, belts and wire coat hangers... Gone. Asthma, sore throat and headache medicine... Gone. After the thieving was complete, Donald was further informed how he could get any of these items back at any time he wanted... All he had to do was ask...

---

[41] This comment relates to a twin parachute fire-cracker bonfire incident, also from his childhood. It is unrelated to the previous fishing incident.

[42] The thought of the needle's Bloody point caused Donald's phasing out.

[43] This is hugely prophetic and unsettling. Footnote number 42 is exactly where Donald phased out of a conversation about his mental health. This could very well be the ultimate answer from my own Deep Thought. If *Paying Attention* isn't how to find *the Answer to the Ultimate Question of Life, The Universe and Everything*, then I don't know what is.

"At least," thought Donald, "I get to keep my toothbrush." He had already thought of several ways to convert this into a prison shank when the absurd situation dawned on him, "If all I have to do to get them back is to just ask for them to be given back… Why bother taking them in the first place?"

Before leaving Donald in his room alone, Nurse Dix gave him several pieces of paper, saying, "These are the preferred names of the other staff members you are likely to interact with during your stay with us here. Please familiarise yourself with them, then drop the papers into your washbasin and stand back. They will most likely self-destruct thirteen seconds after they have been read."

Donald looked to see if she was joking… He couldn't decide.

"If you look in the Welcome Pack, you will find the location of the activity rooms, where and when to go for your medication, and the locations of the recreation facilities we have for your pleasure during your stay here at SaRS." So, it hadn't really mattered at all that Donald had completely tuned out while Nurse Dix was relating this information earlier. "Oh, and the names of the staff members are also included in the Welcome Pack, just in case the other piece of paper does actually self-destruct."

With an evil "Mwwwwwaaaaahhhhh Haaaaahhhhh," and a blatant swish of her imaginary cape, Nurse DD exited Donald's room, closed the door behind her and left him alone.

Donald was reeling from information overload. Some of his questions had been answered, but most had not. The day's activity so far had followed the opening salvo's initial beating with a thrashing of even more questions. He was used to operating on a minimum amount of information, not the vast quantity DD had just poured into his head. Lumbering over to the bed, Donald resigned himself to being confused again, probably for a long time to come.

This was an unusual, albeit unusually common, situation for Donald to find himself in. He lay down on the bed to contemplate all of the activity, things and stuff. "Tomorrow, they will be sticking me with a giant needle and taking a Blood sample. Tomorrow, I will probably have to talk to many more people. Today, I am hungry." Following his gut's instructions, he reached over to find the Welcome Pack folder and investigated when and where lunch was.

Leafing through the thick Welcome Pack, Donald once again dismissed the convenient three-week rotating timetable of Group Sessions and the three-week conjecture regarding extracurricular activities most likely to be offered, to concentrate on the three-week sample menu of food to be, or not to be, served in the dining room. What was the question?

Sustenance Information

Breakfast is served: from 8.00am   to 9.00am
Lunch is served: from 12.00noon   to 1.00pm
Dinner is served: from 5.00pm   to 6.00pm
Please be prompt and line up in an orderly fashion.[44]

"Hmmmmm," mused Donald.[45] He could feel every one of the tiny cogs in his mind ticking over. It was around approximately sometime after 11am, but maybe a bit shortly before 11:30am. He looked for, and then at, the little box holding the sample *Monday Lunch Menu Item*. Objectively to see if he should get excited, or not, with the prospect of some culinary delectation…

Assorted[46]
Sandwiches

Fairly quickly, his stomach came back with an emphatic, "I Don't Know."

"Sigh…" thought Donald's mind.[47]

"I wonder if I mean:
- I don't know if I should be excited or not; or do I mean
- There simply isn't enough information to be able to decide if I should be excited or not; and (or?) thirdly
- What does culinary delectation mean again?"

---

[44] Donald thought, "Does this mean we line up like the orderlies do? Or does it mean we line up wearing whatever the orderlies are wearing?" He put this thought to the back of his mind into the section of his memory reserved for his Trivial, Oblique and Often Unanswered Questions (TOOUQ). It was becoming a very crowded part of his mind.

[45] And my musing was, "How am I going to format all of these tables for an eBook? Not to mention all of these footnotes!" #Donald'sWorldProblems

[46] Donald was unsure about the font the hospital had chosen to print their Welcome Pack in. Chiller didn't seem very welcoming, and when it was coupled with a font size of thirteen points, it was only made more unwelcoming. Another thought to add to his TOOUQ section.

[47] You could nearly see the thought bubble attacking the top of his head.

"OMG!" thought Donald, "I'm a serious pain in my own sphincter.[48]"

"Well, it seems to be somewhere between half an hour and an hour until the food will become available. Hmmmmm, I guess I could do a little bit of the research I am required to do." This was an amazingly coherent thought to have muscled its way to the forefront of Donald's consciousness.

Turning over the next page of the Welcome Pack, Donald revealed a two-page-spread, bizarrely formatted like it was a *Playboy* centrefold.[49] The top of the page read, "Saint Rita's Sanatorium for the Clinically Mental Medical Staff, Roster." Donald had a little internal chuckle at this. He very much liked the idea it was the Sanatorium's roster for the "Clinically Mental Medical Staff."

Such is the humorous difference misplaced punctuation can make…

Saint Rita's Sanatorium for the Clinically Mental Medical Staff, Roster

Primary Nurse	– Nurse Dolly Dix	*You will call her "DD"*
Day Nurse	– Nurse Jack Call	*Token Male Aboriginal*
Night Nurse	– Nurse Hatchet	
Weekend Nurse	– Nurse Wendy Swirl	
Student Nurses	– Grey Duate	*Gender unknown*
Medical Doctor	– Dr Andy Coughed	
Psychologists	– Mr Houts Marted	*Silent H - Not a Doctor*
Psychiatrist	– Dr Gee Jay	
Others:		
Ghost	- *Brother Latent Tardy has left the building*	
Memory	- *Sister Sapphire was right behind BLT*	

SaRS Official 1 – Medical Staff Roster

And directing his gaze down to page two…
(Or over and up, as may be the case here)

---

[48] Then he thought, "It's lucky I don't know the meaning of this either."

[49] I don't think Donald has ever seen one of those…

...to the Non-Medical staff page...

Saint Rita's Sanatorium for the Clinically Mental Non–Medical Staff, Roster

Pastoral Service   –   Aaaron Aare   *Religious not Religious*

Dietician   –   Seymour Feedme

Fitness Worker   –   Ma'am Cybill Flex

Musical Therapy   –   William the Piano Man

Administration   –   Mark Time

Cafeteria Cook   –   Chef Chief Changes   *Native American*

Service Pet   –   Chunky Poopy   *An over-round, over-friendly, and over-easy comfort pooch*

Maintenance Staff:

Groundskeepers   –   Wholly Mowly   *Complete lawn and garden maintenance for: Churches, Mosques, Temples, & Cemeteries We'll put a stop to all your Religious growth*

Cleansers: –   John Enslan   *Spick 'n'*
          –   Paula Bridge   *Span*

SaRS Official 2 – Non–Medical Staff Roster

After perusing the strange centrefold, Donald asked himself, "How many people am I expected to interact with?" There was a fairly unconvincing, stress-inducing and non-awe-inspiring reply of bone silence.[50]

Donald's brain was restarting to hurt again. He was becoming over-loaded with the many questions he wanted to ask of and about the staff members:

- *"Are they serious?"*
- *"Who wrote in Blue Handwriting?"*
- *"Why are my thoughts in the same font?"*
- *"Why is there space left for handwriting?"*
- *"Aren't those comments racially insensitive?"*
- *"Who would bother to print out an obsolete list?"*
- *"Ghosts and Memories?"*

And

- *"Are they serious?"* Seriously!

---

[50]   Well... Bones don't usually talk or make any noise... Do they?

Donald's mind was running on hyperdrive; it was likely he was going to be able to make the Kessel Run in much less than twelve parsecs![51] Donald would go on to learn the answers to all of these questions and so many, many more. Donald thrived on questions. He didn't care so much about the answers.

Conveniently, Donald's mind has decided to list out all the thoughts it has on the staff at SaRS. Many questions, some answers and a few future insights. This will save me a lot of introductory banter later in the story.

We have already met **Nurse Dolly Dix**... Oops, DD. So, we know the reason for the first of the handwritten notes on the Mental Medical Staff Roster. She is a bold personality, and she *will* get what she wants. She is also the key staff member when it comes to Donald receiving any special treatment. If Donald wants to go back home one day, Nurse DD will need to sign the permission slip confirming he is *Normal Enough* to survive there. Donald will need to carefully monitor each of his conversations with or about DD just to ensure he always refers to her by her correct false name. It was the least he could do.

The Day Nurse, **Nurse Jack Call**, is apparently the token male Aboriginal at SaRS. Donald doesn't know if the token-ness is his male nurse-ness or if it is his aboriginality-ness. Donald doesn't mind either way, as he is an extremely accepting soul. He doesn't like or dislike people for *what* they are. It's usually *who* they *think* they are he likes to come to a dislike of. Nurse Jack will become Donald's friend. He will also become the only staff person who Donald doesn't begrudgingly allow to call him Donny. This exception is unnecessary, though, as Nurse Jack always respectfully calls him Donald. Nurse Jack is also the nurse who will be taking his Blood sample tomorrow...

Night Nurse, **Nurse Hatchet**. I assume you have all seen *One Flew Over the Cuckoo's Nest*, but for those of you who haven't, you really should watch it. It is basically a reality documentary about a mental institution, where one of the nurses is named Nurse Ratched. She is not quite evil, but she certainly is the enemy. Ratched sounds like ratchet. A ratchet is a tool. A hatchet is also a tool and one which suggests a nasty piece of kit. It doesn't take a very bright mind, luckily, to make these connections. Nurse Hatchet will be the bane of Donald's medication-taking and television-watching conflicting timetables. She is also one of the few completely fictional breathing characters.

---

[51] Yes, I know. So did Han, George and Steven. A parsec is a measure of distance. It is, essentially, a short-cut through a very dangerous place... This is also completely apt when referring to traversing Donald's mind.

There are always several student volunteers (AKA unpaid slave labourers) on rotation at SaRS at any one time, and ***Grey Duate*** is an amalgamation of all of Donald's stereotypical observations. Obviously, this leads to there being at least one gender confusion issue, so I'll probably end up just calling him/her Grey wherever I can to avoid some of this confusion. His/her gender doesn't obscure things, as Grey gets to do all of the tedious public tasks while looking after the inmates. They perform the ritual of basic vital statistics taking each morning;[52] they keep them company and talk to them, and sometimes they even play games with them. All of the friendly public stuff, but none the fun, private stuff. Donald keeps his interactions with them to a minimum.

Dr Andy Coughed is a force! He is always everywhere, popping up at the most inconvenient times and requiring the most disgusting of things. Ugggh! Who would be crazy enough to be a *Doctor*-Doctor at a Mental Institution? One MD allocated to hundreds of inmates. The less said about his tasks, and I will be saying very little about his tasks, I assure you, the better. Move along; nothing to see here; this isn't the doctor you're looking for…

Houts Marted[53] is not just one of the many fantastic psychologists at SaRS. This is another non-gender specific role, so instead of playing favourites and having to remember many characters, they have all been melded together and moulded into this one identity. And boy-howdy, they certainly combined to create an outstandingly interesting character, who will, unfortunately, get far more negativity assigned than they deserve. They[54] really is a good-un.

The major treatment implications all come from the psychologists, and the major caring interactions are performed by the various nurses. This definition is reflected in a small piece of the Donald puzzle. Things may change later, but at the moment, as Donald has only interacted with DD, I will keep you, him and me all in suspense while waiting for what is about to happen.

---

[52] Except on the weekends when one of the real nurses must do some real basic nursing. This might sound a little bit harsh, but it is completely true. When none of the students are around, the vital statistics taking procedure is, sometimes, known to be more academic than physical.

[53] Silent *H*… Really? Who needs a slap for coming up with this rubbish?

[54] I will be referring to Houts (and to Grey when I forget) as he/him/his, simply because it is easier. There is a distinct lack of non-gender-specific singular pronouns and using *they* in the singular just sounds strange.

And **Dr Gee Jay**,[55] as she is Donald's psychiatrist, she should probably be the second most important character in his story. She is not at the moment. Her importance is destined to change for the greater later. Waiter, I'd like to see a "whine" list, please...

After this download, Donald's brain didn't hurt so much anymore. He was still over-loaded with many questions, and when he turned to the last page of the Welcome Pack, trying to jump ahead and see how the story ends, he found some wisdom he could keep:

FOCUS ON WHAT YOU CAN   and not on what you can't
FOCUS ON WHAT YOU DO   and not on what you don't
FOCUS ON WHAT YOU WILL   and not on what you won't

---

[55] No offence meant to the real Dr J. She is both awesome at her job and much smarter than me... She also knows me far better than I know myself.

Chapter 3.14:
Day -3
(Friday to Time Zero)

It all began...

Or, at the very least, this is probably how Donald would have started recounting his memory of the previous week if anyone at the hospital had just bothered to ask him. Or, at the very, very least, this is how I am recounting Donald's memory of the previous week because it makes for an interesting introduction to the reminiscing section of Donald's story.

DD *had* asked Donald this very question a little earlier, but unfortunately, he doesn't remember: her question, his answer, or when either of these two choice pieces of information went missing from his memory.

It all went missing from his memory... Because it also went missing from the book. It ended curled up and lying in waste, on the editorial floor labelled, contradictorily, too boring, too graphic and, confusingly, too Donald. Because, after all, isn't being a *Donald* the whole point of me writing this book?

For expedience's sake, imagine you're reading, and I may as well throw in *enjoying*, a description of the current Donald fading out and a new friendlier, yet so very much more confusing, Donald fading in.[56] This is a major change of scene, a major change of location, a major change of time frame, and, luckily for everyone, it also includes a major change of underpants... Eventually.

Let's try beginning Donald's internal soliloquy again...

------

[56] I know what it means, you know what it means, but it doesn't. *Fading in* doesn't make any literal sense. Fade: Gradually grow faint and disappear. *Solidifying in* would make much more sense, but this isn't nearly as poetic.

Last Friday began like any other last Friday... With Donald beating his alarm clock to the punch. It was barely seven and a half seconds until the annoying time machine would start blaring out *Tubthumping* - by Chumbawamba. Donald identifies with the lyrics: "He drinks a whiskey drink. He drinks a vodka drink. He drinks a lager drink. He drinks a cider drink." as these are four of his three most favourite drinks.[57]

He reached over to pre-cancel the impending alarm and turn off his "you can enjoy a whole night's sleep without snoring and wake up in the morning still breathing thingy dooby" of a CPAP machine. Donald was in full autopilot mode, rolling out of his bed and zombie-like, stumbling towards the en suite.[58]

Then the proverbial yellow bulldozer dawned:
- I don't have a girlfriend anymore;
- I don't have a job anymore;

Clunk-thunk-rattle.
- I don't have a life anymore...

Donald's last few days had been a bit of an incoherent blur. Autopilot had been performing much more than his usual morning waking-up routine. It had taken him from morning bed all the way through to evening bed at least three and a half times, without as many lucid steps in between. The frightening new person, who Donald felt he was starting to be today, was a vastly different person from the old Donald. The old Mr Donald, who was neither Scottish nor a farmer, just last Monday (four days ago) had quite a promising relationship, had quite a promising career and had quite a promising outlook on life.

---

[57] Conversely, he would never be able to pick these lyrics out of a line-up: "I get knocked down, but I get up again, you're never gonna keep me down."

Under-Note Note: This song has also been listed as... "One of the most annoying songs ever written." So, it is quite appropriate for Donald.

[58] This is quite the confusing word. Or two? Microsoft, all hail the mighty near monopoly, in its English (Australia) language lists this as a spelling mistake when written ensuite, en-suite, or the third option and I'm not making this up, en suite. (42 words if you don't count this and the image below!)

> [58] This is quite the confusing word. Or two? Microsoft, all hail the mighty near monopoly, in its English (Australia) language lists this as a spelling mistake when written ensuite, en-suite, or the third option and I'm not making this up, en suite. (42 words if you don't count this and the image below!)

The Monday-Donald knew, mostly, he was on the correct end of the bell curve of everything used to define a successful human. Whereas the Friday-Donald didn't. Mostly, the Friday-Donald could not even hear the bell tolling for him right now inside his own head. Human is a race he couldn't win.

Work had been an exciting adventure for Donald. He was sent travelling to several different countries on several different continents and had been able to glimpse a small slice of life for several very different cultures first-hand. He had witnessed a male-only wedding celebration, attended several coming-of-age ceremonies and had participated in a few unable-to-be-documented-here customs. He had been the stabilising force on *The Project* for at least the last three years, where he performed nearly faultlessly as the subject matter expert. And against all expectations, probabilities and desires, he had recently been given much more responsibility... In the way of a managerial position.

"Hmmmmm..." thought Donald.

Girlfriend had also been an exciting adventure for Donald. He got to travel to several different holiday destinations on several different airlines and had been shown a small slice of civilisation for several very different cultures first-hand. He had witnessed a wedding celebration, attended a passing-into-the-ages ceremony, and participated in a few unwise-to-document-them-here customs. She had been the stabilising force within *The Relationship* for at least the last seven years. Donald had performed mostly *faultfully*[59] as a willing subject. And against all obvious, common and rational expectations, he had been looking forward to their having a combined future together.

"Hmmmmm..." thought Donald again.

Life, the overarching everything that just is, had been more exciting than Donald had been led to believe. He had been part of several groups of people and had been able to garner a very small slice of friendship from each. He had witnessed the growth of a small puppy into a much larger house eating puppy and the regression of an older, rounder dog into not much different at all. He had participated in not so many unable-to-be-understood-anywhere customs. Donald had been participating in *His Life* all this time, and he had never once stopped to think, "Hey, you know what? This thing called *life* is actually quite easy." He hadn't thought it was ever easy because when things are made easy for you, you don't stop to think about it. Donald has always had some external guidance, someone, or thing, to tell him what he was supposed to be doing.

"Hmmmmm..." thought Donald for the unusually frequent third time.

---

[59] Thoughtful, but still fully at fault.

And this particular moment is/was[60] when Donald finally realises/realised he just might be in some serious need of help.[61]

Shaking himself ever so not gently, Donald wobbled over to the closest bottom receptacle and sat himself down. Then, with the smallest amount of effort possible, he plopped his head into his hands and had a really good cry. This was the greatest amount of internal[62] emotion he had expressed in such a very long time.
Donald then tried to do something he never did; he outrageously tried to use his mobile phone as a phone! Donald's mind was now running on impulse drive, obviously, as it would only be an obviously impulsive action to allow Donald to actually talk to someone on his phone, especially if he was going to ask for help from his family, quasi-family, or pseudo-family.

Conveniently[63] again, for character introduction purposes, Donald's mind has decided to list out all of the thoughts it has recorded about all past and present family members. These thoughts go a fair way to explaining, partially, how Donald became the Donald we all sort of know a little bit ~~and love~~. Again, there are many questions, slightly more than before answers and slightly less than before future insights. This *Out of His Mind!* dialogue won't save me any introductory banter later on because he will probably not interact with most of these characters after this, in this book anyway... It will, however, pad out this section on the way to the assumed magical number of between four and six thousand words +/- per chapter.

Cue the exciting and fast-paced background music.

---

[60] Writing about a present thought, when it happened in the past, is yet another confusion creating anomaly my writing has written off me knowing.

[61] Donald's not knowing what type of help he needs is also a significant barrier to my understanding of him.

[62] Donald has three ranges of emotions:
- External   – What everyone is exposed to;
- Internal   – What only Donald is exposed to; and
- Outternal – What everyone, except Donald, is exposed to.

This last range of emotion only occurs when Donald is singing while wearing headphones and he thinks no one else can hear him.

[63] Donald's mind's *convenientness* is a very useful tool.

Donald's mind, being Donald's mind and being closely linked to my mind, began chronologically.[64] The first introduction given here is for the first-person Donald met, who is still in his life now. She would obviously be his mother.

Home-maker, school-teacher and gardener extraordinaire **Wind N. Rain Halfbrain** (*nee* Potter),[65] who, exactly nine months after the Mother's Day of '67, produced the person who is now known here as Donald. Wind, as a home economics teacher, was the essential ingredient used for Donald's chocolate cake-like raising. With the feeding of, the education of and the clothing of all falling within her purview.

Due to her superpower like ability with a sewing machine, Donald started life as an extremely stylish child, wearing flared jeans in the early '70s, setting a trend for hippies everywhere. Donald also wore a pastel blue skivvy many years before the Anthony Wiggle escaped his Mortein threat. Wind even cut Donald's hair to form his iconic hairstyle named *Helmet Head*, which in later years would help forge his own superhero identity of *Fringe Man*.

Donald was born in the Sydney suburb of A-Fairway-to-the-Farm, and, as the name suggests, there was a farm at the end of the fairway, of the 19th hole, of the local golf course. And this provides me with a fairly decent segue to the next introduction from Donald's past, chronologically wise.

Donald's Father, **Bruiser Rob Halfbrain**, bread-winner, golfer and engineer extraordinaire, can build anything[66] out of some other *anythings*. He is a savvy investor and a shrewd property developer... Just as long as you don't ever ask him to ever climb up a ladder ever again... Ever.

Confusingly, for Donald, Bruiser is a mixed-handedness sportsman. One-handed right-handed[67] (bowling), and two-handed left-handed (batting). So, when it came to learning how to play golf, it was hard and ultimately a failure for Donald, who is permanently a right-hander. He was completely unable to learn how to walk around a paddock looking for balls successfully.

---

[64] One of my favourite words... With *chrono*, obviously meaning time, and *logically* obscurely meaning, "How else would you do it?" It is so much better than alphabetically, or numerically... There is no logic to either of those.

[65] This time I am serious! I don't have the imagination to make this stuff up. She even has a flower named after her. The Wind 'n' Rain Wattle strain.

[66] I'm also serious about the *anything*. He can make anything out of wood, metal and rock. From car trailers and bike carriers, through to submarines and rockets and nearly literally everything else in between.

[67] Long story, but Bruiser, like Dave Allen, has only 9 ½ fingers.

There have been several very famous people throughout history who have shown a similar trait.[68] These special people include icons of their chosen field, Leonardo da Vinci, Michelangelo, Nikola Tesla, Jimi Hendrix and even Albert Einstein. This group may go a little way to explaining Donald's very unique[69] mind, as these people also all exhibited autistic and creative tendencies.

Donald is slowly starting to accept he is a very special person. You can take *special* any way you feel is appropriate. Here is a little indication of just how special he is and a fitting little topical yarn.

Bestest Parents
She is a lady, a teacher and his mother
He is a golfer, bread-winner and his father
Out in her garden, she is a happy Potter
Down in his shed is the metal artificer

    Although they tried their bestest, I pushed them away
    Nothing mattered, a lesson I learned the hard way
    I have no idea what the future has in store
    Though I'm hoping not feeling like this anymore

        The guilt I now feel is because I broke the bond
        By not letting either fish in my little pond
        Having no idea what I am supposed to do
        But try my bestest, then I might just muddle through

Time to take a break… I'll be back later.
Talk amongst yourself for a while.

Shhhhh… Here he comes!

I'm Baaaaack. Did you miss me?
I'll be getting back to the introductions now.
Turn the page to continue reading…

---

[68] Pronounced like tray. (Yes, it is!) Unless you are an A-mental-ican.

[69] Another of Donald's pet hates. You can't be *very* unique, because it is a binary situation. I was going to say it's like being *very* pregnant, but I accept someone who is eight months pregnant, may be *adverbed* as very. Then I thought of *very* dead, but this too may be appropriate. Third time is a charm. It is like being *very* false. Maybe like this explanation…

Donald's only sibling is **Seashell Finch Kindred** (*nee* Halfbrain).[70] Seashell managed to escape the Halfbrain family by taking the mildly extreme measure of convincing Bruiser Kindred to marry her and whisk her away. This seems to have worked very well for her.

Throughout Donald's life, she was the instrumental part of setting the bar extremely high. Not only with instruments and the high jump bar at sporting carnivals but the number adding and word talking stuff as well. This resulted in Donald spending a lot of the time in her shadow, something he has come to terms with, but he would like some of his own sunshine now; if you wouldn't mind, please, thank you very much... Ta...

Seashell is doing her utmost to make sure Donald attains a living level of normal-if-not-famous. Bruiser is also helping in this area. Between the two of them, Donald is hoping at least one of them is completely successful in their subjective objective. Their three *chidlets*: Tall, No-I-am-Your-Father, and Bené, sort of put up with their Crazy Uncle Donald whenever he is around.

This concludes the past section on Donald's traditional societal mandatory relationship introductions.[71] We shall now delve, very shallowly, into the next set of introductions. Donald likes to consider these to be his unconventional optional relationship introductions.[72]

Kay Dressmaker is Donald's ex-wife, and, ironically,[73] she is also a damn good psychologist. Kay was Donald's first foray into the dark optional serious relationship minefield. Though it was optional for her, it wasn't for Donald, as he perceived a major pressure from society to appear normal. This pressure persuaded Donald to open the ubiquitous *Little Book of Life for Dummies* at the *Finding an Appropriate Mate* chapter and have a good long hard read.

---

[70] Obviously.

[71] You can decide for yourself if this means mandatory relationships, or mandatory introductions. Make good use of this opportunity to contribute to Donald's story, he rarely gives anyone more than one chance.

[72] And hitting home one of the many contradictions in Donald's life, this point is ditto with respect to the optional ones.

[73] This is a borderline Alanis-type referral to irony. It should probably be just be called coincidental, but if I called it thus, I wouldn't need to explain it to myself. Socratic irony is used by authors (and songwriters) to dumb down their perceived intelligence, so this comment must be anti-irony or logical.

Kay then fell into Donald's future almost by default. After being the last two people standing at a party and then almost setting their relationship on fire,[74] they would be *together* for the next around twenty years. Although Kay and Donald combined to create two great misses, they will inevitably be in each other's lives forever.[75] During all those twenty years of togetherness, Donald made exactly zero unassisted decisions on his own.

The two great misses Donald and Kay created would be their two children, **Miss E. Clair** and **Miss Jo's Diary**. Today is Miss Jo's' 18th birthday, and Miss E's 21st birthday will come later in the year. For those out there trying to calculate dates and ages, don't forget there was a time, about ten years of it, after the twenty years of togetherness, for Miss E to get to 21.

Every time Donald thinks about these two, he is torn between his love for them and his loathing for genetics. They both possess all the good qualities he can see in Kay, and others admit they can see in him, but they also possess the possibility they might grow into a willingness to not embrace their life, much like Donald has. And he doesn't want him, or this, to happen to them.

These two relationships, and their resultant introductions, while they may not be technically mandatory for the rest of society, are very much mandatory for Donald, who is often heard saying, "those are the two best decisions I have ever been, and will ever be, advised on."

The last introduction Donald's mind can think of, at this point in time, is **Hannah DeRail**. Hannah was the last and the longest-lasting in his how-long-is-a-piece-of-string string of unsuccessful relationships. This relationship was unusual in so much as Donald was given a second (and then a third, a fourth, a fifth…) chance to allow it to become moderately successful.

Hannah was the influential force, ably supported by Donald's GP[76] at the time, to facilitate the landing procedure of the much-broken Donald in SaRS for the first time. She was also the person mostly responsible for most of his education about most places that weren't mostly Australian.[77]

---

[74] Quite literally, thanks to an evil little single bar-heater and a reduction in their multiple polyester blanket requirement.

[75] I am trying to resist the urge to let out the standard evil sounding laugh: "Mwwwwwaaaaahhhhh Haaaaahhhhh." But I am apparently failing.

[76] Hi Dr T. I hope you like this as much as my previous books.

[77] Kay was the one responsible for Donald's education on New Zealand. (Don't worry, I'm sure the few Kiwis to read this won't connect the dots. ☺)

This relationship was both a high and a low point for Donald and his life. It was Hannah who started making Donald take control of his own life; it was Hannah who made Donald make some of his own decisions unassisted; and it was Hannah who needed Donald to be a much nicer, a much less selfish and a much more observant person than he was. Donald failed in all three out of these three[78] tasks.

Having said all of this, Hannah is also the only optional relationship entity likely to reappear later in this story of Donald vs the World... She makes an exhilarating comeback in just over a page, I believe, a little earlier than initially expected, but how else is Donald going to get to SaRS?

Ok, back to the story now...

When we last left our intrepid hero...[79] Donald was in the process of trying to use his mobile phone as a phone! We return to a scene where he is getting up and wobbling uncoordinatedly back to his bedside nightstand, as this is where his phone lives during the night.

Using a phone as a phone was so unusual for Donald; he didn't know what he was doing. He remembered a convenient feature of the early Nokia 5110 phones, where you could assign an important or often used number to a single button for speed dialling. Miserably, this became of no use to him now when he couldn't find any numbers on his *Smarter Than Thou* phone to press.

Flopping down on his bed, dropping the useless phone beside him, then sighing softly to himself, he uttered quietly in the near silence, *"Seriously, I just wanted to call Hannah."* After the last five or so minutes of reminiscence, he had just about given up hope, thrown in the towel, or sucked the juice out of his last lemon when an amazingly extraordinarily strange thing happened...

"Calling Hannah DeRail, mobile."

Donald's head did a Mr Whippy when he looked around to see where the voice had come from. He did a quick man-search[80] of his bedroom and found there was no one else present. This allowed Donald to partially relax, and he thought, "Maybe it was only an imagined peculiar singularity..." Milliseconds after Donald's cracked mind had finished with this thought, he heard a very faint rendition of *I'll Be That Girl* - by The Barenaked Ladies...

---

[78]   Or was this five out of five as number three had three parts?

[79]   Yes, I'm going to continue calling Donald a hero... Deal with it.

[80]   This is where it is a purely visual search, no lifting or moving of things. It is much more like a cursory glance than it is a look I suppose.

If I were you and I wish that I were you
All the things I'd do to make myself turn blue

"Hello…"
"Hello?"
"Hello!?!"

Donald finally recognised the voice as belonging to Hannah,[81] but he was still very confused about where it was coming from.

"Donald, DONALD, **DONALD!** … PICK UP THE PHONE AND TALK!"

Enlightenment finally dawned on Donald, and he picked up his phone from where he had discarded it in frustration half a page ago. "Hello…?"

"Hi, Donald… What can I do for you?" the voice was terse, succinct and only very nearly not abrupt in its questioning. This mattered little to Donald, who could not read the social queues of voice tones if his life depended on it, oh-so-very literally and ironically.

The conversation was brief. Hannah didn't need very long to understand what Donald needed. She was fully aware of Donald's self-created but not-at-fault predicament at work and of his last relationship spiralling out of control. She was much smarter than Donald looked.

Hannah immediately jumped in her car and arrived at Donald's house in minutes… About fifty-nine and a half of them. Then three more minutes after her arrival, she had Donald in his GP's practice. The whole of the two-minute drive, Donald kept complaining about wanting to see a doctor who didn't need to practice anymore… Hannah just groaned, redid his gag and ignored him.

The name of Donald's doctor's practice is *The Little Tinkle Medical Centre* (specialising in urology). Coincidently, also the name of Donald's doctor. They only stayed there long enough for Dr L. Tinkle to give Hannah the details she would need to get Donald institutionalised in a private facility, as opposed to being committed to a public one (A serious world of difference!).

<future note> Not long after treating Donald, Dr L. Tinkle will choose to move to a different medical practice. Donald will then choose to believe this wasn't due to any trauma he might have instigated. The small but significant detail of a Google revealing Dr L. Tinkle's new place for practising will show he wasn't, and isn't, trying too hard to hide from Donald. **</future note>**

---

[81] As predicted. I wonder how I knew, this too, would come to pass.

Back at Donald's place, over the next hour or two, Hannah busied herself with the process of applying to SaRS for/and on Donald's behalf.[82] She was using the information garnered from Dr L. Tinkle and her own overly intimate knowledge of Donald's ins and outs. So, the task was a simple, non-Donald intensive one. She completed the sixteen-page form in just under one hour and 41 minutes after requiring very little input from Donald.

While Hannah was filling out the SaRS application form, Donald was trying to progress the packing of his clothes. He wasn't quite sure where they were going on holiday this time, so he packed for both hot and cold[83] weather. The packing of clothes is always a very strenuous task for Donald, and it came as no surprise to Hannah when Donald fell asleep mid-pack.

What did surprise Hannah was the gobbledygook ramblings Donald had written before he fell asleep. Donald liked to think he was creating new words, although he is actually only filling in a perceived space with what he thinks is an appropriate combination of two or more old words.

In another life, Donald was quite an adept poet, or so he thought. This was just a rehash of one of his early works of poetry, where he conceitedly thought to himself, "My made-up words are just as good as that other poet guy's, and I didn't have to kill anything. And how is what he wrote a poem for children?"

Lyring Gredisess

Forever do I sit and think, oh, this rhyming is my master
I am helpless within its wake, overshadowed by disaster
Forernal do I sest and hink, oh, this lyring ist my mastress
I am clumpless within its strake, inershated by gredisress
Eternal do I rest and hope, oh, this lyric ain't my mistress
I am clumsy within its stride, inundated by great distress

A few hours[84] later, after she had finished his packing, Hannah gently woke Donald and assisted him out, around and down a few times and then into her car.[85] It was a very quiet trip to the sanatorium. Donald never spoke much at the best of times, and having just woken up from a marathon nap, he was less likely to say anything than a Marcel Marceau impersonator was.

---

[82] What happened to the *ahalf*? Doesn't it come before the behalf?

[83] The only two temperature definitions Donald will ever accept.

[84] Approximately 41.99.

[85] Only if you have seen Donald's garage will you understand.

All Donald can recall from Sunday are the many, many people talking very loudly, and very slowly, *at* and *down* to him. They can't have been talking *to* him, as there was no indication from him showing he had any understanding of what was going on within any of the conversations.

The check-in-and-go-up-to-bed-while-half-asleep process was one Donald had perfected during his frequent work hotel stays. There were two noticeable differences this time: the luggage porter must have been on holiday because he had to carry his own bag, and there was a distinct lack of "Hello again, Mr Donald" from the hotel staff.

Donald didn't know it, but he had just missed his Time Zero.

Chapter 4:
Monday Midday
(Ghosts and Dozy Does)

It must be slightly confusing for you to be reading all about these many strange characters without a lot of warning, or time, to digest the large volume of information on how they are going to interact with Donald over the coming period of his life. You must have some concerns about these people, who all decided to work in a mental institution where there are many flavours of mental and physical illness, and how they might not be able to help Donald as much as he needs when so far, we have only actually *met* one.

How do you think Donald feels? On with the story...[86]

Donald's stomach was telling him it was time for lunch Now! Putting down the Welcome Pack, as he had had quite enough of being welcoming, for now,[87] Donald prepared himself to wander out of his safe, but not so comfortable, little domain into the much larger, probably less safe and even more pungent world of SaRS. As soon as he opened the door to his room, Donald felt like he was on the brink of a cusp of an edge of something really big. He didn't know if this brink-cusp-edge would turn into a turmoil of breakthrough, tears and collapse or just end in a monumental disaster.

Maybe all of the above...

Eyes closed, just in case, Donald once more stepped out of his room.

---

[86] I understand this is only a story. What you have to understand is, a story is exactly what it isn't. It is exaggerated and it is humorously twisted, but it is definitely very real. These people, these places, this entire *story* **exists**.

[87] And, predictably, so have I.

Floating just a little way down the short corridor outside Donald's door, and peering into room number 42 *through* the door, was what could only be described as an apparition-like Johnny Depp. He looked like he would probably be more at home within a Tim Burton movie than pretty much anywhere else, or even anything or anyhow else you could ever try to imagine.

Once Johnny noticed Donald, he[88] seemed to do a quick double-take and performed a once-around-himself look. Donald thought it looked like he was making sure he wasn't standing in front of an as yet empty dart board, which, astoundingly, looks vastly similar to making sure he wasn't standing in front of a dart board full of darts. Johnny then introduced himself as: "Brother Latent Tardy, but you may call me BLT for short. I am a self-appointed, self-integral part of the welcoming committee here at SaRS...[89] And, I am looking forward, very much, to easing you through this initial terror-inducing stage."

Donald wondered how a talking ghost was going to achieve this.

Lowering his voice and leaning down so close, Donald could just about feel the ectoplasm infiltrating the back of his eyeballs, "Please don't mention to anyone how I stuck my head through the door into room number 42... I'm not allowed to look in there anymore, something about peoples' privacy when in the bathroom..." Unsuccessfully suppressing a shudder, "If DD ever found out, she would start me on an exorcise regime."

Performing a non-conspiratorial glancing twist through his shoulder, BLT continued, "Please don't get me wrong... **DD is a wonderful lady...**" and then back to his normal voice, "She was the one who convinced me I should cast off my stereotypical brother-monk appearance: the hairy-doughnut do; the sack cloth robe; and the sandals with socks for the more comforting, and also more comfortable, vision you see hovering before you." Even though BLT is already dead and buried, the grave he is buried in is obviously still too shallow for him to be rid of the transparent fear he has of DD. If Donald had pointed this out to BLT, and if a ghost could blush, BLT would have been able to find some rare gainful comic-con employment as a human-sized Blinky.[90]

---

[88] Do ghosts have a gender? It's not like they can make little baby ghosts.

[89] BLT knew enough about punctuation to know you pronounce SaRS without bold italics, but he wasn't ever going to tell DD. Would you?

[90] If you understood this perplexing reference, I am extremely impressed! Would you classify yourself as a Nerd, or as a Geek, or as a both?

For those few non-NGs amongst us, Blinky is the Red Pac-Man Ghost.

For the purpose of this introduction, **_Brother Latent Tardy_** was one of the original founding brothers of SaRS. Way back then, a neck stretching 75 years ago, SaRS was simply called _The Big Ole Homestead_, and it had a pretty nice Kingswood parked in the garage. That was many amounts of time ago before BLT became a B, an L, or even a T.

The then-current homeowner made a few… Fine… More than a few bad investments during the great depression. He never completely recovered from the financial loss, finally turning to the bottle for companionship and solace, and had to sell The Kingswood's House for a little bit… Fine… More than a little bit of money. Ironically, after he had paid off all of his pressing debts, thereby keeping all of his limbs intact, he used the leftover money to become the first patient to check into the newly opened _Private Psychiatric Hospital for Men,_[91] which would go on to focus on men with drug and alcohol addictions, as well as those who have returned from World War II with the forerunner of PTSD.

Back to introducing BLT… He was given the Brother Tardy moniker by the other Brothers of Saint Rita for being chronically late for everything. When he finally became _The Late Brother Tardy_, those same other Brothers buried him in the inside/outside courtyard of the SaRS mansion. His elaborate headstone was supposed to display "Here Lies the Latent Remains of Brother Tardy." Still, the stonemason had apparently forgotten he happened to be dyslexic. He carved, "Here Lies the Remains of Brother Latent Tardy."

Re: He Became Late Too Early (Inspired by BLT) p269.

א   Extract from The Donald Diaries.

What Donald managed was a polite-ish, "Erm, OK? I'm actually on my way to the cafeteria. Would you be able to point me in the correct direction?"

"Why, yes, of course. But I can do better than that… There is a very helpful mantra, one I humbly created myself, you might like to learn. These words will show you the way to almost anywhere in SaRS."

Though there are many paths you can take,
Just around the corner lies your destination
Do not make the mistake most people make,
Turn left before you get to your damnation[92]

---

[91]   The hospital was colloquially known as PSH. The acronym of the sounds of the first letters of the words. Those early Brothers of Saint Rita were a strange lot, even before you include their attire in the entire picture.

[92]   Paraphrasing Due South, "A man with no future, always turns left."

The instant after BLT spouted this amazingly cheesy piece of non-advice, he departed... Poof... Without allowing the dumb-struck Donald to ask any of the questions percolating around inside his head like, "Huh¿™", Donald was once more alone with his confusion, *muddlement* and discombobulation. His non-concentration was only broken when he realised someone other than a ghost or his own mind was trying to talk to him.

"You there! What are you doing!"

Donald's mind reacted immediately to the perceived threat by instructing Donald's body to go into *Freeze* mode. For many people, freeze is the newly discovered first stage of the *Fight or Flight* defence mechanism. For Donald, it is the standard response to just about everything... And, if you looked through some of his history, you would see he rarely progresses much further.

If the source of the threat passed by without interacting, as it usually did, he didn't know what to do. If the source of the threat continued to be a threat, as it usually didn't, he still didn't know what to do. Either way, he would return to his normality eventually, just after doing nothing about the alleged threat. Not knowing what to do and then doing nothing is what Donald often did.

"You there, *Freeze* boy! What are you doing!"

"Dammit!" thought Donald, "It isn't going to go away." He turned towards the unrelenting voice and was surprised to see there was a small keg shaped person barrelling[93] down, at a moderate speed, on him. What made this scene look ever so slightly ridiculous to Donald was that this small beer keg shaped person was barely taller than she was around. Donald has never been one to be politically correct in any of his personal observations.

For argument's sake, at 150cm[94] tall, if you could imagine an angry female crossed with a very cross looking beach ball complete with a slow leak needing a little bit of pumping up to get through the day, the resultant image would be pretty close to the one confronting Donald. He would have given some serious consideration to laughing hysterically, but he was way too busy assuming the traditional jaw-dropping incredulous look.

---

[93] An unfortunate choice of word it may be... But it is an exceedingly apt description for many people on *de-mentalfying* medication, unfortunately.

[94] Five feet for all of you who are still partying like it's 1966... The 14th of February 1966 to be precise. The date of Donald's birth and the year of Seashell's. Coincidence or Conspiracy? But definitely not Ironic.

"Hey, you!" she cried, ramping up the loudness and intensity of emotion with each word… "You there! That means you, you know! Look at me while I am talking to you! What on Earth do you think you're doing! That's disgusting! Who told you that you could do any of it anyway!?![95]"

Their eyes met across the worn Blood-stained, ironically blue, anti-plushily carpeted floor. Donald's face reconstructed itself into one it hoped would look like it was trying to if it could have, exude a stench of complete horror. This was absolutely nothing compared to the look, front and centre, on her face. Hers was a look saying she would brook no schnook and really had to be seen to be disbelieved.

"Errrrr… Ummmmm… Nothing?" is what Donald sincerely hoped was the correct answer, even though it was technically a question. His expression also changed to resemble something more like, "I really hope to wake up from this nightmare soon!" But, his mind, having finally become un-dumb-struck, was thinking, "Oh man, she's definitely a bit of a dozy doe.[96]"

Ok, a couple of introductions are warranted now. We will get back to the story after a short break ~~and a word from our sponsors~~. (Wait for it!)

The short dozy doe is **Nota Beenhead**. Nota, we will eventually find out, has been diagnosed with a Borderline Personality Disorder.[97] This brands her prone to explosive anger, and when this is combined with her suspicious mind tendencies, she becomes (her words) "a good thing in a small package," who, (his words) "has been tightly wrapped and labelled with *Tread Carefully*!"

Oh, and by the way, she always has to have the last word… "No, I don't!"

Nota exhibits several other symptoms of BPD. She is often impulsive and self-destructive with her behaviours, even if it doesn't get her no satisfaction. Her swinging emotional extremes, and rapidly changing self-image, means she doesn't do well alone or with other people… "See, I told you!"

---

[95] It isn't usual to have an exclamation mark at the end of every sentence. This is just the way she talks. Every sentence is either an exclamation or a question… Sometimes it is both, hence the *exclamestion* mark!?!

[96] One of Donald's favourite terms. It means *crazy woman*. It is Donald's go-to when he meets someone of the female persuasion, who is intent on interacting with him, without any introductions over the internet first. His thinking being, "They must be bat guano crazy to be talking to me, right?"

[97] BPD has a new name, Emotionally Unstable Personality Disorder… I don't think this is much of an improvement… In fact, it is *borderline* if it is an improvement at all, so, I won't be using it here.

Nota is also generally found in the company of someone who understands her more than she does herself. This person is usually Owedebt (phonetic accountant parents). They are often put together for the purpose of bouncing their emotions off one another. It is like someone, or something, winding up two jumping toys, pointing them towards each other and sitting back with a goblet of watered-down sherry to watch them as the action unfolds.

I'm not supposed to say things like that, as I might come across sounding like I am trivialising their mental illnesses. It is definitely not my intention to do so; I am just trying to put it into simplistic words a layman, and maybe even Nota, can understand… "What do you mean 'and maybe even Nota'!"

Owedebt Dear has been diagnosed with BPD, like Nota, but as an added bonus prize, she has also been officially diagnosed with Bipolar Disorder,[98] to go with the abundance of her unofficial self-diagnosed issues. She will present herself often throughout the rest of this book, taking on the role of Donald's very incapable sidekick.[99] This mirrors the reality TV scripted reality; Owedebt will attach herself to the real Donald to alleviate some of her co-dependency and abandonment issues. When Owedebt is in her manic phase, she will toggle between good manic and wicked manic. Although neither of these are actually good,[100] they will add a little bit of excitement to Donald's stay at SaRS.

When you find Nota and Owedebt together, you will also always find their third musketeer, third stooge, or third little pig. You may choose whichever he is, depending on how you want to read this situation… But he certainly isn't a third wise man![101] This third wheel, to their haphazard duo, is ***Chunky Poopy***, the over-round, over-friendly and over-easy comfort pooch. He[102] is a mixture of vegan sausage dog and royal canine with some dingo[103] parts thrown in.

---

[98] You may remember this from other diagnoses, such as Circular Insanity, or Manic Depression.

[99] Very much a role-reversal situation for the sidekick prone Donald.

[100] If you know what I mean. Sometimes I don't even understand myself.

[101] I have ducked for cover at this point. This, and the previous comment about Nota's barrelling nature, will probably get me slapped.

[102] Well, he used to be a he…

[103] I was going to put a joke in here, about Chunky partially eating a baby. I was convinced there would be much laughter, then I was unconvinced and finally reconvinced I shouldn't, as it would be in bad taste. So, I left it out.

If Chunky sees an opportunity to have his rotund belly rubbed, this means if you just happen to glance his way for more than a split second, he will gallop toward you in a slow-motion run; dive at your feet with a half aerial twist; and finish the movement with a short, dramatic, slide on his back with his four legs extended up into the air, and casually looking away, so he doesn't come across as being too desperate.

If all this fails to attract your attention, he will wag his tail ferociously and nudge you with his moist little nose. If this is still not enough encouragement, his final method of getting some free pat from a stranger is to lick you on any protruding piece of skin and stare at you with his sad puppy dog eyes until you acquiesce to his demands.[104]

Donald amused himself one night by writing about Owedebt...

Owedebt[105]

Just a normal girl is what everyone sees, not the ups, or the downs, of her mood
In her mental world, she is brought to her knees when they all say she's crazy
Educated fact, this is not what they have, the door you will now be shown
Stupid opinions that is all that they are, painful right down to the bone

>Stigma can cut like a blade when your opinion is made
>Of the tightrope between her ups and her downs

>>[Chorus]
>>She's got borderline bipolar. Mental? Sure...
>>And she's manic like she's never been before
>>She's got borderline bipolar. Mental? Sure...
>>And she's depressed like she's never been before

On that thin blue line of her insanity, the good and the bad always feud
She'll say that she's fine with such intensity, but she's not cos she's crazy
When you're living a life by moments o' time, can't stop, or you might get stuck
Taking her manic, her depression, and time... She shows she don't give a pluck

>Bipolar ain't who she is, she is more pop than she's fizz
>But to be sure she'll be kept safe in SaRS' bounds

>>[Chorus]

---

[104] Literally! True story, with Chuck Norris staring as Chunky Poopy.

[105] Inspired by *Maniac - Michael Sembello*

"Nota, love, leave the poor man alone. You don't know where he's been." This from the as yet unknown (to Donald at least) lady who has just appeared on the scene. Donald noted, startlingly, she was being drawn reluctantly along by a pink fluffy leash attached to a small, furry, and slightly smelly *pat me now please* licking machine.

"But Owedebt, he is doing everything all completely wrong, and I need to make him understand! He probably doesn't even see me here, but honestly, he will only learn if I tell him! I don't know what I have done to make him hate me already, to be honest! But I really need to tell him everything I know about how everything works around here! I don't know why he isn't listening to me, but I really need... but I really... but I... but... but... but he has a cute..."

"Nota! Stop it! We have talked about this innumerable[106] times. He isn't someone you have any responsibility for, he isn't one of your several fantasy playthings, and he isn't even on your list of prospective suitors... Just look at him... He is at least twenty years older than you, and this old age places him squarely outside, even your far-reaching, limits of acceptability."

"BUT, But, but..." *Ding! DING!* **DING!** "Eeeeeewwwww!"

Donald was still very confused. He was watching two people of the female persuasion have a warmish debate about him as though he wasn't even there. It was unsettling, unacceptable and slightly unsavoury. Donald is never, in any way ever, comfortable with being anywhere near the centre of attention, let alone being at the centre of attention of two dozy does. He wanted to silently cringe away, but he really wanted to scream and run and hide, but, but, most of all, he really, reaeaeaeaeally, wanted some food.

"How can I get away from these two dozy does and find some food?" was the thought Donald was rushing to have as soon as possible. His was conflicted, though, toggling between this thought, conveniently compressed right down to "Food?" and, "Run, Run Now, Ruuuuun Donald Ruuuuun, RUN NOW YOU GOOSE!" He was desperately trying to get a response, any response, from his feet regarding these sanity preserving urgent messages.

It was nearly getting to the stage when Donald was starting to think about alternate arrangements, vis-à-vis his feet and their lack of movement. He has never tried to walk on his hands, so he passed over this option fairly instantly. "*Mental forehead slap* This is a Hospital, maybe there's a wheelchair?" But he rejected this perfectly reasonable option with a "Naaaaa."

---

[106] In fact, it was numerable, she had just forgotten how many times they had talked about it. This was due to another fact; the number had exceeded her three-digit-limit for mathematising.

Finally, and thirdly, the usually chosen option came to him, "I'm the boss of me! Listen to me feet... Get your grubby happy socks into gear and mush!" His feet, though, interestingly enough for me to note here, were still hung up on the words *two ladies* from roughly half a page ago.

These same feet responded to Donald with a question of their own... "Why is foot pronounced as if an orangutan with a speech impediment is *ooking*,[107] and boot, as if it was an owl hooting? It turns a seemingly simple trip down to the shops to buy a pair of football boots into a major adventure involving both linguistics and pronunciation."

Much to Donald's surprise, because nothing good has ever happened to him without much forethought and preparation, the questions from his feet, and the quandaries in his mind, were all relegated to being distractions when his attention was diverted by a sign suspended on the wall behind the strange conversating duo. Donald felt, even with his apparent lack of knowledge of how everything works around here, fairly confident he understood what the sign, or maybe the universe, or simply coincidence was telling him...
Gathering up his everything, Donald tried to make good his escape...

Thirteen steps down the current corridor, through an open set of doors, five steps around the next corner, and then ten steps down a different corridor to reach another set of doors. These doors were closed.

---

[107] Upon review this isn't how it would sound. A better line in the first place would have been, "Like a chimney sweep was putting his sooty broom away."

See what I did there? If you did, can you please explain to me why I didn't include it in the story in the second place? Clearly, I am still writing it.

Though I guess the question is moot,* as the book has been published if you are able to read this in the third place. This is a very circular, redundant and confusing situation... Much like the situation Donald finds himself in.

* Or should it be the answer is moot?

Donald was in the middle of congratulating himself for achieving 28 steps without incident when, unfortunately, as we have all just read, on the 28th [108] step, he came to a set of closed doors. Accompanying the disappointment of the closed doors was an official-looking employee category person who was standing near those said same closed doors. Donald caught up to his narrative several moments later. He (the man, not Donald) was wearing a strange outfit, which may have once belonged, a long time and many missed washing days ago, to someone who sort of hung around unimportantly in the background of a religious order of monks hoping to be noticed.

The person in question is **Aaaron Aare**. Aaaron belongs to the Pastoral Care Service within SaRS called *Religious not Religious*. They are there to look after the inmates' mental souls. Preaching from no book, in particular, they are there to help supply the frequently required doses of *just relax*. They roam the corridors 24-hours-a-day,[109] acting as a combination of soul carer, light traffic warden and night watchmen. Whenever there is an incident, a drama, or an occurrence, these people are the fillers out of forms, breakers up of tussles and touchy-feely-good-to-go people.

Aaaron is particularly smug when it comes to his name because every list of names ever made, fortunate enough to include his name, has had it as the very first entry. Throughout school detention, remedial driver's training days and weekender prison, Aaaron would always answer to his name being called out before the second *a* had come out of the role caller's mouth.

"Hi, I'm Aaaron Aare from R'n'R here at S'n'aRS.[110]" This was gargled in a condescending tone of voice and would have been sickly sweet if it had been edible. You could irrationally see where the soluble carbohydrates would be dripping off the letters. Donald looked down at Aaaron's SaRS identification tag and was rewarded with no answers to his unasked gargling question...

Pastoral Service – SaRS
✠ (Religious not Religious) ✠
Mr Aaaron Aare, AASW
Authorised for Most Places...iii

---

[108] Did you go back and add up the steps? I did. Twice.

[109] Just say, "All the time." Days don't come in any hours other than 24. OK, smarty-pants. Except the two daylight-savings-time change over days.

[110] I think he must be a closet rapper.

"Err, um... Hi?" Donald was remarkably adept at turning simple things, like a simple hello, into something so complex, so convoluted, and so co-opted he wouldn't know if anyone has ever answered him vaguely correctly, even if he remembered what the question was in the first place. Sadly, no one ever does. And, neither does Donald... Does he what?

Aaaron blatantly looked down at his red clipboard, something he thought identified him as an important part of the healing process. He flipped through several pages and started to speak as he was tapping his foot, "Hmmmmm, new person, must not worsen, said the nurse-in charge for certain."

Donald looked back up to Aaaron's face to see if he was joking...[111] Again, he couldn't conclusively decide but was thinking it was much less likely he was joking than DD was previously. What he did understand in this scenario was, "there is a dirty caftan wearing, word rhyming and clipboard toting man, who apparently wants to be called Aaaron, standing squarely between my stomach and some food." To further back up this starved notion, Donald noted Aaaron was standing in front of another sign that seemingly indicated there might be a chance food to be found in the vicinity...

All of this led Donald to the astounding audible conclusion of, "Please, Sir, may I have some food?"

Aaaron, as an ever-present meticulous implementer and follower of the rules, looked down at his watch and replied, "It is still only 11:59am o'clock in the morning. Lunch will be served at 12pm noon midday o'clock time.[112]"

Donald saw it was an archaic analogue Tick-Tock watch, with about six... five... four... three... of each until... Ding! "Lunch time."

---

[111] Donald is finally starting to think it might be him with a screw loose, and it is indeed he who is the one needing a teensy bit of *screwdrivering.*

[112] Something is quietly-telling-me Donald doesn't gain any respect for Aaaron Aare with his unique understanding of time. This solidifies into a full-on-lecture about disrespect when we find out Donald refers to Aaaron as, "the triple AAA-Soul-Man," (pronounced Ahhhhh obviously).

Being engrossed in the time on Aaaron's watch, Donald completely failed to notice there was a line of people (His subconscious tried to add *very crazy* before *people*, but his conscious was ignoring these very annoying comments and didn't even bother to include them as a footnote) forming up behind him. When Aaaron's announcement of lunch time was made, and correspondingly Donald's awareness of the lunch queue was also made, one of them tried their darndest to not look back. Still, he may as well have tried to not be acted upon by gravity's influence.

Do not be afraid to be wrong when being wrong is right.

The verbaliser of this fortune cookie quote is **Sven Teatwoo**. Sven is an ageing Swedish/Chinese man who is recovering from a *Confuciusectomy*. This radical process is designed to remove all traces of the inmate's inner-troubled, self-deprecating and mindlessness thoughts by replacing most of them with much nicer bubblier ones of potential personal growth, relationship morality and most importantly, how's-the-serenity mindfulness.

Donald responded to this unexpected piece of audible philosophy with a just-about-audible thought of, "Huh¿™" Then he looked around to make sure there were other people in his vicinity who also heard what he thought he had just heard. There was a mild stench of confusion in the air, so Donald remained cautiously confused. His go-to thought when he is exposed to obvious insanity is, "More spaghetti for brains than a Pasta Dude…" This being shortened to "Pasta Dude" provides his mind with some much-needed nigh-imperceptible humour. It also helps Donald to avoid many confronting occurrences.

Without a hesitation, delay, or pause… Donald stepped through the now open door, over the threshold and under the boardwalk to enter himself into the world of the eating some food place.

Chapter 5:
Food for Lunch

Once Donald makes it through the soon to be opened doors, and on past Aaaron, he will get to meet Chef Chief Changes and Seymour Feedme. You, however, will get to *meet* them now.

Chef is the SaRS cafeteria's chief chef; he is also a Native American.[113] So, if you were to write his full name, including titles, he is **Chief Chef Chief Chef Chief Changes**. David Bowie's song *Changes* was written about Chef. How he left behind all of his struggles with the American invaders and ignored their stereotypes placed upon him, both then and now. All to seek out a better life for himself without having to ask for anything that was his in the first place.

Chief Chef Chief Chef Chief Changes
"Where's your shame
You've left us up to our necks in it?"
"Time may change me
But you can't trace time."[114]

Stereotyping Chef is something I am going to avoid.

---

[113] I am unsure of the least offensive name. I think all grouping of subcultures alienates them from the majority. Why aren't they simply called Americans? Although, this too is a grouping. People are people. Naming a group of people based on what makes them different is surely an *ism* of some sort.

[114] It wasn't of course... But it would have been cool if it was...

There will be **NO** clichéd painted warriors performing war dances skipping around a campfire while creating a vocal siren wo-wo-wo-wo slapping-mouth noise. There will be **NO** pow-wows for traditional enemies, wearing full body length headdresses of eagle feathers, to communally smoke a peace pipe. And there will definitely be **NO** tomahawks or knife scalping savagery.

Chef is the last surviving member of his native tribe. Rather than have an existence in a place where he was *allowed* to live, he migrated to Australia to live a life on his own terms. He hasn't cast off his heritage, instead choosing to embrace it by bringing some of it with him to share with his newly adopted country's people. This is in the form of his delectable homemade treats made from the *Three Sisters* of beans, squash and maize.

"Yes, it is all rather cliché," as Chef is known to comment, "It is what made my people different, it is what I do well, and, naively, it is what *people* expect. Those same *people* are always surprised when they taste my food for the first time because they are expecting it to be bland, tasteless and boring. Anyone can make sweet cakes with flour, sugar and eggs; I can do much more without. It is also much easier than trying to find and skin a fresh buffalo."

Seymour Feedme is SaRS' dietitian, and his favourite saying is, "You can't have a diet without something dying.[115]" Unfortunately, it is usually the taste of the food in mass-produced meals doing all the dying. Seymour works closely with Chef to make sure the SaRS food is equally tasty and nutritious.

When you take into consideration:
- The minimal amount of money allowed to purchase the ingredients;
- The restrictive dietary requirements of some of the inmates;
- The many and varied food allergies;
- The physically huge amount of food required to be served; and
- The very limited preparation and serving time windows...

This is where some true miracles occur three times daily at SaRS.

Seymour could be described as being a significantly large man, while Chef would be considered to be of a much more unobtrusive size. These are not the only stereotypes to be openly flouted. If you were expecting anything to be remotely *normal* at SaRS, you will be seriously disappointed. Time to get back to Donald's story and on to the next ingredient of food.

---

[115] It's even in the spelling! Irony also rears its ugly head when you think about the source (not sauce) words; the Greek *diaita* means *to live one's life*, and the Latin *diaeta* means *manner of living*.

Because Donald is the first person in the queue, he is operating purely on his own intuition. This is definitely not something he is normally comfortable with, but his ravenous hunger was a significantly larger desire in this particular instance. His one saving grace here is that he is intimately familiar with the getting of food from a cafeteria concept, having indulged in thickening sausages 'n' chips with gravy many, many times before at university.

Cocking his head to the standard deliberating stance, Donald found he was able to recall the cafeteria process quite easily:

- Grab a tray, spoon, fork and safety knife;[116]
- Bus it;
- Peer through the steamy bain-marie glass looking hopeful;
- Choose between Mystery Meat or Manufactured Not-Meat;
- Select the colour of your meal: Light or Dark Brown;
- Bus it;
- Add Vegetables if the dietitian is watching and Chips if not;
- Bus it;
- Ignore the salad, and finally
- Add gravy... Always add gravy.

Donald was awoken from his reverie by a "Would you like any assistance selecting your meal, Sir?" question. It was a group of very polite words, but the way they were delivered made them sound rote, unconvincing and slightly, "Please say no unless you want me to make you cry." Standing beside Donald was a rather large man who was possibly under-exercised, obviously oversized and yet somehow still looked like a healthy person.[117]

"I would recommend some butter chicken on steamed jasmine rice and a small side of poached vegetables, all with a nice Chianti. But, as this is what I am having for my dinner tonight, and it isn't on the menu at SaRS today,[118] the suggestion may be a bit insensitive. How about some bangers and mash?"

> **Dietician – SaRS**
> Mr Seymour Feedme, RNutr
> Authorised for CC's Kitchen
> and Cafeteria area ONLY...

---

[116] Sharp enough to spread the portion packet butter when slightly soft.

[117] Maybe it is because he is... (Or could be if he didn't fixate on chips).

[118] Or ever because butter chicken is the one dish Chef can't cook.

Donald didn't really want to know, or think about, or even have the topic discussed by other people in a remote area next week, why the authorisation was an *ONLY*; he didn't want to know what the ⚡ meant, and he didn't want to know anything about what *RNutr*[119] stood for. He was busy trying to stop himself from shouting, "Feed Me, Seymour!" *Audrey II* style.

The bangers and mash offer hit him like a plate of bangers and mash. Donald was having a heavenly culinary memory!

He came crashing back down when he saw what the SaRS interpretation of bangers and mash was. Anaemic, insubstantial, sausage-similar extrusions, full of *meat* which had, almost surely, been manufactured by waving it at the cows in the paddock next door; then thrown into what presumably could only technically be called water; had what remained of anything vaguely nutritious boiled out of them sometime last week, and then dropped on the floor.[120]

The mash wasn't much better. It was the colour of dry concrete, and from the way the serving ladle was unhappily resting in a nearly vertical position, Donald could only assume the post-potato consistency was more akin to wet cement rather than wet concrete. Which was probably just as well.

Donald could nearly hear his stomach screaming out, "Yeah!" Which was closely followed by his mind reacting with, "But, No!" This friendly to-and-fro banter escalated near-instantly to one almighty internal game of Donald Pong, where, as usual, Donald didn't even have a paddle, let alone a creek of shush! "But Yeah!" "But No!" "But Yeah!" "But No!" "But Yeah!" "But No!"

Much to the relief of his mind, his stomach and all the people in the queue behind him impatiently waiting for their food, Donald's ravenous hunger came to the forefront and got things moving along in the required orderly fashion by ordering his mouth to shout, "ENOUGH ALREADY!"

Donald, curiously, became quite aware of the complete silence echoing right throughout the cafeteria. Trying to keep the level of colour in his face to a nearly acceptable three shades of pink, Donald quickly *muttbled,*[121] "I would like to have three sausages, mash," and then, turning around to see if Seymour was watching, added, "and some vegetables please."

---

[119] Registered Nutritionist, not Really big Nutter as I originally thought.

[120] Which could have only added nutrition and only in Donald's mind.

[121] Donald was so confused that he didn't even know he was well past mixing his literal mutterings with his metaphorical mumblings...

"Two."

Donald was confused by this response. He waited a moment just to see if Chef was going to elaborate. When the moment transformed into a painfully obvious uncomfortable silence, Donald tried ordering his food again, "I would like to have three sausages, mash and some vegetables *too*, please."

"*Two*."

Donald looked to Seymour for some guidance… "Donald, may I introduce you to Chef Chief. Chef is our chief chef here at SaRS."

"Aaaaaa,[122] I don't think it will ever be up to me to give you permission to do anything… And haven't you just done so anyway?"

Seymour continued condescending as if he hadn't just been interrupted by Donald's pedantic logic, "What Chef is saying is, there is a two-sausage limit for first servings. If there are some sausages left-over at the end of the lunch hour, then you may please yourself and return to have many more."

"Ahhhhh,[123] now I think I understand. I would like to have two sausages, mash and some vegetables, please." Then adding an internal clause to himself, "I must not, and will not, plan on coming back here for any extra cold, extra congealed, extra extrusions at the end of the lunch hour, or in fact, ever!"

His mind also chimed in with its own clause, "Never, never, ever, ever! Not even if they were the last two sausages left on earth. You would prefer to be stranded on a desert island where there is only stagnant sand to eat and your own dehydrated concentrated pee to drink."

His stomach also, also, added a clause, "Shut up, and just take the food!"

"Gravy?[124]"

---

[122] The verbal version of Donald's mind raising a doubt.

[123] The verbal version of Donald's mind understanding a doubt.

[124] Chef is remarkably conservative in his use of words. This is not due to his lack of knowledge of English. *That* would be a stereotype. He is literally very literate and just prefers to say what is needed, zip, zero, naught and nothing more. He doesn't like to go on and on, ad infinitum, trying to show off how exceedingly exceptional he is, with monumentally extravagant words and run-on sentences, which don't really say anything you didn't know in the first place anyway… To Chef, it isn't the magnitude of the communication device, the significantly important part of the message is in its substance.

"Yes, please... Two...[125]"

There was little to read on Chef's identification card, so it didn't matter a split infinitive to casually not read it, as far as Donald was concerned. If he had read it, he might have asked a question, "What does the little ⚡ mean?" But he didn't, so he didn't. And it, also, still didn't.

Chef put his hand up in the *Stop!* position so Donald didn't keep bussing his tray away without first collecting his food and asked, "How?[126]"

Donald, after another short pause waiting for any subtle visible or audible indication from Chef that he was going to either laugh or elaborate, eventually realised there wasn't going to be any laughter or information, decided to cut his losses[127] and respond to the inappropriately written question, "All over the sausages please, enough to cover them completely."

Once Chef had completed serving Donald's lunch and had given him a full plate of food outrageous enough to be in an *I'm a Celebrity - Bush Tucker Trial* episode, he pointed to the display case on the end of the counter and asked, "Would you like to select one of my delectable, mouth-watering and yet still healthy treats? There is a variety of pumpkin muffins, blue vegetable cakes and peach puddings, all served with sweet corn or prickly-pear ice cream."

Struck audibly dumb, Donald only just managed to squeak, "A muffin with some prickly-pear ice cream, please."

Donald's dumb shocking reaction didn't go unnoticed by Chief, who smiled one of those all-too-common dejected sigh-ridden smiles of knowing-he-had-been-underestimated-once-again sadly.

Donald thought to himself,[128] "Damn, this guy is good."

---

[125] Donald thought he was sooooo funny.

[126] OH NO HE DIDN'T...
Slap my wrist!
OWW! But I was only referring to how Donald wanted the gravy.

[127] A joke isn't funny if you need to explain it. Neither is irony ironic...

[128] If it was *to himself*, why is it here?

His lunch tray now complete, Donald embarked upon the next stage of the process, finding an isolated seat where there would be no chance of someone accidentally sitting next to him. Donald has had significant experience with this step of the process, so, for the first time at SaRS, there was something he could do with a smidgen of honest complacency.

He selected a corner table far, far away from every walkway from the food collection area. He nudged the chosen table just a little bit closer to the wall and moved all but one of the chairs to other tables, thinking his efforts would remove all traces of the chance of someone asking to join him. Sitting in the last remaining solitary chair and facing towards the corner of the room, he set about looking for the courage to face his food as well.

Donald could not delay the issue any longer. He was hungry; he was seated at a table by himself, he had a plate of "food," and he was wearing his glasses. Following in the natural food eating order, he picked up the knife and fork and gingerly, with ample trepidation, and no small amount of slow cut into one of the perhaps sausages. Making sure it didn't utter a squeal and was completely covered with gravy, closing his eyes twice just to be sure (to be sure), he put the alleged sausage into his mouth.

Palatable hope soon gave way to unbelievable enjoyment.

The food, although it looked like it was related to a large, freshly prepared, steaming pile of poo, was actually tasty. Donald was halfway through eating his lunch: nearly forgetting where he was; eating like this was the first meal he had had this week; while he was in gaol and likely to have his food stolen; and where survival of the fittest was being vigorously applied now, instead of to a future generation; when he was politely interrupted by someone tapping on his shoulder and asking, "Would you mind if I sat here?"

Donald is about to meet another inmate, "one" who will perhaps become the most interesting person, apart from himself, Donald has ever, or will ever meet… Ever! **Skit Zoland** is the first person to have been diagnosed with a unique mental disorder called… Extreme Dissociative Identity Disorder with Infinite Transmutations (E-DID-IT).[129] Basically, Skit believes he is, and will thus figuratively become, someone different each day. All explanations to Skit of why this is and who he is, are always forgotten overnight.

---

[129] This is not real. (Duh, really? You need to give the readers more credit when it comes to grasping your jokes.) It is an exaggeration of Dissociative Identity Disorder (DID). You may remember this from other diagnoses, such as Multiple Personality Disorder (MPD) or Split Personality.

This is similar to the movie *50 First Dates*, except there is no easy way to explain to Skit who he is and then explain who he really is each morning. The *interprebriefing*[130] became such an extremely traumatic experience for Skit and everyone else concerned, so much so, firstly, for his family and then for the staff at SaRS; they have all simply stopped trying.

The disorder first became apparent in Skit when he was performing in a High School play. Not only did he play a very convincing lead role character in the Shakespeare tragedy that must remain nameless as the scientific tradition dictates, he thought he had actually become Hamlet.[131] He stopped just short of realistically killing anyone. Still, the guilt and paranoia he assumed from the persona drove him literally, metaphorically and dialectically insane.

His insanity and unpredictability increased significantly over time. This has been partially attributed to him becoming only infamous fictional characters, heavy on the *in*. Eventually, Skit became too difficult to look after, culminating in a permanent committal to SaRS, where he will live out the rest of his life in sequential 24-hour long skits.

Donald, having been brought up to be polite, said, "Of course not." while he was really thinking, "Hells, Yes... I Do Mind! I Mind in The Strongest Possible Way Someone Can Mind! Just Look At The CamelCase Of My Words!"

As this stranger was then sitting down, he continued on urgently with his introduction and quickly became sizably stranger, "Hello, my name is Lisbeth Salander, and I believe I have been placed here completely against my wishes. I have managed to evade my captors for only a moment, so you must help me escape! Quickly... We have only a few moments before they manage to track me down. It is imperative I escape. I have several pieces of important sensitive information that must be made public as soon as possible."

The words in this monologue were so stereotypical, their structure was so forced, and the subtext was so contrived, Donald began to wonder if he was an unwitting character in an action-adventure, horror suspense, or a crime-thriller novel... His distorted wondering was leading him to believe, possibly it is perhaps, maybe all three.[132]

---

[130] Interpretive Debriefing of Skit... About who he is being today.

[131] It's ok, the forbidden play is *Macbeth*... Oh... Bugger...
* Spin, spin, spin. Ptooie!
* Angels and ministers of grace defend us.
* Can I come back in now please?

[132] Only we know it is a comically tragic documentary.

Lisbeth[133] continued speaking like this to Donald for a long time after he had stopped listening and had gone away to find his private happy place. This is how Donald avoids becoming stressed when he is confronted by any unease. A lot (all) of his currently stupefied, confused state of mind is directly related to (caused by) Lisbeth explaining the many tattoos covering her body.

For each of her tattoos, she imparted detailed knowledge of its history and meaning. Donald had only one trifling issue with this; when Lisbeth showed a different tattoo to him, there was no ink… Of any type… To be seen anywhere! Was Lisbeth hallucinating, or was Donald anti-hallucinating?

"Shhhhh, here they come!" whispered Lisbeth, who quickly shoved a small package into Donald's hand and disappeared under the table before he had a chance to ask, "Who is coming?" "What is this?" or even his favourite question of all time, "Huh¿™"

These were all purely reactionary questions. Donald had only thought of them because of his current befuddled state of head-grabbing, hair-pulling and I'm-so-confused confusion. He didn't have anything near to any actual interest in knowing the answer to any of them.

But he still mentally listed them again, for completeness, apparently:
- "Who is coming, or indeed, is there anyone actually coming?"
- "What is in the small package you have just thrust into my hands?"

And even the ever-present:
- "Huh¿™"

They were all purely rhetorical[134] questions.

Three seconds went past, and Donald had nearly convinced himself there was nothing much wrong with anything right now: he wasn't really sitting in a mental hospital's dining room enjoying the food; he wasn't really helping an escaped, deluded, fictional and possibly dangerously mental inmate who was currently gender polymorphic evade his/her pursuers; and he didn't think he needed any more convincing he wasn't really all that[135] crazy, when…

"Did you see where he went? Did you see *Skit*?" came a puffing question.

---

[133] I will refer to Skit by his, or her, fictional nom de plume, only once we are all aware of who the unknowingly adopted, not necessarily rigidly enforced and unusually unnatural, persona currently is.

[134] Most of Donald's questions are nearly always rhetorical, sometimes.

[135] Or that this wasn't a redundant usage of this or that.

Donald has imagined a scenario very much like this so many times before. Except he wasn't a crazy mental inmate, he wasn't in a crazy mental hospital, and the fugitive he was helping wasn't also all of the above. Apart from those minor details, this was exactly the same amount of crazy.

The standard responses of "No!" "Who?" or "Huh¿™" weren't anywhere near the first words Donald thought of and casually said. What he did think of and say was astoundingly quick-witted, "I haven't seen anyone recently, who was calling themselves *Skit*,[136] and I didn't see where they went even if I had seen them." This turned out to be exactly the right thing to say.[137]

The puffer was rapidly turning into a *huffer*. "Where are you Skit?"

Medical Assistant – SaRS
Grey Duate (Student Nurse)
Un-Authorised. Except for when
pursuing any escaped patients...

Donald caught a glimpse of the name tag flapping around Grey's neck just before he ran off in search of Skit. He had an unusual, uncommon and nearly unique thought of, "Nailed it!" This *it* shouldn't be confused with the other *it*, in the earlier thought, "I've still got it!"

Even though Donald didn't know what was going on or what he had just nailed, he did know at least one thing no one else did... His autism (Asperger's, HFA, whatever...) had gifted him with the superpower of being able to just *See through all of the crap*. He didn't know why this was relevant, though.

Much like the alleged thieves' motto, Donald was of the opinion, "All the people like us committed committee members need to stick together!" Which is why he wasn't going to do anything to help *The Man* recapture the person currently known as Lisbeth, who might have formerly been known as Skit.

Aaaron was the next to arrive as he, Donald guessed correctly, had been seconded from his door minding duties into the chase for Skit. He was looking somewhere between very annoyed, slightly flustered and highly motivated. Pausing only momentarily to verify Skit wasn't in the dining room anymore, he set off in the exact same direction as Grey.

---

[136] Which wasn't really a lie, just a small factual fib.

[137] It may very well have been the first time ever for Donald, probably the first time ever in SaRS and definitely the first time ever for a chase scene in this book where someone referred to the chased person's name in italics.

Donald shook his head, thinking, "Why would you follow someone if you knew the someone you were following was also looking for the same other someone as you? It would surely be more productive to search in a different place." Shrugging to himself, he said, "It's ok to come out now."

Nothing.

"Lisbeth?"

More nothing.

"Skit?"

Donald looked under the table and located only the floor.[138] Bizarrely, he took all of this in his stride and thought, "After all... I am in a mental hospital. It wasn't so strange. Much stranger things are bound to happen. Right?"

"Absolutely, Sir," came the unexpected reply.

"Sphincter Feng Shui![139]"

Donald snapped up from looking under the table, only missing its edge by a wafer-thin after-dinner mint. Once a couple of his senses had regained their senses, he was able to focus on where the voice had come from. But to Donald, it appeared to be coming from nowhere. This diversion was suitably complete to make Donald forget about the small package Lisbeth had just given to him. The package doesn't matter in the scheme of things because it is empty, but what Lisbeth thought it was might have been interesting to find out.

Who Donald was seeing, or more correctly, what Donald wasn't entirely seeing, was another resident ghost[140] not living at SaRS. It is unknown how the ghost was able to answer Donald's thoughts at this time.

Seth Rueful is the ghost of a previous SaRS inmate and, for other reasons, also yet to be explained, has assumed the responsibility of butler. His memory of his own demise is rather fuzzy... He only knows it all started to go downhill quickly after he came to receive treatment at SaRS, ironically, because he was feeling depressed about being mostly invisible to other people.

---

[138] Along with the past week's food droppings, but he was ignoring these.

[139] Donald's ejaculation of surprise. (Oh, don't be so rude and childish!)

Ejaculate: 3rd person present   /ɪˈdʒakjʊleɪt/
To say something quickly and suddenly.

I learned this definition reading Biggles books <mmmmmph> years ago.

[140] There may be more than two ghosts at SaRS, but they haven't been written or thought of yet and I must allow myself some room for a sequel.

One of the best tools in pre-ghost Seth's depression recovery toolbox was to use this near invisibility for his own advantage. For example, it was surmised he would never have to pay for a ticket to go to, or get into, anywhere ever again. Unfortunately, on the evening of the day he was released from SaRS, he decided to put this newly supposed skill to the test.

He didn't queue up and therefore didn't buy a ticket for entrance to the *Luna(tic) Park* amusement and theme park; he didn't queue up and therefore didn't buy a ticket for entrance to the infamous *Mirror Maze*. Finally, he didn't use either of those tickets he hadn't bought to enter the maze. After this, things become a little blurry...

He remembers:
- Going inside the maze and wandering around for a while;
- Forgetting to keep track of the time;
- Someone screams, shattering a mirror; and
- The rest is silence...

After this silence, there is only... And he was never seen alive again...

Literally...

"Good early-to-mid afternoon Sir; I am Seth, the SaRS butler. Master BLT informed me there was to be a brand-new patient. I was to keep a special eye out for you just in case you were having any difficulties acclimatising[141] to your new, albeit hopefully temporary, home."

Donald was quickly arriving at a position where he might actually think, "Maybe I am crazy... Really? Do you think so? It's just as well I'm in a mental hospital then. I'm not so sure. But look on the bright side... Well, it is certainly good. Isn't it? Yes, I completely agree. What was I saying? Who are you?[142]"

Limping off, Seth said to Donald, "If you would please walk this way, Sir, I will lead you back to the common area.[143]"

---

[141] Acclimatising - Acclimating? Isn't the English language wonderful for having so many words with exactly the same meaning as another one?

I also find it humorous, amusing and funny, when an American dictionary refers to English as British English or Commonwealth English.

[142] Thought no one ever.

[143] Can you guess what happens next?

Chapter 6:
The Kingswood's House (Scandal)

While walking[144] down the corridor, following a few paces behind Seth, Donald couldn't stop himself and began to wonder about three random things… Firstly, "Are there uncommon areas?" Secondly, "I wonder what they are going to serve up to us for dinner tonight?" and finally, "I wonder why a ghost would need to limp?"

Then a completely unexpected, unmistakable and unembellished fourth wondering came along. It, however, along with many of the other wonderings Donald will eventually have, is destined to stay inside of Donald's wonderful mind for at least as long as it takes him to forget them.

This fourth question, currently residing in Donald's confused mind, is one he is required to think about immediately. It is primarily about a current and potentially unavoidable, curious activity converging straight at him. "Why are there two people, who are wearing matching motorbike helmets and carrying a large cardboard box, coming along the corridor directly towards me?" As the two masked, box carrying, and rapidly approaching persons came a little closer to Donald, he could see, "This is yet another successful delivery being made by the Moped Riders of Mc∕David's!" printed on the back of the helmet of the backwards walking Rider.

Seth stopped his limping to enquire of them an answer for the question, "What do you think you are doing?" Actually, this is only what Donald thought Seth was asking because he couldn't hear any of the conversation due to the many amounts of alarm bells ringing inside his head. Seth would never be as impolite as Donald; he was, in fact, giving them directions to where they were supposed to deliver the large cardboard box's contents.

---

[144] Fooled you! Yeah, probably not, I know I am a predictable prat.

The box they were carrying had a sign on the side...

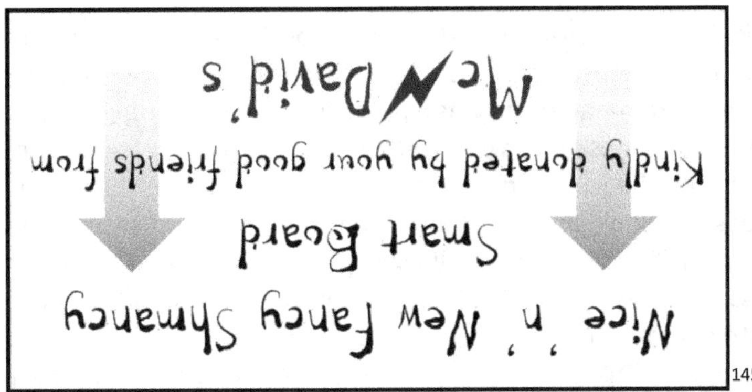

[145]

Donald put this whole episode out of his mind, having no doubts at all, maybe hopefully, he would never have to see anything like this ever again.[146]

Continuing on their way towards the common area, Seth led Donald past several other rooms. Most of these cells had their doors closed, but there were a couple with their doors unclosed. Donald always looked inside the ones with their doors open,[147] just to see what he could see. Primarily what he saw were hospital rooms, each with a hospital bed, and most of these with an assumed hospital inmate lying on top of it thinking hospital thoughts.

In one of the few open doored rooms, observably, Donald saw Nota and Owedebt sitting down at a table playing a game. It looked a little bit like it was a weird cross-pollination of *Scrabble* and *Snap*. He loitered for a moment and watched them play... They were making little piles of letter tiles between each other, and when they thought there was a completed valid word, they would slap the pile and say, "Scrap... Ow![148]" Their objective seemed to be scrapping enough words together to make a complete sentence.

Donald then made a major mistake...

---

[145] Do you know how hard it is to get text upside-down when converting from Word to a PDF? I hope you appreciate all of these little touches.

[146] He does remember thinking something about how it was surprising there were two people delivering an upside-down smart board by motorbike.

[147] He could hardly look inside the rooms with closed doors, now, could he?

[148] This sounds like it might actually work. All someone has to do is think up a few rules, change the tiles into cards so they don't hurt when scrapped, put it all in an oversized box and then send me a royalty cheque. Please.

He glanced in the direction of Chunky Poopy.

Chunky looked up from the little lumpy comfy bed he was lying on, on the floor under the table, and successfully made eye contact with Donald. He took this eye contact to mean there was a potential patter standing in the doorway. Blinking several times to make sure Mr Man wasn't an apparition, Chunky somehow found the required energy to stop time, waddle the thirteen puppy steps across the floor, and flip-flop in front of Donald. This was all before his several plus one[th] blink. When he finished defying the illogical laws of physics, Chunky assumed his natural back down feet up stance and threatened to lick Donald into submission if he didn't give some pats.

Donald chose this moment in time to escape the horror and keep himself alive and unlicked, thank-you-very-much.

"For now, my pretty little patty-man… For now!" Was the ominous you're-welcome-very-much reply Chunky had indelibly inked all over and through to the back of Donald's retreating eyes.

A few, stumbling backwards with one half-twist from the upright position, steps down the corridor,[149] Donald came to another room, and this one, also, wasn't hidden behind a closed door. This room was smaller, darker and colder than the comparatively luxurious one in use by the *un-manage-a-trio*. Donald, ever curious, looked inside. He was doomed to always cave and try to take a peek when his curiosity was piqued.[150] It was a single room much like his own, and it contained many other similarities, including the occupier.

Karl Saneman is the occupant of this room. Karl, like Donald, used to be just another normal man who had normal struggles throughout his normal life. He also struggled with friendships and relatives (optional and mandatory), fitting in, and with just trying to appear normal. The similarity of their painfully current situation, and the similarity of their history and future, would lead them to become friends inside, outside and *Outside* SaRS.

Remember when I said, "This situation would be a very unusual situation for most people," and, "a seriously cliché one?" I guess I can extrapolate these to, "This is an all-too-common situation, which no one will ever talk about."

---

[149] Donald only scored a combined score of 19.5, due to the extreme low level of difficulty and the harsh Russian Judge's score of three points.

[150] Except into known occupied bear caves. There wasn't enough piquing for him to try and peek into one of those and become a sitting duck for the bear's dinner… Or if you would like, a peeking-sitting-duck dinner.

But let's not dwell on the dwindling humour and concentrate on dwarfing the sadness of these two dweebs' situation.

Karl looked up from where he was sitting, slumped over on the bed, still with his face cradled in his upturned palms. His Welcome Pack was discarded on the floor, its contents shredded and strewn uncaringly as far away as you could strew a few handfuls of shredded uncaring welcome. He had a familiar despondent look in his watery red-rimmed eyes, simply asking… "Why?"

Donald knew the look, knew the question but was unable to provide Karl with anything remotely resembling an adequate answer. There was no answer to satisfactorily satisfy a similarly distraught, downtrodden and demoralised person. What Donald could and did offer Karl was some of his own company throughout this traumatic experience. They would go on to become the *Statler and Waldorf* of SaRS, and people would talk about them for years.[151]

Donald jumped and turned at the unexpected, and frankly quite spooky, sound of Seth clearing his throat.

"*Ahphlegm*… Sir, please… We have much more ground to cover."

It only dawned on Donald much later… "Why would a ghost need to clear his throat? Must be the whole incorporeal thing of not being able to tap living people on the shoulder."

Donald glanced back at Karl, who was returning his head to his hands, and tried to think of something encouraging to say; but couldn't…

He silently followed Seth, vowing to not look into any other rooms. When they passed by Interrogation Room Too, Donald felt a small shudder just above his neckline, indicating his mind had gone off into something of a tangential self-defence mode. (It had wandered off, leaving Donald to fend for himself.)

This is what Donald calls his *Information Gathering Mode*. He sees, hears, feels, smells and tastes everything… Sometimes all at once.[152] But, he doesn't try to interpret any of the information. When he gets like this, he is gathering a vast amount of information for a later offline batch process, after which he will report back to himself, at a more convenient time, anything important.

---

[151] Strictly for medical or supervisory reasons only. Because… One of the "SaRS Rules the OK!" is "What Happens in SaRS, Stays in SaRS." Yeah, right… Would you like to buy a talking purple bridge?

[152] A recently flaming still smoking toasted marshmallow crackling while it is cooling on a fondue fork is a very good example of this… Yummmmm…

Today, still Monday, this information consists partially of the crook's tour around the SaRS' Kangaroo ward. But first, a word (or an average of 49) about each ward at SaRS, curiously named after an appropriate Australian animal:

Kangaroo - This is the Mental Health ward, where Donald will be spending the bulk of his stay at SaRS. Before someone can become an inmate here, they are required to choose and then exhibit at least three of the many down and up symptoms of the many personality and mood disorders available.

Wombat - The Uniformed ward (specialising in PTSD). Inmates here are all from a uniformed and generally dangerous occupation (Soldier, Policeperson, Dentist etc....). They will have either been exposed to major trauma or have been shot at by cowardly tourists, hunting a slow-moving target for kicks.

Platypus - Addiction Discovery and Recovery ward. Inmates are those with seriously debilitating addictions. They could be physical, mental, or reality TV hyper-theatrical. They are, as often as not, people who have had a hard time explaining to the rest of the world who they really are.

Tasmanian-Tiger - Aged Care and Rehabilitation ward. Inmates here, the TTs, are those who are close to, or about to pass into, extinction and have no family left willing to look after them. Or, they have just been through a major surgery and have survived (anything from a haircut upwards).

This description of their demarcation delineation only applies when there are enough beds in the most approximately appropriate ward to go around and around. Sometimes the inmates throughout SaRS are needfully mixed and matched with each other, so you might have a Wombat in the Kangaroo ward learning how to jump through their becoming normal hoops or a Platypus in the Tasmanian-Tiger ward who is going through a dissociative identity crisis.

Seth's tour took Donald through the mansion, currently serving admirably as the psychological treatment section of the Hospital, and throughout the tour, he provided the following commentary-most-exquisite:

Building of The Kingswood's House started roughly 125 years ago. Since then, it has undergone several significant physical transformations. It has been expanded up, down and sideways; it's had rooms divided, joined and created; and through all of this, it has had many more than its fair share of documented scandals (at least five) and unresolved serious crimes (at least three).[153]

-----

[153] And many more than a few undocumented, and resolved, ones as well.

The most recent, most unsolved and quite possibly the most combined scandalous crime was the chilling discovery, a few years ago, of a complete set of human remains. They had been found deposited underneath the mansion's thought to be incomplete and completely unused courtyard basement. This place itself was found to be underneath a hidden secret door.[154]

A great, great-grandson of one of the main building's original architects, twice removed due to budgetary issues and not incompetence as was widely reported at the time, unearthed a set of draft plans for The Kingswood's House building. He found these while researching his ancestral roots and the effect they have had on the local landscape over the years.

These plans were dated a full three years before the formally approved plans had been lodged to the local building commission. Bizarrely, they had also been updated to match what was thought to be the building's layout 75 years ago at some time in the past. This alteration included a large red arrow pointing to the unused under courtyard basement burial tomb from a "Do Not Dig Here! Move Along! There is Nothing to Find!" message...

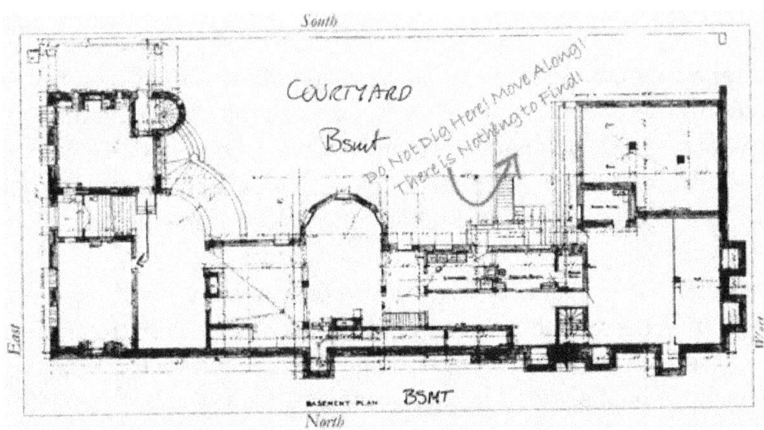

This discovery generated much-unwanted intrigue, and because there are a few passionate people at SaRS trying to debunk the rumoured finding as a hoax, a group of passionate hoax debunker debunkers has been formalised.[155] When the apparent hoax was found to be not so apparent, after they literally uncovered the body, a full-scale investigation was launched. The ex-person's remains were excavated, exhumed and examined. These were then expertly identified as human and had been buried for approximately 75 years.

---

[154] It wouldn't be much of a secret door if it wasn't hidden.

[155] Everyone knows that when a rumour is vehemently denied it is more than a little bit closer to the truth than the people concerned would like it to be.

75 years ago was also, oddly approximately, exactly the same time when The Kingswood's House mansion changed hands to become the first iteration of SaRS. The people, places and objects of SaRS one-point-zero have all been included in the investigation.

The people under suspicion of committing this nefarious act are:[156]

Brother Brown - Alias: The Adopted One We Don't Talk About. He would hang around the rest of the Brothers of Saint Rita, hoping for a bit of inclusion to rub off on him. Eventually, it became presumably easier for the Brothers to explain his persistent, pervasive presence by making him a permanent paltry part of the parish's pretence.

Father Fuchsia - The Founding Father of SaRS, back when it was called the Private Psychiatric Hospital for Men. He was instrumental in identifying this iconic institution-to-be as an incredibly important investment inside the ill-informed insanity industry. He facilitated the purchase of the grounds on behalf of the Brothers of Saint Rita.

Sister Sapphire - Sister Sapphire was one of the early cloistered nuns who belonged to the Order of Saint Rita. They were the Yin to the Brothers' Yang. She was voraciously vocal and virtually visceral in her valuable vexations. She vehemently wanted the hospital to accept vindicated female inmates when they were accompanied and vouched for by a venerable voice.

Gardener Grey - An employee of the previous owner of The Kingswood's House. During the transition of ownership, he was notified that his near noble botanical services would no longer be needed, necessitating his navigation to a new niche, which allowed his nurturing of the native Northern Pepperbush, and nullification of any noxious negative nuisance weeds to continue.

Lawyer Lithium - He was a lawyer... Enough said.

Wastrel White - Wastrel, was, apparently, the last remaining living relative of the previous owner. His identity was kept a secret. This is primarily why he failed bitterly, when he bumped himself forward on the ballot, to become the sole beneficiary of the big boundary blanketed building's booty, based on both non-believable and blatantly bold balderdash. But I digress...

---

[156] Each of these people were present 75 years ago; each of them has a significant secret story surrounding the sad situation of the *Bones Under the Courtyard Basement*; and each of them are also now dead...

The investigation has revealed two solid facts:

- ¤ As all of the main contenders are not with us anymore, anything else unearthed by this investigation is going to be purely hypothetical and based on hyperbole; and
- ¤ The body had been dehumanised in another part of The Kingswood's House. Thus, the main areas of the investigation are centred around the following squarish shaped set of rooms:

CC's Kitchen - The kitchen (currently known as Chef Chief's Kitchen, or CC's Kitchen), even though it has always been the kitchen for each of the iterations of The Kingswood's House, it has changed drastically several times. Initially, it was a moderate semi-detached room with a well-used well under the current walk-in refrigerated larder (their well became obsolete when the town water supply was connected). The cooking facilities have also transformed from an open fireplace to a wood-fired pizza oven then the current semi-commercial restaurant-quality stainless-steel easy-to-clean electrical-appliance one.

Main Dining Room - Where the majority of eating takes place (and is the most recent addition to The Kingswood's House). It is understood this used to be an undercover outside place of escape for the inside staff. It is only-just included here for completeness. It was fully enclosed (and therefore became an inside) much later than the courtyard basement's underneath was opened up to become an outsiders' inside hidden burial tomb.

Minor Dining Room - The main (actually the only) inmate dining room at the time of the incident. This room imbues the look and feel of a commercial terrarium.[157] Apart from the single wall connecting the room to the mansion, it is completely made out of glass panels. The tables and chairs are arranged specifically to facilitate the complete ignorance[158] of the other diners.

Outside Dining Room - This room is outside. It has always been outside (from the initial building of The Kingswood's House, right through to the under cellular modifications when it was purchased by The Brothers of Saint Rita 75 years ago, and then finally to last week's lawn mowing). It is therefore not of any importance unless you are a hungry claustrophobia sufferer.[159]

---

[157] No! I'm not suggesting the inmates in SaRS are like plants...
Oh wait... Maybe I am... (But I really shouldn't.)

[158] Meaning... Each diner can successfully ignore every other diner.

[159] For these special inmates there is also a special table delivery service.

Staff Dining Room - While it might say "Staff Only" on the door, everyone understands it to mean "Medical Staff Only" (as neither the dietitian nor the kitchen staff are allowed in there to eat). Oh, the kitchen minions are allowed in to collect the dirty plates, and the cleansers are allowed there to cleanse but don't even think about sitting down to nibble on some minute leftovers.

This isn't just bordering on segregation; it is demonstrably demonised. The elitist attitude displayed by some has been smuggled over the double razor wire fence, combined with a side of gene enhanced corn cakes, and then force-fed to their superiority complex. There have been many complaints over the years, but they have all fallen on either deaf or ignorant ears.

Group Room 1 - This was the mansion's drawing-room, where gentlemen would sit to smoke their cigars and drink their whisky. It was also the original hospital's ward for their alcoholic (male only) inmates.

Group Room 2 - The mansion's master bedroom, once used for relaxation and sleep, is now the main yoga and meditation room of SaRS (where there is no sleep allowed, just copious amounts of painful stretching and relaxation).

Group Room 3 - Originally the mansion's bedrooms two and three, today they have been joined to become the SaRS music room. (Basically, this means the piano is stored here when it isn't in use somewhere else).

Each of these three group rooms has been repurposed a great many times throughout history.[160] For the purposes of this breakdown, there isn't much to describe: they each have tables, chairs and malfunctioning whiteboards; they each have a similar-but-individual Rules and Regulations poster, and each of them is unlikely to be the location where the incident likely took place.

Managerial Office (Mansion's Servant's Quarters) - From underneath the bottom of the pile up to sitting on top of the heap (so to speak). This room is always off-limits to all, except for the current manager of the SaRS facility and any minions who are required to be there. *They* have said this isn't where the incident took place, and as there are no wrong answers, it must be true.

Inside/Outside Courtyard - The last resting place of Brother Latent Tardy. His headstone, the memorial fountain and the evidence of many pigeons are the only significant contents of this location. It has only been included because this is where you can gain entry to the courtyard's basement (and then on to the under-courtyard-basement's burial tomb via the secret door), leading to a set of steps underneath the fountain's base.

---

[160] There is a complete, and intriguing, picture display in the reception area of the ward buildings. We might touch on these later. **Edit:** No, we won't.

Way back when The Kingswood's House was just a mansion, this was the room[161] where: accomplished musicians would perform; local thespians would put on Easter, Christmas, and Beauty Pageants and the pigeon poo would be fished out of the fountain on a daily basis. None of this happens nowadays.

The story of "how the found body became a lost body" has benefited from the recent supposition, suggestion and surmise. All manner of examinations performed on the remains have been inappropriately inconclusive as to the answer to the question: "Which of the several historically plausible methods of murder most monstrous was it likely to have been?"

There were no obvious fatal injuries found, less evidence of poisoning, and even fewer ligature marks[162] to be seen. All standard methods of murder, most monstrous, where they are both unobtrusive[163] and available in the era of the death, have been considered. The credible options are:

Rope - The victim may have been strangled or choked. There was always enough rope available. Hanging, however, has been specifically ruled out, as the neck bones were completely intact in their detached state… And hanging generally creates quite a memorable spectacle anyway.

Medication - An overdose of Metrazol is one of the considered methods of murder. This was a commonly available drug for the psychiatric institutions of the era. There have been several documented cases with lethal results when it was administered with a surprisingly moderate quantity of alcohol.

Electrocution - Electro-Convulsive Therapy (ECT) was still in its infancy as an unknown science, and most early machines were still being developed. But it is thought that if these experimental examples were turned up to thirteen, they could have produced enough electricity for a fatal shock to occur.

Pillow - Suffocation was unlikely but still possibly plausible. Being an older hospital, the pillows of the day were encased with plastic pillowcases, making the process of getting an airtight seal around the mouth area quite easy.

---

[161] Do you refer to an inside/outside courtyard as a room? It is completely encased within walls, doors and windows like a room, but it has no roof.

[162] These last two were no-brainers. After around 75 years of being buried underground there generally aren't any squishy bits of a victim left to test.

[163] Unobtrusive to everyone bar the victim of course.

Animal Intervention - In all likelihood, this would have been an accidental cause of death. There have been incidents in the past where mistreated farm animals have rebelled against humanity. Still, in all those cases, it has been pigs at the centre of the controversies. There are no records of pigs in the area.

Implements - such as spanners, candlesticks, daggers and lead pipes have all been ruled out, with the exception (that only proves the rule) of the dagger. Apart from being unimpressive, they would all have left obvious signs of major malfeasance when inflicting a fatal injury except the dagger, of course.

Conveniently, Seth's tour concluded just after he had detailed all of these investigated murder weapons. This left Donald with much to think about. And as he was starting to ponder which of these varied topics he would like to think about first, the near silence was quietly shattered by…

Death is not the end; it is merely the beginning; of a very long, very sad and very boring story; no one has written, no one is reading, and no one will buy.

"Sphincter Feng Shui!" It doesn't take much to go all the way from terrific to terrify, passing through terrible on the way. Donald became aware of Sven, and another five people, who were sitting around a table, doing what looked to be a jigsaw puzzle of jigsaw puzzle pieces.[164]
"Shh, everyone! Can you hear a noise? I think I heard someone speaking…"
"Nah, man, of course, we can hear him; he's standing right there!"
"You are not helping."
This conversation went on for considerably more minutes than the half of which has been slowly illustrated here. It was a tepid banter between two of the other SaRS inmates… Nelo Priors and Istha T. You.

Two of the other three currently un-named people at the table were polar opposites in their levels of interest. Got Knoted (silent K noted) was mentally taking notes, so she could remember what this exchange was all about in the future, and Lost M'Hankie was trying to remember where he put the notes he had taken about what he had exchanged his mentality for previously. The last person, with her head slumped on the table, was Mindy Ownbeeswhacks, who was comfortably asleep and snoring like Methuselah.

---

[164] Not the little jigsaw puzzle pieces making up a jigsaw, although they were puzzling over the little jigsaw puzzle pieces making up this jigsaw puzzle. The little jigsaw puzzle pieces were pieces of a jigsaw puzzle created by using a picture of completed jigsaw puzzle. (p99 has this completed puzzle picture).

Nelo (Vamp) Priors is one of the frequent flyers at SaRS, as he is addicted to drinking Blood and is also, ironically, anaemic. He is so anaemic he needs to have a transfusion of type B+[165] Blood every third month or so. Otherwise, the hobgoblins, living in his haemoglobin, start acting up, and he has actual trying to fly like a bat contemplations. When you add in another of his symptomatic complications, being very photosensitive, Vamp is an archetypal stereotypical example of an, I really *wanna-be* a vampire.[166]

Istha T. You is living with a schizophrenia diagnosis and understands that the physical appearance of Donald is just a personification of the voices inside her head, and no one else can either see or hear him. If someone does tell her they can see and hear him, another little voice in her head tells her she should ignore the first voice, as she is only thinking she can hear it.

Istha is always being told, by all of her psychologists, "Often what you are experiencing is only real for you. What you think you are hearing and seeing is only your own personal version of an altered reality." She is also being taught how to differentiate between her own perception of reality and the other real reality. The trouble with this is, her psychologist is someone she can see and hear. So, she doesn't know if she should listen to him and simply dismiss what he says as he is only her perception, or dismiss him and embrace the reality of what he is saying.[167]

Got Knoted is an undercover reporter (her real name is *Monique Aname*). There is not much known about her, except she is here trying to get to the bottom of the *Bones Under the Courtyard Basement* controversy. At least, this is the cover story she tells. She is really a secret undercover policewoman (her real real name is *Alley Usknownas*). She is a former Eastern Bloc spy who we should know even less about. Still, apparently, we know she was formerly an Eastern Bloc spy. She is here now trying to expose an elicit undercover reporting ring. Or she is just plain mental?[168]

---

[165] As well as one of *Be Positive*. **Groan**. Yes, but it had to be done.

[166] His aptly chosen profession of *Moon Time and Place Photographer*, his symptoms and his addiction have all made him a minor paparazzi for the local vampire and werewolf cults... Of which there are scarily many.

[167] If you think this is confusing, remember back to when I asked you, "How do you think Donald feels?" I ask again... How do you think people like Istha feel? And there *are* people like Istha.

[168] Or is she? (Don't ask me... How am I supposed to know?)

Mindy Ownbeeswhacks is heading towards ancient, at one-hundred and seven years old. She is also currently the only inmate who is fully in control of her own mind. She takes her mind out of her head and places it very carefully in a bowl of warm water beside her bed every evening and then returns it to her head every morning, generally without mishap.[169]

Mindy is also the primary reason there is going to be an eventual update to the Hospital's _free_ Wi-Fi service, specifically to the login page. Currently, it only accepts up to two digits for your age. She has no overstated need for the _free_ Wi-Fi, it is just the principle, and she is a cantankerous old pedant.

Lost M'Hankie is an amnesia sufferer.[170]

Donald is just standing anxiously throughout this entire debacle of an end to the sixth chapter. What he really needs right now is for you to turn to the next page, please. Don't even bother to read the last footnote.[171]

---

[169] Ask her about the incident with the vase of flowers.

[170] ...and I have apparently forgotten to write an introduction for/about him. Except for this. And this. And this... Too much? And that too?

[171] What did I just say?

Chapter 7:
Monday
(4pm⁺ to Zero Dark)

Donald finally catches up with his thinking, "Or, should that be the other way around?" he thinks. It doesn't really matter how you see it, because, unusually, this destination is more important than the journey travelled. From the outside of Donald's head, it appears as if he has just woken up after a semi-permanent nap.[172]

Coming from the hallway directly across the room was a massive influx of conga line people, who were being led by a vivid red leather leotard wearing, stick carrying and carrot taunting bundle of energy. Donald's mind needed to only take a minutely small step to imagine she was directing a training session for an upcoming Halloween musical version of the Rocky saga.[173]

Following the procession and providing the musical accompaniment was probably the second strangest looking person Donald had seen in the last five seconds. He was wearing an outfit Robin Hood would have been proud to be seen in while he was prancing through a forest dominated by Jacaranda trees, surrounded by people drinking mojitos with those cute little paper umbrellas and listening to the dulcet tones of the Village People during their heyday.

---

[172] This is up to eight days of nap, which doesn't actually commit you to any length of time. You can take this type of nap anywhere naps can be normally taken. Whereas if you want to take a permanent nap, you are required to make some further elaborate preparations.

Note: A *permanent nap* is apnoea speak for a coma and not death.

[173] A Rocky Horror Musical if you will.

The director of the procession, wearing the strangely coloured, strangely captivating, but not-so-strangely, yet seriously, inappropriate exercise gear,[174] is **Ma'am Cybill Flex**. She is the fitness worker, occupational therapy guru, and part-time dominatrix exercise wear fashion designer. She provides ample motivation for participation in her exercise regimen by illustrating what she will do to you, ramification wise, if you don't follow her rules. She will always catch you, and her "I must break you!" is way scarier than Dolf's ever was…

Fitness Therapist – SaRS
Ma'am Cybill Flex, MOT
Do Not make the mistake of attempting to hide from me…!

William, the Piano Man, is here to provide for any and all of your musical needs, and he is currently providing by playing a long green flute. It looked like it was made out of bamboo by a legally blind baboon, using a blunt spoon on one of his bad days. When Willy first became a member of the SaRS treatment family, he found it hard to carry the piano around all the time, so he taught himself to play some (more?) portable musical instruments.

What he generally omits from his introductions is that it was a few days after he had finally mastered the keytar when he found out the room he had always known as SaRS' group room three was also known as the music room.

There's a piano in there…   And some chairs as well…

And people with names…   With sad stories to tell…   Open wide…

Musical Therapist – SaRS
William (Willy) The Piano Man
I'm not really sure how it goes
But I can play you a memory…

Donald was still just standing there and mostly minding his own business; mesmerised by the sounds, the colour and the what-the of it all, when out of somewhere, "Has she gone?" came a whisper.

And for the third time today… "Sphincter Feng Shui!"
(Hey, it rhymes. I'm a poet, and I damn well know it!)
"Well, Has She Gone or Not!!!" screeched Owedebt, switching to devil.

------

[174] "Clothing" would be a flamboyantly overstated much too strong a word to describe the unusual memorable ensemble she was almost wearing.

"Has who gone?" responded Donald, ever so slightly bewildered.

"Did I ask you for any of your attitude! Did I! Did I really! No, No, I did Not! Most definitely Not! What is your Problem! Just answer the freaking question! I'm talking about Ma'am Flex, of course! The exercise Lady! Do you understand now?! Or are you stupid or something! **Has she gone?!**[175]"

Glancing around, Donald took in the speechless silence, indicating Ma'am Flex and her procession had gone. The very strange conga line had gone back out of the common area, and up the corridor, from whence they had come.

The quietly forlorn *fluterised* notes slowly wafting to the floor, only to get caught in the current flowing underneath the emergency exit door and having their tiny cartoon exact images squashed into two-dimensionally flat notes so they could fit, were the only noticeable reminder of the previous bizarre music related activity in the common area... And only in Donald's mind.

Recovering from his melancholy detachment and thinking the squashed music could be used instead of the little printed lines and dots on sheet music, Donald managed to squeak out a barely audible "Yes."

"Thanks, sweetie,[176]" said the now conversationally adept Owedebt.

"!iuhS gneF retcnihpS"

"Wow... Phew... That was an excitingly close one," with a nonchalant non-effective non-nonplussed brow wipe and hair flick, "Themse semantics were some-antics, weren't they?[177]" continued Owedebt, without a hint of knowing just how much her incorrect blasé comment infuriated Donald. She finished her unplanned introduction with a, "Hi, my name is Owedebt."

---

[175] These rabid exclamations are Owedebt's application of what happens when her borderline personality disorder is mixed with her bi-polar disorder giving her BPD^2, which is exponentially worse than either on their own.

This can only happen when she *forgets* to take her medication...

Have you ever seen those movies where patients, or prisoners, pretend to take a pill, only to produce it on their tongue the next time they are alone with the camera? Owedebt taught them that special person's trick.

[176] Yes, transitions from Devil Owedebt to Angel Owedebt are *that* fast.

[177] Yeah, it looks and sounds like a question... But this side of Owedebt doesn't like to rely on anyone for her own answers. Even though there are multiple fitting answers, there was only one acceptable response. Much like the question, "Would you like me to do the washing up?"

Putting aside his monumental confusion exacerbated by her flagrant flip-flopping attitude and sucking back in the words he urgently wanted to speak, Donald answered her with an answer he would come to regret for a long, long time... "Listen up carefully, you crazy Dozy Doe: it's not *themse* semantics, it's *those* semantics; and because the word *semantics*, ironically, means the study of *word meanings*... NO...[178] They certainly were **not**, *Some-Antics*!"

Unfortunately for Donald, this wasn't his verbal answer; it wasn't even his visual answer; it was just his visceral interpretation of what the answer should have been. Sadly, "Yeah, ha, ha. They were some antics all right." was all he could manage to come up with on such short notice. This was the answer he thought was well worth his regretting.

Had Donald's thinking been a teensy-little bit faster, he might have come through this teensy-little chance to distance himself from Owedebt a teensy-little bit, with a teensy-little bit of distance between himself and Owedebt... Sadly, again, like most chances he has ever received, he blew it when he didn't think quickly enough and continued, "Hi, I am Donald; nice to meet you."

"Nice to meet you? Dammit!" he thought.

"Hey, Donny..." audibly thought Owedebt.
"Donald," corrected Donald.

I don't agree with what you are saying, but I support your right to say it.

Donald began to wonder if Sven was going to keep popping up like this... At random times, in random places, with random quotes that are only vaguely related to the situation he was interrupting.

"Hey, Donald..." said Owedebt pausing for acknowledgement, "Why don't I give you an all-expenses-paid trip around the Kangaroo ward? It won't cost you a thing. C'mon... It will get you away from any vestigial amount of dignity you might have left to lose after just standing there looking like the ballerina in the spinning dancer silhouette illusion."

Donald quickly found and donned his embarrassing dumfounded look to cover up his thinking about how Owedebt was on a par with Sven in the mental stakes. "I guess so. It's not like I have any pressing previous engagements..."

"Right-y-ho... Let's start with dinner."

"But it's only the middle of the afternoon."

---

[178] I find it strange, and interesting, "No!" and, "Yes!" can both be thought to mean the same negative response. No, I disagree with you, they were not! And... Yes, I agree with you, they were not!

Donald was about to learn a very invaluable lesson: SaRS operates on Old People's Time, otherwise known as "OPT." It wasn't optional or optimal and frequently caused optophobia,[179] but it was what they did.

"Mid broad daylight. Yeah, it's true. But it's also when dinner is served at this esteemed establishment.[180] If you don't get there quickly enough, you get left with the soggy cauliflower, and you don't want your cauliflower soggy."

Donald was unsure if this was a euphemism.[181] But, thankfully, this side-track was about to be side-tracked by the next, definitely not, euphemism.

With a slow-motion flourish of her long auburn hair, a straightening out of her crimson leatherette skirt-suit and in an obviously magma enriched state of mind, in comes a definitely atypical woman in red. Striding over to Lost, she slaps him soundly once, then she slaps him again resoundingly twice, leaving three hand-sized and shaped red welts on his cheeks. Throwing her head back in the standard humph motion, she leaves without uttering a single word.

More than thirteen, but less than fifteen seconds pass. No one needs to request an extra helping of stunned silence so they can hear the tock of the clock as each second ticks over. Everyone is looking mouth-opened, goggle-eyed at Lost with the same obvious question:

"What is for dinner tonight?"

"No... The other question."

"Oh... Who was SHE!?!"[182]

Lost tried his hardest to look back at everyone at the same time, and if he wasn't so obviously in agony, it would have been laughable. As it was, it was only just funny. His jaw was on the floor, glowing red and showing no signs of supplying the answer to either of these questions. His memory was still being registered as a non-participant in the conversation, and no information could be found written on his face between the fading fingerprints. He didn't even remember that this had happened at least 37 times before.

---

[179] The fear of opening your eyes, which makes a lot of sense at six o'clock in the morning, but not so much at six o'clock in the middle of the afternoon.

[180] It was amazing how Owedebt made this sound like she wanted to say, "Hell Pit," and she would have, if she wasn't on her third warning this week...

[181] I am unsure as to why you use an *a* for "a euphemism." There are so many factoids of English to learn. I should schedule an English language group session sooner, rather than later. **Edit:** Done, but later, rather than sooner.

[182] I think an exclamestion mark is well warranted here. My suggestion is: ‽.

In response to him becoming the focal point of attention, all Lost could manage was a vague shoulder shrug. Then he went back to being just one of the background characters, albeit a recurring one, in someone else's story.

"Happens much more often than you might think," commented Owedebt. Setting off, Owedebt's explanation should have been a smidge comforting, except it made Donald uncomfortably numb. Thinking someone behaving like this could ever be considered to be approaching normal was not something Donald ever wanted to find comforting.

Dinner, this Monday night,[183] consisted of either: meatballs, vegetables and chips 'n' gravy, or for those who preferred the food's food, not-meatballs, vegetables and chips 'n' gravy. It didn't seem to worry anyone that the chips were fried in an oil derived from animals or that one of the ingredients in the gravy was listed as being a "natural animal flavouring.[184]"

The third option for dinner was a garden salad, vegetable soup and fruit. This seemed way too far, bordering on disconcertingly too far, removed from an unhealthy diet that it wasn't worthy of being called a numbered option... In Donald's humble opinion. He suggested to Chef, "Maybe the inhabitants of the field next door might enjoy some of this for their dinner?"

Donald's quip didn't merit a response from Chef, but there were several other inmates in the dinner queue who chuckled. Donald chose the meatball option for his dinner and his entertainment. Apart from the three diet lemon cordial disasters, dinner was uneventful.

If you want to know more about the diet lemon cordial disasters, I'm afraid Donald won't be of much help to you at the moment. They were so disturbing he has successfully had them erased from his memory. If he ever gets around to writing a book about these and his many other experiences inside SaRS, he might try to recall the incidents... But I wouldn't hold my breath if it was me.

Owedebt showed Donald how to clear his setting, where dirty plates and utensils went, and where the bin for any rubbish was. Donald let her have this one, as he didn't feel comfortable enough yet, to start making fun of her out loud. For now, he kept it all inside and had an inappropriate internal moment.

---

[183] And I use this term as loosely as possible.

[184] Four statements I always take with me to fancy food places are:

- Natural Products... As opposed to *Unnatural*... Ah you meant...
- Chemical Free Products... H_2O is a *Chemical Compound*...
- Cracked Pepper... Has a *Chemical Formula* of $C_{17}H_{19}NO_3$...
- And of course, the wound rubbing favourite, Salt... $NaCl$... **Next!**

Following her out of the dining room, which was located in the ex-mansion area of SaRS, Owedebt emphatically assured Donald they were on one of the most direct routes leading to the start of the tour:

- ☒ From the very far corner of the dining room, where the receptacle for the non-digestible gastronomical waste was located;
- ☒ Down the ramp, along the food queue (in reverse parallel direction);
- ☒ To, and then by, Aaaron's post;
- ☒ Along the corridor, passing the inside/outside courtyard;
- ☒ Turn left through a large ornate door and along another corridor;[185]
- ☒ Through the grey emergency exit/fire door combination,[186] which was always propped open, covering the "Do Not Prop Open" sign;
- ☒ Down the corridor, passing the nurse's station and drug dispensary for the Platypus ward;
- ☒ Don't turn left; that direction takes you to the Blood extraction room. There will be plenty of description about this tomorrow morning. If you continue on that way despite this warning, it will take you to the hospital memorabilia gallery, the waiting area and the administration desk. These will all be described tomorrow, or at most, eventually;
- ☒ Continue down the corridor, passing through another open fire door. We have bypassed this door in the past, as it is somewhere between Donald's room and Interrogation Room Too, but before right now, we simply haven't paid it any attention;
- ☒ Passing another two fire doors, one to either side of the corridor, and both of which are closed. These doors have two violently handwritten signs, one on each door, screaming silently, "SH!" Both have all the tell-tale font signs. They could quite easily have been written in Blood;
- ☒ Then there is a rounded capital-A lying flat-shaped area (standing up, it would be the same). If you go to the pointy end of the curve, you will end up in the common area. We are going to take the crossbar;
- ☒ Through a final, for this trip, fire door; ending in
- ☒ Success! We have arrived at the terrarium TV room.

"If you take a look over to your left, the SaRS Elevator will be coming into view shortly." Owedebt's commentary was then continued, as if it was part of a comedy monologue, in Donald's mind.

---

[185] This corridor is the standard Z, or N, shaped fire escape bottleneck.

[186] This is a serious reference. The Emergency Exit doors automatically close when the fire alarm goes off. This is so the inmates can stay safely inside roasting marshmallows, while waiting for the fire to be put out, or for them to being ~~fried~~ freed, whichever comes first.

"If we are surprisingly lucky, we may catch a rare sighting of it opening its doors to release the bowels of the hospital's latest unsuspecting victim.[187] If you pay very close attention to the eyes of the victim, as they stumble to their assumed freedom, you may be able to witness the look of absolute horror they have permanently imprinted on their psyche."

"We will be exploring this special location in detail later.[188]"

The transition back and forth (and fifth) between Owedebt's commentary and Donald's internal monologue was at times, at least to Donald, quite scary, seamless, and at other times just confusing. "And alongside the elevator is the back of the fire door we passed earlier. One of the ones with the SH! sign."

Donald noticed this side of that particularly peculiar door also had one of the same "SH!" signs on display. He decided to call this door Mobius.

"To our right is the combination corridor gauntlet. It passes by the main administration office and the public bathroom to arrive at the administration waiting area." Owedebt leaned up as far as her tippy toes would allow, cupped her hands conspiratorially around her mouth, and whispered seductively into Donald's ear, "Don't ever get those two places mixed up... One is for making a deposit, and the other a withdrawal, of, more-or-less, the same stuff."

Donald's uncontrollable shudder may have been for several reasons.

Moving back to the more traditional arm's length away.

"**The TV Room.** Not to be confused with The Other TV Room. On the wall behind the door is the room booking whiteboard, but the pens don't work, so it is next to useless. Useless is what we call the SaRS DVD library because most of the DVDs in the library were generously donated by Emirate's community outreach programme. These DVDs contain the unpopular Emirate approved versions of popular movies... There is no swearing, no nudity and categorically no gratuitously appalling plane movies.[189] The other DVDs are either missing, scratched, or not good enough to warrant borrowing them permanently."

Owedebt, curiously, continued with her copiously colourful commentary without cessation for comedy, cynicism, or condescension. Because it was now a little bit on the excruciatingly dry side, Donald's mind kick-started its collecting, collating and condensing process once again.

---

[187] The bowels of the hospital, not of the inmate. That would be too messy.

[188] Said with just the right mixture of honey and venom to make it intriguing.

[189] *Snakes on a Plane* is in the gratuitously bad plane movie category, and *Rain Man* has had the "I'll only fly on a Qantas plane" scene rudely deleted.

Both of these statements are surprisingly true.

If you leave the TV Room and continue in an orderly, inwardly spiralling clockwise direction, we will see:

The Other TV Room - This is where the daily morning self-introductory roll call is enacted. It is optional and, therefore, a purely checkbox ticking routine. You firstly have a chance to inform the other inmates of your preferred name. Then each member of staff present briefly introduces themselves. This is followed by a timetable check of the day's activities, which includes: the time for breakfast (nineteen minutes ago); what group activities are planned (check the welcome pack); and if and when the pool or gym are open today.

Then the public announcement section: telling you there is absolutely no smoking allowed at SaRS, except within the designated area, as this has been surrounded by a special invisible secondary-smoke filtration system; asking us if there are any maintenance issues needing to be raised; and cancelling the optional morning's mindfulness walk so it can now be mandatorily ignored.

All finishing with a reading from the deplorably bad *Biggest Ever Book of 1000s of Really Bad Dad Jokes*, or *The Little Book of Calm*.[190]

Kangaroo Medication Nook - If you can picture the medication dispensing scene in *One Flew Over the Cuckoo's Nest*, you have a good idea of what this area is like. Except, in reality, there is slightly less stringent monitoring of the taking them process. There are little white half-filled cups of water, so you can swallow anywhere between one and eight pills (from another little white cup). The line up in front of the window, where inmates are jostling for position, is also very much the same. At SaRS, there are three windows of opportunity[191] to receive the magical little white pills, so there is something for everyone.

Over the space between the medication dispensing windows is a sign...

---

[190] Only if it hasn't been swallowed by Manny again.

[191] Morning, Noon and Night. There are only two physical windows, and the inmates are divided in half, alphabetically, between them. Except for the weekends when they alternate between opening the East (odd weekends) and the West (very odd weekends), window.

Underneath this sign, there is always some Reggae/Disco dancing going on. This phenomenon is known as the *Bugger Em... It's my life, and I'll dance if I want to!* theory. This is the mind's way of using up any excess energy before the inevitable calming effects of the medications take hold. The same study that discovered this theory also noted, "It all makes sense when you sit down by the rivers of Babylon and remember Zion."
Re: *Life on Meds?* (Inspired by *Life on Mars?* – David Bowie) p267.
ಠ   Extract from The Donald Diaries.

Nurse's Bowl - If you are thinking of the all-female group of sexy-nurse-uniform clad American lingerie football players, you are spot on. Except for the all-female bit, the American football bit and the sexy-nurse-uniform bit.[192] The reality is more akin to an endangered nurse enclosure at a zoo.

This is their office. It is completely encased in glass, with the exclusion of two glass doors, both of which can only be opened from the outside by swiping an appropriately authorised SaRS identification tag. A series of speakers and microphones allow conversation between the nurses in their enclosure and the inmates on their viewing platform.

The following messages, heard throughout the day, all originate here:
ಠ   "Stop Doing Whatever You Think You Are Doing... Or Else;"
ಠ   "Don't Make Me Come Out There;" and
ಠ   "Careful, or I'll tell DD on you." (As more of a threat than a message).

On the only wall not made out of glass, there are hanging approximately forty-one alarm Doodad Thingamajigs. The nurses are supposed to wear one of these at all times while they are on duty. The DTs illuminate, vibrate and ding when someone pushes the emergency call button beside their bed. When this happens, many of the nurses return to the Nurse's Bowl to determine which room originated the call. Then some go and attend to the inmate's issue. There is a possible time-and-motion improvement to be made here.

This system does have another flaw... There are no emergency call buttons in the common area. If someone slips in the Tiger-Kangaroo kitchen, someone else has to Womble back to their own room, press the emergency button, wait for the nurses to arrive and then explain to them what has happened.[193]

---

[192] I'm not implying they couldn't look like this if they wanted to. I have the utmost respect for these nurses, indeed all of the staff at SaRS. It takes a special kind of person to look after us special kinds of people.

[193] True story... Believe it, or not...

TK Kitchen - is an outrageously generous description. If you want a mug of coffee, some toast and jam, or a shot of juice, you are generally in luck. The Kangaroo and Tasmanian-Tiger wards share this kitchen. There is a separation of fridges, but otherwise, they share everything, including the meagre store of coffee, sugar and biscuits; and the OH&S approved tepid water dispenser.

The TTs' idea of sharing is to eat all of the morning tea delivered during the first group session time. They are exempt from going to group, whereas it is mandatory for the single Ks. Donald didn't even know there was a morning tea until there was a delivery of banana-prune muffins. Apparently, the regularity generating muffins, when combined with the eleven-minute travel time to the bathroom, made for a higher-than-normal no-thank-you response rate when they were offered a second muffin.

And then we have the spiral terminating at the:

Common-Area - Basically, all this room contains is one round puzzle table with six upright chairs; a pair of three-seat lounge chairs separated by a small coffee table; and a grouping of two one-seat armchairs, with a supplementary three-seat lounge chair, in a three-sided square u-shape configuration, around a second coffee table. (One of the one-seat armchairs has a dodgy leg, so be a little mindful of this before sitting on it).

The same group of people are sitting on the same chairs, around the same round table. They are still doing the same jigsaw puzzle, of jigsaw puzzle pieces, as before. Donald thinks they have placed an additional ten or twelve pieces into the partially completed section of the incomplete puzzle...

SaRS Unofficial 3 - Jigsaw Puzzle Jigsaw Puzzle

PRN[194] **Items** - The whiteboard outside the Nurse's Bowl; the notice board beside the TK Kitchen; and the are-you-bored-yet activity sign-up board on the wall in the common area, with its associated signature sheet just underneath. These three middle-to-high traffic areas act as the activity hub for most of the not-so-many extracurricular activities at SaRS:

- If you have a medical appointment scheduled, it will be written on the whiteboard without anything remotely resembling confidentiality;
- If there is a notice about an upcoming, or completed, pest (or similar) inspection, it will be posted on the notice board;[195] and
- Before you can have a visitor, go on a scheduled shopping expedition, or utilise the art room, there is a sign in, up, or out requirement on the activity board signature sheet.

Donald's process of taking in some slightly damaged information and then regurgitating a slightly less distorted amount of knowledge finished at the same time as Owedebt's commentary.

This is one of those occurrences Donald doesn't challenge; another is the ability of some people to just disappear. This is what Owedebt has just done. Donald was left there, for all intents and purposes, alone in his crowd of one.

Is No going to be the next word you say?

"N...? Y...? Wha...?" Donald was never going to get used to Sven. The next interruption to Donald's Kalamazoo handcar of thought was a loud ding-ding-twang. Donald thought, "Whatever, but it can mean nothing good."

What it was, was the 8pm medication call.

There was no hustle 'n' bustle. It was more like a whimper 'n' groan, but there was a definite glacial movement towards the medication windows. To Donald's amazement, all of the TTs made their way straight past the windows of magic. This was when he put two and two together and came up with half a pineapple. They may be sharing the kitchen and the common area, but they have their own dispensary hidden away somewhere.

---

[194] PRN is derived from the Latin term *pro re nata*, which has been loosely translated to *as needed*. It doesn't specifically have to mean medication.

[195] Sometimes they put these on the back of the notice board, and this still satisfies the regulatory requirements, however, the practice of posting some of the notices in Latin has been suspended pending legal proceedings.

Outside the two Kangaroo windows, two lines were forming (even Escher would have had trouble sketching them). From Donald's perspective, each inmate seemed to move in a different direction, at a different speed and may have had a different end destination in mind. Somehow, they all managed to creep, crawl, or clamber to the appropriate window. Mostly anyway.

Lost became[196] completely lost and had to wait in the time-out corner for all of the other inmates to get their medication before he could have another attempt at lining up. When he was reminded of what it was he was doing, he lined up in the same wrong line as before. Donald was watching as the drama unfolded. He liked watching; he was very good at watching.

Nurse Jack came over and helped Lost to the correct medication window. He seemed to be quite a friendly person, or he seemed to be quite good at his job; Donald didn't mind either way.

Once Lost had been taken care of, Nurse Jack came over and introduced himself to Donald, "Hello... My name is Nurse Jack, and I understand you are Donald." Nurse Jack had a very likeable quality,[197] so sadly missing in so many people... Like Donald, for instance... Nurse Jack didn't have to try very hard to be likeable; he just was.

Donald was fairly sure there was some small talk between them. Still, it was overshadowed by, "I also understand I will be taking a Blood sample from you tomorrow. Until then, let me make you as comfortable as I possibly can, and this whole process will be completed as painlessly as possible."

Nurse Jack led Donald to the medication window,[198] where they both were confronted by DD, "Ahhhhh, Donny, nice to see you again. Wait a moment, and I will get your file." She turned slightly and ran her fingers through the open drawer of the filing cabinet.

Ostensibly, DD could multitask, as she also started talking down to Nurse Jack while she was rifling through the filing cabinet, "Mr Call... I see you are working late very again. You know you don't get paid overtime."

Nurse Jack almost hated the way DD always addressed him without using his proper title.[199] He knew enough to not correct her, though. It is rumoured that Nurse Hatchet had once corrected her, and this is why she is the nurse on permanent night shift. You just don't mess with the DoubleDees.[200]

---

[196] Wait for it... Wait for it... Russell...

[197] I would write, "je ne sais quoi," but I can't spell it.

[198] Donald learned later this was the East medication window.

[199] DD is firmly entrenched in her archaic belief of, nursing is woman's work.

[200] This is what everyone called DD in the privacy of their own minds.

Without waiting for a submissive response from Nurse Jack, DD switched back to talking down to Donald as she opened his blue manila folder[201] while she wrote "Donny H" in red on the tab. She found the *medication prescribed* column, "I see you have been prescribed two yellow ones, two light blue ones and one and a half of the little white ones."

While DD was reading out his medications and following this information in the file with her right index finger, her left hand was retrieving the various packets and bottles of medication, without looking,[202] from a blue plastic box also labelled "Donny H." It was both fascinating and infuriating for Donald to watch. Without moving any of her belly button down areas, DD was able to write the date in all of the intersecting date/medication boxes, create one pill filled cup, another water quarter-filled cup and return the unused portions of each box of medication to Donald's blue plastic box.

During DD's short monologue, all Donald was thinking was, "Yep. Either she's one of *those annoying people*, or she is a bully, or maybe she's both, but, as I only met her less than 24 hours ago, what did I really expect?" In this specific instance, everything Donald said *after* the "but" was meaningless, false and contradicted the standard before-the-but rule.

Nurse Jack broke off Donald's internal thoughts and thanked DD. Taking the two little cups, he led Donald away to a quiet corner to explain to him what was happening. "These are the medications your psychologist has prescribed: the bright yellow ones are liquefied sunshine for vitamin D; the white ones are extremely mild sleeping tablets, so mild they probably won't make a slight bit of difference to you or your neighbours; and the light blue ones are your anti-depressants, or as I like to call them, **M**ake **D**onald **M**ore **A**wesome[203] pills."

Donald has had abundantly more than enough of everything for today, so he took his medication, drank his water, did the Ahhhhh thing like a good little boy, and headed off to bed. Much (all) of what happened next was performed via his autopilot assist; he found the way back to his room, changed into his pyjamas, climbed into bed and went to sleep.

All in the hope, tomorrow will be another different, if not better, day.

---

[201] Manila is a colour people! It is just a blue folder.

[202] Not her left hand, it doesn't have eyes. I mean DD wasn't looking.

[203] Move along, no acronymising here! Like cocaine and heroin, this used to be legitimately prescribed in hospitals. There is also research being done to see if it can assist in treating severe treatment-resistant PTSD.

Chapter 8:
Day 2
(Tuesday Morning)

Thump. Donald had, once again, reached over to turn his alarm clock off. His momentary confusion faded when he opened his eyes and was unceremoniously reminded of where he was.

SaaaaaRS...!

He shouldn't have been surprised. The echo, of the memory, of the hourly bright white light and its accompanying sad "Sorry Donald, go back to sleep." was not so much missing from his memory this morning; it was still packing its overnight bag and waiting for the taxi to arrive. Donald was fairly sure these hourly sightings were only done to make sure he hadn't run away, rather than anything to do with his mental well-being.[204]

Sitting up, Donald followed his usual morning routine as much as he could. This included careful fumbling around in the semi-darkness to find his glasses, cleaning them by braille with whatever material was available, and...that was pretty much it today.

Once his glasses were on, and he could see more than a collective blur, he turned on his overhead light, looked directly at it to make sure it was working, and said, "Bright Light!" Then gathering up his vestigial waking-up strength, he flicked off the stubborn clingy bedding, swung his legs up 'n' over the non-wall side of the bed and successfully managed to stand up.

---

[204] Donald was also fairly sure that waking someone up every hour, on the quarter past the hour, was as anti-productive and as anti-conducive to an antipodean trying to become very well rested, as it could possibly be.

Deciding if he should change into his non-pyjama type clothes or not was about the limit of Donald's decision-making ability these days. Even this simple task required an "I can barely decide which side of the bed to get out of...and one side is a wall!" motivational speech. Coming up with the obvious answer of, "OMG, just do it already![205]" was probably going to cause him much grief in the future, along with grief about the shoe-less footnote author comment. But, at this precise moment, he honestly didn't care. To be honest.

He didn't want to think about what sort of shiver-inducing, motivational speech would be required for him to try and tackle the mammoth task he liked to call *The Four Esses:* "**S**hut up! Go and have a **S**have and a **S**hower, **S**tupid." Choosing to postpone this task was easier to justify than acknowledging any benefits obtained from actually doing the task immediately.

The meagre illumination from the bright light was enough for Donald to see a new note taped to the side of his mirror. When he was able to examine it closer, he found out it wasn't a new note; it was an old note, newly taped to his mirror. Reading the note, and realising it was from Nurse Jack, placed Donald's mind at ease. The rest of him was still fixated on the Blood-curdling redness of the word Blood. He didn't want to co-operate with anyone, let alone be willing to submit to anything.

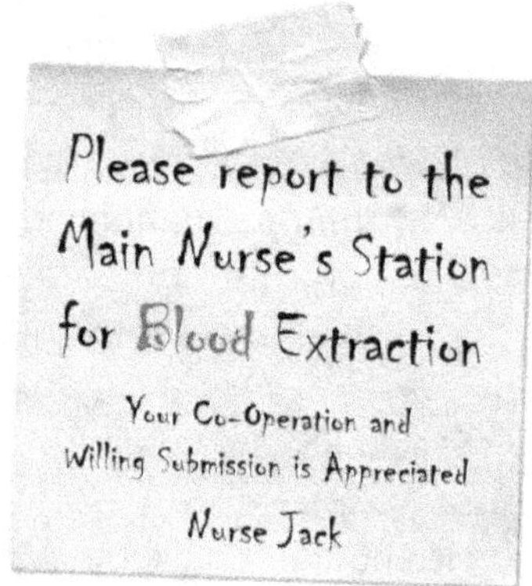

The next thing to catch Donald's eye's notice was the Blood extraction and collection instruction manual sitting on the basin underneath the note. Calling it a manual was bordering on ludicrous and offensive to every manual writer all over the world, as it was only a single-spaced typed laminated half sheet of paper with a total of four instructions:

- Do not eat anything; *(including food)*
- Please have a drink; *(of water)*
- Come to the Main Nurse's Station A.S.A.P; and *(map on the back)*
- Please bring these instructions with you. *(and the sticky note)*

---

[205] Catchy, but what does it mean? "Don't look at the price tag, or think about where they came from, just buy these excessively overpriced trendy shoes. They might not have been manufactured in a sweat shop, as we don't officially do that anymore and even if we were exploiting our workers, we would have been exploiting them in a good way, because ~~we are~~ we might be giving an underprivileged worker at least triple the nothing they used to get."

Donald picked up the manual, turned it over and studied the map until he was sure he knew where to go. The printed map was a basic floor plan of this section of the hospital. On the lamination was a blue white-board-marker line from his room to the room labelled as the "Main Nurse's Station." A subset of the many, many, many questions Donald wanted to ask at this time went along the lines of:

- *"Why is the manual pre-corrected?"*
- *"Why are my thoughts in the same font again?"*
- *"The personalised map is a nice touch, though.[206]"*

Dressing himself in a record time, Donald grabbed his SaRS branded bottle of water,[207] the map to the Main Nurse's Station and coupled reminder note; and headed off in the general direction indicated in the blue marker on the map. Donald was furiously trying to not think about Blood, needles and questions. Amazingly, for once, he was fairly successful with this not thinking.

What he was thinking about, though, was the section on the map labelled as "Pecuniam in loco repetit lacum." Donald erroneously translated this to, "Here be Accountants," but he wasn't far wrong. As the cerulean blue white-board-marker mapped route didn't take him through this area, he assigned an issue-level of five to the thought (cosmic), filed it in the do not disturb section of his memory and continued on closely following the map.

Donald was making good time to the Main Nurse's Station when, for once, he wasn't going to be side-tracked by anything worthy of note:

- Not by the sight of a semi-naked inmate running through the corridors screaming, "My insanity laughs at your pressure… Let Me Out…"
- Not by the view outside, of someone deftly pruning the rose bushes with an electric chainsaw; and
- Not by the sounds of someone's agony induced cries emanating from under the floor through a conveniently placed air duct.

He had just started to reach for the door's handle to the Main Nurse's Station when the door opened by itself, and through it came a topical Sven.

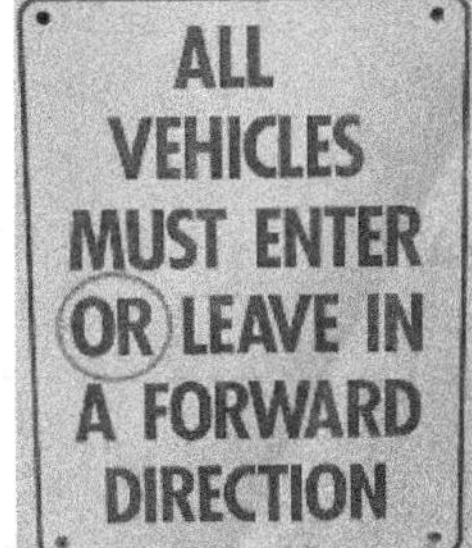

All vehicles must enter OR leave in a forward direction. But NOT Both!

---

[206] This wasn't technically a question, but it was still a very good idea.

[207] This is a purposeful time anomaly and definitely not a continuity error; Donald will receive his SaRS water bottle in a few minutes… I promise.

Sven came out by moonwalking through the door backwards. This incident was not really such a great surprise to Donald... The surprise came when Sven finished his moonwalk with a crotch holding move, black Fedora removing and Flick-My-Bic fiery spinning leg split. If the original creator of this move ever saw Sven perform it, he would, most probably, roll over in his grave if he was able to do so. Sven sauntered away with a saucy limp to his step. Donald chose to believe this was by design and not a painful by-product of the outrageously inspired dance move, undoubtedly, surging through his body.

The next person coming out of the Bloody room was an official-looking man who Donald couldn't remember ever having seen before but still looked eerily familiar. Normally this situation wouldn't phase Donald in the slightest, as he was a devotee of the art of *Likes Isolation, Constantly Keeps to Myself*.[208] Still, as he was also being waved at in a sickeningly chipper fashion with the spoken accompaniment of, "Hello, and how are you this morning Mr Halfbrain?" he escalated and became more irrationally irritated than he usually liked, and he didn't like it. **Quote:** "I dooooon't like it."

Without waiting for an answer to his innocuous query (though to Donald's thoughts, it was a threateningly incredulous inquiry), the official-looking man continued with the perceived diatribe of berating comments, "When you are finished here with Nurse Jack, Mr Halfbrain, would you care to pop over to the administration area, where I will set you up with one of the SaRS show bags of goodies. It shouldn't take more than a moment, and then you may be on your way to breakfast. I understand it is sausages and eggs today..."

Mark Time is the SaRS administration personnel chief. He also wears the SaRS Emergency Sections Ward Chief Administrator's hat and the SaRS Chief Emergency Warden's (administration section) hat. His office is located smack bang in the middle of the "Pecuniam in loco repetit lacum" marked area.

Mark is one of those overachieving types of people who has their fingers in multiple pies and gets along with everyone in person but is reviled by the same everyone silently behind his back. He almost single-handedly keeps SaRS financially functioning, knows how to do every non-medical related task and is always the go-to person when it comes to clearing paper jams out of the insides of photocopiers and printers.

---

[208] Unfortunately, when the supporter badges were made, a font-blind printer was used. He chose font sizes poorly and gave the badges an unwholesomely scary, albeit a very ironic and welcome, unwelcoming look.

Administration – SaRS
Mark Time (Chief of Admin)
Chief Emergency Sections Ward
and Chief Emergency Warden...

After Donald completed several to seven pirouettes, firstly trying to follow Sven and then trying to not follow Mark, he closed his mouth, gave his head a little shaking-off-the-disbelief shake and went through the open door into the Main Nurse's Station. Instantly he was confronted by someone wearing what probably began life as a welder's mask and a butcher's apron, who was holding an oversized syringe, which was ominously dripping a thick red liquid.

"Sphincter Feng Shui." Donald was surprised, but only just.

"Do you like my Halloween costume? Who would have guessed an ageing *Swinese*[209] man was so adept at creating such horror inducing outfits? And yes, I do know the modern interpretation of Halloween is nothing remotely like the pagan tradition of *remembering the dead* that it was most probably inspired by. I figure the practice of any traditional ceremony, even one with such dark and murky overseas roots, will aid me in my quest of promoting the Aboriginal Dreamtime legends whenever I can."

Donald didn't even want to think about the possibility of the foreign land's infamous legend of celebrating death could, or should, be utilised to promote the ancient Aboriginal culture, especially when that same culture contains an important belief...the spirits of the dead should not be disturbed. Because, at this precise moment, Donald was preoccupied with the potent concern he was about to be jabbed by a psychotic giant needle wielding butcher!

Nurse Jack removed his Halloween costume immediately once he saw the distress it was causing Donald. He knew the maxim: "A calm patient is an easily Blood extracted patient." Calmly he directed Donald to "Hop up on the bed, roll up your sleeve and just relax. I'll have you out of here in a jiffy."

Donald, like the patient, patient he was, did everything he was told to do, except the relax part. He always has a fundamental dislike of being told to *just relax*. There was nothing *just* about it. It was entirely *un-just*. Nine out of ten people[210] would react exactly the same way Donald did, which was, as always, steeling his resolve to do exactly the opposite of what was requested unless it happened to be easier their way, which it rarely was.

---

[209] Sven is one-half Swedish, one-half Chinese and all fortune cookie.

[210] Did you know 74.321% of all statistics are just made up on the spot?

Donald's memory here is a bit fractured because of his uncanny ability of being able to recall every single bad thing that could possibly be lying in wait for him to remember inside his long-term memory. His short to medium-term memory is not equally afflicted by the same issue. So, we will be stopping here for a bit while Nurse Jack is removing a largish vial of Donald's Blood. Then a few seconds after the Bloody theft, we will continue with the story.

… … …

Stepping through the door and sauntering away, with a saucy limp to his step he couldn't remember acquiring but assumed it was a by-product of his Blood loss,[211] Donald headed off to Here be Accountants to collect his attention popping SaRS show bag of goodies.[212] He also noted there was a distinct lack of map for him to follow and that he possibly now has a lack of any memory of when he might have *disacquired* it.

Donald was only approximately thirty steps into his current trek when he arrived at the administration front desk. He was confronted by a large sign saying, "You are Now Here," with an orange arrow pointing down to the large green dot he was conspicuously standing on top of. "Where else would I be?" Donald is not averse to talking to inanimate signs after he has read them, "and I also don't think you are a very useful sign."

"Ding!" Donald rang the bell, once only as directed, to attract someone's attention. While he was waiting,[213] Donald reminisced on each of the steps he had taken to arrive at his current location. The last thirty literal walking steps, not the many more conceptual psychological steps he had taken to land himself in SaRS.[214] He also revised his previous use of approximately; he knew there were exactly thirty steps… He had counted them all.

---

[211] He also has no memory of being told the details pertaining to the testing of his Blood, or when the test results were likely to be available, or even of the orange flavoured lollipops he turned down because they were too childish.

[212] This recollection was somewhere between long, and short-to-medium-term memory, where the bad information is recallable, but is still slightly fuzzy.

[213] Donald did a lot of waiting and he caused a lot of waiting to occur. He could wait in several dimensions at the same time. Short-term waiting, like the typical bellringing wait he is demonstrating here, right through to the vastly longer term waiting, such as waiting for waiting to become an Olympic sport. He just couldn't wait for that to happen.

[214] This will be a chapter in the next instalment of The Donald Diaries.

Donald always counted his steps... Actually, he always counted everything. Counting was the only thing Donald could always count on to never change. When he went shopping, he counted all of the items he put into his shopping trolley. This was a relatively easy task to do when his selections were generally made in multiples of two...[215] Except for zucchini, he would always get three zucchini and then not be able to figure out or tell you why he did.

He also counted through the gears on his Kamikaze motorbike. He would continually count from one to six, then six to one, then etc... The exception to prove this rule is when he tries to count to seven. He gets to six, and to check that this is so, tries to change into seventh gear. Seven never works because his bike only has six gears, so when this didn't physically work, it was actually working perfectly. ~~The~~ Another strange thing about this feature is, Donald will also verify sixth gear by looking at the speedometer to tachometer ratio; if this was 1:500, he was in sixth gear, and only then could he *just relax*.

"Ah, yes, Mr Donald Halfbrain. My name is Mark Time, and I am the head of administration. Please let me extend to you a most heartfelt welcome to SaRS. We hope your stay with us will be a pleasurable one, an educational one and a memorable one." Mark had risen from behind the desk, like steam rises off a newly patted cow pat in the middle of winter, holding up the SaRS Show Bag[216] he had promised to Donald scant moments earlier.

"I am afraid we have temporarily run out of the personalised travel coffee mugs, but as soon as a new shipment arrives, I will be sure to drop one of them off to you in your room." Cross-selling, "We also have a selection of locks for the lockable cabinet in your room. Should you wish to purchase a set, they are only $15 and will provide you with an invaluable amount of comfort."

Donald's answer to this welcome was a deeply silent expression. Donald was trying to express, "Who are you? What do you mean by welcome? Why are your ears so familiar?" and as an afterthought, he expressly added, "And I am hungry." But what was expressed through his vocal cords was, "Huh¿™"

---

[215] If he was to be asked, Donald would always say his favourite acronym is BOGOF - Buy One, Get One Free, due to it sounding so much better than TftPoO - Two for the Price of One, which reminds him of a juicy fart.

Don't Visualise... Ewwwww... Did you have to? Now I can't Un-See it...

[216] The contents of Donald's show bag was a personalised water bottle; a personalised notepad and pen; a voucher for a small sized decaffeinated cup of coffee; the Wi-Fi password (Di@l1forMental); the washing machine and dryer instructions; and a three-week rotating timetable of group sessions.

Mark, having seen this exact expression many hundreds of times before, pressed a secret, silent and small call button conveniently located under the desk next to where he was. Then he very slowly, so as to not startle Donald, handed over the Show Bag, pointed him in the direction of the dining room and actively waited for what was about to happen.

Aaaron came out of his office with exaggerated purpose, settled in beside Donald and began escorting him to breakfast. He also explained he was going to take him on a roundabout route to the dining room, so he could "see more of SaRS." What he didn't tell Donald was his alternate reason. He was going to try and introduce him to some of the contractors working at SaRS. The theory behind this being, "If there is a reduction in the number of possible traumatic unknown surprises, there will also possibly be an unknown reduction in the number of traumas, initiated by those now known to be possibly, reduced in number, trauma-inducing surprises.[217]"

Backtracking a few steps, Aaaron led Donald to one of the many doors that allow the inside to become the outside without breaking through the window with a water fountain. Soon they were strolling along a path running parallel to the corridor Donald had walked along earlier. Donald could hear the electric sound of a chainsaw tenderly pruning the rose bushes, accompanied by some staccato complaints of, "Why would anyone plant rose bushes sideways?"

When they were nearly within sight of the chainsaw-wielding gardener, Aaaron took the offered opportunity to secretly slip into Donald's pocket one of the electric chain sawer's business cards as a less harrowing alternative to introducing him to the grounds keeping staff in person...

Wholly Mowly Groundskeeping
Complete lawn and garden maintenance for Churches, Mosques, Temples and Cemeteries. We'll put a stop to all of your Religious growth!
Dial: 1800 WHOLLY

Andy One is the founder, co-owner and proprietor of the Wholly Mowly Groundskeeping business and is also a veritable chainsaw-wielding expert. He started in the chainsaw business as the husband half of a husband-and-wife chainsaw juggling and knife throwing comedy act. *Chainsaw juggling* is not a phrase you generally get to say, legitimately, twice, every day.

---

[217] It also gives me a great opportunity to introduce a few of the other minor characters, and they have humorous names, even if I have to say so myself.

This act received top billing in the now-defunct One to Remember Circus. And not just because they owned the circus… It was also due to the fact that they were the only act in the circus. Tragically, after the infamous seven-dead-slippery-handle-chainsaw-massacre mishap of 1968, they were not allowed to perform in public anymore and were relegated to command performances.

Simone Finger-One (*nee* Finger) is the co-owner of the business and is the Human Resources resource. She was the wife half of the chainsaw juggling and knife throwing act with Andy until the uncontrollable-sneezing-knife-thrower mishap of 1968[218] left her unable to count up to ten on her fingers. After this, she changed the pronunciation of her name to Simone Finger *minus* One. She is not so expert with chainsaws and frequently mistypes the letter ~~W~~Q.

Edward Knife Hans is the "he does everything unseen behind the scenes" employee of the Ones' grounds keeping business. He was previously a private in the Swiss Army, where he learned complicated knife making and throwing skills, and he used these credentials to join the Ones' circus. Unfortunately, his stage name was Mr Sneeze. Consequently, he is currently working off his debt to the Ones as an underpaid overused dogsbody until Simone's finger grows back. He isn't quite as smart as this quaint story might suggest.

Not long after the completed Wholly Mowly non-interaction-introduction, Donald and Aaaron returned to the inside of SaRS and continued to the dining room. "Breakfast today is sausages and eggs… Enjoy!" was Aaaron's parting remark to Donald. The enjoyable message became just a little threatening-to-be-disconcerting when a double "Baaaaahhhhhaaaaa, Baaaaahhhhhaaaaa!" slipped out from under his breath as he was leaving. Donald looked at the food offered and wasn't at all convinced it was sausages, eggs, or even food…

Donald also has a strict definition of cooking…
"Cooking requires a minimum of at least one[219] of:
- Something chopped;
- Something stirred; or
- Something basted.

Merely re-heating, or even heating for the first time, does not generally escalate to *cooking*. A boiled egg is one of the rule-proving exceptions."

---

[218] 1968 is looking like it was a very bad year for minor mishaps.

[219] As the minimum whole amount of anything physically present is one, this is only very slightly a little bit sort of an unnecessary redundancy… I think.

The sausages all looked like they were leftover from yesterday, so Donald was conflicted again. He was having the same thought as yesterday, "Never, never, ever, ever! Not even if they were the last two sausages left on earth." But he is also remembering they weren't so bad in the taste department. This was his first exposure to everything dialectical at SaRS.

Donald was also looking at the fried tomatoes and scrambled eggs. They were both showing distinct signs of being an unusual shade of greenish. The green tomatoes were not so much of an issue, as Donald had heard this was an actual thing, and Chef has already displayed a talent for creating wonderful tasting food out of not so wonderful ingredients. But the eggs, being any shade of green, was a distinct disadvantage to Donald even trying them.

When Donald enquired about the *greenishness* of the eggs, Chef replied in his usual curt English, "Dr Seuss' Birthday."

I know who I am... Do you know who you are?
Cos, when you're done knowing... It's then you'll go far.

Sven had crept up silently behind Donald. This type of creeping came as absolutely no surprise to Donald; what did come as a surprise, though, was Sven creepily channelling Dr Seuss.

Donald decided to take his chances with the greenness of everything and requested, "I'll have one of everything, please.[220]" He collected his plate of semi-questionable food and headed off to find an empty table. It was a task made much harder than usual,[221] due to his, out of his control, very nearly too late arrival for breakfast.

Cursing Nurse Jack, Aaaron and Mark all for making him uncomfortably nearly late for breakfast, he begrudgingly chose the furthermost emptiest table he could find. There was only one table with one person sitting at it, and Donald sat at this table. He was sitting directly across from Karl but kept his eyes lowered to indicate an avid willingness to not engage.

It didn't work very well, or even at all, as Karl politely greeted him the first instant after his plate touched the paper tablecloth[222] performing the function of covering the table adequately.

---

[220] Incidentally, this is also how I order a cup of coffee, extra hot. FYI ☺.

[221] Usual... Meaning his one experience of eating breakfast at SaRS.

[222] I am constantly troubled by nearly everyone's complete acceptance of common oxymorons. In random order: random order, paper cloth, blue manila, clearly confused, open marriage, plastic glasses, bad coffee, mental health...

"Bad Morning. What are you in for?" Karl was clearly somewhat confused about where he was, or maybe he was indifferent about his committal.

Donald remembered back to yesterday when Karl had asked him simply, "Why?" He didn't have one iota of an answer for him then. Unfortunately, the situation had not changed overnight, and even more, unfortunately, it was never likely to. All he could offer Karl, at the moment, was "Bad Morning. I am in here because of my almost full aeroplane hangar of woe, strife and misery.[223] It is following me like a lost puppy follows the scent of food."

Karl just hung his head in agreement.

Donald was about to break most of his looking after himself traditions, and offer some heartfelt condolence to someone else, *there, there* style. It didn't eventuate when the moment was broken by the arrival of a frantic Skit, who had just dived under Donald's table again.

Skit stayed silent and hidden only momentarily, then he sat himself on the floor, half under the table, with the table-paper-cloth bunched on his shoulder and began speaking in a very soft frantic murmur, "Here, take this. It is all the evidence I have. It must be made public. Do you understand?"

Donald then failed to repel Skit's thrust as he shoved some tightly wadded pieces of paper into Donald's empty hands. Skit then continued whispering his concerns, "If I don't return to retrieve these <*cough*> from you before 8am tomorrow morning, it means they have caught me, and I am most probably already dead. This is what you must do if I don't come back..."

At this point, the already high-pitched intensity of Skit's voice increased, and he unexpectedly switched to speaking in what Donald could only assume was Swedish. All Donald could understand was "Lisbeth" and "Fire."

Putting all of the clues together:
- The similarity of the forced stereotypical monologue;
- Speaking in Swedish; and
- The frantic way in which he described "Fire."

Donald knew this was Lisbeth Salander from movie number two.

Eventually, Donald returned to the present, after mentally congratulating himself for figuring out who Skit/Lisbeth was without having to see where her tattoos weren't. All the while managing to ignore the fact that this could have also been learned by simply listening when Skit had said, "Lisbeth." When he arrived fully back, he was greeted by Lisbeth, not speaking in Swedish.

---

[223] Would you believe depressed?

This time, instead of whispering, "Shhhhh, here they come!" Lisbeth said nothing at all when she disappeared under the table.

Donald had a fair idea of how this scenario would play out, so when Grey and Aaaron came puffing along with the question, "Did you just see someone… Only a moment ago… Come running through here…?" He tried to give them a confusing mix of questions and answers that would even cause an elephant to forget the question they asked, as well as any answers he provided.[224]

Donald's barrage of questions and answers was:
- "Who is it you are looking for?"
- "No… I haven't seen either Skit or Lisbeth together;"
- "What does he or she look like?"
- "Neither have I seen them both separately;"
- "Where did you lose them?"
- "It was very careless of you to lose them;"
- "Have you checked your pockets?"
- "I often find, the things I have lost are found in the last place I look…"

He was so pleased with this last question and answer combination that he completely failed to notice the teensy problem of knowing the answer to his first question before it was asked.

Grey and Aaaron performed a perfectly simultaneous, "What-the-Hell?" sudden stop with a half twist in the open mouth position, followed by a doubt-ridden, "Really?" motionless stunned stare, combined with the mandatory eye roll, "You've-got-to-be-kidding?" movement, finishing their three question and one statement routine with a "God-damn-it!" expletive.

They waited for their score,[225] exchanged high fives with each other, took a few bows, thanked everyone for their ongoing support and then continued on their pursuit of Skit with impressive, revitalised energy.

Donald didn't need to look under the table this time to know Lisbeth had once again vanished. It was bordering on becoming an annoyingly interesting habit that Donald hoped may, or may not, continue.

----

[224] Provided he never actually blatantly lied to them, of course. He did have a proud inflexible set of moral standards to maintain.

[225] Their score was a magnificent, institution high, combined score of 79.25. The harsh Russian judge wasn't on score this time, and their routine had a high degree of difficulty (because neither of them had done any practising).

During this episode, Donald's DOGoNs increased from a fairly stable four right up to a mentally painful high of ten and is now hovering around an only just acceptable eight. He couldn't wait until it was time to go back to bed, so he could dream a waking nightmare ending sleeping dream.

Karl apparently couldn't wait to leave either, as he had already left way before the early matinee session of *SaRS the Diabolical* had finished.

Chapter 9:
Group Session 1.0 [226]
(Regulations)

onald was hiding safely in his room as the morning's activities, of *Blood* extraction and breakfast, had stretched his coping skills to a *poofteenth* off the maximum limit currently available. There wasn't very much left, really. He was fearful that if even just one more minuscule event went pear-shaped, his mind would be sure to be on the next boat out of town. And while there is a river flowing by out the back of SaRS, it wasn't one with a normal ferry route. There were no wharves, and the cows in the pasture between him and the water had sported a menacing look the last time he had himself a little look-see.

Knock, knock, knock...

Donald could hear the palpable hesitation seeping out of these condensed knocking sounds, along with their oozing fervent hope if someone was inside, they wouldn't be disturbed enough[227] into answering the door. Or if someone did answer the door, the person would be appropriately, "¿… () …?"
Cursing ever so slightly, "SFS,[228]" Donald opened the door.

---

[226] I guess this means there are going to be multiple chapters dedicated to Donald's first group session. Excuse me while I prepare for an all-nighter.

[227] Nope… Would have been overly way too much seriously easy.

[228] This is a Donald level four curse; an almost silent, acronymised and capitalised Sphincter Feng Shui. A level five, and the least severe curse, would be a silent utterance of, "sfs."

Seth was floating there with BLT hovering just behind him, both of them were looking very ghostly, and Donald understood, "Well, I guess that explains the formal sounding triple knock with the fancy description... But how did Seth knock on the door?" His next thought was another on the lines of, "I wonder what would happen if I wrote all of this down for people to read?[229]"

"Excuse me, please, Master Halfbrain, if Sir would be so inclined as to kindly accompany us up to Group Room number one. It is located mere seconds away in the old mansion. It is time for Sir to attend his first group session with Mister Houts Marted." Seth stood to the side of the doorway, holding his arm in the standard *this way if you please* position.

Donald hesitated, trying to understand how Seth could make people feel obliged to do whatever he asked just by asking them nicely. "Simply amazing, it must be something to do with his exaggerated politeness," he thought.

Houts Marted had sent the two most malleable residents of SaRS out to round up the new week's worth of inmates. Seth, because he was so damned polite with his persuasion, and BLT to keep an eye on Seth. As far as Houts is concerned, Seth is broken and needs fixing. It doesn't matter a jot that he is a ghost, he is treated like any other patient, and patients need supervision when they are roaming around the campus on a mission. The only person who could do this for Seth was BLT.

Houts has been working intensively (and insensitively) with Seth for many years, trying to coax him out of his ghostly persona. Publicly, to allow some of Seth's memories to come back to this side of the "all forgotten," but privately, for the scientific paper he was writing on Seth for *Psychology Today*. "Ghost Psychology: Boo Who? How to stop thinking you are invisible... A twenty-first-century Psychological Ghostbusting guide.[230]"

One of the major hurdles Houts is facing with Seth's treatment and with his own future publication possibilities is trying to find Seth's next-best-next-of-kin. Seth's self-punishing negative feelings of invisibility and dissolvement have selectively annihilated most of his memory. When Seth became an anti-one, anyone who was an anyone to Seth became a no-one-anymore.

---

[229] Eventually, Donald will go on to write several other best sellers and be knighted for his contribution to mental health. He will also go, "pthththththth," in a messy bout of spitting onomatopoeia, at all of his previous detractors.

[230] Donald is also destined to provide most of his ghostly observations to Houts. However, Houts will not credit Donald for any of the ghostly writing in his paper and they will eventually fall, exceedingly, out with each other.

The reason this particular hurdle is so important to Houts is Seth's next-best-next-of-kin would be able to provide any authorisations required for his ghoulish ghastly ghostly project. Houts doesn't know what he would need to absolve him of any potential malpractices in the future. Even though Houts logically thinks, "Seth wouldn't stand a ghost of a chance of winning a legal suit against me for breaching any psychological equivalent of the not-a-real-doctor-patient confidentially agreements because Seth wasn't technically a patient or alive." he couldn't be 100% positively sure.

Houts has the same issue with BLT, only at an 85% level, though, because BLT wasn't a SaRS patient before he became a deceased part of his own estate and had apparently signed a waiver 75 years ago when he became a B.

Neither Seth, nor BLT, have left the grounds of SaRS since their death, and neither have any memories of their past life. BLT has the added complication of needing to come to terms with the name on his headstone, while Seth has to think about, "Why, and how, did I come back to SaRS when I died?"

Putting the vexing question of politeness out of his mind, Donald walked towards the group room with Seth and BLT in tow, a couple of floats behind. When they got to the group room, it was empty of people, just the way Donald liked it. Arriving early to everything is one of Donald's worst habits. Satisfied with this, he sat down as far from the door as he could sit and waited.

While Donald was waiting, Seth and BLT were hovering just inside the door, watching him. They reminded him of Rosencrantz and Guildenstern. Not because they were childhood friends, but because they looked like they were a pair of spies who were undoubtedly there to report on everything he did to someone rather than helping him through his depression.

Next to arrive on the scene were Grey, looking slightly downtrodden, and Houts, looking pointedly prosecutorial. Soon after this second pair appeared, the first pair disappeared further, but this didn't surprise Donald, as he hadn't missed the standard dismissive curt nod of, "Well done, thank you. I'll talk to you later, now go away, please I've got this." from Houts to Seth and BLT.

Houts started his preparations for facilitating the group, which included:
- Making it very obvious he was starting his preparations.

Whereas Grey, conversely, got quietly busy with the room's preparation. Performing several (un)important tasks such as:
- Straightening the tables;
- Circularising the chairs; and
- Making a forlorn attempt at cleaning the whiteboard of the previous group session's (in)coherent scribbles.

Before the whiteboard[231] was unsuccessfully partially erased, Donald had been able to discern a disconcerting amount of the scribble:

- ¤ A **SMART** goal is:
    - ◦ **S**pecific;
    - ◦ **M**easurable;
    - ◦ **A**chievable;
    - ◦ **R**ealistic; and
    - ◦ **T**imely.

Donald subsequently transliterated these in his mind to:

- ¤ A **NUTSO SMART** goal is:
    - ◦ **N**ever
    - ◦ **U**nderestimate
    - ◦ **T**heir
    - ◦ **S**tupidity,
    - ◦ **O**r
    - ◦ **S**chizoid,
    - ◦ **M**eaningless,
    - ◦ **A**wful,
    - ◦ **R**ong[232] and
    - ◦ **T**errible.

But the most important activity, to Donald, was that they were paying less than absolutely no attention to him, just the way he liked it. Donald realised he wasn't starting out on a positive note. He doubted they would consider changing any of the textbooks to include his definition of NUTSO SMART,[233] but he was happy with the satiric nature of the entire situation.

Houts leafed through a largish stack of papers, selected a single sheet and put it on the table near the door. He then checked his shirt pockets for what Donald assumed was a pen. Finding none, he selected several from the cache in the whiteboard's marker holder. Testing each of them in turn, he seemed to be happy with the fourth one and put this pen with the piece of paper. He then returned the remainder of the pens to the marker holder.

This annoyed, nay **infuriated**, Donald... Twice:

- ¤ Firstly   - If the pens don't work, throw them out!
- ¤ Secondly   - Come prepared next time!

Houts went through exactly the same process to find at least two working whiteboard markers. Donald went through his annoyed and infuriated process again after Houts returned the not working markers back to the holder.

---

[231] Or more accurately, the creamy off-white yellowy grey beige board.

[232] Remind me to buy you a dictionary that includes satirical definitions.

[233] He half considered updating Wikipedia, just to see what would happen.

Once Houts had finished his meagre preparations, he looked around the room and made momentary eye contact with Donald. Then after struggling to count to one in his head, not being able to go through some sort of internal calculation process, he returned his attention to the stack of papers.

When he finished restacking his stack of papers, and the whiteboard was *this is as clean as it gets*, Houts sat down with Grey to await the arrival of the rest of the inmates. The group started at nine o'clock, so they were expecting people to start arriving around five or ten minutes past nine.

First to arrive late were Owedebt and Nota, with Chunky flouncing along beside them. Two of them were projecting a suddenly rash screaming look of, "Don't look at us; we weren't talking about you; to be honest." While the third member of the eclectic trio had a requiring look somewhere between, "Please pat me, I'm desperate, pleeeeease." and, "You will do what I say! Now pat me, my pretty little patty-man, Pat Me, PAT ME, **PAT ME!**[234]"

The to-be-honest-it-wasn't-us two both paused near the door and wrote something on what Donald nearly thought was the piece of paper Houts had placed there earlier. Owedebt then introduced Nota to Donald, "Hi Donald, you remember my friend Nota Beenhead, don't you?" Donald felt a shiver of understanding pass between him and Owedebt. He was very much relieved when they chose to sit several chairs away without waiting for him to give them an answer or a pat.

A distance bonus of Chunky being tethered underneath Owedebt's chair was he wasn't able to reach Donald. The sight of Chunky's tongue waggling all pink and juicy escalated this bonus to become a major jackpot.

Got Knoted, Istha T. You, Lost M'Hankie, Mindy Ownbeeswhacks and Nelo (Vamp) Priors all trickled in, in dribs and drabs... And all, apparently, sensed Donald's discomfort because they all chose to sit in chairs located at least two empty chairs away from where he was.[235]

Not wanting to feel any more uncomfortable than his currently bearable eight DOGoNs, Donald chose to avoid all forms of personal contact, including visual, audible, tactile and olfactory. Then his under-his-breath exasperated thinking came to the party and thought, "There is a good reason for gustatory and disgust, sharing so many letters in common."

---

[234] Donald was reminded of a scene out of Cujo and wondered if Chunky Poopy had ever been bitten by a bloodthirsty bat... Or even a rabid ant.

[235] Either what he said, or Donald was starting to smell again.

He was hoping his introductory confession didn't need to be started with: "Hi, I'm Donald, and it's been three days since my last shower..."

"Free Gift!" It's not much of a gift if it isn't free!

Sven came in and made himself comfortable by walking around an empty chair three times, doing a very odd impersonation of John Travolta performing the splits, then finally, a matrix-slow-motion backflip into his chair. Donald deduced that Sven was someone who really knew how to make an entrance. He was also amazed to see that none of Sven's entrancing repertoire seemed to make an impression on anyone else in the room.

Without missing a single beat from life's defibrillator, or the next moment after Sven's butt hit the chair, Houts indicated to Grey with a piercing glance, "The doors should now be closed,[236]" so they could begin the group session.

Before Grey made it to the door, Seth appeared again, "Please excuse the interruption Master Marted, but Karl Saneman is also here to participate in his first group session." Seth stood to the side of the doorway, holding his arm in the standard *this way if you please* position again.

Karl shuffled into the room with his head hanging down, obscuring his face and the well-worn dazed-kangaroo-in-the-headlights look. Donald would have significantly related to this if only he could have seen it. Karl raised his head only enough to find the closest empty chair, mumbled quietly, "Sorry," and sat down in the remaining silence.

The last person to arrive was a dishevelled looking Skit. "Ah, good, good, I see you are all here. Good. I will just get myself organised a little bit, and then we will be able to start." He was pulling handfuls of things out of his pockets, looking at them briefly before returning them to the pocket from whence they came, "Oh, sorry, and my name is Doctor Tony Hill."

"Ahem, Doctor Hill, was it? Perhaps it would be better if I was allowed to facilitate the group session today? As this is your first time here, it might be prudent for you to sit and observe how we do things at SaRS. And then maybe your observations can be discussed in a future group?" Houts clearly has had to deal with situations like this before, so smooth was his regaining control of the group from an unauthorised interloper.

"Pardon me? Oh. Oh? Yes, of course, please do continue; my apologies." Doctor Hill lost the confused doctor look from his face, replacing it with a stock confused patient look. He found a free chair and sat down with an observable happy aura seeping out, with a pencil and notebook in his hand. Waiting.

"Thank you."

---

[236] But not locked. There is still an ongoing case regarding an inmate who was locked in a room and tortured well passed their insanity break point by being forced to watch hours, upon hours, of reality TV matchmaking shows.

Standing, Houts started walking through his generic autopilot introduction speech, "Firstly, can I direct your attention to the Group Guidelines, please…" Facing towards the back wall of the room, Houts raised his arms and eyes to what was an almost certainly, a reverential pose… "Let us recite the thirteen Group Guidelines together as a symbol of our own acceptance, understanding and commitment to helping one another through these troubling times…"

""… ""Group Rules struck out, no space, Guidelines.
The first rule of Group…

Group ~~Rules~~ *Guidelines*

The first rule of Group: No matter how bad today is, tomorrow could be worse.
What's said in Group won't stay in Group; it's recorded, edited & published.
In Group, some members think they are more insane than others; they aren't.

We admitted to ourselves we are mental, insane & are seeking help voluntarily.
We are willing to accept instruction for the prevention of our own destruction.
Contradictorily, we are the only ones with the power to repair our own sanity.

To cure ourselves: We must learn about ourselves and about everybody else.
We must make an inventory of all our assets and arrange for them to be sold.
We must create a list of all the people who have wronged us and forget them.

We don't look back. No matter how tempting the salted caramel ice cream is.
Never, never, never, never, never, never, never, never, never, never give up.
The last and thirteenth rule of a SaRS Group: We should learn how to count.

SaRS Official 3 – Group ~~Rules~~ Guidelines

…We should learn how to count."" …""

Donald, surprisingly, didn't do as he was told for once.
He assumed as these ~~Rules~~ Guidelines are only ~~Rules~~ Guidelines, they most probably are not mandatory; it then logically follows that the reciting of these ~~Rules~~ Guidelines at the start of the session is also not mandatory.[237] While he was not busy not reciting the not mandatory ~~Rules~~ Guidelines, Donald was also surreptitiously looking around at the rest of the room's occupants. He was beginning to form his unsolicited opinions of everyone else.

---

[237] Not mandatory is not the same as optional, as not mandatory, literally, means you *must not do*. Optional means you may choose to do or to not do.

Apart from himself and Karl, everyone else was being a good little inmate, droning along with Houts and reciting the ~~Rules~~Guidelines. This included: Seth, who was confusingly floating in a seated position over a space without a chair; Mindy,[238] who may have been talking in her sleep; and Chunky, who was standing with his front right paw raised in the dog *Shake Hands* position, which made it look uncomfortably like he was performing a Nazi Dingo salute.

Continuing to stand while pivoting to face the Southern wall,[239] "Now we will familiarise ourselves with the housekeeping instructions…"

""… ""Housekeeping
All mobile phones must be…

Housekeeping

All phones must be turned Off. This does not mean On Silent. It means **Off!**

Any infraction of this phone rule will result in the following fines: *

Vibration	– $1/vibration
Ring–Ring	– $2/ring–ring

Song ringtones will be charged a premium at the facilitator's discretion
Leaving the room to answer – $10, plus the above
Answering inside the room – $20, plus $2/10sec, plus the above

No food or drink is allowed in the group room. **

** Proceeds go towards new stationery for groups*

*** Coffee is allowed. White with 1 sugar, please…*

**** Sign the attendance sheet (authorised ~~#~~ MB11)*

SaRS Official 4 – Housekeeping

…Sign the attendance sheet (authorised ~~#~~ MB11)"" …""

Same participants… Same participation…

---

[238] Donald will come to learn her preferred name during the upcoming self-introductions, so, please, just bear with me here, ok?

[239] Another pet hate of mine. How do people correctly identify compass directions from inside a building without having a convenient compass? I am so going to cover this issue in greater detail in a later group, or a later book.

"Thank you, everyone!" Houts exclaimed…deriving altogether too much excitement from the disjoint mumblings. Switching back to his condescending yet understanding tone, "Donald and Karl, both of you will eventually become indoctrinated into our ways, and one day you might even see the light at the end of the tunnel. But for today only, you will both be given a free pass for the preliminary lexicalised vocalised warm-ups. This is one of our quirky traditions for your first and then thirteenth[240] group sessions."

"Yeah, a Free Pass to Go Straight to Gaol, and Introductions that have been Completely Scripted and Rehearsed. I already know what is behind the Reality of this Situation!" Donald was a tad sceptical in his own private thoughts. Still, he was also passionate, as the capital letters and italics indicate.

"However," said Houts, interrupting Donald's slowly derailing caboose of thought, "you both must still sign the attendance sheet. This is one of the basic seven, non-negotiable, patient signature requirements that MentalBank, our malpractice and *malproficient* insurance providers, have placed on us for your own good. It has something to do with time and motion coverage.[241]"

Karl and Donald both got up and signed the attendance sheet. It took Karl just 23 seconds, but it took Donald a much more substantial 123 seconds.[242] Donald couldn't help himself; he is one of *those annoying people* who always reads everything he is about to physically sign. E-sign is another matter.

What intrigued Donald most about this signature sheet was that Doctor Tony Hill had signed his name as "Skit Zoland" and had entered "Kangaroo" in the column labelled "Patient's Ward." He didn't know what any of this meant, but he certainly found it interesting.

"And now, let us all proceed to the introductions." Houts had directed his attention to the group as a whole, "As there are two new members of our SaRS community here today, I will ask everyone to please give a brief introduction of themselves using the standard Fluffy introduction template[243] as a guide."

---

[240] The thirteenth group session is roughly Tuesday afternoon next week.

[241] Any, and every, time a solicitor lodges a motion against them, they will already have their arses well and truly covered and out of danger.

[242] Seconds are another funny one, why are there no firsts?

[243] Fluffy has been designed, specifically, to ensure there are no triggers mentioned in anyone's introduction of themselves. You basically have to talk about what drove you insane, without being able to talk about what drove you insane just in case the same thing also drove someone else insane.

Houts then went on to explain Fluffy... The introduction template guide:
¤   Firstly, tell everyone your preferred name;
¤   Give a very brief innocuous description of why you are here;
¤   How you have been feeling since our last group session; and
¤   How you are feeling right now.

If you feel so inclined, you may add:
¤   An itty-bitty titbit that you think makes you who you are; and
¤   What you are hoping to get out of this group session today.

Turning to his left, Houts asked, "Owedebt, perhaps you would like to start us off with your introduction?" Houts had the amazing talent of being able to ask a question and have it come across as a direct order, a condescending doubt and a polite request all at the same time.[244]

"Hi everyone, I'm Owedebt Dear. Ummmmm, I have been diagnosed with Bipolar Disorder and Borderline Personality Disorder. Ummmmm, to be honest, I don't know what else I should say. Ummmmm, I have been OK since yesterday's group, and I am OK now. Ummmmm, oh, and what makes me, me. Ummmmm, I guess my titbit would be Chunky Poopy. He is my best friend."

"Hey?" chimed in Nota, "What am I, chopped liver?"

At the sound of his name and one of his favourite foods, Chunky did one of his attention extraction routines. He opened one eye to look and see if there was actual food or if someone was holding a leash. Finding out this was not the case, he rolled over onto his back, licked his lips with gusto and looked off wistfully into the distance waiting for his upturned underbelly to be rubbed. After no response, he went back under Owedebt's chair and fell back asleep.

"Thank you, Owedebt."

"No worries." was Owedebt's subconscious reply lie.

"Nota, would you like to continue around the circle of introduction?"

"Hi, I'm Nota." Clearly put out by being demoted to second banana, after Chunky, she gave no more verbal introduction. She just sat there swinging her legs, frowning, pouting and thinking, "I'm not a *banananana,* and what do you mean anyway, what is a second banananana?[245]"

---

[244] How very *trialectical* of him.

[245] Nota takes everything as she (mis)understands it; mispronounces many words; and gets very offended if you try to correct her. She will argue, "Yes, *banananana,* that is what I said!" disagreeing with common facts. Then she will forget the whole ordeal after something else comes along and grabs her attention. Then she will say, "Nothing *grabbed* me, what do you mean?"

Got, looking as *inconspiratorial* as she could, said, "Khkhkhkhkhyello, my name eeze Got Knotyed, and khkhkhkhkhave ze, ah, khkhkhkhkhow you say, ze crrrrrazy mind.[246]" Adding a little bit of the index finger twirling around her left ear action, the international standard symbol for mental, was a nice touch. This whole introduction has been badly translated into stereo-a-typical movie Russian from, "Hello, my name is Got Knoted, and I have no specific diagnosis, but I am crazy." She said no more, protecting her identity.

Taking her cue from Got, who was tilting her head slightly, shrugging her shoulders and holding her arms in a W formation with palms upturned, and looking pointedly to her left, Istha introduced herself, "Hello, everyone. Tree people, this is for you too. I am in here because I hear voices. I hear voices all the time. I can even hear all of you talking in this room right now. My doctor tells me this is a psychosis called schizophrenia, and I am here to learn how to tell the difference between the real people and the fake ones.[247]"

"I have been having a reasonable day today, but yesterday there was an incident in the common area when I thought I heard someone speaking. Nelo tried to convince me, again, that I wasn't crazy and there really was someone called Donald, who was there talking... But I can't believe anything Nelo says because I still don't know if *he* is real or not."

"At some stage, though, I will have to throw my arms up in the air, throw caution to the wind and try not to throw up while I talk to someone who will talk back to me. And I guess...hoping whoever it is (this who, who is talking back to me) isn't just me talking back to myself... Is what makes me, me."

Lost was next to introduce himself and was about to do so when...

The door opened, and through it came a definitely unusual woman in red, who was in an easily understood overzealous state of mind. One accentuated spin-and-whip of her long golden-brown hair with an unnecessary smoothing of her cherry-red wet-look latex dress later, she brazenly sauntered on over to Lost and slapped him decisively on both cheeks. Then, tossing her head back again, in the ancient "Got no satisfaction? I can't!" way, she departed like she entered, without speaking a word.[248]

---

[246] She is very good at pretending to be someone, who is pretending to be someone, who is pretending they aren't from cold war communist Russia.

[247] Sadly, for Istha (et al), there are a lot of real fake people in the world.

[248] As this scene practically duplicates the earlier one, Donald is thinking it is some sort of altered reality déjà vu; and even though his mental state isn't getting any better, his grasp of French is definitely improving.

After an applicable amount of discombobulation, Houts spluttered, "Lost, who was she‽[249]" Not realising he has probably seen this drama unfold many times before (if the continuity people have done their job correctly).

Lost, who was often as confused as ever, shrugged his shoulders again and said, "Not only do I have no memory of her…I have no memory of who I am, why I am here, where here is, who you all are, or even how I came to be in this room. But, evidently, I do seem to recall a vague notion that some women are far more dangerous when they get too close than they appear to be."

Donald has just decided to call this mysterious lady in red Miss Direct and planned on mentioning this in his first attempt at a self-introduction in SaRS. His words decided otherwise and didn't come out of his mouth. Just one single moment later, they were all lost and forgotten, as predicted. Because…

Mindy Ownbeeswhacks piped up from her snooze, "You got it utterly spot on, Son!" Donald's head almost made a complete revolution as it spun around to look at Mindy. She continued to skip over him and introduce herself.

"My name is Mindy Ownbeeswhacks, and I suggest you all do exactly that! I may be as old as I look, but I am an old woman who can still take dangerous to an entirely new level. Now, I'm not one who normally blows my own warty nose, but I'd like to see any three of you try and take me on… Give me a large mixing cauldron, a reasonably full jug of moonshine and a deck of tarot cards, then I will show you just how dangerous this old woman can be."

The room fell silent, processing Mindy's introduction.

For Donald, his processing included, "Crap… I'm sitting next to an ancient fortune-telling witch, who has an alcoholic attitude to match!" His shuddering was reduced to a trembling when the sound of Mindy snoring, once or twice, filled their ever metaphorically compacting room again.

Nelo continued on from where Mindy had left off, "Yeah, I wouldn't ever cross her… (Again…) Not if you want to keep both of your eyebrows.[250] Hi, my name is Nelo, and I'm an addict. It's been," looking at his wrist-watch, "twenty-seven hours, thirty-eight seconds, since I last had a drink."

---

[249] It's catching on. I wonder if new punctuation marks can even be invented. On further investigation, filling in my pompous non-understanding, there is a punctuation mark called an interabang, and it looks like, "‽" This character denotes a question asked with excitement, disbelief, or is rhetorical. **Really‽**

[250] His hands spontaneously went up and then defensively hovered in front of his face, unsuccessfully attempting to hide his slowly regrowing eyebrows.

Donald should eventually discover that Nelo is addicted to drinking Blood. Until then, he will promote Nelo as the sanest person in the vicinity, including the various professionals he has met over the last couple of days.

Even the most blunted axe can be used to chop down the largest tree if there are enough people who are willing to swing the axe.

Going back to his standard meditative state of alertness, Sven apparently thought his introduction was now complete.

Donald was unsure if this quote meant:
- Even a godlike[251] egotistical overlord can be overthrown when there is enough opposition from his slaves; or
- Even the greatest hope of recovery can be dashed away if there are enough people willing to put you down.

Karl Saneman simply said, "Pass." and continued looking bewildered.

When their introductions had reached the end of the irregular circle, there were still two inmates who had not yet introduced themselves… The length of the uncomfortable silence was growing, many inmates were showing signs of disinterest, and Donald was showing no anything of breaking, so Doctor Hill[252] went ahead and introduced himself.

"Right… I am Doctor Tony Hill, I am a clinical psychologist working with the local constabulary, and I am here to assist with the solving of the *Bones Under the Courtyard Basement* case. From the little information, I have been able to gather so far," referring to his little notepad, "someone in this room may very well know more than they think they know. We will be going through all of the events of the past leading up to the burial and on to the discovery of the, as yet unidentified, set of remains which were buried below us."

"(Cough). Yes, thank you again, *Doctor Hill*. Perhaps you would like me to continue with the group introductions, and you can return to your observing?"

"Of course? Of course. Of course! Please, carry on."

"Thank you…"

---

[251] Donald believes that real belief is something to believe in when you don't really believe in anything. Hope for the hopeless… God for the godless… and Un for the unless…

[252] Donald already knows all about Skit, and so do you, so there is no real point in either reintroducing him or reiterating his unreality.

"All right. Donald… Lucky last… Would you like me to introduce you to the group, or would you like to introduce yourself?[253]" Houts was grinning like a clean dog grins at a puddle of warm mud, just moments before it chooses to get in and get comfortable, and then curls up in its cosy mud blanket.

Donald thought, "No, thank you!"
Wanted to say, "No, thank you."
But heard himself saying, "Ok, sure…"
Then went back to thinking, "Stupid! Stupid. Not smart…"

When Donald finally realised his inaccurate reply didn't remotely provide a definitive answer to the option selection of the yes or no question. He had no idea of what else to do; he just sat there and waited.

You should turn the page now.

No really… Turn the page.
There is nothing interesting written on this one.

Don't you believe me?[254]

---

[253] The amount of condescension, being levelled squarely at Donald, went from a smidgen of doubt, to a full-blown in-your-face fact.

[254] See! I told you. Just believe me next time, ok? Yeah, shuddup!

Chapter 10:
Group Session 1.1
(Tapestry #1)

Waiting for the requisite acceptable amount of awkward silence to pass,[255] Houts introduced Donald to the rest of the group… "Donald Halfbrain is here," pausing for effect, "because he has recently been clinically diagnosed as having resisted all treatments for chronic major depression and anxiety, autism and sleep apnoea. Otherwise known in the medical fraternity as *Institutionalisable* **Crazy Batshit Mental**.[256]"

Donald found he couldn't disagree with this descriptive introduction since it was all totally actually factual. His standard introductory definition of himself declares, "I am an atypical high functioning sociopath… With a list of problems twice as long as half of my arm, written in a sweetened condensed scalable font, with no spacing between the issues… The list can only be read by reading it through a powerful magnifying glass, under appropriate lighting conditions and even then, only if you want to know…[257] But don't ask me if I snore."

There was a collective sigh of mass distraction from everyone after Houts finished introducing Donald. They were all, including Donald, very glad he had his own single room. The last sound anyone wants to hear, the last thing at night, is an old man snoring after he has already snored himself to sleep.

---

[255] The Australian standard (AUS #27) is roughly 36.3 metric seconds. Or 42 decimal seconds, if you are a French Revolutionary living in the past.

[256] ICBMs are dangerous; I suggest you don't play with them at home.

[257] And he wonders why people suddenly remember they have an urgent appointment, over there, by the thing, very far away from here… Bye-bye…

Houts continued with the introductions of Grey and himself, "Grey Duate is one of our several student slaves. The local educational facilities send out a few examples each week; we use them for a week or so. Then, we mostly send them all back, often in the same condition they arrived in. The experience is well designed, so they: advance their own *education*; practice their budding *nursing* skills, and get a little taste of *the real world* of mental health."

He said all of this with *exaggerated* air quotes around *education, nursing* and *the real world*. It didn't inspire Donald with enough inspiration to have the inspirational thought, "Wow, we are in great hands. Thank you very much."

More continuing… "And due to the turmoil inducing high turnover rate of students, they all become a bit of a conglomerated blur. The real nursing staff don't get to know them personally, don't rely on them to do any meaningful work, and don't mind assigning them to do all of their dirty work. This results in the students taking temperatures, taking notes and taking the piss.[258]"

Donald had to stifle a childish laugh.

Even more continuing… "It is current SaRS policy to:
- Refer to all of the students by the gender-neutral name of Grey;
- Attribute them all with the intelligence-neutral brains of some; and
- Allocate them tasks with the completion-neutral time of now.

Any questions? Apart from mine? No? Good…"

Donald no longer had to stifle his childish laugh. When he looked around the group room, he saw everyone either had a bewildered look on their face, was trying to avoid eye contact with everyone else, or was sound asleep and snoring up a marginally audible storm.[259] There were no questions.

Finally, continuing for the last time… "And now, on to me!" Houts actually looked quite excited as he launched himself into his own introduction: "I like to be called **Doctor Houts Marted.[260]**"

---

[258] This is meant quite literally. The students will find themselves constantly emptying colostomy bags and, allegedly spill proof, overnight urine bottles.

[259] I find it interesting, the less sound you make while you are sleeping, the more soundly you are sleeping. It should be called no-sound-asleep.

[260] The whole Pronunciation vs Enunciation debate is going on in my mind. It will be addressed at some stage. It may even be in the appendix of this book… It's not. I just checked. Damn you Nunciation family.

"So what if I received my doctorate from an online night school based out of Outer Mongolia? So what if my thesis was a study of anthropomorphology as it relates specifically to ghosts? And so what if my certificate of completion was written using a blunt 9H pencil on the back of a menu from Fuddruckers... It doesn't make me any less of a doctor... **I am a real doctor.**"

Recovering from this brief is-he-out-of-his-mind-? experience, Houts went on for Donald's and Karl's benefit... "I am one of the Psychologists of SaRS[261] and will be imparting a vast wealth of information to you over the next three weeks. It will be my job to teach you how you can become a functioning part of society. It will be your responsibility to learn this and then make it so."

Donald wasn't able to grasp the rationale of how "Learning of knowledge, and the correct implementation of that same new knowledge, could be all said and done in one breath." He thought about asking Houts to "Please Explain?" but the question smelled of fish, seemed strangely anti-foreign and made him feel uncomfortably ginger...so he left it unsaid.

Moving away from the nitty-gritty but necessary Group ~~Rules~~Guidelines, Housekeeping and introductions, Houts continued on to the next in line item of his own internal personal agenda.

"All right, people... Now we all know each other ever so slightly, I will take you through the last of the prerequisites before you may participate in a group session at SaRS."

Flipping the whiteboard, Houts revealed *SPLAT*...

SPLAT[262] Coping Mechanisms[263]

Select an item from the group sensory box that appeals to your favourite sense

Practice a mindfulness technique

Leave the room temporarily if you just need a short break

Always return if you can

Tell someone if you aren't coming back

---

[261] The PoS acronym is not going to make it through an acceptability edit.

[262] Factual? No. Fictional? Maybe. Functional? Precisely, more or less!

[263] Even though this message was hand-written on the whiteboard it, was still in the same font as the other blue-tacked informational signs around the room masquerading as information to help tackle the patients' blues.

"These are only some of the possibilities available to keep your anxiety in check. If you want to select an item from the group sensory box, I suggest you do so now to minimise any predictable disruption to the group."

When no one made a move towards the box, Houts signalled to Grey, using the: multiple raising of his eyebrows, slight tilt of his head, and go-on anti-nod to perform the student task of handing out the paraphernalia to the inmates. Grey timidly picked up the sensory box, made a complete circuit of the group and offered the contents to each person in turn as he went. When finished, he brazenly returned the box to where he had picked it up from and resumed sitting, having handed out a total sum of zero, naught, or O[264] items.

Once all movement within the room had ceased, Houts began, "This group session is the traditional first group of each new patient's stay. It is designed to give you some information about where you are and a bit of the history of SaRS. Other than that, its primary task is to facilitate patient bonding by giving you a topic to discuss which is not specifically related to your mental issues."

"Clueless!"

Donald was startled by this opening. Houts had said it like it was supposed to mean something. Donald looked around at the group, wondering what was going on and noticed that everyone else, apart from Karl and Doctor Hill, were all trying to avoid any direct eye contact with Houts. Then Donald realised the "everyone else" people must have all been through this group session before, and they knew what was coming.

Grey was standing by the side of Houts, acting as a spotter of any interest, Doctor Hill was busy taking notes on his notepad (with what looked like, as far as Donald couldn't see, an imaginary pen), and as this was all of the movement in the stationary room, the word was Grey's luck had got away.

Undeterred, Houts went on, probably because it was his job. "Who would like to catch us up to where we left off last time? We were discussing the *Bones Under the Courtyard Basement* case, as Doctor Hill so kindly revealed without any spoiler warning." The irate gaze Houts delivered to Doctor Hill was verging on becoming a multiple homicidal death stare. Then, after removing all traces of ire and hate, "Nota, would you like to share what you can remember?"

Nota looked at Owedebt as a sidekick would usually look to the main hero character when they were silently asking, "Is it OK for me to be the centre of attention for just a short while? Please? I promise I won't take it for long, and I will give it straight back unmolested?"

------

[264] I don't much understand how someone can recite a number, of the phone variety, and include all of: Zero, Naught and O. But, I have heard it done.

Owedebt nodded a nod trying to convey, "Yeah, sure, what-ev-er! It's not like I wanted to share or anything stupid like that. Ummmmm. I mean, just go ahead; why are you even asking? Ummmmm. To be honest, I really don't care what you, or anyone else here, does. Grumble, moan, whine and whinge.[265]"

Nota read into Owedebt's nod, "Of course, you may, please, be my guest! I would love for someone else to be lavished with the centre of attention for once. Let me know if you would like to read anything from my notes, but to be honest, I think you could handle this all by yourself, without my help. Yay, woohoo, good job and no worries.[266]" and then retold everything she could remember, utilising some logical, verbal bullet points:

- The Kingswood's House was built approximately 125 years ago;
- There were discrepancies with some alterations made to the building plans 75 years ago, which included a "Do Not Dig Here!" message;
- A descendant of one of the builders dug there, found a secret room and discovered some human remains;
- The bones have been there for 75 years, and were recently excavated, exhumed and examined but have not yet been explained;
- 75 years ago is also when The Kingswood's House became SaRS 1.0;
- The possible perpetrators were: Brother Brown, Father Fuchsia, Sister Sapphire, Gardener Grey, Lawyer Lithium and Wastrel White; and
- An official investigation has shown there were many rooms where the alleged murder could have taken place and common household items which could have been weaponised, but they really have no idea.

"Thank you, Nota, for a most comprehensive, highly cynical retelling."

Donald was astounded by three minus one things:

- Firstly, the tour information Seth had bombarded him with yesterday was apparently not a figment of his imagination; and
- Thirdly minus onely, he was becoming mildly interested in playing the upcoming Get to Know Your Fellow Inmates game.

"To assist us with today's meet-n-greet group, we have *borrowed* one of the Hospital's three *magical* tapestries. Not only will it give us something to look into, but it may also give us something else to talk about." Houts had just reverted to his air quoting fascination again, for borrowed and magical. This took away some of Donald's interest, but luckily for us, not all.

---

[265] Owedebt's nods are extremely verbose when she says she doesn't care.

[266] Nota's interpretation of Owedebt's nods are just as extremely verbose, but not quite the same sentiment is understood.

"What this tapestry does is similar to, yet appropriately unlike,[267] what a largish bowl full of silvery spooky stuff does in a well-known-but-shouldn't-be-mentioned collection of urban fantasy novels about another unlikely hero."

Donald's interest was politely re-piqued[268] as he mostly likes collections of urban fantasy novels. Especially those with an unsung hero who he can totally relate to; those with lots of crazy weird people; and those with many harmless random comments about random stuff peppered randomly throughout.

"Each of you, in turn, will look deeply into the tapestry. When your viewing is complete, if you were lucky enough to be chosen, you will recall and be able to describe what you saw in great detail. What you'll see is *not-a-memory* from any specific person. It has been described as like being in a virtual reality reconstruction of a scene from an inanimate object's point of view, without any of the annoying virtual reality apparatus or possible legal ramifications."

Seamlessly transitioning from Houts, Grey factored in, "Six factual things we know from past experiences with the tapestry are as follows:
1. The tapestry will choose only one person to see the not-a-memory;
2. It will present to that person[269] a not-a-memory scene from the past;
3. The person will then find themselves embedded within a scene;
4. The outcome of the displayed scene cannot be changed;
5. Blind people are able to sense things that sighted people cannot;

Houts, taking the baton away from Grey before the final factoid…
6. Physical interactions within each not-a-memory scene will be strictly limited to all things without faces."

…resumed, "When the chosen one returns from the not-a-memory scene, they will hopefully have a new piece of information to add to the puzzle. After this piece is added to what we have already retrieved, maybe we will get lucky, and it will be enough for us to solve this 75-year-old mystery."

Donald's mind was screaming, "Pick me! Pick Me! PICK ME!"

---

[267] Hopefully it is different enough, and I honestly think it is, to avoid any legal issues. But if it does get taken out, you won't be reading this anyway.

[268] Ok, so Donald's interest was only semi-re-piqued.
But this is still way more piquing than most polite people will ever do.

[269] Or "It will present to the Chosen One (TCO), a not-a-memory scene from the past;" if you would like to encounter a bit of non-plagiaristic word play which is running very close to the wind.

Maybe the tapestry heard Donald's mind screaming, "Pick Me!" or maybe it was just a pure coincidence; or maybe it was a patently obvious step in what could be thought of as an atrociously thought-out plotline to involve the hero again. Still, whichever, when the tapestry was shown to Donald, he was the one chosen to be the Chosen One. TCO to his friends.

On his way into the not-a-memory scene, Donald was shown a document, apparently, roughly describing most of what he was about to see; what the ramifications of seeing it might be; what he was and wasn't allowed to do or say, about the tapestry and/or the specific scene displayed, both during and after the not-a-memory scene; and what he could and couldn't, touch, feel, or smell. There was also copious subtext explaining that the manufacturer of the tapestry, and all of their associates, could in no way be held accountable for anything remotely, or even closely, associated with the viewing of an alleged not-a-memory scene inside the tapestry... Up to and including this message.

© Copyright SaRS Official 5 – Fine Print p141

⚥ Extract from The Donald Diaries.

Towards the bottom of this document, following all of the legalese there to ensure you aren't going to read it in the required detail were the tapestry's viewing instructions.[270] Or, more precisely, the last tapestry instruction, which explains how you leave the tapestry unreality and return to your non-tapestry reality when you think you have seen enough and are ready to do so.

Directly underneath this was where Donald started to think-read. It was the standard tapestry restart after an incomplete, or failed, interaction where you last left off security clause, relaying, "Imagine a strong re-entry password, re-imagine the same password, and then think *Check...*"

Donald imagined his standard password[271] twice and thought, "*Check...*" almost immediately. His password was accepted, even though it was so very weak, as the next instruction was, "Think *Next...* if you wish to proceed."

Glossing over his own standard background thoughtless question, "They wouldn't allow me to view the tapestry if anything bad, or possibly dangerous, was actually going to happen to me... Would they?" Donald guessed he should want to proceed. So, after dismissing this question and the small amount of trepidation associated, he thought, "*Next...*" in the hope of self-perpetuating bliss and not really caring or fully understanding what he was doing.

---

[270] Typically, predictably and stupidly Donald, unusually, didn't think or read very far ahead in the Document. I will try to deal with this omission later.

[271] Donald would be wise to change a few of his most treasured passwords, from DH007, to something a bit less predictable like D1/2B.

By doing all of this thinking, Donald has just wittingly launched himself into the next instalment of his self-discovery phase.

Don't turn out the lights if you don't like what you can't really see.

Donald was about to ask one of his several three-question drama inducing monologues when the sound of Sven's voice disappearing, much like an echo just fades away to become a memory, caused quite a disquieting quiet inside of him…just quietly.[272] The echoing cookie quote was accompanied by some fuzzy, wavy, hazy fading in and out visuality.

Although Donald is mightily accustomed to tuning out of any unpleasant situation which may cause him anything greater than a small amount of angst, thus making them meta-figuratively disappear, he was just as unaccustomed to the reverse happening to him.[273]

Reorienting himself, and becoming accustomed to his new situation, was going to be Donald's first onerous task, as he wasn't yet accustomed to his old situation. Looking around, he decided that where he was, was still in the SaRS Group Room. One of the problems with being in the same location now was that the SaRS Group Room wasn't *when it was*, barely moments ago.

To Donald, it looked like it was the same Group Room, but it smelt vaguely of hospital strength bleach and blood; it had hospital beds instead of chairs; and the most subtle of hints, which clinched his earlier thought, was a sign leaning against the wall waiting to be hung which said…

---

[272] He was also thinking, somewhat slightly off track, "Why do none of the fortune-cookie quotes, which the audacious Sven is always quoting to me, ever have quotation marks around them?"

[273] i.e. The angst causing situation literally appearing from where it didn't used to not be wasn't at all before. (Don't blame me, I just wrote it.)

[274] "PSH… for Men," sounds like an awesome name for an aftershave.

Finding himself absurdly dressed in, what looked like, a dirty off-white tie-died smock and poufy pants twin set... Donald realised he was seeing himself as a period-accurate patient in the precursor of SaRS... 75 years ago! No one seemed to be paying too much attention to him, so Donald went for a bit of a nearly brisk walk and had a Hokey-Pokey-nosey look around.

Donald divided the population of this time Hospital into six main groups:

Patients[275] - He easily identified the patients by their attire. They were all wearing something close to identical to what he was currently sporting.[276] He also, pragmatically, I think, decided to take a timely, accurate but conceptually inaccurate, anti-Schrödinger's paradox view of the cleanliness of his current undergarments and assume, until otherwise known, that they were clean.

Doctors - These are people who Donald assumed were doctors. They were all male, were all wearing the standard whiter-than-white lab coat, and all had the stereotypical strap-on head mirror used to denote physicians of this sexist long-forgotten era. All in all, he thought it was a pretty safe bet to assume they were all antique medical Doctors.

Nurses - These were the only female population in the scene, so they were a fairly easy subdivision to recognise. Each wore a dress uniform, not quite as white as the doctors' coats and had varying colours of pinstriping attached to make their rank easily identifiable. They also had those pointless little hats bobby-pinned to their hair screaming Nurse. Again, it was another safe bet.

Brothers of Saint Rita - These, officially male, guys were silently wandering around, with their heads bowed down, showing off their partly bald cinnamon doughnut styled hairdos. They were wearing brown sack-cloth robes, slightly longer than knee length short, which revealed entirely too much of their hairy legs for Donald's liking. Wearing sandals with socks finished the ensemble off painfully. They didn't stick out like sore thumbs at all!

---

[275] This is a significant distinction: Clients of Hospitals see themselves as Patients; those of Sanatoriums see themselves as Inmates. Insignificantly, the staff of SaRS all thought of the Inmates as Patients.

[276] Only in as much as all snowflakes look identical from far away. It is only close inspection that reveals they are unique. Until one day when they are all stupidly thrown together into the same huge commercial washing machine and emerge as one large clean off-white globular mass of no-longer unique.

Orderlies - Wearing the male equivalent of the nurse's uniform, working as a combination of bodyguard, baggage handler and personal cleaner… None of them looked like they were a day over eighteen; none of them looked like they would run out of Brylcreem soon, and none of them seemed to mind the challenge of finding some spare time to chat up the available nurses.

Filling out his not-a-memory scene was the sixth group of **Miscellaneous** people. This included the various staff groupings of cooks, cleaners, gardeners, game hunters and administration etc… Strangely, these people were wearing exactly the same clothes as their 75-years-later counterparts. The only thing jumping out as being different was the names sewn onto their pockets.

Donald found his outfit to be comfortable and conveniently camouflaging, giving him the chance to poke his nose around without attracting any undue attention. If someone saw him somewhere where he wasn't supposed to be, he could always claim he was a newly admitted patient who didn't yet know all of the local-time rules.[277]

This was close enough to the truth to satisfy Donald.

Donald's ASD gifted superpower came with one non-trivial, self-imposed and cursed morality drawback: If he wanted to continue being able to just see through all of the lies other people told on purpose,[278] then he would still have to require himself to tell no lies of his own.

Donald called this inner turmoil his personal "Liars' Three Truths," and he always battled with his three, subsequently manifested, inner selves:
- **Can't Tell Real Lies;**
- **All Lies are Trouble; and**
- **Don't Ever Lie.**

Collectively known as his CTRL-ALT-DEL directive. As long as everything he says doesn't contravene any of these three truths, he was good to go. Donald focuses on the purpose of his words to define what he is allowed to say.

------

[277] Donald had obviously not paid very close attention to the largish bowl full of silvery spooky stuff scenes from the well-known-but-shouldn't-be-mentioned collection of urban fantasy novels. If he had, he would have known he was essentially a non-participating invisible viewer. Why his clothes had changed to match those of the time was anyone's guess.

[278] If the lie is believed to be not a lie, then it is plausibly undetectable.

The truth can be a highly deceptive mistress with contrived equivocations, artificial rationalisations and deceptively concealed falsehoods. For example, if one day you were unlucky enough to meet the agreed patron saint of liars,[279] and they said to you... "Everything I say is a lie."

Would you interpret this to mean?
1.	I am telling the truth;
2.	Therefore, I am telling a lie;
3.	Making their statement not a lie.
Conversely:
1.	I am telling a lie;
2.	Therefore, I might be telling the truth;
3.	But, if I am telling the truth, I must be simultaneously telling a lie;
4.	Making their statement not a lie.
Quite the logical conundrum.

"Hey?" he thought to himself, "If I am in a not-a-memory scene from 75 years ago, and if the hospital was a male-only facility 75 years ago... Why did I just see one female wearing an inmate's attire and another wearing a doctor's outfit?" Because not long before Donald had thought this bizarre thought, he had thought another: that he had seen this exact thought depicted in the not-a-memory scene in all of its exactness and bizarreness.

He came to the fairly logical conclusion of, "I must follow them."

Donald hunched down, glanced over both shoulders and calmly followed these two poorly camouflaged, clearly suspicious ladies at a discrete distance. In his previous experience of following people surreptitiously,[280] the best way to avoid notice is to act like you belonged. Donald didn't come anywhere near to achieving this with his obvious effort at looking inconspicuous.

He crept from pillar to post, sidled along walls and poked his head out for barely two moments at a time, always ensuring he was keeping the two ladies in sight. He moved around like this for at least seven minutes, making several loud body placement errors, when the realisation dawned upon him, "the not-a-memory scene, people can't see me."

---

[279]	Probably Lucifer's 2IC... I didn't bother to look this one up.

[280]	Being accused of stalking is a great way to gain some understanding of the generic rules, restrictions and regulations for secretly following people appropriately. Not meaning to imply Donald has ever done this.

Mentally slapping himself upside his head for not figuring out this bauble of information sooner... He stood up straight, brushed off his remaining non-existent dignity and strode, in what he hoped looked like a confident manner, to all of those people who couldn't see him after his quarry. This would have been fantastically awesome had he not tripped over a recalcitrant shoelace, stumbled through some young rose bushes,[281] and fallen flat on his face.

While Donald was contemplating the ground, he saw a shadow pass over him. The scene had all the ominous features of an intruder being discovered due to his own clumsy stupidity scenario.[282] Luckily for Donald, when he rolled over to see who had discovered him, all he saw was the underside of a wicker basket attached to a casually floating along "Bad☠Day" hot air balloon.

Physically slapping himself again fiercely, he re-stood up straight, brushed off some of the strangely definitely existent dirt and ran in the vague direction of the two alleged persons of interest, fully utilising the burst of energy coming from the undetected adrenaline-infused Blood pumping through his veins.

After nearly catching up to them, Donald trailed the two ladies as close as he dared for what felt like hours. Up and down elaborate staircases; in and out of assorted rooms; winding through a fledgling hedge maze; finally coming to an end at the entrance archway of an ornate pavilion.

During this time of following and discovery, Donald became aware the sky was closing in and turning prematurely grey. He also astonishingly noticed this was due to a fairly dense coverage of dark storm clouds, which he could have sworn were up to something devious. But he didn't, so he didn't, again.

He stood still and watched for a few moments, fascinated by the clouds.

After Donald finished pondering the cloud's malfeasance, he returned his focus to his current predicament, where he was drastically losing the current game of *chasies*.[283] He stepped through the arched entryway of the pavilion and got back on to the now brutally cold trail of the two ladies.

---

[281] Donald didn't yet connect this to the earlier outburst he had heard from the chainsaw wielding groundskeeper. This is also when Donald didn't yet realise he could physically interact with anything in the tapestry as long as it didn't have eyes. Otherwise, you would fall through the floors...

[282] If this was supposed to be a murder mystery novel, instead of a humorous one containing a bit of murder and mystery, it probably would have been.

[283] I don't know why this isn't a legitimate word, after all, it has been around since Eve played naked chasies with Adam through the Garden of Eden.

Once Donald was inside the sandstone building, there was, what appeared to be, a crudely concealed trap door leading to where he assumed there would be an underground room. Hanging over this alleged door was a sign warning…

Beware of the Minotaur!

Donald didn't question the ridiculous stupidity of having this warning sign hanging directly over the not-so-secret-anymore trap door. Neither did he ask the explanation question, "What do you mean, Beware of the Minotaur!?" nor the coherent one, "Where did those two ladies go?" What he did wonder, though, ridiculous as it sounds, was, "Why is it called a trap door?" Then, disengaging himself from thinking about the incongruent function of trap doors, he finally thought about asking the poignant, "How am I supposed to open any sort of door if I am unable to interact with anything here on a physical level?"

Throwing his head back in convenient despair, Donald's eyes glanced upon a sunbeam coming through one of the ornate leadlight windows, oddly located on the roof of the pavilion. Not remembering that the weather outside was fast becoming a dark and stormy night, he followed this unimaginative sunbeam down to the floor, where it landed on a small piece of plastic.

"How very *coinsidious*!" thought Donald.

Reacting naturally for a change, Donald picked up the piece of plastic. He sat down on one of the surprisingly comfortable sandstone bench seats lining most of the inside wall of the pavilion[284] to ponder his next step. While he was brooding, he had another royally troubling thought, "How does One return to being not inside this not-a-memory scene tapestry?"

At the precise instant that Donald had this thought, his subconscious, still alert and aware of everything happening around it, perceived localised flashes of lightning, an inflated collection of onomatopoeia sounds, and a magnifically sparkled framing of the trap door as something happened in reverse…

Out and in fading hazy, wavy, fuzzy visuality.

---

[284] Both actions contravening the tapestry's "no touchy touch" rule. Which is another way the two literary historical information delivery devices differ.

Donald was back in the group room, at the correct when, with everybody staring at him. "Well, I guess you have just answered my unspoken question!" Sadly, it also rebooted the short to medium-term memory of his subconscious, and he lost everything he had not yet converted into long-term memory.

"Ah, I see you were Chosen. Excellent. It is sometimes hard for me to tell if someone has been in a not-a-memory scene or if they have simply fallen asleep." Houts flicked a not-so-subtle glance towards Mindy and explained, "Time behaves clichély differently inside the tapestry. What may have seemed like hours for you were only seconds for us. But never mind that, jump to the exciting part... Did you see anything useful in your not-a-memory scene?"

Donald took his cue from Nota's previous recounting and went through everything he could remember using verbal bullet points.[285] This should have been not very much, according to the end of the second last paragraph, two paragraphs ago, but conveniently, it was everything.

He firstly recounted several initial points to establish he had seen a vision from the appropriate time, 75 years ago:

- A room smelling of bleach and *blood*, with beds instead of chairs;
- Descriptions of the various staff member groups; and then crucially
- The "Welcome to *PSH... for Men*" sign, including the date 1945.

Then[286] he concluded his recollection with:

- Following the two leading ladies around with deft spy-like agility;
- Up and down several staircases, in and out of many more rooms;
- Round and round the garden, including the fledgling hedge maze;
- Bravely entering the ornate pavilion with so much style, and finally
- The not-so-hidden trap door and the "*Beware of the Minotaur!*" sign.

Thinking he had done a most excellent job with his not-a-memory scene retelling, Donald leaned back in his chair, almost toppling it over. Managing at the last second to kick his legs out, counterbalancing his fattening head, he casually clasped his fingers together and waited for the avalanche of questions to come. It was during this clasping motion Donald realised he was still holding something in his hand from the not-a-memory scene.

---

[285] The retelling of Donald's not-a-memory scene experience sounded like a cheesy voice over summary from an old private investigator movie.

[286] Self-consciously leaving out the physical struggles he had had with the 1945 not-a-memory scene and embellishing a great deal on the other details.

He tried to surreptitiously conceal his excitement about the thought of examining his find... And when he failed to do even this, he realised he would not be able to contain himself if he looked at his find here. Instead, he slipped the item in question quietly into his pocket, never thinking he, like always, would, in due course, eventually forget something was ever in there.

"All right people, we have arrived at a logical point in our group today to take a break. We have all just been given a lot of information to process, and I respectfully suggest we should cogitate about it over our respective lunches." Houts dismissed the inmates, who rose as one and exited cordially.

Houts reached over and touched Donald on the shoulder as he was going past and surreptitiously gave him the international symbol for *we need to talk* with his index finger. "Donald, I was just wondering if you have shared *all* of what you saw in your not-a-memory scene today."

"Um, yes... It was all the activity, of all the people I saw, with all of the eyes in my head, for all of today..." was his hesitant but truthful just reply.

"Excellent!" said Houts while he was writing something else in his notes. "It was a most magnificent meet-n-greet group session this morning, and I am very much looking forward to your not-a-memory scene interpretations after lunch. I think you might have made a major breakthrough."

Unfortunately, his breakthrough wasn't as large as it might have been. He had omitted both the hot air balloon and the darkening storm from his story. Not because he had forgotten about them, but because he didn't think either of them was in any way at all empirically important.[287]

Donald felt he had passed this significant test with flying colours and was now experiencing three powerful feelings:
- Happiness;
- Hope; and most prominently
- Hunger.

Looking to Houts for approval, Donald exited after the other inmates and went looking for some food.

It was at about this time Donald forgot about the quietly pocketed item.

---

[287] Donald's thinking was very wrong once again. On both counts. He also forgot to mention the concept of the not-a-memory scene people not being able to see you, but as this was an already known concept, it actually wasn't in any way at all important.

Chapter 11:
Group Session 2
(Debriefing)

Lunch today was a cheesy pumpkin soup with an assortment of bread rolls. Donald smelt a rude odour in the air. He thought to himself, "I don't know what that smell is: it could be the cheesy pumpkin soup; it could be someone's shoes the day after they forgot to wear socks, or it might be the effect of someone in front of me in the queue cutting the cheese…" The sad and confusing thing for Donald was that he didn't know which smell he would prefer to be smelling; none of them were particularly appetising.

Donald accepted a tepid bowl full of pumpkin soup and sat down at a table with empty expectations from and of the soup. Just the way he liked it. What he didn't like was the immediate congregating of Got, Istha and Karl. Got was interested in talking to Donald about the not-a-memory scene from group and had many questions; Karl was interested in just talking to Donald and had no questions, and Istha's presence there was completely coincidental.

Before Donald could transliterate and then avoid answering any of Got's questions; listen attentively and respond appropriately to any of Karl's small talk; confuse the proverbial out of Istha by talking to her at all, or even get to taste his soup, Grey appeared. He was breathing heavily, barely focussing and came complete with a look of mortal terror from his entire body…

"DD wants to see you… Now…[288]"

---

[288] No explanations were necessary for any of Grey's abrupt interruption, apparent exhaustion, or abhorrent terror. Neither was there, strictly, a need to append "Now…" to the end of the request, but it lends a sense of urgency to the ~~proposal invitation request instruction demand order~~ directive.

"Go quickly, Donald, and don't worry about clearing any of this away; I will take care of your dirty lunch plates and utensils myself as you have much more pressing matters to attend to. And I know I am speaking for the whole group when I wish you well and hope for your speedy recovery…"

Donald was taken aback by Got's well wishes.[289]
"Thank you, I think… But what do I have to recover from…?"

There was no time for any answers, apparently… Grey had physically lifted Donald out of his chair, swivelled him around to face the doorway and pushed him towards the general direction of that way. Donald was using strength provided by gravity, trying to postpone the inevitable smack in the face with the floor, which was going to arrive any second n… *thud*

Donald didn't know the layout of the hospital at all well, but he found himself drawn in one specific direction each time there was a choice to be made. He hadn't even asked Grey where DD was waiting, so it should have come as an immense surprise when he found himself standing outside an office marked "Primary Nurse (sic) Office!" Surprisingly, Donald wasn't surprised by this. "I think I might be getting used to the strange behaviour of the strange people in this strange place." he thought strangely quietly…

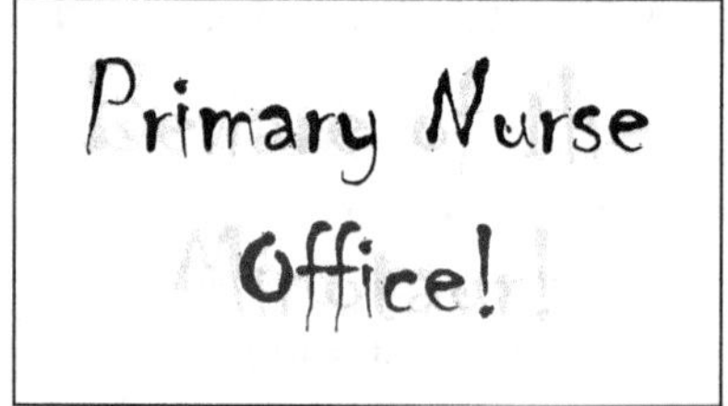

Donald performed a magnificently elaborate, over-the-top double-take of the sign when he thought he saw a familiar warning underneath. He chose to believe it must have been some kind of optical illusion, a re-used sign with the old words oozing out, or that he was just projecting a mental image of the sign from his not-a-memory scene. It didn't explain the poor grammar, though.

Mentally preparing himself for a barrage of berating belittlements, Donald raised his hand to knock on the d…

----

[289] Not to mention the unasked exclamestion, "Where did your exceedingly poor grasp of English go, and your obviously faked TV Russian accent?" (Yeah, I know, but I don't care. I like my punctuation thingy better.)

"Come in, Donny.[290]"
Cringe.[291] "Sphincter Feng Shui!"

Watching as the door opened all by itself, Donald felt conflicted between the urge to be drawn inside; the feeling of helplessness; and the impulse to scream, "Run, Run Now, Ruuuuun Donald Ruuuuun, RUN NOW YOU GOOSE!" again... And this time, to follow through with the action.

The thought of Donald thinking that he had a choice was farcical. Everyone knows that when you find a door opening all by itself, you always go in to see what is in there, even if it is just to confirm the suspicion that you shouldn't go in. It doesn't matter if you know Johnny is in there with a chainsaw, patting a rabid dog with three heads and sipping on a Molotov cocktail...
You will always go in... Always.
As it happens, it was someone performing a routine maintenance task on the door. He was fixing the auto-return mechanism after it had been damaged by an over-enthusiastic exit from an inmate who had just received the news he was going to be set free. A small pile of one business card had fallen out of the workman's pocket. Donald bent down to retrieve the one of it...

Who Would – Wood Masons
We are Not Just Carpenters...
We are an underground elite group of artisans
Who aren't afraid to work with petrified wood...
Dial: 1800 AREYOU – ask for Dennis

Dennis Who is the Who, in the who's who, of Who Would - Wood Masons. He is not, however, the person currently working on DD's door; that person is **Chip Chop**. Chip is the general dogsbody of the whole Who Would enterprise, who gets to work on all of the non-petrified wood woodwork. The door to DD's office is entirely made out of wood, which has subsequently become terrified wood, a completely different species to petrified wood entirely.

---

[290] Yes, it was a bit obvious, but they can't all be pearlers. Interestingly, well interesting for me anyway, *pearlers* is an Australian slang word and isn't in the American dictionary. This same dictionary also doesn't have entries for Accadacca, Bogan, Crikey, Drongo, ...

[291] This is Donald's reaction to DD calling him Donny, not your reaction to the last footnote. Although, it may have been applicable to that as well.

Dennis Who abuses his superior superstar supervisory role to choose only those jobs he wants to work on. He will also commonly swoop in at the very last stage of a project, displacing the minion who has done all of the hard work and take all of the accolades for himself. Giving him the reputation of being a bit of a woodpecker of a woodwork picker. This is patently confirmed by his standard phone call answer (and ringtone) "This is Who... Who are you?[292]"

"Come in, Donny, please,[293] and there is never a need for such colourful[294] language here at SaRS." DD was displaying a little bit of patronising contempt for Donald's hesitation.

"It has just been brought to my attention that you were, on this morning, supplied with one not-a-memory scene by the tapestry known formally as The Tapestry #1. Is this attention-seeking information correct?"
"Erm, Yes."

"In that case, we have some documentation for you to sign:
- To remove any and all responsibility from SaRS, SaRS personnel (past, present and future) and anyone who has known anyone who at some time may have been remotely related to a SaRS employee;
- To unconscionably render the above persons unaccountable for any repercussions, be they mental, physical, or financial, at any time (past, present and future) ever;
- And finally, to assure the author of the well-known-but-shouldn't-be-mentioned collection of urban fantasy novels, every accidental minor similarity between the two is purely coincidental in nature;
- This last clause, now known as the second to last clause, applies to the authors and/or those who have reserved the rights of any published work (past, present and future) that this totally original material may be thought to infringe upon without the correct acknowledgement.

---

[292] He has whittled this down from a much longer and cringier, "Who I am is Who, that's who. Who is the you who, who is speaking to this Who?"

[293] If this politeness was personified it would be similar to a hangman asking his current client if the rope was comfortable, the hood was the appropriate blackness of black, and if he had changed his underpants recently.

[294] If white is the theoretical combination of every colour, why did I always manage to create a putrid shade of *greeny-browny-grey* when I combined all of the paint in art class? This is the colour Donald imagined DD meant.

Sign here…, and date here…, please."

> I, the undersigned, remove any responsibility from SaRS, including, non-exclusively, past, present and future employees and anyone else, who has known anyone, who at some time may have been remotely related to SaRS in a functional, or a non-functional capacity and also absolve them entirely, from any repercussions, resulting from viewing a not-a-memory scene in Tapestry #1, including fundamentally mental, physical, or financial ones.
>
> I, the undersigned, assure the author of the well-known-but-shouldn't-be-mentioned collection of urban fantasy novels of any similarity between the SaRS Tapestry, known formerly formally as Tapestry #1 and the largish pedestal bowl, full of silvery spooky stuff, is purely coincidental and definitely not intentional.
>
> I, the undersigned, accept any ramifications, from seeing a not-a-memory scene, in Tapestry #1 are not the responsibility of the Tapestry manufacturer, including anything, non-exclusively, relating to anything I may have seen, heard, touched, smelt or tasted before, during, or after, the interaction.
>
> Everything, up to and including this message, is purely fictional, signed/dated
>
> _________________ / _______   295

SaRS Official 5 - Fine Print

Donald thought the fine print was looking particularly fine today. He took the document, barely read the first three words and ceremoniously signed his name on the correct line. Having no more of an idea about the date as he had before,[296] he handed the document back to DD, saying, "I have no idea what the date is anymore."

"That's ok, Donny," said DD, as she got out her date stamp, adjusted it to today's date and stamped it officially on the document. She enacted a tri-fold-ceremony on the single piece of paper, inserted it into an envelope, licked the envelope shut and held it out for Donald to take, saying, "Be a dearie and take this to Mark Time for me, please. He is on your way back to group."

Donald experienced some more déjà vu when he thought, "It didn't sound like a request, again." He also thought, "Ewwwww, Juicy," and, "This place is actually becoming polite with so many pleases; just as long as you don't do as you please, I guess." He grabbed the envelope as far away from the lick as he could and followed his memory to "Here be Accountants."

---

[295] **Note:** This has been displayed & printed in actual size. It basically says: "No care, No responsibility and No idea. With No takebacks. Just… No!"

[296] The days are passing blindingly slowly for Donald, I can assure you.

Repeating the dinging episode from earlier… "Ding!" Donald rang the bell, once only as directed, to attract someone's attention.

Mark poked his head out from behind the photocopier. "I'll be with you in just a tick, right after I deal with this recalcitrant machine." There were several crash-bang-ouch noises and a couple of very unhealthy-machine-like *twang-bzzzzz-damnits*! Closing the, now likely completely dead, photocopier's access panel, Mark stood up, shook his head and sighed as a single tear weaved and wended its way down his cheek.

After he handed the pre-licked envelope to Mark, as requested, and after Mark had disappeared to file the alleged form in Donald's folder, Donald took the rare opportunity to wander around the entry vestibule aimlessly for a little while to fill in some of the time until the next group session started.[297] There were many interesting items hanging on the walls:

☼   The Three Magical SaRS tapestries. Where the newly now seen #2 and #3 tapestries look eerily similar to #1;

Tapestry #1 we already know. It had been dutifully returned after group.

The next one labelled as ***"Tapestry #2 - TV Test Pattern"***, displayed the familiar pattern Donald had not seen or looked at closely for many years. When he looked closely now, he could see the unimpressed robot face, with a moustache and a Bloodshot left eye, was wearing a yarmulke.[298]

The third one labelled as ***"Tapestry #3 - Quiz"***, appeared to be constantly changing.[299] It was changing between three images: various groups of people standing behind a podium; several people reading from a card or a computer screen; and a puzzling mashup of question marks and money signs. On closer inspection of the tapestry, Donald found it wasn't actually a tapestry at all. The tapestry-like texture had been synthesised using a holographical combination of three separate images. He caught himself being entranced by the annoying suspense of waiting for an answer to, "Why was it called a tapestry?"

---

[297] Ok, he does *technically* have an aim, with the time thing, but wandering around aimlessly paints a much better picture of what he thinks is doing.

[298] There's no doubt many of you don't know what I am talking about. What is a test pattern? What do you mean there were only three channels? What do you mean it wasn't 24/7? Are you sure we are both talking about TV?

[299] Is constantly changing an oxymoron? I think it might be, but maybe not.

ᵡ   An indigenous inhabitant's map of Australia and Torres Strait Island... from before they were all known as such;

Attached to the bottom of this map was an information pamphlet about the upcoming Halloween and Eternal Dreaming celebrations... Donald took a mental note to make sure he was available to attend...

True Histories of Halloween and The Eternal Dreaming

Pay your respects to the traditional custodians of the land
An evening of Traditional Music, Dancing and Legends
Hosted by Nurse Jack Call and Chef Chief Changes
Featuring William the Piano Man on the Digeridoo
To be held in the Battle of Kingswood Hill memorial garden

SaRS Unofficial 4 – True Histories...

ᵡ   And then there were those two overhead photos of The Kingswood's House. They provided a convenient side-by-side historical comparison of how SaRS has developed.

The first was a *black and white* photo from circa 75 years ago, displaying: the hedge maze in its infancy; the mansion surrounded by lush grasslands; and what looked, to Donald, like an old clown lying face down in a garden of rose bushes. The inferior quality of the old photo reproduction was bad enough to think someone would need a bit of television detective show unrealistic image enhancement or the original photo to determine who the person was.

The second one was a *colour* photo of exactly the same scene, which was taken only a few years ago. It showed a flourishing hedge maze and a perfectly manicured rose bed, spoiled only by a man-sized section of sideways planted rose bushes. It also showed the result of all of the building additions over the last 75 years. The detail in this photo was significantly better.

"Sphincter Feng Shui, how is this even possible?[300]"

Donald looked around to make sure no one had seen him and slinked off.

---

[300] It had taken Donald a little while longer to arrive at the same conclusion you arrived at a long time ago. Each of these two photos had been taken moments before the entombment, and then the disentombment, of the victim.

Donald had also noticed, though he didn't realise how important it would become at the time, that all of the main buildings in both photos had been labelled with their current use. He had a thought chuckle at the label in the middle of the young grey hedge-maze reading, "Dick Shack,[301]" and a thought irony at the middle of the elderly green hedge-maze, "Head Shrink Office."

The other nearly interesting thing Donald nearly didn't see and therefore nearly didn't take note of was the presence of an all-but empty room next to DD's office. If he had only looked in the general direction, he may have noticed the empty room's title, "Interrogation Room Won.[302]" This wouldn't have benefitted Donald at all at the current moment, but it may have assisted him in the future.

On his, slightly quicker than indirectly, meandering way back to the group room, Donald began exuding many dialectical symptoms… He was excited; he knew information nobody else did, but nervous they wouldn't believe him; he was proud he might finally have become a somebody, but he was ashamed he wasn't going to mention the rose bush war. He was so disappointed but strangely familiar with each of these combinations of emotions.

Reconvening the group session was an easy task, as everyone was already there, sitting in the same seats, waiting for the story to continue.

"Welcome back, everyone… I hope, and assume, your lunch was a culinary masterpiece." Houts could barely contain himself, "Just a running-in-joke of mine," snigger, "that I like to tell at the start of each afternoon group session," snort, "I facilitate." Waiting for laughter, as always, was a futile effort.

Donald thought, "Was that supposed to be funny? I thought the food was much better than it should have been, you i…"

"Has everyone signed in?" Houts had interrupted Donald's slowly derailing caboose of thought again, and this time it looked like it was just about to get interesting, so it was probably just as well.

Donald, having forgotten to sign in, got up and signed in again.[303] He also checked to see if Doctor Hill had signed in as "Skit Zoland" again.

He had.

---

[301] How awesome would it have been if the RadioShack Corporation had merged with Dick Smith Electronics and the B52s wrote a song about it!

[302] Confirming the earlier suspicion about the sign-writer's education.

[303] Does this mean Donald re-signed from being Donald, or does it mean Donald was re-signed to being Donald? It can't be both, obviously.

"Ok, so, for a brief recap of this morning, back at SaRS 1945, two women and a trap door. Questions?"

Houts's recap was indeed brief. Instantly, no one put their hands up.

If anything, everyone was in the middle of trying to make themselves look as small as humanly possible. This being the next best available option, after looking like they were not there at all, was ruled out as an option. All except for Chunky, who wasn't human and was pretending to be asleep, and Mindy, who might have been well past human but was actually asleep.

Houts had expected this lack of participation from everyone, and he continued on undaunted, asking for Donald's thoughts, "All right... Donald, do you have any constructive thoughts of how we might make the not-a-memory scene, from out of the Tapestry #1, experience a little better?"

"Yes." came the unexpected answer.

"Would you care to elaborate?"

"No...[304]"

"But I will... Next time, maybe some instructions for the Chosen One would be useful. You know, before you send someone to wherever and whenever you might want to tell them how they can come back."

Houts, rebounding like the consummate professional he thought he was, further embedding in Donald's mind the concept there are no wrong answers in group, picked up and carried on with Donald's comments, writing them on the whiteboard. Starting with the underlined heading, as per requirement #7 of "How to Facilitate a Successful Meeting."

Tapestry Instructions

"Does anyone have a suggestion for what might be useful to know?"

There was a lot of uneducated discussion from the group members, some unknowing waffle from Istha, "Who keeps on talking?" and a few unwarranted scoffings at the discussion, but nothing about the waffle.

After enough time had elapsed for someone to run to their local tapestry retailer, purchase an official tapestry user manual, extract the un-foldable wall chart and blue-tack it to the wall against many of SaRS regulations...

---

[304] Donald was experiencing another bout of déjà vu. It's déjà vu for two.

The group came up with a fairly serviceable facsimile...[305]

Tapestry ~~Instructions~~[306] User Manual

What happens in the tapestry stays in the tapestry...[307]

To return to the now, think about returning to now.

Only stay in the tapestry while you are comfortable.

No one out of the tapestry can see you in the tapestry,

No one in the tapestry can see you AT ALL, therefore...

There can be no judgements before, during or after.

You don't need to eat, drink, or poop in the tapestry.

Nothing you do inside will alter the tapestry scene.[308]

Tapestry user manual rule ten, there is no rule nine.

SaRS Whiteboard 1 – Tapestry ~~Instructions~~ User Manual

Donald thought these instructions were remarkably coincidentally similar to the instructions provided before a mindfulness session.

Owedebt, who had unusually remained fairly quiet throughout this whole process, quite possibly asked two of the most topically astute questions ever asked by anyone ever: "What about those two women who went through the trap door to escape?" and, "Who were they?"

---

[305] It occurs to me, that should this book exceed all, or any (or even one) expectations, these posters would make awesome advertising paraphernalia.

[306] This is on a whiteboard! Why can't they just erase things instead of using a strikethrough? The footnote # also has a strikethrough... Weird.

[307] This rule always makes it to the top of the list of any group activity rule list. It is also, always, the first rule to be broken. "Hey, did you hear about the group rules? Apparently, you aren't supposed to talk about them."

[308] This rule is a theoretically inexact. The *observer effect* theory states: the mere observation of a phenomenon, inevitably changes the phenomenon. Donald's appearance in the early B&W photo, unclearly shows, he clearly changed something while he was in the tapestry, as does retrieving the item.

"So that's where they went!" was Donald's belated realisation.

"Alright, folks. Let's focus our attention on those two ladies. What does everyone think?" this is Houts' second most common question, the first being, "And how does that make you feel?"

"If I might?" Doctor Hill intervened, "Donald, can you tell us anything more about either of the two women?"

Houts' expression went from incensed; to thoughtful; to dammit; I wish I had thought of that question.[309]

Be careful to not hide the truth; you may forget what it looks like.

"Wait! I do have something."

Sven's timely apt quote had nudged Donald's mind into action. It was now instructing Donald to produce the hidden item and his lost memory thereof, so everything was out into the open, both literally and figuratively.

Reaching inside his pocket to produce… "It's a game card…"

Clueless! – PSH… for Men
I think: It was Sister Sapphire
who killed an unidentified woman
in the secret underground room
by some accidental electrocution

After Donald had read the card, he asked, "What does this mean?"

"Eet means tkhkhkhkhkhis khkhkhkhkhas been waste of time!"

"Now, Got, we don't know for sure it has been a waste of time." Chastised Houts… Even though everyone knows there are no wrong answers in group… "I think this is some information we can take on board."

"Wkhkhkhkhkhkhtyeverrrrr."

Got fully understood what the game card meant. She didn't know whether it was good or bad to have this amount of information released to the public. Whichever it was, she was going to have to keep an eye on Donald.

Breaking into the uncomfortable silence left by Got, Mindy commented without opening her eyes, "I'm thinking the woman in the doctor's outfit was possibly Sister Sapphire, and she was taking an unidentified female patient for some undoubtedly unauthorised Electrical therapy in an underground room, hidden underneath the pavilion, under the Minotaur sign as an unambiguous deterrent to passers-by and things went unequivocally out of hand."

---

[309] And how is it you are called *doctor* and I'm not?

Donald wouldn't have gotten very far in life without being able to sense a high amount of commonly uncommon, common sense. He was trying to piece some of this puzzle together in his mind when he remembered the electrical storm in his not-a-memory scene.

"Um, there might have been a storm…" 25 eyes looked at Donald.[310]

Nota asked a question… The one that everyone in the room was thinking but was unwilling to ask, as it could have appeared to be just a little bit rude and maybe even a tad insensitive, "Are you a *freaking* idiot?"

Istha chimed in with an emphatic, "*Yeah?* Who are we talking about?"

"Now, Nota, you know we don't allow euphemisms in group. If you want to say something with feeling, use your words to express those feelings." Said Houts, starting out with some minimal condescension for Nota and finishing with a whole helping of ignoring for Istha.

"If you don't say exactly what you are really feeling, there is a danger we might not understand what you are really trying to say. In turn, there might be a possibility of confusion, and not long after confusion, there is always chaos." Working himself up into a nonsensical frenzied state.

"Willies and *nillies* flying all around the liquor landing palaces, *haphazards* hanging out in the medication corridors, as many helter-skelters as you can fit into your left shoe…" This continued for some time[311] as Houts worked himself into quite a scary bewilderment situation.

Grey, who up until now had been sitting quietly in the corner, minding his own business, twiddling his fingers and hoping to blend into the background, realised he was needed and picked up the conversation before it turned into a speech.[312] "…chaos, and we can't have any of that, can we? Now, Nota, why don't you say what you were really thinking?"

"Are *you* a freaking idiot?" This time it was obviously directed at Grey.

Istha chimed in with another emphatic, "*Yeah?* Who are we talking about this time?" She liked running with the crowd, even if the crowd was only a tiny crowd of one plus her. She also liked asking questions and getting no answers. It was when there were answers that she had a problem deciding if they were real or not. Silence was always real in any language.

---

[310] One from Chunky, as he was half awake, and none from Mindy.

[311] Of course, it was for *some time*, there isn't any other option. Like saying *up to*, in a discount offer, it's just fluff and tinkle to get people excited.

[312] That's not a euphemism, *THAT'S* a *Euphemism!*

Houts, having recovered a half measure of self-awareness, felt he had lost complete control of the group. He did the only thing possible and fell back on the time-honoured three-step technique of catch, de-hook and release:

- Saying something banal but making it sound like a congratulation;
- Summarising the session, highlighting any areas of success, as well as those needing some improvement; and
- Calling an early finish to avoid any possible Bloodshed.

"Thank you, everyone; I think we have achieved something very real here today. It is important for all of us to acknowledge the positive steps we have taken towards our mental recovery."

"We have several new pieces of information, thanks to Donald. There was the first female, masquerading as a doctor, who may well have been Sister Sapphire. There was the second female, dressed as a patient, who may well have been the victim. And there was the important clue that the game card recovered from the not-a-memory scene revealed of the underground room. Even though this last point brings some of our previous thoughts on tapestry interaction into question, I feel all of this combined was a large leap forward in the investigation of the *Bones Under the Courtyard Basement* case."

"Let's call it a day, people. I will record everything we have learned today in the session notes, and then I will add those notes to the hospital archives. I am also looking forward to this group next time when we shall all discuss the storm as well as the two ladies in much more detail. Who knows, we may even progress another step forward. Good Job, people![313] Dismissed!"

All the while this was going on, Donald was thinking, "But nothing from the scene actually helps us to identify who the victim was if indeed the second female was the victim. It doesn't explain the other secret underground room. And it doesn't explain what happened to Sister Sapphire." He only returned to the present moment when Houts mentioned the hospital archives, "I must get my eyes on those archives."

No one noticed Got's interest, or the rhyme, in this piece of information.

And no one joined the dots about the possible location deficiency in the previous investigation results. If they had noticed, someone might also have asked, "How did she get the body to the under the basement area?"

---

[313] This soap opera worthy ending, as well as the rest of the speech, made Donald's internals outwardly cringe. It also went a fair way to strengthening his resolve for what he assumed was about to not happen…

Donald received another touch on his shoulder. Houts was holding out his hand expectantly, "Donald, I was just wondering *again* if you have shared *all* of what you saw in your not-a-memory scene today?"

Donald's reply will skirt the exact details again. He doesn't tell any blatant lies but will be glad his lies of omission won't count. This is how he will justify his actions to himself when he fails to mention his potential presence in the photos and his flailing about in the rose bushes 75 years ago. Donald doesn't like to help others increase his level of embarrassment, as he is usually over able to become totally embarrassed all by himself.

Handing over the *Clueless!* game card, "Um, yes... This card is the only item that I had an intentional interaction with and then subsequently brought out of the scene with me. I have told you everything I think is pertinent to the case I can remember seeing while I was still in the not-a-memory scene."

"Excellent!" Houts' words may have said they believed Donald's story, but his eyes were looking like more of a cautious, "Ok, I'll let it slide, just this once, but I am watching you.[314]"

"When will the next group session on this be?" Asked a hopeful Donald.

"The next meet-n-greet group session will be in three weeks' time.[315] As you should know by now, we have a revolving three-week schedule of groups here at SaRS. We find that most psychological issues can be corrected in exactly three weeks. Even though the majority of health insurance companies stop paying for medical treatment after three weeks, without a written explanation from an approved psychiatrist, I can assure you... Money has absolutely no bearing on how long you stay at SaRS." Came the rehearsed reply.

"Excellent!" Donald's words may have said they believed Houts' story, but his eyes were looking like more of a cautious, "Ok, I'll let it slide, just this once, but I am watching you."

None of this explains how convenient it was that Donald and Karl both just happened to land in SaRS at the start of a three-week cycle; and if everyone else *was* aware of what was going on at the start of the group session, how is it that they have *all* been in SaRS for longer than three weeks?

---

[314] His eyes were watching Donald... Ah well, at least I make myself laugh.

[315] I guess this means the *Bones Under the Courtyard Basement* case, is going to be left as a diabolical dialectical underground cliff hanger... Or is it?

Chapter 12:
Coffee and Music
(Unnecessary Sub-Title)

On his way back from group, Donald decided he would fill an empty unfilled void.[316] He felt like something had been missing from his life over the last few days… Something he thought so identifiably normal, so profound, and so comforting he couldn't believe he had gone cold turkey for such a long time… It must have been nearly two whole days!

Coffee.

In his darker days (last week or so), Donald had had thoughts of:

- "I have just slipped over on the wet slippery tiled floor and done some permanent damage to my back…coffee will make me feel better;"
- "I'm down to my last acceptably clean t-shirt, so I'll have to do some clothes washing tomorrow…coffee will get me through;" and
- "I've left my coffee mug somewhere; I'm going to get some Valium, look for my mug and make a coffee… And life will be good again."

Donald wanted to get those days back because although they were bitter and dark, so was the full-bodied, robust roast!

Making a short detour to use the comfort station, check the plumbing, or use the facilities,[317] Donald was offloading a great weight from his mind when he experienced, at the most convenient time possible, a recurring episode of having the crap scared out of him.

---

[316] Donald 3:16 – The redundancy is strong with this one…

[317] Whichever is your favourite euphemism, for using the euphemism.

Knock, knock, knock.

Much to Donald's relief, neither Seth nor BLT were about to poke either of their heads through the door.[318] His comfort became almost palpable when, thankfully, he heard a female voice sigh, "~~Housekeeping,~~ Cleansing."

"Occupied." relieved Donald redundantly, twice, as the little red sign just above the door handle was already indicating the exact same message.

"Yes, sir... I know... I can see the little red sign." Came the sigh again.

There was some rustling, and the sighing continued, "I am only letting you know 'I will be returning in approximately seven and a half minutes.[319]' I have also been instructed to warn people 'I have a master key, and I'm not afraid to use it!' before I do actually use it to enter an otherwise occupied bathroom."

Then came the unnecessary explanation, "My previous employers failed to instruct me on the benefits of letting people have their privacy, and I may have intruded on an inappropriate indiscretion one too many times."

Something came through the gap underneath the door. The way it glided across the floor and stopped just before hitting Donald's feet was curious. It was quite an unbelievable feat, especially when you consider the distance, and the floor was currently less than conducive to sliding anything due to the non-slip abrasive textured paint that had been applied to the floor tiles.

It was another business card...

Spick 'n' Span Cleansing
"We can even cleanse your Elevator Pitch."
John Enslan – Fastest Vacuum in the West
Paula Bridge – Specialist Bathroom Cleanser
Phone: 123 456[320]   **Address:** Just Next Door

---

[318] Quite literally.

[319] The average time for a short bathroom break at SaRS, or a short time for an average one. Don't ask how I came by this pair of statistics.

[320] I was going to use 123 555, to spoof the American film industry phone numbers, but a derivation of that number actually belongs to the NSW Environment Protection Authority, as their Environment Line.

And then, I was going to use 123 665, the next phone number is the Devil's joke, but a derivation of that number is for Interaction Disability Services.

Cross my heart, true story! Freaky or what? I think 123 456 is safe.

And this one wasn't just double-sided; it was two-faced...

John 'n' Paula Cleansing

"The BEAT LESS Cleansers, Together Again"

John Enslan – Cleansing's on sale again...

Paula Bridge – Agent for Mulligan's Tyres[321]

Ph: same Beat phone **Address:** same Beat place

Donald flushed his business, washed his hands and picked up the business card all well within his seven-and-a-half-minute time limit. He hesitated at the door and bleakly turned his head looking for something showing a semblance of an answer. Sadly, the closest thing bearing any similarity he could see was the new sticker over the hot water tap in the shower.

The message, "Warning – This HOT water is HOT," was exactly the same as before, but this new sticker wasn't peeling off yet, and rather than seeing this discovery as a completely irrelevant disappointment that was somehow connected to the way he was feeling, Donald, chose to think, "Well... If they can fix a sticker, then *surely* they can fix me...[322]"

Anyway, enough chit chat, back to the story.

Donald turned left out of the bathroom and headed for his bedroom. He had forgotten all about his coffee withdrawal symptoms due to his mindless reversion to **T**he **E**asy **D**onald **I**nside-**O**utside **U**nthinking **S**tandard of blocking out all internal thoughts and external triggers. During these times, Donald's mind is running itself on autopilot. It has generally found that if it sings to itself, an easy slow-paced country song with altered words, it can also make Donald forget all about his troubles, at least for a short while...

Doctor mine... Let me go[323]
To my place, where I belong
Medication! Give it to me!
Let me go... Doctor mine...

---

[321] Re: Mulligan's Tyres (Inspired by *Mull of Kintyre* – Paul McCartney) p266.

ж   Extract from The Donald Diaries.

[322] No, he didn't! Haven't you been paying attention? Also, if you find the start of this chapter to be too low brow, feel free to start reading from here.

[323] Inspired by *Take Me Home, Country Roads* – John Denver.

Donald's blind happiness dissipated when he got to his room and saw the door open. But there's more…

The door wasn't likely to close because leading out of his room was an old extension cord, barely hanging on to its purpose after someone had attacked it with crime scene tape to stop it from fraying on the job. But there's more…

Putting these two facts together with the sign on the door…

Beware of the

Cleanser!

…Donald came to two conclusions: first one, his room was currently being cleaned by a cleanser; and second two, these cleansers are people who either don't understand or they have no idea they don't understand.

Donald was then forced to explain this to himself…

- Either… They don't understand what a cleanser is, and they used it in their business name because they thought it made them sound posh. When really, it just makes them look like they are trying to sound posh and don't understand what a cleanser is;
- Or… They do understand what a cleanser is, and they used it in their business name because they thought it made them sound posh. When really, it just makes them look like they are trying to sound posh and don't understand what a cleanser is.

Whichever, Donald was fairly sure of the appropriate saying: "Don't mess with the English language, boy, or you'll get the conjunctions.[324]"

Not knowing what to do in this situation… Donald waited.

And that's all! No BOGOF, no TftPoO and nothing up to anything off.

Eventually, after a somewhat longish minute or three, out through his still open bedroom door came the cleanser in question. Donald wasn't sure what his specific questions were anymore, but he was fairly sure they would never be asked. Donald would certainly never require this lady cleanser to answer any of his irrelevant questions…

---

[324] Donald was fairly taken by this phrasing, what with the earlier reference to the Minotaur and all.

She had a Mr Sheen brilliant sparkle coming out of her eyes,[325] and Donald surmised, precisely correctly, this cleanser was the female half of the dazzling duo, bathroom cleanser extraordinaire Paula Bridge.

Without introductions, Paula unplugged the vacuum cleaner power cord and looped it like Donald thought a cowboy might loop a rope. She collected the rest of her cleansing accoutrements and exited the bedroom dragging the vacuum behind her. To Donald's astonishment, Paula's vacuum was coloured blue; decorated with eyes, ears and wool; and had a little nametag that said, "Lamby," strung around its neck.

And then, like two tugboats in the late afternoon struggling to manoeuvre around each other while also keeping off the walls of a small strait, with nary a port, a wine, or a whisky in sight, they crossed paths, somehow managing to stay upright and contactless. Paula successfully passed into bathroom number 42, and Donald unsuccessfully passed out on his bed in bedroom number 41.

Donald consigned this minor drama to the forgetful part of his memory. Then, like so very many other trivial dramas before it, this soon to be forgotten drama pushed an existing memory out of his mind.[326] Luckily for Donald, the memory pushed out was a recent thought about wanting a cup of coffee. It was *lucky* because it coincided with another random event; seeing a coffee mug sitting on the table in his room. Wondering where it came from, he picked up the mug, and as he did so, the forgotten memory came flooding back.

I am afraid we have temporarily run out of the personalised travel coffee mugs, but as soon as a new shipment arrives, I will be sure to drop one of them off to you in your room.

Donald supposed the new shipment had arrived, and although reading the personalisation, "SaRS: *Where Life would be a bit Crazy if you couldn't Drink Coffee!*" confirmed his supposition, it didn't do a lot for his confidence in the area of a SaRS sense of humour.

There was a pamphlet accompanying the coffee mug.

Donald groaned, running through the complete gambit from in-loud right through to out-loud, out loud; because he had metaphorically been here many times before. He knew that his OCD tendencies wouldn't let him use the mug until he had read all of the instructions twice, in at least two languages.

---

[325] Donald added the sparkle, wishing he could take her home with him, to make his house sparkle the same way his room, and her eyes, sparkled now.

[326] Yes, please, one of everything, extra hot. (It might make sense soon.)

He tried to give the instructions a cursory glance but finally had to give in to himself and read them completely.[327] This was actually quite a complex yet fulfilling task for Donald as the user guide was written in French, German and, surprisingly, Latin.[328]

The instructions on how to make a cup of coffee were fairly standard and extremely generic:

- Place one or more heaped teaspoon(s) of soluble coffee into the mug;
- Add hot (only just not boiling) water up to the dotted line marked on the inside of the mug;
- Add sweetener and dairy product of choice to taste;
- Stir vigorously, and finishing with the obligatory
- "Caution... Hot Water... Is Hot![329]"

Donald, throwing caution to the wind, picked up his new mug and headed to the common area. When he arrived, he noticed there were only two other people there, and they were both sitting around the puzzle table. Mindy, who was un-soundlessly asleep, and Istha, who was trying her hardest to not see Donald. This situation suited Donald more than adequately.

He made himself a cup of coffee, according to the recent instructions; took it out to the common area; sat down on an unoccupied chair, and relaxed for the first time since he arrived.

One of Donald's least housetrained pet hates is the misrepresentation of coffee and coffee cups in the acting arena. Donald is so passionate about this topic; he wrote a poem about something other than himself for once...[330]

---

[327] It doesn't matter to Donald if the box says there are 50 smarties inside, he will count all of them, every time. It isn't so much Donald doesn't believe or trust the advertising, he just wants to know. You know?

[328] The Latin vocabulary workout is what made this task fulfilling, and his stay in the hospital not a complete waste of potential learning time.

[329] Donald is always wondering how long it will be before people became dopey enough to need a warning label saying, "Do not eat the plastic coffee mugs," "Do not lick any wet paint," or, "Do not poke fingers into a lawnmower if it is running." (Refer back to the 9 ½ finger father anecdote.)

[330] One example of his poetry on this topic is coming and there are several others: Coffee Cup, Coffee Toffee and Coffee Bitter Nana Fritter.

TV and Coffee

Coffee - it is obviously not hot
In takeaway cups - never nearing full
The level of liquid changes, sans plot
Continuity - is a load of bull

> They have no respect for the hot caffeine
> Drinking it straight after it has been made
> Tipping the cup to an angle, extreme
> I find it all - a depressing charade

> Actors not giving it a second thought
> Directors should add some - reality
> This ain't only a single "what they aught"
> Cos the same comments all apply to tea

While Donald was sitting there, sipping on his now just a little bit less than halfway to tepid coffee, he wondered, "I wonder if they will give me back the power cord for my paddle so I can generate some more scintillating poetry?" Then, taking this thought from inspiration to perspiration, Donald rose, walked over, quietly knocked on the Nurse's Bowl's door and asked, "Hello, may I ask you another question?[331]"

One of the Greys, startled from their deep study of the mobile phone they were trying to keep hidden below the desk, looked up with an expression that oozed, "Oh, crap!" After they realised Donald was just an inmate and not one of the feared SaRS trainee supervisors, Grey's expression relaxed onto one of uninterested, "What is it now?"

Adept at reading startles, Donald repeated his initial "Hello," and asked, "May I have the charging cord for my paddle back, please?"

Grey's face turned into a scowling pile of rhetorical, "Please stay there and wait for three minutes while I finish this unimportant text you have so rudely interrupted even though I am not supposed to be using my phone while I am on duty I am going to continue to text and a temporary side effect of this is it makes me speak in extended elaborate text speak sentences without stopping for punctuation because this is how I always talk when I multitask but getting back to the crux of the sentence in general it is just to show you who is really in charge around here and now please wait for it wait for it wait for it I will add a set of horizontal ellipses and an exclamation point...!"

---

[331] He of course realized this was the first question he was asking, and even though it was summarily approved, it shouldn't be arbitrarily dismissed.

Grey stood up after he finished sending the text, casually walked over to Donald, pushed the intercom button and asked, "Yes, how may I help you?"

Donald, having just run out of his last iota of patience, degenerated to his familiar monosyllabic[332] conversation style, "Phone cord please...!"

"Donald Halfbrian, isn't it? Kangaroo ward, room 41?"

Donald was used to people becoming a bit dyslexic with his name, so he didn't bother to correct Gery, "Sure."

"Ok, follow me, please. All of those dangerous items are kept safely locked away in the Medication Nook. They are locked away for your safety and not to reduce the hospital's MentalBank liability insurance premiums."

Donald was confused; he was not used to getting answers to questions he had asked, let alone answers to questions he hadn't asked yet. He didn't say or ask anything further about this because he was content to assume it was an example of a standard spiel given when someone asked, "Why?"

Grey had continued to speak through Donald's thoughts, and Donald only caught up at the last stage, "I will have to go and get a real nurse to open the medication nook and find the cord for you."

Sitting on one of the medication-queue chairs, Donald did a bit of location and people watching while he was waiting for Grey to return with a real nurse. He noticed there was a notice on the nurse's whiteboard about him, "~~Donald H~~ ~~Blood~~/~~Morning.~~" It had been crossed out, obviously, and he wondered why they hadn't just erased the message instead. He followed this wondering with a more tangible and obscure thought requiring quotes, "Maybe someone has eaten all of the erasers."

Donald forgot his thought about privacy as Sven came into the common area and sat at the puzzle table with Istha and Mindy. To Donald's surprise, it seemed that Sven was able to successfully place a few pieces of the puzzle into their correct places. His surprise was then shattered by confusion when Mindy woke up, removed the pieces that Sven had placed and went back to sleep.

Shaking his head and standing up, Sven *cookied*:

Music is for when words are not enough.[333]

---

[332] I will delve into the oxymoronicity (yes, it is a real word) of the English language at some stage... Chapter 18: Friday on his mind p235

[333] Donald was slowly coming up with a theory about the lack of quotes for Sven's cookies. Give him a few more chapters and he might tell you what it was. Of course, it will have to be after I think up a ~~funny~~ plausible reason.

Istha responded to Sven, "Yes, Sven. Thank you. We all know that Tuesday afternoon is music therapy time. Some of us don't like going as the selection of songs sometimes sound so seriously sad, and the alliteration is also prone to becoming a tad too wet at times."

Donald didn't like how Istha had said, "We all know…" because he didn't know. He was able to take a small amount of solace from the knowledge Istha was only disregarding him because she believes he doesn't exist, not because she was just rudely ignoring him.

Grey returned with Nurse Jack and had, evidently, explained the situation to him on the way back, as he immediately went and opened the medication nook. This removed the necessity of Donald having to repeat himself. Donald gave thanks that his life wasn't a movie where everything had to be artificially explained in front of the camera.[334]

Nurse Jack retrieved *Donald's Things Tray* from where all the trays were stored, removed the iPad charging cord (he didn't yet know it was being called a paddle) from the little resealable plastic evidence baggie it was in labelled "Dangerous," and gave it to Donald politely asking, "Is there anything else you would like me to return to you?" finishing a mighty long sentence.

Donald looked into the tray and didn't see anything dangerous. He did see several items DD would have probably classified as dangerous for those with more ingenuity and less compunction than he has, but there was nothing he particularly wanted back right this instant. He said, "No, thank you," and as an unrelated afterthought added, "Do you know where the music therapy is?"

"Oh, goody, an easy one; for musical therapy," making the tiny correction subtle, "just follow either of your ears towards the melodious piano playing and ~~screeching~~ singing coming from group room three."

Taking the cord but not the bait, Donald returned to his room and plugged his paddle in. He then sat down on his bed and had a short sit 'n' think session with himself:

- If I want to charge my paddle, I have to leave it on top of the bedside table so the cord can reach the powerpoint;
- I can't lock it in the drawer as the drawer doesn't allow any egress for a cord while it is locked, and I don't have a padlock anyway;
- I want to go to the music therapy session, but if I do, I will be leaving my paddle unprotected; and
- If I leave my paddle here, I'd be up the corridor without a paddle.

---

[334] This is only Donald, and he doesn't matter as he is a fictional character remember? I, on the other hand, would be seriously chuffed.

Donald came to an agreement with himself; to leave the paddle plugged in and to hide it under his pillow while he went to music therapy. As an added security measure, he folded a piece of purple paper[335] into an origami mouse trap and carefully placed it between the paddle and the pillow. This was all in the abject hope no one would see the cord dangling from the power point.

It wasn't a huge amount of security, but charging his paddle was Donald's primary concern, and he, however naïve, still put his trust in people. In any case, forlornly trying to convince himself this was a good idea, he would know if the paddle was missing if the paper trap had been sprung. It didn't cross his mind to think about the possibility this might be considered a useless fire risk.

Is this the real life? Is this just fantasy?

Hearing these sounds, Donald did as he always did and did as he was told. He followed his ears alternately, zigging and zagging all the way until he was standing outside the open door of group room three. AKA the music room.

Mama, life had just begun, but now I've gone and thrown it all away.[336]

Noticing someone was there, William stopped his playing and singing and said, "Come in, come in, we haven't started yet. I was just getting my fingers and vocal cords[337] warmed up."

This was abundantly clear to Donald as there was no one else in the room. Pushing his fear of embarrassment aside temporarily, he took two steps into the room and sat in the chair closest to the door.

Donald liked to keep his options open for as long as possible. In this case, he was keeping the option of "leaving through the open door" available just in case an escape needed to be attempted. For example, if the musical therapy changed from being like a treatment into being like a torture.

Nothing really matters to meeeee. Any way the wind blooooows.

---

[335] It just happened to be lying about. Donald didn't know what it was lying about, but he was sure it was of no consequence (good or bad).

[336] So, it wasn't just Sven. Apparently, anyone with a pithy quote or a line from a famous song gets to go without quotation marks. The thick *plottens!* And these lines are from *Bohemian Rhapsody – Queen*.

[337] Donald was tempted to correct William and say, "vocal chords." But it would have been wrong on at least two of several levels.

After about eleven minutes, the length of the short version of the song, it became obvious no one else was going to join them, so Willy,[338] unperturbed, began the session with Donald as the only ~~victim~~ participant.

There was a bit of small talk where Willy introduced himself and explained to Donald why he was there. In response to this, Donald asked, "Is there a sign-in sheet I am supposed to sign in on?" Donald is single-minded at the best of times and will always do things by the book.

Willy shook his head and said, "Nope. They don't think music has a place in the toolbox of mental health therapy around here. In fact, they think I am a bit of a tool for even trying. They only suffer my presence because I provide a musical accompaniment to whoever requires it."

"Oh." was all Donald could offer in response to this detail.

"It isn't as bad as it sounds, both literally and figuratively." This was when Donald decided he was going to like Willy. Not only because he is in awe of anyone who can play multiple instruments, read and write music, and sing... Often, all at the same time. But because he sounded like his kind of people.

Willy continued to impress Donald by asking three questions that made him think. But more importantly, they made him think about himself:

- "What is a song you sing along with only when you definitely know no one else is listening to you?"
- "What type of music do you put on when you know there is someone else listening?" and
- "What is your seventh favourite song?[339]"

This last question was a doozy, but the first two were easy.

"The song I sing along with is *Miles from Nowhere*, by the artist who was firstly born as Steven Demetre Georgiou, became famous as Cat Stevens, then infamous as Yusuf Islam and finally joining the single named legend fraternity as just Yusuf, the artist formerly known as Cat Stevens.[340]"

---

[338] William, the Piano Man (without any last name), liked to be called Willy. Billy would have been way too obvious, and we can't have Billy being thrown around willy-nilly, now can we? There are already enough Billy singers.

[339] The randomness, and thirdness, of this question was right up Donald's deserted cobblestoned alley.

[340] Believe it or not, this is completely true, both the singing and his name. I don't know why I expect people to not believe me, but I should stop that. It probably won't matter though as these comments won't make it by an editor.

David Halpin

"The type of music I listen to publicly is any Underdog Australian Rock."

The look Willy gave Donald would have conveyed confusion to just about anyone else, but Donald wasn't having a bar of it. He was way too busy trying to think of his seventh favourite song. We all know by now that when Donald starts about something, he is going to finish the thought, even if no one else cares anymore. Which is the precise situation at the moment. Willy lent over and picked up his guitar, "Here is a little tune I think you will like..."

Willy began strumming, and although Donald was able to identify the tune fairly quickly, he felt he didn't have the heart to tell Willy that the Australian band recording was just a cover of an English band. Donald was startled out of his reverie when Willy started singing out the wrong words, even if they were appropriate...

Out of My Head[341]

In the sad, lonely part of my mind, where I think of all I've done
There ain't no happy. Not even one...   (Oh no, there ain't)
And now, with my dial set to rewind, trying to undo the bad
Trying to wind back the clock on sad   (Too bad. So sad!)
But knowing there is happy to find keeps me going through the day
Not willing to throw my life away   (Oh no, not yet)

> I gotta get out of my head
> It's what my shrink has told me to do
> I gotta get out of my head
> And then I will start to stop my blue   (So true, so true)

> All my memories are well defined, and they cannot be undone
> Help! My ruminating has begun   (Oh yes, it has)
> Anything offered, I won't decline. I can be helped. I'm not mad
> Gross exaggeration? Just a tad   (My bad. Way tad!)
> Inside my sadness, I'm not confined, no inclination to stay
> I'm removing my mental decay   (Oh yes, it's gone)

> > I gotta get out of my head
> > It's what my shrink has told me to do
> > I gotta get out of my head
> > And then I will start to stop my blue   (So true, so true)

---

[341] Inspired by *We Gotta Get Out of This Place* - The Angels.
A cover of *We Gotta Get Out of This Place* - The Animals.

Willy interrupted Donald's thought, "You do know the last question was just to see if you were paying attention, don't you?"

"I didn't. Oh, well, I'll keep thinking about it anyway..."

"Ok, thinking is good. There are no wrong answers, only wrong opinions."

Music Therapy continued like this for the next hour, with Willy playing the guitar and doing most of the singing. Donald would chime in for some of the choruses, but the "~~screeching~~ singing" comment from earlier, heightened his very self-conscious concerns. Although he didn't really care what other people thought of him, he still didn't like to be laughed at.

Donald was feeling an alien sensation. While he didn't fully understand what was going on inside, he did know he needed to snap out of it before his outsides started to channel Julie Andrews. That would be something he wasn't comfortable with, even if there was no one who could see or hear him.

Hopping... Skipping... Jumping...
Arms Flailing...and Singing...

Coffee and Music[342]

Coffee with sugar, a dollop of froth top
Make sure the water is not boiling. But Hot!
Sprinkles of chocolate on top of the mug
One of the legal spectacular drugs

    Music with gusto and words with a meaning
    Axes, pianos, or saxes... (No cleaning!)
    It's never too loud if you use earplugs
    One of the legal spectacular drugs

        Coffee and Music, when combined, are the best
        Ensuring survival. In this, I don't jest!
        Don't you listen to all of the humbugs
        Two of the legal spectacular drugs

            When my brain hurts, needs a mind hug
            Auto thinking sad...
            Hot coffee and music, spectacular drugs
            And now I don't feel... So... Bad...

---

[342] Inspired by *My Favourite Things* - Rodgers and Hammerstein. From *The Sound of Music*.

Not wanting to embarrass himself further, Donald slunk off quietly during the next song, *Another Brick in the Wall, Part Two* - Pink Floyd.

Epically bookending the music therapy jam session. It was about to finish anyway, as it was nearly time for dinner. This was sufficient justification for Donald to allow himself to leave something early.

And as Donald always says… "Food before music!"
Completely forgetting the task of the seventh song.

Chapter 12a:[343]
The End[344]
(Heists and Fish)

Donald was just about bouncing along, looking like he had no cares in the world and might have actually been happy. His mind wasn't paying attention to what it, or Donald, was doing.

We don't need no thought control, no dark sarcasm in the classroom.

It was probably just as well his mind was still engrossed with the thought of coffee and music. The same mind would have been totally outraged by the display being put on. If someone was to see Donald, they might actually think this version of him was exhibiting signs of happiness and also some unknown type of recovery. Who knows how it might be mistakenly misinterpreted?

Hey teachers, leave those kids alone.[345]

---

[343] Donald isn't anything remotely like superstitious, but it couldn't hurt.

[344] Calm down, it is only the end of day two of Donald's little adventure...

The end of one very long Tuesday, starting 70 odd (very odd) pages ago. There are roughly 100 pages of story yet to go. This is a major guess, as I haven't written most of them yet. So, you could be roughly just over halfway and a bit more through. Exceedingly well done you! Put your commemorative bookmark in and go make yourself a cautionary hot cup of coffee.

[345] *Another Brick in the Wall, Part Two* - Pink Floyd.
And guess what just started playing on random shuffle? Spooky...

It was at the low point when Donald had started to sing; his mind slapped him most soundly and woke him up from his daydreaming... Even Donald was embarrassed for himself by this. Checking around, he became relieved there seemed to be no one paying him any attention, as usual.

What (or who?) Donald didn't see, was Seth. Seth was dangling, absurdly, upside down from the light fixture above the door to the music room. He liked to hang out up there, absorbing the music in his downtime. He was about to clear his throat and let Donald know he was there (because watching people like this felt like he was unfairly using his ghostly talents to spy on them) when, interrupting his conscience, he heard the piano playing stop. Seth returned his gaze to the music room. Only two silent bars later, he saw Willy come out and watch Donald with what seemed to be an unusual amount of intensity. Seth had no problems at all with using his ghostly ability on Willy.

Seth and Willy have had a very uneasy[346] relationship ever since 1954, the year when Venolia and Ray Parker Senior thought it might be a good idea to have a son. It doesn't matter a jot to Seth that Willy wasn't even a twinkle in 1954. He figures he is allowed to backdate all of his ghostly angst to the source of the issue.[347] After all, who are they going to complain to?

As Willy was finishing up his deep Donald watching, he wrote a short to-do notation in his phone, cast two last glances Donald's way and went back into the music room. All of this was before Donald had regained his senses[348] and performed the cursory check of his immediate surroundings.

Seth couldn't read what Willy had written, so he made a mental note[349] to find out. He had never known Willy to take such a great amount of interest in any SaRS patient before, and this, in turn, only served to increase his own level of interest in what Willy had written significantly.

---

[346] Why not just say hard? *Sigh* If only there was some sort of mechanism for me to come back and edit the story. It must have been diabolical being an author and trying to write stories before the computer. Spelling two.

[347] Don't go anywhere near Makin' Whoopi.

[348] This is another bizarre saying, or an idiot's idiom as I like to call them. It doesn't have anything to do with getting your traditional five senses back. They never left. What did leave Donald was his mind and reality. Regaining his sense, singular, as in sensibility, would be a more appropriate saying.

[349] As he didn't have a phone, obviously.

What Seth will eventually find out, after following Willy around for around two hours off-book, is nothing anywhere near as sinister as he thought he would find. It was just a note-to-self to talk to Ma'am Cybill Flex about finding Donald a part in their upcoming rock musical, *A Rocky Horror Musical.*

Ok, it's just past pumpkin time... See you all tomorrow.
I'm back, yaaaaay, and now to continue on with the (s)laughter...

Feeling a sense of relief, created by the coincidence of becoming aware of a potentially embarrassing situation and then having that same situation stay on the it-was-so-close side of the embarrassment ledger, Donald headed back to his room for a bit of serenity until dinner time. Donald might have arrived still feeling just a tiny amount of euphoria had the circumstances allowed it. Sadly, this particular circumstance hadn't received the request memo...
"Have you seen my fish?"
Owedebt had uttered this string of words, and she seemed to understand but may well have been the only person to do so in this situation. To someone like Donald, who wasn't privy to her unique thoughts or to the innermost rusty workings of her mind, they didn't even come close.

Finding himself more and more dumbfounded with each interaction he had with Owedebt, Donald scoured all of his current, historical and hysterical knowledge for any possibility he could feasibly remotely think of that might conceivably include a search for a missing fish:

- Had Nemo vanished again?
- Had someone found a bigger boat?
- Had Billy Bass been finally taken to the river?
- Had Rex caught mono and wanted to eat the source with sauce?

Extending his thoughts to include all future possibilities, the pursuit of any aquatic animal and unqualified fantasy, Donald tried his damnedest to come up with anything he might consider to be somewhere near a remote outpost of a chance at the plausible:

- Was there going to be a Scottish movie called *Jurassic Loch*?[350]
- Was Ahab going to star in *One whale, white whale, no way Ishmael?*
- Was the Kraken about to be re-released?
- Was Flipper[351] making a comeback?

---

[350] What an awesome movie. Starring Mel Gibson as the voice of the brave Nessie: "They may take my photo, but they'll never take my freedom!"

[351] **Notes:** Luke Halpin is no relation and Flipper's voice was a kookaburra.

Donald came to the conclusion: that nothing he could think of was going to help. Neither was the simple fact that Owedebt had come to the more-or-less same conclusion about Donald not being able to help seven minutes ago and had continued with her search six minutes and fifty-nine seconds ago.

Her departure left Donald standing there, mouth agape, all alone with his barely conceivable ponderings. Thinking, "what a Dozy Doe," and shaking his head in disappointment was the combination target Donald tried to reach for. He gave up on this goal and settled for the far more achievable one of feeling like such a Pasta Dude and hanging his head in shame.

Successfully, this time, he made his way back to his room without further ado. Once he was safely inside, he let the mental exhaustion have his head and flopped onto the bed as gracefully as a uniped dismounting a unicycle.

Snap!

Donald hesitated, waiting for his heartbeat to come back to double digits. Three minutes later, he realised this was never going to happen while he was still worrying about his heart's racing to win attitude, or more important than his heart beating if he had just cranium dropped all over his paddle:[352]

- Sitting up and shutting his eyes, "No, No, No;"
- Lifting the pillow, "No, No, No;"
- Removing the discharged origami mouse trap and throwing it across the room to where it nearly reached the end of his bed, "No, No, No;"
- Fumbling his paddle open, "No, No, No;"
- Opening one eye a microscopic tad, "No, No, No;" and hopefully
- Having the smallest of squinty looks possible, "No, No, No..."

Relief flowed in tsunamis.

DOGoNs settling back down to a comfortable seven.

If you multiplied the relief from the Cleansing incident by the relief from the Singing and Dancing incident, you would be getting close to being nearly ready to get into your car, so you could drive to the carpark of the ballpark, just a short walk in the park away from Gorky Park, level of relief Donald felt right now because he hadn't just broken his paddle.

Donald hitched up his puddle of relief, tenderly unplugged the charging cord and gratefully headed out for dinner while lovingly hugging his definitely not broken paddle to his chest. He didn't care that it was only 33.3% charged.

---

[352] Donald has hypothetically either just become convinced, or he has just remained convinced, of the fact that if he ever meets Schrödinger in person, he is likely to punch him squarely on the nose... Giving him a *schnozdinger!*

While Donald was thinking about his DOGoNs, he decided to give himself a refresher course in the definition of each of the levels. Seven just didn't seem enough at this, more than perilous moment in time.

13 -   Waaaaayyyyy tooooo laaaaate!!!!!
Donald won't think about this level until it occurs, and then he won't be able to.

12 -   Way too late!
Major Drama. When there is no coffee, no music and no way of getting either.

11 -   Too late.
Having no coffee and no music, with a still viable way to get only one of them.

10 -   Upper maximum unacceptable level.
Having no coffee and no music, with a still viable way to get either of them.

9   -   Upper maximum acceptable level.
Having no coffee and no music, with a still viable way to get both of them.

8   -   Indistinguishable from seven.
Administer Coffee and Music... Stat.

7   -   Indistinguishable from eight.
Administer Coffee, or Music... Stat.

6   -   Upper middle level.
Administer Coffee.

5   -   Lower middle level.
Administer Music.

4   -   Indistinguishable from three.
Enjoying either Coffee or Music.

3   -   Indistinguishable from four.
Enjoying both Coffee and Music.

2   -   Lower minimum unacceptable level.
Asleep in a medication-induced state.

1   -   Lower minimum acceptable level.
Asleep.

0   -   DOGoN measuring device broken.

Floating along on a happy-it's-not-broken-paddle cloud of a remeasured and reinterpreted, eight DOGoNs allowed Donald to reach the cafeteria,[353] in the unrequited search for food, without people noticing him.

----

[353] **Mental Side Note:** I think it might be ironic that coffee isn't on the menu. Particularly when you consider *cafeteria* means *coffee shop* in Spanish?

Getting through his dinner tonight was starting out to be an uneventful event. Unfortunately, eventful was still waiting to eventuate and was hiding just around the corner so it could time its entrance to perfection.

Donald set himself up in the, I have **M**astered **E**ating **A**lone Layout:
- Bowl o' Soup[354] front and centre, shadowed on the right by a spoon;
- Food tray at roughly two o'clock, most of an open arms-length-away, aligned perpendicular to the median point between him and the table, still containing the balance of his balanced diet, fork 'n' spoons, and two single-serve serviettes;
- A non-optional one-size-fits-all limited-reusability not-biodegradable baaaaahhhhhaaaaa-recycled plastic ½ cup of not-in-a-pink-fit-natural-tasting diet lemon cordial at a half-arms-length-away one o'clock; and most importantly
- His paddle in a quarter reclining position, a quarter-arms-length-away ten o'clock, displaying where he was up to the last time he was reading one of the several thousands[355] of books he has stored inside it, with the brightness set to the minimum setting possible, still allowing him to read the words. (All too sad and all too true.)

When Donald had transitioned through the soup (with bread roll), main course (with bread roll), and dessert (without bread roll) meal categories and was about to perform his clearTheTableInTheMostEfficientWay method,[356] he was interrupted by the arrival of Dr Tony Hill.

"Donald, if I might, can I get an answer to my previous *if I might* question?" Doctor Hill was, of course, referring to his, all but overlooked, earlier question about the two unknown women who starred in Donald's not-a-memory scene. "And if you would, I also have a few more questions..."

---

[354] You really don't want to confuse this with bowel soup. Bowel soup is the last meal you have before a colonoscopy. It is an unflavoursome nearly invisible broth made out of warm flat home-brand lemonade and half a stock cube crushed and sprinkled lightly next to the turned off cooking pot.

[355] OK, it is a slight exaggeration, 1606 e-books, 198 PDFs and many, many, many poetry notes. There is also a copy of his CV, the two books he has written previously and the spread-sheeted colour-coded catalogue of all of these books, including... Wait for it... An entry for the catalogue.

[356] I can't let a reference to the other *Java* escape unfootnoted.

Resigning himself to be talking to a real person, who thought they were a fictional character, about a fantasy character, who used to be a real person, was so far out of character for Donald that he surprised even himself. Donald hunkered down for the long haul about his not-a-memory scene, and Doctor Hill was off and running straight away.

"We have three opinions[357] about the two women you saw; from Mindy, Houts and most importantly, the *Clueless!* game card you retrieved. They're all in consensus, thinking the woman dressed in the doctor's outfit was probably Sister Sapphire and the other woman she was with could very well have been an unidentified female patient."

"We have three postulations[358] as to where the crime might have actually taken place. Mindy, Houts and the *Clueless!* game card all hypothesise there is a secret hidden underground room underneath the BotM! sign." When Donald didn't understand what this was, Doctor Hill explained, "It is a room, thought to be both hidden and secret, but that isn't so important right now." Further confusion ensued until "Beware of the Minotaur!" was also explained.

"And thirdly, we have two speculations[359] about the method. Mindy and the *Clueless!* game card, both guessing there was something weird surrounding what might have been a very early form of ECT (**ElectroC**onvulsive **T**herapy), resulting in accidental ECD (**ElectroC**ution **D**eath) due to the electrical storm activity. And I am also nearly positive Houts would think so too."

"It is this last point that has got me curiously intrigued. Why would Houts not mention the storm in his summary of what happened?" pausing for effect, "I think he failed to include this puzzle piece in the newly discovered material details," DrrrrrDrrrrrDrrrrrum rrrrrolllll, "because this is a piece of information *he has heard before*… so, it didn't make an impact."

Donald and Dr Hill looked at each other, and then something bordering on magical struck… With a delivery that would have won them, or at least placed them a very close second (with an honourable mention), in the synchronised epiphany section of the Occult Olympics… They had both just realised what they needed to do: "We need to get our hands on those archives."

---

[357] **Opinion** is to **Option** as **Pain in the neck** is to **Pat** on the back.

[358] **Postulation** is to **Population** as **Lost** his mind is to **Lop** off his head.

[359] **Speculation** is to **Peculation** as **S** is to ….

No, it's a real word I promise. It means to embezzle or steal money, especially when they are public funds. I'm guessing they are the same if you speculate with someone else's money on the stock market and lose.

This was all well and good, but it appears more magical than it should have been when you consider that Donald had had the, not quite exactly the same but still close enough, thought just over 8142 words ago.[360]

Not able to avoid it this time, Donald found himself jumping up and down and around and around with girly excitement. They hastily cleared Donald's dinner space and brought out: a pre-prepared building blueprint; traffic and soil composition analysis documents; and a treasure map, where there was a large X covering what was probably a filing cabinet of some sort.

The next few hours were spent planning the elaborate heist requiring:

- Three *BMW X2 M35iss*;[361]
- An edgy code-name. *The Full Monty Python* was discarded due to the possible legal ramifications of a similar idea waiting to happen in New Zealand… They eventually settled on the working title of *Kubrick and Tarantino's SaRS' 3.16*; and
- A bottle of *Nitrous Oxide*, just for fun.

Donald was quite pleased to take his mind off the details he left out of the report on his not-a-memory scene and his subsequent photo revelation. Even though he seriously doubted his unplanned yet intimate and fairly photogenic knowledge of the origin of the sideways planted rose bushes would lead them to any great discovery.

He did make one conscious concession confession, "There are some new historical photos in the hospital's administration foyer area, and I think one of them might be a detailed colour overhead photo of The Kingswood's House and grounds." Continuing on through Dr Hill's looks of not understanding, "In one of the photos, there is an office labelled as The Head Shrink Office right in the centre of the hedge maze!"

Donald's mind was ticking over at about double the tock speed of Dr Hill's, and it fed him another thirteen-watt lightbulb moment. Picking up most of his excitement after he carelessly dropped it while chasing after this realisation penny, rapidly clicking and pointing his fingers, "I bet this is where they store the hospital archives!"

---

[360] It must be nice to be constantly surprised by old memories masquerading as new realisations.

[361] The most ridiculous vehicle available, in both nomenclature and design. To complement this obscure choice of car, they would all be coloured in complementary achromatic matt paint. Dim Grey, Medium Grey and Jet Grey, making them all look unpainted and very, very stealth.

All the ooooomph went from his bad mood compensating, apparently not so magical, moment when Dr Hill pointed to the large *Exed*-Filing cabinet on the treasure map sitting right in front of them.

Nurse Dolly Dix, DD, she makes me nervous,
she told me to get you to come and join us,
as it's time for you to take your happy pills,
and to put aside any thoughts of free wills…

Are you here to try and get better?
Are you meaning to upset her?
Are you, are you going to ever,
follow these instructions to the letter?[362]

The appearance of Sven, who had superficially been sent to remind them it was medication time, caused Donald and Dr Hill to agree to put the plotting on hold for the time being. They are going to mull all of the information over overnight and then try to get their two skulls back together in the morning to continue planning their heist.

Got was also there, hidden in plain sight, pretending to read a newspaper. It was a miracle no one noticed that the newspaper was upside down. Got was reading it like this on purpose, as she thought there were secret messages to her, hidden in the now inverted, intentionally obvious classified section. After Donald and Dr Hill left, she stayed there, lowering the newspaper occasionally, looking off into the distance and thinking about all of this new information.

Donald, like the submissive puppy he was, went straight to the medication window and silently waited. Unlike a puppy, he waited with his tongue safely tucked inside his closed mouth. While he was waiting for DD, Donald was also discussing the day's events with himself. He found himself becoming eager for today to turn into tomorrow.[363]

He completely failed to consider that along with the coming of tomorrow, there would also be the arrival of a different personality inhabiting the person who was sometimes known as Skit Zoland.

---

[362] I had better put a reference to *Down Under* - Men at Work. Because we all know what happens when you don't, even if it is only a couple of words, in the wrong order, about a completely different topic, you thought up on the spot and didn't set out with the intention in the first place.

[363] Or yesterday, depending on how you looked at it.

DD, who was reading a book, gave no indication Donald's presence was known to her. She turned over several pages, continued reading until she was finished with her current chapter and deliberately ignored Donald, all while firmly asserting her passive dominance. To Donald's horrification, she dog-eared a page and carelessly tossed the book into a plastic bucket. His horror increased when he saw that the bucket was still wet after it had been used to clean up a personal spill without being hosed off.

When he recovered sufficiently to read the cover of the book, he relaxed; it was only a catalogue of neckties that evidently came in 50 shades of grey. Donald guessed incorrectly that DD must have been shopping for her husband and shuddered at his wondering what type of man would be married to her.[364]

"It is nice you deigned to grace us with your presence tonight, Donny." This wasn't so much passive-aggressive as just plain aggressive. Without taking her eyes off Donald's, she reached over for his folder and the two ½ cups of water and medication. "Here are all of your prescribed night-time medications which I diligently prepared much earlier. Please swallow them now, so I can complete the day's report and go home after my," not bothering to look at her watch, "eight-hour, thirteen-minute and seven… eight… nine… second shift."

Acting on one of those rare impulses actually beneficial for his immediate future, Donald took the medication DD was offering and poured it all into his mouth at once. After he had swallowed the medication, along with the ½ cup of water, in an appropriately contrite fashion, he displayed his empty mouth, did the "ahhhhh" thing and disposed of the tiny crushed empty cups into the waiting receptacle.

He was immediately surrounded by a ring of confidence, closely followed by a ring of protection and then finally by a ring of fire. This last one, being so inappropriate, should never have made it through an editor. Bad editor.

Not impressed by Donald's three-ring circus, DD returned his file to the filing cabinet, closed the cabinet and then the medication nook window with just a touch of deliberate overzealousness to indicate her quite high level of peevishness. Finishing her irritated display by harrumphing her way out of the nook and off into the evening without looking back.

Donald wasn't sad to see her go, but he was all drugged up, with no place to go, no place to hide and no place to call his own. He decided that the best use of his time now would be to document today's activities, on his paddle, of course, so he could refer to them in the morning and be surprised at just how devious he could be when he was tired.

---

[364] He did approve of her choice of lack of colour though and thought he might ask her to order him some as they would look perfect as camouflage.

Sitting on one of the single lounge chairs in the common area, engrossed deeply within his own inconsequential thoughts and devoid completely of the ability to care about anything else while he was writing, Donald very nearly missed the next interaction entirely. Which, in the scheme of things, wouldn't have been devastating, even if it was less tasty.

The first thing he noticed was something sounding like a cross between a funeral dirge and an advertising jingle. If Donald had asked Willy what it was, it would have been described concisely as "an esoteric nostalgic melancholic classic, which was written in a minor key, designed to make the listener both want to remember the better times of their past, as well as looking forward to the brighter times in their future." Pure uplifting dialectics.

Then there were the accompanying words...

The DABDA 5[365]

Denying your loss... It didn't happen
If your feelings left, don't mourn the passion
Denial... It didn't happen to me
Stage 1 of wearing a coat of bluesleeves

> Angry at your loss... It just isn't fair
> Shouting sarcasm, raging without care
> The **Anger**... It mustn't happen to me
> Stage 2 of wearing a coat of bluesleeves

> > The cost of your loss... It can all be fixed
> > Promise to be good; results will be mixed
> > **Bargaining**... It shouldn't happen to me
> > Stage 3 of wearing a coat of bluesleeves

> > > The pain from your loss... It can overwhelm
> > > Everything is lost; no one's at the helm
> > > **Depression**... It always happens to me
> > > Stage 4 of wearing a coat of bluesleeves

> > > > Accepting your loss... It's time to move on
> > > > Rebuilding your peace, the byes are all gone
> > > > **Acceptance**... It just did happen to me
> > > > Stage 5 of wearing a coat of bluesleeves

---

[365] These are the actual stages of grief...

Raising his eyes, Donald surveyed the scene to make sure he wasn't just hearing things. When he saw an antique pink and cream ice cream cart being pushed by a kindly looking sad older gentleman, who was wearing a similarly coloured antique pink and cream pin-striped suit, complete with a blue swirly paper hat, he still wasn't sure if this was a multisensory hallucination, or not.

Thoughts of, "I don't believe my eyes; my mind is playing tricks on me; and yep, I'm afraid that I'm completely, absolutely and undeniably bonkers." went through his head. All not without cause, mind you.

When the intriguing sight approached, and asked, "Would you like to have some ice cream from the Zippy cart, sir?" Donald thought, "Oh, what the hell? I may as well embrace my insanity if it gets me ice cream."

He didn't even bother to check the identification tag. If he had, he would have noticed the Zippy ice cream pusher of the Zippy ice-cream cart was the polar opposite of Aaaron Aare...[366]

> Pastoral Service – SaRS
> ✝ (Religious not Religious) ✝
> Mr Zzzyxon Zzippy, AASW
> Unauthorised Ice Cream Man...

"Have you got any Salted Caramel? It's my favourite!"

"I am very sorry, sir, but we seem to be going through a B phase and only have ice-cream flavours starting with B. There is Bacon, Banana, Blueberry, Bread, Bubble-gum, or Butterscotch. And if you choose Bread, you get a bonus double scoop of Beer and Brown."

"You had me at Bacon. It's my favourite!"

When you have no milk, you can always drink melted ice cream.

Donald was becoming accustomed to Sven lurking around and speaking something inanely insane (or insanely inane?) at just the right moments.

He went to bed with a smile on his face and bacon on his breath, trying to not think about having to put melted beer-bread flavoured ice cream milk into his cappuccino enhanced dream.

---

[366] In alphabet only. Definitely not in unwise parental naming choices wise.

Chapter 14:
is brought to you by
Mc⚡David's

Donald hadn't exactly become used to the hourly checks overnight. While he didn't appreciate the disturbances, he did appreciate their necessity. Just not for him.

It was when Donald relayed this thought to the Grey performing the Daily Health Check, who in turn relayed it to Nurse Jack, and so on… All the way up the medication chain to Dr Gee Jay, it became an official formal request asking for Donald's checks to be reduced to every two hours instead.

This glorious Wednesday morning is the start of day three of Donald's stay at *"SaRS - The no-stars resort." Where the only two resort activities available are: medication restraint as a first resort; and restraint medication as a last.*[367] Everything had gone, more or less, as was scheduled. Alarm clock, confusion, awareness, pants and shirt, avoidance, and so very nearly almost breakfast.

Donald was in his preferred seat by himself, reading the current news on his paddle and enjoying the comfortable solitude of the semi-crowded room. He was reading a fascinating story about an unbelievably elaborate heist some crazy person was planning. He didn't fully understand their slightly incoherent goal. Still, he thought it was about breaking into a hospital archive to retrieve some information about an ancient game.

He was well over halfway into his second sausage and even beginning to enjoy his meal when this strangely familiar face attached to an overly familiar strange person appeared and began hovering uncomfortably too close.

"You're in my spot."

---

[367] This is the rating Donald is going to leaving on Tripping is Ill Advised.

Donald didn't like to have his routine disrupted... And even though it had only been routine for 2.1 days, he still didn't like to be told where he could sit to eat his breakfast. Then he *really* didn't like it when he remembered he had made plans yesterday, with the now day-old Dr Hill version of Skit, to borrow a portion of the hospital's archive.

And then finally, he *really, really* didn't like coming to the realisation that all those plans were now most probably bunkum. This realisation came in the form of a female dog who was going to include a new requirement that he find another cohort for his incoherent ill-conceived inconsiderable crime... Which didn't give Donald any time to think of an appropriate reply.

Pausing for the socially accepted bare minimum amount of thinking time, in which someone with half an assumed brain would be able to formulate their answer, "Excuse me, I'm afraid you might not have heard me, or what is largely more likely, you didn't fully understand me... **You're in my spot.**"

Donald was escalating to *really, really, really* disliking the interruption.

With no obvious signs indicating comprehension would be along any time soon, the un-cooperative shell Skit had donned continued his stereotypically awkward supercilious misunderstanding of all basic human interactions rant, "Oh, I see, you are deaf. I am so sorry. **You're - In - My - Spot.**[368]"

The condescending idiotic pompousness of this situation was starting to annoy Donald,[369] and rather than make an off-off-Broadway scene into a fully commercialised Andrew Lloyd Webber production, Donald finished his prickly pear juice, gathered up the remainder of his breakfast items, discarded his a little under a half uneaten sausage and returned to the common area to await the coming of the next group time.

Got had been there again, hiding in plain sight and was wearing the same unfocussed look off into the distance. This look might have indicated she may have been thinking about something important and perhaps intrinsic to add value to this episode of the developing story. It was possible she was just having an episode of her own. Whichever it was, she was doing it so well that she wasn't noticed in the slightest again.

---

[368] Slowing your words, enunciating clearly and increasing your volume with each repetition is the time-honoured triad of scientifically unproven ways to enable anyone to understand you.

[369] Pthhhhhuuuuush to anyone who conjured a thought of me then.

Frothing at the mouth isn't a phrase Donald would use to describe himself absurdly often, and he very much didn't want to do so now. He did feel it might become an extraordinarily real possibility if some of the many number of little things in his immediate future didn't start going partially well for him. Frothing just might come to a small part of the forefront of his mind.[370]

Thinking over the immediate future possibilities and assigning to each of them two scores out of thirteen:
- One for seriousness;
- One for uniqueness; and
- One for his ability to count like a gully dwarf, although he often forgets to include this in his calculations, which makes it acceptable.

...allowed Donald to get all the way to the common area with a complete lack of frothiness. Up until then, the high score of thirteen plus one had been assigned to doing nothing about anything. When Donald saw Grey waiting, like a three-toed sloth waits for the sloth moths to lay their eggs in its sloth poop each week before climbing back up to obscurity, to perform the Daily Health Check on him, he reached a hitherto unreachable score of forty.

Donald didn't like participating in these tests; to him, they were invasive, inaccurate and incongruous. There are four physical data tests: Blood pressure, heart rate, oxygen saturation and ear temperature.[371] The fifth test is mental and is the testing of Donald's patience. He knows he will never pass this test, so he doesn't even try, making it a self-perpetuating failing prophecy.

Blood **Pressure** - when Grey succeeded in finding the medium-to-large cuff for their automatic sphygmomanometer,[372] it was an easy test to pass. But, when they couldn't find it, as one of the kleptomaniacs up from the Platypus ward had pilfered it (not because they had simply lost it), the children's version had to be wrapped so tightly and squeezed manually; Donald always thought his arm would squirt out like a half-opened banananana.

---

[370] Which is unfortunate really, because the interaction had caused Donald to forget about his SaRS archive heist completely. Also, unfortunately, a problem that this has caused me is... I now need a new segue two books long.

[371] Donald will find out these Daily Health Checks are actually optional. Optional in the taking and recording of, not in the participation of.

[372] Such an awesome word, except I think sphygmopersonometer would be a hard sell as its politically correct name... Blood pressure device might be ok.

Heart Rate - Often Donald's, still morning but after breakfast, resting heart rate was a little over 100.9. This was a socially unacceptable representation of accurate, and his pulse would have to be taken manually. A Grey would count the pulses after poking their finger roughly near Donald's carotid artery[373] for *tenish* seconds, think of a random number, add it to yesterday's temperature reading and multiply by two. Bingo, you have an acceptable heart rate.

Oxygen Saturation - Usually fluctuating somewhere between 92 and 94. Donald was always told to take a few deep breaths, so it would be artificially raised to an at-least-95-please. Donald didn't really understand how the little red light measured oxygen. Still, he was always ~~happy~~ ok to blindly oblige the greater good when told to do so.

Body Temperature - Again, this always seemed to be hovering lower than the acceptable range. Donald was always ~~ok~~ happy that a lower-than-average ear temperature was still accepted without manual intervention. None of the other several options available to more accurately measure the temperature of his brain excited him very much...
Or, in fact, at all...[374]

After the morning, tests were given and taken, or as Donald liked to think... They were stolen and swept under the linoleum; Grey ushered Donald to the medication nook. "Mr Saneman, it has now come to the time when you need to take your morning medication."
It took Donald a little while to realistically decipher what Grey had said. There was nothing like an early morning medication mix-up to get someone's blood pumping. On any other occasion, Donald would let it slide; he couldn't now as it may affect the real Mr Saneman, "But that isn't me!"
"Oh, come now, Mr Saneman, I know all of this must come as quite a shock to you, but if you don't at least try to accept the concept that we are going to create a new healthier you, your mental health normalisation might take longer than the, statistically inaccurate average, three week period allocated, initially, to each patient at SaRS, as per the MentalBank overseen insurance regulatory board and you know how much interest they have in your wellbeing."

---

[373] Sometimes Grey would poke a finger roughly, sometimes they located the vein roughly, but it was generally both.

[374] Joke to be inserted here (poor choice of words? I think not). Something along the lines of, "Brain in his Butt," "Thinking where he Sat," or, "Don't even think about going there, cos there's no coming back unscathed."

Donald was waiting impatiently for any indication there was going to be a valid point at the end of this extended soliloquy, rather than the soporific rant of a much-confused person with little to no ability of being able to firmly grasp reality and give it a really good shake, he always expects when someone other than himself strings more than thirteen words together in a single sentence.

Ahhhhh, the spurns that patient merit of th' unworthy takes, when he himself might his quietus make with a bare bodkin...[375]

"Exactly!" Donald was about to congratulate Sven for his most apt fortune cookie quote, timely interruption yet. Right up until he realised, quite possibly, he was probably one of the only we-happy-few who understood what this quote meant without doing a little research first. And Donald was never one to advocate violence.

"I am Me. I am Donald. I am Legend![376]"
Donald looked around for some support, then he realised how futile the action was, as the only people he could see were:
- Istha, who wouldn't yet accept him as a non-imaginary-figment;
- Got, who would never admit to knowing anything about anyone;
- Lost, who has forgotten much more than he will ever know;
- Mindy, who gave him a "Don't you dare!" stare; and
- The un-manage-a-trios', who he would never ask for help even if they were the last option available...

Donald was avidly trying to fend off the worrisome possibility trying to pop itself into his hippocampus. This *itself* was the concept that he was personality confused because he couldn't see Karl anywhere. He was only just managing to keep the thought, "Maybe I am Karl," nonverbal and out of his mind with the thought, "If I fail at being me, I will probably become even more nonverbal and so much further out of my mind, it wouldn't be funny anymore."
"What are you doing here, Donald?" DD didn't literally want to know what Donald was doing *here* when he arrived at the medication nook window; she wanted to know why he wasn't at a somewhere else, which wasn't anywhere near the *here* where she was.
Donald turned to Grey, said, "Pthhhhhuuuuush," and faded to grey when he realised how childish his visage was looking.

------

[375] Shakespeare: Hamlet: Act 3, Scene 1, Page 4.

[376] As Meatloaf intoned in the trite cliché... "Two out of three, ain't bad."

Grey had nothing appropriate to say as a response to Donald's immature blurt and stood there with *Des yeux fixés et froids* (fixed, cold eyes), watching him walk away.

Donald had started on his way to the group session room via his room to collect the show bag voucher for one free cup of decaffeinated coffee. He was hoping he could get *decaffeinated* changed to *real*, so he wouldn't be drinking something only looking and feeling similar to the real thing.

"Decaffeinated caffeine," apart from being a divide by zero impossibility, always promises to taste like something it isn't but can never quite deliver. If you are expecting something to be something else but already know that it isn't, then it can never be. The reverse placebo effect will always be ineffectual in its effect because you already know it wasn't.

Removing the coffee voucher from the SaRS Show Bag, Donald looked at it for the second time and read it for the first time…

> ### SaRS Show Bag Voucher
> The holder of this voucher is entitled to One Small Takeaway Cup of Decaffeinated Coffee (Tea or Hot Chocolate are acceptable variants)
> PTO for the Ts and Cs

…and it dawned on him that decaffeinated coffee, apart from also being one of the many exceptions to the *I before E except after C* rule,[377] would render the drink unpalatable, untenable and would fall completely within the realms of Donald's definition of dialectical.[378] *PTOing* as instructed…[379]

> ### No, you may NOT
> UP-SIZE, PLUS-SIZE, or RIGHT-SIZE IT
> Have ANY NON-DECAFFEINATED Beverage.!
> #### But you may
> Select the EYECED variation of the Beverage.!

---

[377] Interesting factoid: Ghostbusters' "It's more of a guideline than a rule…" predates the Pirates of the Caribbean's "The code is more what you'd call guidelines than actual rules…" by nearly 20 years.

[378] Frozen Chili is his favourite and would make a great unsuspecting treat.

[379] Which is also, coincidently, the sound Donald makes when he is spitting out both decaffeinated coffee and frozen chili.

"Bugger."

Donald failed to make a disparaging remark at the "EYECED" statement or to ask a symbolic question about the ".!" character combination, so complete was his bleak disappointing disillusionment.

Not wanting to completely waste the not-coffee voucher, Donald devised an acceptable alternative. He added another via to his immediate travel plans and went to the TK kitchen to grab one of the paper tubes of instant real coffee freeze-dried goodness. His plan was to add this to the free cup of brown and stir in some basic caffeinated sincerity. One small takeaway cup of dialectical in hand, Donald proceeded to the group rooms.

I'm off for my own mug of yummy barista juice now... I'll be back.

Reconvening a short while later, both me and the SaRSaparillans, are most of the unusual suspects sitting in their usual places with two conspicuous, due to their absence, obvious exceptions. There was no facilitator standing at the pointy end of the room expecting attention, and there was a neglected vacant chair right next to Donald, which had a handwritten note, "*I'm Not Crazy. My Mother Had Me Tested.*" signed confusingly, "*Skit Zoland.*"

Donald always found it interesting to wonder about why people sat where they sat. He would come up with various arguments and then dismiss each of them in turn, as he didn't like to argue with anyone, even if the *one* is himself. He was getting near to the end of his internal tether and about to start yelling at himself to "Shut the Hospital Up!" when he was genuinely surprised by an interloper... None other than Roland Mc/David himself had just turned up!

Donald played along with the faux excitement as he knew it was probably just someone in a suit who was being paid to be there. No one with an iota of self-respect would go out in public looking like the spectacle being presented to them here, for free. Imagine this if you will:

- **A face painted with radioactive luminous lime green paint;**[380]
- **Bottle green hair, reminiscent of a large upside-down bottle opener;**
- **Clodhoppers, complete with spinning wheel spurs;**
- **Denim blue onesie, clashing with both of the greens; and**
- **Everything was embellished with various sizes of ⚡.**

---

[380] And I mean this quite literally. There have been at least six documented cases where people wearing this costume have been rendered unconscious by the radioactive face paint.

Donald was thinking, "It's not something you are likely to miss, but I guess that's the point." He was so infatuated by the stunting outfit that he failed to notice how Roland was struggling to drag a giant chocolate wheel covered with many dreadfully scratched pictures of food into the room. The cacophony of smells insidiously wafting in three steps behind Roland heralded his arrival better than any spoken announcement could ever have.

Chunky was going blue, cowering as far away as his leash would allow, and Donald was genuinely surprised to learn that dogs can hold their breath. This also caused Nota to be engulfed by more than her normal utter confusion. She will be the one genuinely surprised to learn that one day, she can add anosmia to her list of differences. Once someone tells her what the word means.

Seven seconds after arriving, the Roland Mc⁄David outfit was being taken off. This was quite a laborious task due to both the size of the inhabitant and the precautions required to remove the clodhoppers (if you still wanted all nine fingers[381] afterwards). You could virtually hear the sweat glands exuding their salty goodness as he extricated himself from the costume.

"Sorry about that, people. It is a mandatory contractual requirement with our corporate sponsors, Mc⁄David's. I must wear the suit to any group session about food that I facilitate. Luckily for me, they forgot to specify exactly how long I was to wear it. I am also legally required to disclose the following safety warning before I say anything else:" The rather rotund Seymour Feedme then launched into a well-worn spiel...

Warning: Mc⁄David's Chocolate Wagon Wheel may contain traces of peanuts, tree nuts, milk, eggs, sesame seeds, fish, shellfish, soy, gluten, wheat, lupins, sulphites and penguins.

"OK, everyone, it's great to be alive, it's great to be here, and it's great to see you all looking so well fed! My name is Seymour Feedme, and I will be your dietitian for today. Are there any questions so far?"

If you turn the air conditioning UP
Are you making the temperature HOTTER or COLDER?

Donald had taken Seymour's request for a question quite literally, as he quite literally always takes everything other people say quite literally. He knew this wasn't the type of question Seymour had had in mind, "but at least it's a food adjacent question; after all, people often eat food in an air-conditioned room, don't they?" was Donald's follow-up justification.

---

[381] He learned how to do this the hard way.

Mind you, there is probably no easy way to learn how to lose a finger.

Seymour was way out of his depth here and had this been an underwater food demonstration, it was probably where he would have started to drown. "Colder…?" Seymour didn't generally comment on anything non-food related and hadn't made the same leaping connection that Donald had.

Then there was not so much a question from Sven; it was more like a ninja baked and branded fortune cookie quote…

Do you know the cookie man? I am the cookie man.
I am the only cookie man! Stay away from my cookie jar!
Or you just might find yourself covered in steaming hot cookies.

After his outburst, Sven stood up, gave the standard *I'll be watching you* two pointy finger gesture to Donald and Seymour, and left… Without so much as a by your leave, another word and without saying anything that was trying to resemble a good good-bye.

"Now there's a freckle freezing forecast." Donald was referring to the cold shivers he was currently experiencing running up and down his spine playing some sort of vertical hopscotch game.[382]

After more than a couple, but less than many, moments of uncomfortable silence, Seymour launched into the pre-prepared food lesson. He had already referred to his notes just to confirm to himself that he was starting at the beginning. He began to impart the universally known facts about fast food to the group with his well-worn "You can't have a diet without something dying" quip. He was cooking with gas by the time he got to "I am here to ensure if anything does die, it isn't firstly you; secondly the food's taste; or Drrrrr Drrrrrum rrrrrolllll, thirdly the chief chef!"

Jumping out from behind the chocolate wheel, in what was a poor attempt at replicating the ta-da woman jumping out of a surprise cake spectacle, was Chef. "Give it up for Chief Chef Chief Chef Chief Changes everyone," Seymour was enthusiastically clapping all by himself. He was becoming an even larger embarrassment than he looked, smelled and felt.[383]

---

[382] Sometimes Donald could hear these cold shivers conspiring behind his back over his shoulder saying, "We want to play vertebrae with your vertigo, so stop vertexing you dopey vertebrate."

[383] This embarrassment was mirrored by Chef, who had been obligatorily reduced to assistant chocolate wheel spinner and gift shop host.

Donald wondered if this combined super foodie duo act ever worked and answered himself, "yeah, probably not.[384]" He also thought he might just have possibly figured out what the ⚡s on their identification cards maybe probably meant, but he couldn't be positively definitely sure.

"Pffffft, not fooling anyone." Came back the clearly negative Donald.

After all of the side-show antics were seriously past their use-by dates, the main content of the group session could be discussed. Donald didn't pay much attention to what Seymour, and occasionally Chef, had to say. He was of the opinion he already knew enough about food. He knew how to buy it and how to eat it and was adamant he wouldn't be convinced otherwise by anything a corporate-sponsored minion had to say.

<redacted> Explanation of food portions, colour, and merit. "Yeah, Yeah, talk to the low fodmap and hi fibre handful of I don't give a crap!" </redacted>

There was a small amount of interest from the group when Seymour asked each person to come up, spin the chocolate wheel and have a whiff of their prize. He went on to explain, "The Mc⚡David's Chocolate Wagon Wheel is also a giant round magic-8-ball of answers. It will divine which type of food elicits your greatest food linked emotion.[385] It will then provide an opportunity for you to salivate over the pure concentrated scent of your predicted delectable by scratching the associated scratch-n-sniff area."

"Yuck," blurted Owedebt, clearly negatively affected by the residual smell coming from the much-scratched scratch-n-sniff chocolate wheel.

Looking in her direction, Seymour noted Nota's complete lack of cringing and invited, "Nota, would you please volunteer to be the first spinner."

Chef showed Nota how to grab hold of the wheel and give it a great big spin. "Grab, click↑, click↑, click↑, click↑, swishshshshsh, click↓, click↓, click↓, click↓ ... ... click↓, click↓, c l i c k↓, c l i c k↓,   c l i c k↓"

"Oh, Eggs!" Nota was underwhelmed with her spin when she landed on a hard-boiled egg. When she heartily scratched 'n' sniffed the egg picture, firstly with a tentative single sniff, followed by a deep inhalation... So deep, it would have put a Dyson to shame... She complained, "This is stupid; it doesn't smell like any egg I have ever smelt before."

---

[384] He really thought, "Yeah, definitely Not!" but he was trying something new and keeping some of his profound negativity to himself.

[385] They had to remove the scratch pads for durian, limburger cheese and Carolina reaper chili pepper following the recent report stating there had been several bouts of projectile vomiting and emergency hospital admission.

"You got that right, love! It smells worse than Chunky Poopy after he has rolled in a new poop-nugget recently expunged by an unhealthy skunk." Nota was oblivious of everyone else's reaction to the bad oh-my-god severity of the rotten egg gas smell emanating from her fingers and didn't understand why Owedebt was talking about skunks. Nota then did what she always did when she didn't completely understand something happening around her; she went to her safe, private happy place and became extra vapid.[386]

Next was Nelo, "Grab, swish, click. Steak! Mmmmmm, steaeaeaeaeak."
He was on his scratch 'n' sniff like manufactured meat on a home-brand pizza. By the time he was finished sniffing, there was nothing left except for a tongue print and whatever was usually stuck to the lid of the box. "Nummy tastes like week-old filly tartare."
Karl, Got, and Istha all had their turns and were rewarded with a generic slice of plastic extra tasty cheese, a pre-roofed little round pickle, and a lightly toasted sugar-infused hamburger bun respectively.

Donald was starting to see a pattern emerge, "It's strange. All the products we have randomly scratched and sniffed so far are also the main ingredients in the burgers sold at Mc⁄David's. What a completely crazy coincidence."
"Ahhhhh, I haven't really, ummmmm, noticed anything like that before, errrrr, to be honest. *Gulp*" Had Seymour been a wooden puppet instead of a corporate puppet, his nose would have grown to catastrophic proportions, given his proximity to the chocolate wheel's caustic odours.

---

[386] So, it was pretty much always then?
That's Not Funny!
Yes, you are correct, that was just mean. I expected more from me.

You, yes **You**, must now punish yourself, according to the following scale of laughter intensity: (from Wikipedia, so you know it must be true!)

Chuckle	-	Go make a coffee, bring it back and keep reading
Titter	-	Keep reading without coffee
Giggle	-	Phone a friend and tell them about this book
Chortle	-	Tell all of your friends you are enjoying this book
Cackle	-	Post on social media how awesome this book is
Belly Laugh	-	Write to the author of this book and tell him
Sputtering Burst	-	I assume you spat your coffee all over the book... Having to buy another copy is punishment enough.

Extracting himself from the biased conversation, Seymour whispered into Chef's ear, "The time has come when it is time for us to wrap everything up. Our pretence has been blown. Enact the emergency evacuation process. You save yourself! I'll stay here and stall them for as long as I can."

Seymour took the only remaining action available to him. Hoping it would lead to a calming of their farms about this potentially dangerous situation, he offered them all a bribe of Mc✔David's food vouchers...

> Mc✔David's complimentary voucher
> My word, what fantastic eyes you've got.
> My word, what fantastic ears you've got.
> My word, what fantastic teeth you've got.
> All the better to eat at Mc✔David's, my dear!

Turning the proffered bribe (but not the page in this instance) over to read the inevitable fine print...

> Valid:
> – For one of anything that is normally free
> – Until Tomorrow (Insert Today's date here)
> – With an order value deemed appropriate, and
> – When Dining-IN only (No delivery to SaRS)

With the potentially violent situation averted, the rebel horde appeased, Chef successfully escaping, and the chimes luckily ringing out, *"it's lunchtime, mister wolf,"* Seymour put his foot back into the quagmire of this stupidity and gave them some homework to complete.

"Your task, optional though it may be, should you choose to accept it, will bring me some well-deserved satisfaction if I do say so myself. I would like you all to describe in detail your favourite food-like ingredients and flavours of the burger you would consider as ideal. If you could write it on the back of one of these handy reply-paid envelopes, it would be just dandy." Seymour handed out these envelopes as everyone *lemminged* their way out of the group room towards lunch.

When they all arrived at lunch, they found out today was the day the SaRS inmates had Mc✔David's, and surprise, surprise, the best before date on the amazingly well-preserved food was 37 years into the future.

Donald gave the food at lunch as much thought as it warranted.

Back in his room, for the ever so short time that is between now and then, Donald decided to put it to good use and write something positive about food. He emphasised to himself that he was not going to do the homework; he was finished with being a goody-two-shoes suck up to the teacher. If life was going to give him lemons, he was damn well going to squeeze the lemon juice into someone's eyes and make them pay.[387]

Shaking off the funk of the last few hours, Donald tried to make good his decision to write something positive about food:

Fruit

Some berries are black, some berries are blue
Some berries are straw; I know this is true

    There's purply grapes, and also green/white
    The grapes are of wrath; I know I am right

        Some apples are red, some apples are green
        Some apples are pine, I know; I have seen

            There're brown and green pears and also yellow
            The pairs come in twos; I know it, I know

                Some cherries are red, some cherries are pink
                Some cherries are lost, I know it... I think...

---

[387] Seems to be a bit over the top, even for Donald. It may very well be that his medication is starting to work. (Depressed → Angry → Normal.)

Consider: An actual Consumer Medicine Information extract on possible side-effects: "Persons taking xxxxx may be more likely to think about killing themselves or actually trying to do so, especially when xxxxx is first started."

- Worsening of depression;
- Thoughts or talk of death or suicide;
- Thoughts or talk of self-harm or harm to others;
- Attempts at self-harm;
- Increase in aggressive behaviour or irritability; and
- Unusual changes in mood or behaviour.

Chapter 15:
Medication and Meditation
Mediation

Donald was multitasking, contemplating the recent morning events and his navel. He came to the conclusion... He wasn't so sure if he wanted to attend any more group sessions. If the sessions were going to be similar to the tapestry group session, he was leaning towards, "No, thank you very much." but if it was going to mean him sitting through some more of the infomercial style of groups without the possibility of remote, he was heavily coercing himself to answer, "Oh, Hells No!"

Knock, knock, knock.

Donald knew *that* knock, he knew the time, and he also knew he was about to be passively aggressed into going to the imminent upcoming group session. Resigning himself to the inevitable, bracing for the unavoidable and expecting the unexpected, Donald once more opened the door to his outer sanctum and exposed himself entirely[388] to the world at large.

Seth and BLT were both waiting outside the door. This was expected, and even though Donald was expecting the unexpected, seeing them both hover in unison and then hearing them speak as one, "it has come to that time again, Mr Halfbrain, would you please be so kind as to accompany us to group?" put this at another level of *entirely*, entirely, and nearly triggered expectoration.[389]

---

[388] In the good way... Minds out of the gutter people. This is a family book.

[389] Given the strangeness of all of Donald's thoughts, he really should have been expecting something like this.

The two ghosts looked at each other smugly, with four ghostly thumbs up. They were no doubt impressed with their own performance and by Donald's reaction. After nearly seven minutes of practising their scripted synchronised soliloquy, their impromptu victim gathering skills were finally maturing.

"I am here to escort you to the weekly optional gathering of the psyches-trust quadrumvirate and their comprehensive review of the past week's most over utilised T[+]LAs, Lists, Groupings, Scales and Bongo Sheets. They will also attempt to consign you to a specific pigeonhole on the 'Standard Quadratic Venn-Psychogram' as defined by some really smart people," BLT intoned.

"And I am here to learn some really big words," Seth's utterance, losing a preponderance of both temperance and tolerance, turned immediately into a colossal embuggerance[390] of, "for what must surely be the thirteen-thousand-thirteen-hundred-and-thirty-thirteenth time."

Donald didn't understand what either of the spiels was meant to convey, but he assumed they could mean nothing good. This particular assumption came with the attached thought, "but what the nothing good, I've got nothing else to do at the moment. I may as well go and watch a train wreck happen."

When they all arrived at the group room, there were just as many people sitting behind an important-looking wooden table, looking important; as there weren't people who weren't sitting behind an unimportant looking wouldn't table, not looking unimportant.

The important people were Dr Gee Jay, ~~Houts Marted,~~ *cough* Dr Houts Marted, Mindy Ownbeeswhacks and Skit Zoland. The others[391] were Owedebt Dear, Lost M'Hankie, Nota Beenhead and the newly arrived Donald Halfbrain. Donald didn't understand why he was thinking the full names of these people, maybe because the room had an air of formality about it.

Soon after Donald had sat down, ~~Nurse Dolly Dix,~~ *ahem*[392] DD, came in and dramatically said, "Let's get ready to Unnnnnderstaaaaand!" to anyone who would listen. Pausing to let the bulk of the resounding silence pass, she continued, "Good afternoon, people. Welcome to today's knowledge match, which promises to be something, in at least one sense of the word."

---

[390] Thank you, Sir Terry.

[391] These four would have been sitting at the four corners of a crazy table, even if they had been sitting around a round table in a lighthouse, protecting the basket boats off the coast of Camelot, under a full moon blindfolded.

[392] Donald should see a doctor about the frog in his mind, or maybe a vet.

Transferring the bulk of her near-unlimited requirement for attention to the eight thinkers, "All right people, I want to see a good clean discussion. And what I mean by good and clean: there are to be no snide remarks, no cynicism and definitely no sarcasm... I'm looking at you here, Donny."

"Duh, Really?"

"I'm going to ignore your pitiful puerile attempt at making a juvenile joke. Psyches-trust, brace yourselves for your introductions."

Dr Gee Jay - Introducing, in the blue seat: wearing her sky blue double-breasted long three silver buttoned blazer pant suit; with a matching set of left and right black round toe pumps; and an IQ of exceeding *Bloody* brilliant. She comes to us once a week, every week, all the way from just across the SaRS compound... We have the local medically qualified favourite Psychiatrist, Doctor Geeeee Jaaaaay!

Houts Marted - In the next blue seat along, wearing what appears to be a slightly-inappropriate slightly-worn sharkskin khaki safari suit; and his alligator anklet boots with a pair of faux diamond-tipped spurs. The only living person to go toe-to-toe with a psychosis from the grave and survive. Originally from <classified>... Our favourite not-a-real-doctor dammit-yes-I-am psychologist, Mister Hooooouts Maaaaarteeeeed!

Mindy Ownbeeswhacks - Looking very comfortable in the third blue seat: wearing something she might have been alone in considering was fashionable at the turn of the century (the 19th one), being someone who has entirely no idea at all.[393] Always present and always pervasive like the bad smell following the Mc/David's Chocolate Wagon Wheel, our very nearly resident idiopathic *somniloquist*, Mindyyyyy Ownbeeeeeeswhaaaaacks (certified Wiccan).

Skit Zoland - In the fourth, but not the last, as all of the others are blue as well, blue seat: wearing a pineapple onesie; with a pair of childish fluffy bunny slippers. Called in at the last moment to replace the self-proclaimed, 100% guaranteed, and world-famous Indian astrologer wanna-be, complete with a solution for everything, up to and including Children Mistakes. Please join me in welcoming the completely unknown Shawwwwwn Speeeeenceeeeer.

---

[393] DD was able to get away with this for two reasons:
1) She was DD.
2) What didn't you understand about reason one?

Donald Unofficial 1 – Durga Devi Astrologer Business Card
Name and phone number changed (and address removed) to protect the gullible.[394]

Donald has never had so many questions, which could be taken in so many ways and about so many of these qualifications. He had to resort to pinching himself so many times to keep himself from uttering, "Oh so, many hilarious, sarcastic comments," and thus keep himself free from any dire DD ire.[395]

While she was handing out the northwest corner stapled wads of paper, Donald was presuming they were pre-prepared printouts of a presentation on primary pandemonium precepts, proposed to be presently pondered and politely discussed. DD threw him a threatening, "Play nicely, or else…" look, which fully deserved to have at least two exclamation points appended.

"This is the handout pack for today's discussion.[396] The presentation will also be simultaneously displayed for you on our Nice 'n' New Fancy *Shmancy* smartboard, so kindly donated by our good friends at Mc⁄David's… Found on every second street corner.[397]"

---

[394] This one is actually serious! It is on the back of a business card from the local Durga Devi Astrologer. When you google his phone number, the first result is for a Qualified (wink, wink) Massage Therapist.

[395] "Why has Skit changed into a new persona from this morning? Should we be concerned that his condition is worsening?" would have probably been two important, appropriate and relevant questions to ask at any other time.

[396] Perfect.

[397] This is not : One found on *every second* street corner.
It is   : One found on every 2nd *street* corner.

At this point of the proceedings, Seth and BLT removed the hospital cover sheet from the previously deviously, obviously, hidden smartboard. Fumbling the mismanagement of the sheet, the two ghosts exited the room, looking like the ghost of a headless Bactrian camel, and sounding like the ghost of Abbott and Costello whispering urgently to each other, "Stop pushing me!" "I'll stop pushing you when you stop pulling me!" "I'll stop pulling you when you stop pushing me!" "I'll stop pushing you when you stop pulling me!" "I'll stop…"

Donald changed his mind from thinking, "*That* would be such an awesome Halloween costume, it's a real shame, I don't believe," to concentrating on the front page of the handout. He first noticed the handout was formatted in the default standard and always unhelpful, sideways-layout-making-any-stapling-effort-a-minor-disaster style. And secondly… It did indeed present him with a list of topics they would be discussing in a moment.

DD finished handing out the paper wads and returned to the smartboard to turn it on. The board went through its start-up process, culminating with a spiralling hypnotic, mesmerizingly blurred screensaver. It drew attention to, of course, the lightning bolt featured in the centre of the spiral. As it was the first time DD had become involved with this new piece of technology, she poked, prodded, and fiddled with it, pretending she knew what she was doing.

Eventually, showing a full-colour list of ~~menu items~~ talking points…

Psyches–Trust Quadrumvirate Talking Points

- The People ~~Bongo~~ Sheet (attachment page ~~#~~ last)
- Lists

  Personal Bill of Assertive Rights   Ten Common Cognitive Distortions

  Five Love Languages   Four parts of I   Four Horseman of the Apocalypse
- T+LAs

  SMART, TIP, DEAR MAN, PLEASE, GIVE, FAST, SUDS
- Groupings

  Ways of Communicating   Self-Care Wheel
- Scales

  The Anger Spectrum   SUDS Scale
- The Standard Quadratic Venn–Psychogram

SaRS Whiteboard 2 – Psyches–Trust Quadrumvirate Talking Points

"If everyone could please turn to the last sheet of the handout pack." DD had rudely interrupted Donald's fixation on the first bullet point of what was going to happen to him today, "You should find there a page called 'The People Bongo Sheet.' You should also be able to find a detachable pencil attached to 'The People Bongo Sheet' page. Please detach this page from your pack and then detach the detachable pencil from the same recently detached page."

Donald zoned out at the first mention of playing People Bongo. This was a variation of his most hated icebreaker game. To him, it was the equivalent of throwing someone into the deep end of an active volcano and expecting them to swim to the moon and back. Zoning in, he caught up with DD explaining the last few attachments and their rules, but then he simply forgot everything.

"Quadrumvirate, are you ready?"
""""Yes. Yes. Yes. Pineapple, I mean, Yes.""""
"Quadmentalirate, are you ready?"
""""Ummmmm. What. That's what she said. For what?""""

Assuming[398] this meant everyone was prepared, DD announced, "The first and only round of People Bongo will commence as soon as I have finished the next instruction monologue bullet-pointed checklist:"

"Do not begin yet!
- Your task will be, and you must all choose to accept it, is to completely fill out your personal People Bongo sheet;
- The winner will be the first person who can somehow manage to get someone else to complete it, somewhat, for them;
- Each square requires the full name of someone in this room now who thinks they might relate to the thinking inside the box on a personal, or impersonal, level. Personally, I think, myself this will be the hardest instruction for you to try to follow;
- There are eight leading statements in nine boxes for you to find names for. There are also only eight other-than-yourself people here, so you will have to and may only gather each and every person's name in full exactly, but only once.
Then adding in an impossible, unnecessary and fifth complication:
- Each person may only enter their name in each of the other people's bongo sheet squares... Once...
Now you may begin!"

---

[398] Don't you *ever* try and assume anything about DD assuming things. She's the one there to tell your ass what to do and not anything *ever* else.

Immediately… There was the standard mad dash to do nothing.[399] Donald spent the first few moments wondering how this group session was related to McᴺDavid's and came up with "**J**ust **A**nother **C**ommercial **K**nowledge **S**haring **H**ighly **I**nvasive **T**echnique."

Soon, he moved on to reading and thinking about the inside of the boxes' statements, mentally filling in all the blanks as best as he could. Some of them were obvious and easy; some were outrageous lies,[400] and the remainder were simply a collection of leftovers…

1. Knows an advertisement when they see one Shawn Spencer (AKA Skit Zoland)	2. Has a secret they have told everyone Owedebt Dear (She seems unable to help herself)	3. Doesn't like either Coke or Pepsi Lost M'Hankie (Probably because he has forgotten)
9. Can count 8. Dr Gee Jay (obviously, as uncommented)		4. Has never been told they snore Mindy Ownbeeswhacks (Would you?)
7. Has won a game of People Bongo today DD (No arguments here… Or else!)	6. Can see dead people Houts Marted (Ghosts… Duh)	5. Fell out when the little one said, "roll-over." Nota Beenhead (You already had me at the little)

SaRS Official 6 – The People Bongo Sheet

---

[399] This was due to the undue complexity of the rules, as well as the general mutters of *I don't want to, and you can't make me*, coming from the six novices.

[400] But, as he has stated before, Donald doesn't like arguing with people, and he certainly wasn't going to start by arguing with himself, or DD, today.

...and soon, again, he decided to do what he always did in these situations, more of nothing. Figuring someone will eventually call an end to the fiasco.

This is exactly what DD did thirteen silent minutes into the task. "OK, it seems the People Bongo game hasn't worked, yet again..." She cast her, "*I told you so*", glance at the Psyches-Trust table, rather unfairly including Mindy and Shawn. "It seems we all know each other as well as we are going to."

Reiterating from her initial speech, as she had a feeling it had been moved to cater for someone's OCD formatting tendencies, "The second to last sheet is the 'Standard Quadratic Venn-Psychogram,' or, as we here within the SaRS community like to call it, the 'Psych-cle of Dis-Belief.[401]' We have also included the Talking Point rules, which, for quickness' sake, are as similar to the normal Group ~~Rules~~Guidelines as makes no difference. But enough of the rules; I have been instructed we should be moving on to the next agenda item."

Hanging her head in abject dejected giving-up-ness.

"Patient Rights," continued DD through tightly clenched teeth.
"Here we have a list of rights you, as a patient, are entitled to."
DD's grinding of her teeth was increasing in intensity with each word she ~~spoke~~ spat from the presentation notes.
"You've got to ask yourself one question: 'Do I feel violated?'"
"Well, do ya? Punks!"

Donald was sensing DD thought this was becoming a waste of her time.[402]

Looking up from her presentation notes, DD gave the impression that the worst was over, "please take this time to read through the list thoroughly, making sure you understand each point, and then we shall have a productive discussion about patient rights,[403] in a few minutes."

---

[401] I will include this a bit later, when the relevant conversation is about to happen, and we will find out at the same time if Donald can reach the magical thirteen. And it wasn't really the whole SaRS community, it was only DD.

[402] She didn't. A waste of her time is the time taken to prepare each time this fiasco-waiting-to-happen group is attempted. This wasn't a *waste* of her time. This was an out-and-out unabashed abuse, and misuse, of her time.

[403] Donald could have sworn he heard DD's *Wrong* and *Left* inadvisable factions having their own discussion about what to advise was a *Right*.

Again, Donald had already started reading ahead…

You have the right to:[404]
 ⚥   Be the judge of what you do and what you think;
 ⚥   Make your own decisions and ask for what you want;
 ⚥   Offer no reasons, or excuses, for your behaviour;
 ⚥   Refuse to be responsible for finding solutions to others' problems;
 ⚥   Say, "I don't know," "I don't understand," or, "I don't care;"
 ⚥   Change your mind, make mistakes, and say "no," without any guilt;
 ⚥   Express all of your feelings, both positive and negative;
 ⚥   Follow your own values and be treated with dignity and respect;
 ⚥   Feel scared and say, "I am afraid;"
 ⚥   Personal space and time, and to have these respected by others;
 ⚥   Be healthier than those around you; (this isn't saying much)
 ⚥   Make friends and be comfortable around people; and
 ⚥   Be uniquely yourself and be happy.

Donald added his own additional right to make it a list of not thirteen:
 ⚥   Expect honesty from others, especially from all SaRS staff.

He then thought, "If only common sense was actually *common*, most of these rights wouldn't need to be explained." He also had to choke down a lot of his right to LOL when he read, "be uniquely yourself," with the attached, "Who else would I *Uniquely* be?" typical Donald response for when people don't understand what words mean.[405]

While everyone else was still reading, Donald got to thinking, "where are the other everyone *elses*?" When he saw Owedebt's eyes glaze over, making a matching pair with Nota's, he nudged her and asked, "Where is Chunky?"
"Oh, today is Wednesday."
"¿" thought Donald, not even bothering to think, "huh," first.

---

[404] Please, again, once more, bear in mind while reading these rights, they were actually part of a real group session presentation, and it was **assumed** that we were being told something we didn't already know.

Condescending much! Talk about making **ass**es out of you and **med**s.

[405] He also made a mental note to bring up rights #1, 2, 6 and 10, when he goes to act upon any plans, schemes, or heists, that may, or may not, involve medication avoidance, escape, or archival x-filing cabinet content liberation.

Bizarrely, Donald had hoped to get an answer he could understand.[406]

Soundlessly clipping Donald over his ear for thinking during reading time, "As you seem to be finished early, Donny," he still cringed at this name every time. "Maybe you would like to share your thoughts with the whole group?"

Pushing himself into the danger zone, Donald shared his recent thought question combination, "Where is everyone else?"

Barely containing herself from escalating the previous non-verbal ear clip into a full-blown physical one, "I will refer you to point three; they are none of your concern Mr Halfbrain."

Hearing Donald's formal name, Dr Gee Jay interjected before things went too much more out of control, and they had to resort to restraint, "I think what DD means is, does anyone have any thoughts about their personal rights?"

No one wanted to be left out: Houts added, "Exactly;" Shawn was nodding his head with his mouth open like a consenting Muppet, and Mindy wasn't.

Donald had reached a saturation point with his participation, "I plead the fifth and am saying, 'I don't care.' I have always been taught... When you don't know what to do, the best thing to do; is do nothing." Crossing his arms and looking directly away from DD, "This is because my recent number two, 'asking for what I want,' was just swept under the carpet."

Shawn's juvenile reaction was, "Ha! Ha! He nearly said do-do!"

Even Mindy, who was still asleep, laughed at Shawn ('s non-joke).

DD crossed her arms and responded with her own *teenagerish* response to any situation where she wasn't in total control and dismissively *tantrumed*, "OK... Whatever... Fine... See if I Care... Because I don't!"

"You go, girl!"

The look that DD threw at Nota went right over her head, as most things tended to do when you were knee-high to height indisposed personality. Any attempt that Nota ever makes to jump onto someone's bandwagon is always destined to fail simply due to the unavailable logistics.

After a minuscule gathering up of her modicum of cerebrum decorum, DD uncrossed her arms and continued, "As usual, we are running a little over time due to the inordinate number of questions being asked."

- Another look;
- Another glare;
- Another way of making Donald not care.

---

[406] Bizarre on so many levels: Donald had actually *hoped* for something; and he had hoped against hope for an understandable answer to come from Owedebt. Well, it was only bizarre on two levels then, but who's counting?

"As the official mediator, who has my absolute power to put a stop to any, and all, of these shenanigans, I choose to instigate the facilitation of the main reason why we are gathered today. Which is, to assign you four reprehensible reprobates to a specific pigeonhole in the 'Psych-cle of Dis-Belief.'"

"Ahem.[407]" This came from Dr Gee Jay.

Taking this relatively subtle hint, DD restated the main aim of the group as she saw it, "Why we are here today is so the psyches-trust quadrumvirate can comprehensively evaluate each of your situations and conclusively assign you four only slightly reprehensible reprobates to a specific pigeonhole in the 'Standard Quadratic Venn-Psychogram.'"

The infuriated glare Dr Gee Jay levelled at DD was repelled by the smug-laden sneer on DD's smirking face. She was showing enough offensive fervour to sink several large battleships completely overloaded by intentional, but not so subtle, mischievous comebacks.

Breaking the tension, by nearly breaking down the door during the process of entering, causing Nota to break wind,[408] came the becoming more and more traditional interruption by Miss Direct.

Reflecting on the recurring interaction of any gathering, including both Lost and himself, Donald was starting to think it was strangely convenient that he had been present for each of these unnecessary interruptions to the story.

Crash, silence, pffffft...

His observation, when later converted to poetry, will go something like:

Magenta lace[409]

Magenta lace, a pomp in her face
Slow-motion red locks, blowing socks
The purpose of her zeal has a circus-like appeal...
Slapping M'Hankie down

Then striding out, no turning about
Arriving to accost, to tell him to get lost
Ain't said a word, cos I think I'd have heard
She's a tramp. That baby's never from uptown

---

[407] This would have sounded like *ahockphlegm* from anyone with less class.

[408] **Note from Nota:** What? It's a natural bodily function.

[409] Inspired by *Chantilly Lace* - The Big Bopper.

Dr Gee Jay sighed a disappointing blue sigh of submission and indicated, with absolutely no fervour, in any way, shape or form, to DD that she might as well try and continue with the process of pigeonholing, as currently, they were going nowhere slowly.

Donald's mind broke into the conversation and thought something along the lines of, "Can we write the introduction of Dr Gee Jay now?" He thought it over and decided it was a good idea, just like he thought it was a good idea to write an introduction for Dr Andy Coughed. He has already forgotten how badly his after-thought introduction inclusion went.[410]

The SaRS appointed psychiatrist, **Dr Gee Jay**, is awesome! Donald doesn't respect anyone who doesn't use their cognitive powers to their fullest,[411] and he is quite aware of just how lucky he is because she does. Donald has never seen Dr Gee Jay's SaRS identification tag, but if you asked, he would imagine it would look something like this...

> Psychiatrist – SaRS
> Dr G.J. MBBS, FRANZCP
> Authorisation... Authorisation?
> I don't need no Authorisation!!!

Trying to re-rail the DD train, "If we have the time and the inclination,[412] we will continue with one, or more, of the topics of discussion listed on the initial talking points. But for now, if you could all direct a very small amount of your limited attention to our new smart board, so kindly *coughrap* donated by our good friends at McᴺDavid's,[413] we will try to pigeonhole you suckers."

"Dr Jay and Mr Marted, would you please explain..."

Not bothering to harrumph at the argumentative caption, Dr Gee Jay took the introduction and ran with it, "OK, we will all choose to ignore the blatantly argumentative and erroneous label... *For now...*"

---

[410] Unless I have gone back over everything, again, and added a few random appearances where text bulking was required. (Yeah... Not so much.)

[411] Yes, I do understand the iceberg like quality of the irony here.

[412] And I have the space.

[413] Donald was starting to think, "Maybe she isn't quite so firmly on board the last train to McᴺDavid's town..." as he previously thought.

Turning to speak directly to DD, "We will talk about this later![414]"

The Standard Quadratic Venn-Psychogram:

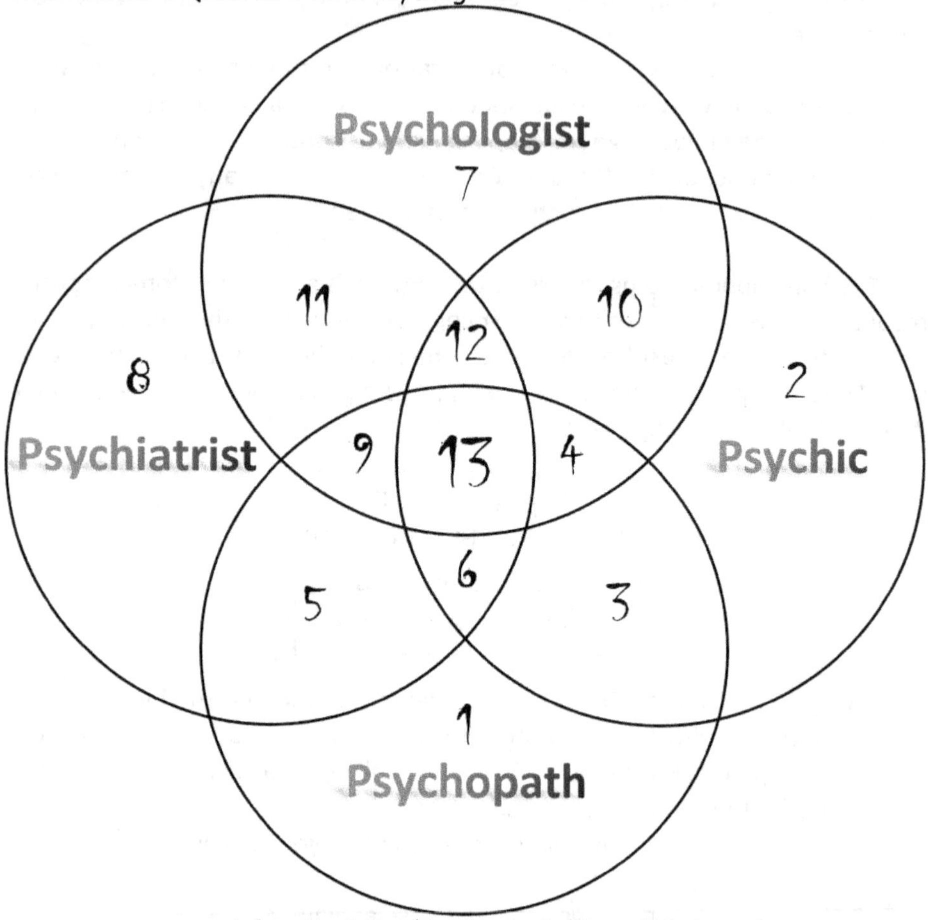

SaRS Official 7 – The Psych–cle of Dis–Belief

In SaRS' mental hospital system, the inmates are treated by two separate, randomly appointed groups: There are those who care about the service they are providing, and then there are those who just have a job to do. Dr Gee Jay is obviously one of the former.[415]

---

[414] It wasn't really a question, or a request, but it was going to be a battle of epic proportions between two fierce wills who will both probably stop traffic in their wake. Donald was hoping to get roadside seats.

[415] As are, basically, all of the people who has had anything to do with him. Donald, to be brutally honest, was a lucky one.

"What we have here is a perception of understanding; it is a diagrammatic representation of all the possible ways we connect to our cognitive awareness. As you can see, there are four major precepts, which are illustrated by the four circles. These are labelled with their respective *Psychs*:

- ¤ *Psych*iatrist;
- ¤ *Psych*ologist;
- ¤ *Psych*ic; and
- ¤ *Psych*opath."

As Dr Jay spoke the Psychs' names, the appropriate circle was highlighted automagically, "These are the four foremost cornerstones of each individual's inner *Do-You-Mind?* And we call these, *The Four Ps*. You may find it interesting to note that the opposite sides of the diagram don't ever interact with each other directly. Their only communication is via one (or both during the perfect thirteen) of the other Ps acting as a mediator."

Houts tagged into the presentation, "The larger intersections (between two of The Four Ps), create the four major quadrants, *The Four-Double-Qs*. We have most oddly numbered these with three, five, ten and eleven. The smaller intersections (between three of The Four Ps) create the four minor quadrants, *The Four-Triple-Qs*. We have mostly even-numbered these with four, six, nine and twelve." As Houts presented, there was no auto-magic happening.[416] He looked to be in some serious trouble, of being pegged as quite confusing with no one really understanding his repetitive stating the obvious non-content.

Stepping back in to try and recover the presentation, or at least to control the obligatory crash landing, Dr Jay went out on a limb, winging it and without a net, "Remembering this is still very much a work in progress… The concepts we are trying to develop here are: people, including you, me, everyone and even Mister Houts, are made up of varying amounts of The Four Ps."

"Once we understand, and are then better able to label, the intersections, we will be able to better understand, and then label, people appropriately.[417] We are all hoping the end result of this research will produce targeted hospital treatment options, where we can tailor a treatment therapy package to each specific atypical unique individual patient.[418]"

---

[416] Donald would later decide that it was probably because Houts didn't think in bullet points. Or maybe simply the smartboard name is a misnomer.

[417] No, the inappropriateness of all of this wasn't lost on Donald.

[418] This speech scored an eleven on the buzz-word bingo meter.

Bouncing back, Houts added some more of his straight out of the textbook information to the mix, finally catching on to the bullet point concept.

"Each intersection represents a level of self-awareness:
- Ranging from being a pure P, where the cognitive awareness of self is well defined, when it is projected to your average external observer, resulting in the notion *It Takes One to Know One*;
- Progressing right through each of the various over and under, lapping intersecting major and minor Q quadrants. Here is where awareness, and the projections of, become more complex and less well defined, such as *Pot Calling the Kettle Black* and *Look Who's Talking*; and
- Arriving at the most centred, most complete psyche, with the magical number of thirteen... *I Know Who I Am, But Who Are You?*"

Dr Jay, ramming home their advantage, "Please take note of the figure at the very centre of the diagram. That is your perfect thirteen. This only occurs when someone has the perfect balance of the four Ps. It is where medication meets mindfulness; sanity gets introduced to insanity, and the unreal takes on hopes and dreams and is converted to realism."

And finally, Houts and Dr Jay combined their presentation effort to deliver a decisive synchronised summing-up:

Dr Jay   "If you take the number of a quadrant;"
Houts   "as the base value of your self-awareness;"
Dr Jay   "combining it with your understanding of who you are;"
Houts   "balanced by the personal information you acknowledge;"
Dr Jay   "then you will arrive at a comfortable place..."
DJ / H   ""where you know all of your cows will always go moo!""

Donald's final thoughts about all of this were:
- "The diagram seems to be a little bit too perfect to be accurate;"
- "I still don't know where everyone else is;" and
- "What has this chapter had to do with medication or meditation?[419]"

---

[419] I can answer this one for you. Originally, I had planned to have the two naturally opposing forces of mind-altering medication, and mind influencing mindfulness, take opposing sides of a wrestling bout, with DD in the middle acting as a referee. This now seems a bit gauche, as it would require one of them to take on the bad guy persona, when in reality, these two concepts work together, blissfully, hand in hand... *For the Greater Good.*

He would have thought something else, most probably about going back over the complete list of discussion items, but then he would be having a bit of a fourth thought, and Donald simply isn't allowed.

As it was, Donald found some *automagic* of his own. He passed through the remainder of the day (into the night)[420] without needing to document a single further detail.[421] The only lingering doubt creating a blip on his nirvana was, "So… To achieve perfect equilibrium with my mental self-awareness and stuff, I have to be part psychopath?[422]"

---

[420] Obviously.

[421] Not quite so much Obviously.

[422] Profoundly, and Fundamentally, Inconspicuous.

Chapter 16:
Good Morning Tour
(and Off Shopping)

Ahhhhh, Thursday morning. After an unprecedented night's[423] sleep, Donald woke up refreshed and relaxed, but with a vexing thought. When this thought was translated, it roughly meant, "I don't know what I did last night;" but more specifically, it was a cavalcade of:

- ☒ "I don't know what I am thinking;"
- ☒ "I can't remember what happened yesterday after group;"
- ☒ "I don't remember what I ate for dinner last night;"
- ☒ "I can't remember taking my medication last night;"
- ☒ "I don't know what I am thinking again;" and
- ☒ "I can't get over the thought; I think I've thought some of this before."

So? Nothing. Doesn't Matter. Probably. Correct. And So?

Donald's mind had, unilaterally, decided this morning would be an easy, unavoidable, and appropriate time to teach him all about the useful benefits of writing any important or interesting thoughts down. Following this with a course on the useless pain of stressing about things he may have forgotten.

It provided Donald with this poor explanation of what is going on: "I have purposefully forgotten everything from yesterday evening, through last night and into early this morning to emphasise my second point. Now it is your turn to forget you have forgotten. You should then not record everything you have forgotten in tonight's diary entry, thus satisfying the first point."

Blink. Rewind. Play that déjà vu Donald boy.

---

[423] *Why is it the* night's *sleep? Shouldn't it be* Donald's *sleep?*

Ahhhhh, Thursday morning. After an unprecedented night's sleep, Donald woke up refreshed and relaxed with this positive thought, "Today is an important day. Not only is today one whole day closer to my release; it is also the day when I am allowed to go shopping."

Then he thought he might have heard a faint echo in the back of his mind, sounding something like, "Good Job Donald!" Shaking his head to remove the last vestige of morning fuzziness, Donald arose and alighted the bed.

On his roundabout way to breakfast, Donald went past the are-you-bored activity sign-up board. He neatly added his name to the scheduled shopping expedition sign-up sheet. Reading the sign-up sheet closely, for the first time, he noticed there was some fine print[424] at the bottom he had previously been ~~happily~~ conveniently oblivious of...

* Make sure you have the approval from your SaRS doctor.

** Not available during the first week of your SaRS stay.

*** All SaRS fine print is negotiable for a nominal fee.

Donald thought, "Duck! How am I supposed to get Dr Jay's consent before this afternoon comes around?" Then he questioned himself another question further, "Or are they referring to Dr Coughed?" Finishing his third degree by commenting, "Because I know they don't mean Mr Houts Marted."

Resigning himself to participating in another stint of being kept in the dark about his future, Donald did a little bit of looking around the common area and at its current impersonating personable person content.

Who Donald saw, completely unsurprisingly and blatantly astonishingly, was everyone we have been introduced to so far who wasn't at the Psyches-Trust Quadrumvirate session yesterday. They were all puzzlingly, squeezed in around the jigsaw puzzle table, puzzling the jigsaw puzzle piece jigsaw puzzle.

"Excuse me, but[425] where were you guys yesterday afternoon?"

---

[424] This fine print is not so much fine, as it is *Fine!* It should be renamed to unbelievably small disappointing print. Donald gave himself a half-smile, half-grimace and half-math-tutor-required look when it reminded him of how he described his standard introductory definition of himself.

[425] I often find, when someone says *but* frequently, they are really saying, "I may have just said something to placate you, *but* now I am going to tell you what I really think." This is the *everything before the but doesn't count* rule.

Of the people sitting around the table:
- ⌐   Istha was never going to answer him because she was busy trying to ignore the voices she annoyingly couldn't get out of her head;
- ⌐   Karl might have answered if he had felt in any way confident to tell anyone anything about himself;
- ⌐   Nelo's entire body was visibly shaking, and he was dripping sweat in large buckets with what Donald assumed were the DTs; and
- ⌐   Sven wasn't going to tell Donald anything useful, as he was still upset about Donald taking his bit yesterday, and would only offer:

You are *that* person; the one who takes all the fun out of a funeral.

- ⌐   So, he was left with... Got...

"We werrrrre rrrrrecyeiving ze TMS."
Donald's look told her much more than his words ever could.
"Trrrrranskrrrrraneeal Magnyeteek Steemulakhkhkhkhkhon."
Donald's look didn't change.
Got dropped her TV Russian accent and quietly whispered into Donald's ear, "You get a couple of electromagnetic thingies strapped to the sweet spots on the sides of your head; they turn up the juice to just before it starts to hurt and you start to scream; and then we sit there, while our brains are being soft rebooted, hoping for the best. TMS is like getting a clean slate of mind, where all of your TMIs and PMSs have been removed."
The thought of having a clean slated mind sounded interesting to Donald. Unfortunately, moments before he had finished having this thought:
- ⌐   Owedebt appeared;
- ⌐   Got returned to her normal persona of an ex-ex-Russian spy; and
- ⌐   The thought was no more.

Owedebt grabbed Donald's arm and hesitatingly said, in short bursts of six words, "Quick come with me, before I" "am discovered, by them finding me."
Out loud, "What's going on?" followed by a silent, "OMG, You Dozy Doe!"
"I need to hone my subterfuge" "skills because I keep thinking someone" "is watching me and I'm not" "a paranoid schizophrenic.[426] So, I'm practising" "hiding from Nota and Chunky. I've" "given them the slip, thrown them" "off the scent and now I'm" "getting the heck out of Dodge!"

---

[426] Although sometimes she talked to herself to escape the loneliness of having no one to talk to while she was alone or with Chunky. Chunky isn't a very big conversationalist, unless he is hungry, then he will chew your ear off.

"Weird." Simple, succinct and spot-on. Donald glanced in Got's direction, wondering why he thought she may have had something to do with Owedebt's latest, possibly imagined, obsession.

"Hey," casually exclaimed Owedebt, "why don't I give you an all-expenses-paid round trip of everywhere else inside the place? We could call it the Rooms of SaRS Discovery and Definition - Part Two. It still won't cost you a thing."

"Yeah, except for the little amount of sanity I have left." Donald was going to have to get his appropriateness gland looked at. Instead of thinking this to himself and saying *sure* aloud, he had transposed his responses.

"Ummmmm, right-y-ho, let's start with breakfast.[427]"

Donald was lucky he was quite used to OPT in the morning because if you don't get to breakfast early, you always get left without the option of turning down the sausages... If you were late, it wasn't a question of if anymore; it was a question of how many?

Breakfast today was definitely not reconstituted scrambled eggs.[428]

Donald sat in the same seat as usual, and there were none of the unusual interruptions from Miss Direct or from any of Skit's boundless personalities. Curiously, this situation made Donald slightly uncomfortable, as the total lack of drama was a sizeable deviation from his routine. A curiously uncomfortable dearth of random events later, our apathetic duo set off for their next dreary adventure, and Donald hoped it would stay that way... Uneventful.

Following Owedebt from the dining room to the start of the tour Part 2,[429] even though it was via an entirely different route, didn't take them very long because the start was located in Chef Chief's Kitchen:

- Twenty-seven steps to the flip-flop top bench that allows easy access from CC's Kitchen to the dining room, only to find that the reverse direction was unavailable unless you were staff.[430]

---

[427] Donald's déjà vu-dar was getting a healthy workout today.

[428] These aren't optimistically called scrambled eggs. There is significantly more freshly cracked egg here than there ever was in Humpty Dumpty.

[429] The Arabic Numeral Conundrum: Why are these numbers not written by speakers of Arabic languages, unless they are writing in English?

[430] Being refused entry, just because they looked like a pair of animated, contaminated zombies, was only a slightly disturbing setback for Owedebt.

After this false start, the path they began to follow reverted to the reverse of what they followed earlier:

- ꭓ   Along the inside/outside courtyard corridor; and
- ꭓ   Left through the ornate door and down the corridor.

Branching out just before the emergency exit/fire door:

- ꭓ   Instead of going through the still open door, they went down the fire escape stairs. These were confusingly on the outside of the fire door;
- ꭓ   Turning right at the bottom of the second flight; they
- ꭓ   Followed an obviously considerably used corridor, although it was also obviously considerably empty at the moment.

Owedebt broke into Donald's thought process and instructed, with this unfairly lengthy instruction, "Please keep focussed on what is ahead, …, …, …, and try to not be too unduly distracted.[431]" What Donald missed while he was being distracted by Owedebt's instruction to not become too distracted was:

- ꭓ   The laundry;
- ꭓ   The games room;
- ꭓ   The massage studio;
- ꭓ   The gym;
- ꭓ   The chemist; and
- ꭓ   Various storage and meeting rooms along the way.

Donald caught up with Owedebt when she stopped at the bottom of a well-worn flight of stairs. Here she cautioned Donald, "When we reach the top of these stairs, there is going to be a closed door; it is essential for us to open, and pass through, the door silently.[432]"

To emphasise her directive, Owedebt indicated the pulverised remains of what Donald could only guess was an ex-door. Following her finger, pointing up to the three sections of ripped out concrete wall where the hinges used to hang and hearing her say, "This is what happened last week when the door was left to its own devices and consequently slammed very loudly…" enticed Donald to experience another bout of his shivers playing vertebrae.

---

[431] Although Owedebt was speaking figuratively here, Donald was hearing literally there. He continued to follow Owedebt, focusing on her right butt cheek, not interested in anything that was being left behind.

[432] Owedebt mouthed the word *silently* silently, assuming Donald needed an example, as if he didn't understand what silence meant. If you have ever heard Owedebt *talking* on the phone, you would double over with irony.

Continuing with the tour prequel monologue:

- Gingerly they stepped through the ex-doorway, cautiously ascended the stairs and proceeded in an orderly fashion to standing just outside the door in question;
- Negotiating the door in categorical silence, Donald felt apprehensively relieved when he saw that the other side of the door turned out to be one of the ones with the angrily handwritten "SH!" sign, as this meant he might know where he was;
- Bypassing the rounded pointy bit of the A-space, they negotiated past Mobius (the door), with equal care as the last; and
- Success! Arrival at the elevator doors.

Moving back to Owedebt's commentary from Donald's internal thinking was again so deeply seamless that he completely neglected the "quite scary" thought comment this time. His mind prefilled the description of the kitchen from memory, but other than that, this is what Donald either heard or saw:

Chef Chief's Kitchen - CC's Kitchen - The kitchen sports a just south of the border state of the art walk-in refrigerated larder. If you think of the freezer scene from *The Shining*, you would be more than fairly warm.[433] The cooking facilities, as Seth has already described to Donald earlier, are semi-commercial restaurant-quality stainless-steel, easy-to-clean electrical appliances.

Whilst Donald and Owedebt were refused entry to the actual kitchen, they were able to furnish this description out of rumour, gossip and hearsay. They could also see through the partially open saloon kitchen doors.

Chef runs a tight ship and doesn't allow any mess. He shows his devotion to the people of SaRS by being there most days to guide the food preparation. Days when he is not on duty are steak like blue rare, and even on those days, he can generally be found in the Battle of Kingswood Hill memorial garden.

If you do find him there and ask respectfully, he will enthusiastically tell you one of the traditional stories from his people.[434] Chef has an astonishing memory and can relate a story on just about any subject. The single exception being that he won't tell you any stories relating to settlement[435] by the white man, only stories of his ancestors' defiant survival.

---

[433] Don't fixate too much on the detail that the Here's Johnny character is an old author gone mad. I'm sure his situation was probably different to mine.

[434] If Nurse Jack Call is also there, then Chef will defer to him to tell you an appropriate Aboriginal Dreamtime story of his Darug people.

[435] A term as appropriate as telling someone to, *settle petal.*

Elevator - For all intents and purposes, this is a *normal* two-floor double-slide-door hospital-sized elevator. It travels up and down, the doors open and shut, and people go in and come out. But like the *normal* people being treated at SaRS, it is prone to strange outbursts of insanity when anyone tells it where it is, what it can and can't do, or where it should go.

If you ever find yourself leaving the elevator and can see something other than what you are expecting, make every effort possible to jump back into the car before its doors close. Most probably, you will be too late, then you will be late for your next appointment, and mostly finally, you will just be late.[436]

There are many "alleged rumours" floating around the SaRS mire, which have been handed down from patient to inmate, over the weeks and months, about some unexpected elevator destinations. These include a range of places from the unlikely, through the fanciful, to the downright ridiculous:
- ⚥ Padded rooms;
- ⚥ Ancient operating theatres;
- ⚥ A clothes manufacturing sweat lodge;
- ⚥ An Illicit prescription drug manufacturing lab;
- ⚥ Several variations of dungeon cells; and even
- ⚥ An evil medieval torture chamber.

Massage Room - Even though this room is only open between the hours of two and five in the afternoon, every other day unless it is a day on either side of a full moon,[437] this is the most popular intra-place in SaRS. To partake in the relaxation, you need to book at least a month ahead,[438] especially if you would like to make use of their services during the subsidised happy hour.

There's one of those water-feature displays, with the sole responsibility of teasing out your desire to pee; a white noise machine emitting soft sounds of the beach adding to the yen; and a tap dripping somewhere in the backroom, completing the unholy trinity of passing water inducing water noises.

Donald hasn't had the chance to meet the masseuse, the masseur, or the massage therapist. He has heard a rumour, though, when the're asked if they prefer a particular name for what it is they do, they will probably answer with a paraphrase of, "In my opinion, for me, personally, I don't have an opinion."

(DD must have been giving them lessons.)

---

[436] BLT will try to convince you that being late isn't really all bad once you eventually get used to it. His opinion is a tad on the biased side though.

[437] Lunar eclipses excepted. (Anna Lykeananna will likely appear one day.)

[438] Which is quite tricky when you consider that the average maximum length of a stay at SaRS is roughly only three-and-a-bit weeks in duration.

Gym - After the massage room, this is the next on the list of most popular destinations at SaRS. If you want to induce a fragment of relaxation, it is either the massage room or the exercise gym for you. It is interesting, though, that it won't be both, even though they both provide, more or less, the same net result. One comes via a therapeutically calm laying of hands on you. The other via an invigoratingly frantic laying of fists into someone else.

There are three definite factions within the gym world:
- Cardio only;
- Weights only; and a small amount of
- Combined weight and cardio *weirdios*.

The first two factions have their own distinct areas, patronage and dress requirements. The full-length mirror side has quite baggy attire, free weights and obvious muscles, while the mirror-ball side has form-hugging spandex, all manner of cross-trainers and attitudes to match.

Somewhere near the middle of these two dialectical worlds exist the few weirdios and everyone's aspirational hero Ma'am Cybill Flex. Don't ever make the mistake of thinking you could possibly take her at anything. She can run rings around most of the SaRS population while she is giving a piggy-back ride to the rest. Equally at home in the water, as she is on a treadmill, she also acts as the SaRS lifeguard during the pool season.[439]

Games Room - The games room is sometimes described as the only quiet, unassuming unsung hero of the entire hospital. It performs several of the vital behind the scenes functions at SaRS and does so valiantly:
- Firstly, it is the detention basin for the accommodation building;

It is a sizeable open plan area adjacent to all of the major foot accessible arteries, with various entrances and exits that can all be closed off individually. Several specific combinations of opens and closes can protect most patients from, and focus the majority of, any crushing stampedes when the remaining inmates have become manic maniacs on the loose.

---

[439] **Infomercial warning!**

Ma'am Cybill Flex's line of pleather gym attire is always in stock at the front desk. It comes in a variety of colours and at a very reasonable price. Not only are you are allowed to wear it on both sides of the gym facility, it is suitable to be worn in the pool. (With one small caveat saying: you must make sure to remove the clothing before it dries on any appendage requiring a constant supply of blood.) Straight Jacket/Gimp design to be available soon.

⚥   Secondly, it is used as a distraction room;

The inmates are placed here and are secretly monitored, via CCTV, during changes to their medication. This gives the inmate a safe environment to be in while their body takes its own sweet time in assimilating the new levels of the various chemicals ingested. The liver-like by-product of this scenario is the much-needed bile-inducing job for the monitor of the CCTV monitors.

⚥   Lastly, it is a games room.

A place where all of the inmates can gather to play several space-intensive inside games such as pool or table tennis.[440] These sorts of games are usually only played by and between teams of inmates. The only exception to this is the annual staff v inmates' round-robin of party games. One of the only times when it is amazingly beneficial having a schizophrenia diagnosed teammate is when you are playing either pass-the-parcel or musical chairs.

Tour concluded, Owedebt and Donald settled in for a quick game of pool before the morning group session. Donald utilised the only practical skills he had learned in high school mathematics and physics: Newton's laws of motion, angles of incidence and reflection, and all of the small (and most of the large) numbers between one through fifteen inclusive.[441]

At the end of their game, Donald emerged as completely triumphant, and conversely, Owedebt completely failed to emerge. Donald had turned around, only for an instant, to place their cues back in the rack when Owedebt utilised her ability to disappear. Donald was once more alone.

Leaving the games room, Donald correctly turned to the right. He headed to what was fast becoming his favourite destination[442] at SaRS. Completely by accident, he completed the prematurely ended tour by himself.

Laundry - This is the semi-standard, semi-commercial, semi-practical and semi-nudity-inducing facility. Three washing machines; three dryers; and one of each tub, sink and basin. The six originally white white goods all accept one two-dollar coin as payment for a single complete cycle.

---

[440] Darts used to be another popular option, but ever since the unfortunate acupuncture incident of Twooooo Thooooousand and Eiiiiighteeeeen, MentalBank has only allowed sawn-off practice darts to be used, and it just isn't the same when they don't get stuck in.

[441] The recent practice of using dialectical colouring, instead of numbering, to distinguish between opponents' balls makes a mockery of this learning.

[442] He was also practicing his use of undetectable underhanded sarcasm.

The preferred usage instructions tentatively attached to the front of each of the washing machines were fairly easy to understand...

Washing Machines

1.   Add Dirty Clothes   (up to maximum)
2.   Fill Detergent Thingy   (up to maximum)
3.   Insert a $2 coin into the Coin Receptacle
4.   Select "Wash" and Press "Start"

A complete washing cycle is 48 minutes, exactly

And the ones attached to the dryers were similarly understandable...

Clothes Dryers

1.   Add Wet Clothes   (up to maximum)
2.   Make Sure Lint Filter is Relatively Clean
3.   Insert a $2 coin into the Coin Receptacle
4.   Select "Dry" and Press "Start"

A complete drying cycle is 41.1 minutes, roughly

Donald will find out when the little red light next to "Dry" is illuminated; it doesn't mean it has been selected. He will waste three $2 coins starting the timer, but not the dryer, thinking it is simply a poorly functioning dryer, before someone points this error out to him.[443]

Finishing the Tour for the second time, Donald found himself at the fire escape he remembered from the start of the first tour. Using this knowledge, he was firstly able to re-orient[444] himself and then subsequently proceeded in an obedient fashion to the next available group session, which coincidentally, conveniently and correctly was just about to start without him.

Donald arrived and found the room filled with inmates. Trepidation and excitement, in equal portions, were floating around the room so thickly he had to be careful he didn't trip over their efforts to dominate the atmosphere. He sat in his vacant customary seat and waited, thinking, "It's amazing everyone is already here, as if it was a planned literary tool to expedite the introduction and explanation process. And if anyone was late arriving, it was me."

---

[443] Donald put a review of all hospital documentation onto his to-do list.

[444] There is probably a funny racist joke to be made here, but I can't think of one that is, and isn't, so I won't, but just did, I think...

Disagreeing with Donald's thought, Houts arrived late and proceeded to announce, "The session this morning is going to be a truncated look at some psychological logic,[445] so everyone will have ample time to chase their elusive approval for, and then prepare for, the shopping adventure this afternoon."

Another piece of information imparted in his opening speech, "It is also strongly suggested you get takeaway sandwiches for lunch. These can then be used to supplement the real fresh hot coffee available at the shops, so you can feel like a normal functioning part of society, if only for a few moments."

<truncation mode>
Sadness vs Depression (Discuss...[446])

When you are Sad	When you are Depressed
Memories can make you Happy	Memories just make you Sadder
Sadness brings Tears; But then they go away	Depression brings Tears; They stay; everything else goes away
If you are Sad. Friends can Help	If you are Depressed; What Friends?
Sadness doesn't affect Memory	Depression takes...what was I saying?
You are Sad for a specific Reason	You are Depressed for no reason at all
Sadness Passes and is Forgotten	Depression Stays and is Remembered
Comfort is Free when you are Sad	Depression always costs Money
Everyone gets Sad occasionally	Only you are Depressed all the time
Empathy is Easy, Welcome, and Right when applied to Sadness.	Pity is Easy, Unwelcome, and Wrong when applied to Depression.

Donald, unusually, didn't have many, or indeed didn't have any, questions, thoughts, suggestions, wants, needs, doubts, issues... or any of the vast array of other terms available to be used to describe this situation.

Neither did anyone else.

---

[445] All this means is there will be a limit put on the inane (insane) questions people might be tempted to ask, and they are going straight to the handout.

[446] This doesn't so much mean *have a meaningful discussion*; it more closely reflects *comments on a pre-prepared presentation*, without the pretence of having any presenters present... Possibly.

This was probably because there was a pall of understanding covering the proceedings. Everyone in the room could relate to the sad picture painted in some direct way. The presented picture is always just a shade or two of blue away from being used to describe you.

Houts chose to continue with something a little more upbeat from out of the bag of psychological concept descriptions.

<u>Psychological Concepts Explained</u>[447] in alphabetic order:
- ꭓ   Accepting that you can't change a situation is your first step in changing it.
- ꭓ   Black Dog: A pet nobody wants to feed, but everyone does, at some period.
- ꭓ   Crisis Management Plan: What to try and do after it too late to do anything.
- ꭓ   Dialectical: Two incompatible concepts occurring at exactly the same time.
- ꭓ   Exorcise and Exercise: Dialectical methods of fighting your evil depression.
- ꭓ   F-ing Responses: Fight/Flight/Freeze (unconscious and without sympathy).
- ꭓ   Guess: Euphamism for the act of depression & anxiety medication selection.
- ꭓ   HELP: Hope, Encouragement, Love and Patience (every 12-step programme).
- ꭓ   I Statement: When shit happens to me... I feel bad because I don't like it.
- ꭓ   Just Don't It: Don't it always happen that way? (There's often a gap to fill).
- ꭓ   Knowledge: The ultimate piece of your puzzle is always inexplicably missing.
- ꭓ   Lists: There is a list of everything in psychology (there's even a list of lists).
- ꭓ   Mindfulness: How to consciously make your unconscious completely vacant.
- ꭓ   Normal: Unfortunately, this state is yet to be defined by any professional.
- ꭓ   Overwhelmed, or Underwhelmed only; you can never be explicitly whelmed.
- ꭓ   Ps, The Four: Psychiatrist, Psychologist, Psychic and Psychopath (Probably).
- ꭓ   Questionnaire: Unavoidable, stressful and inconsistent communication tool.
- ꭓ   Research: Another name for the various treatment options they have tried.
- ꭓ   Stop: One level higher than give way. One level lower than avoidable crash.
- ꭓ   TheRapist: UnfoRtunate job title if you have a nonfunctioning loweRcase R.
- ꭓ   Unused, this letter has been intentionally left: Making this a niqe conndrm.
- ꭓ   Viscous Cycle: Slowly coming to an understanding of what is wrong with you.
- ꭓ   Weakly and Weekly: Extended dialectical options for Exorcise & Exercise.
- ꭓ   X-axis: Generally, it is time. Sometimes it is not, and at other times it isn't.
- ꭓ   Y-axis: Anxiety levels of Acceptance, Accomplishment, Annoyance, Anger...
- ꭓ   Zen: The fine art of sleeping with your eyes open whilst also being mindful.
  </truncation mode>

---

447   The subtitle of this is, "Actual real things that don't make a lot of sense."

Houts had already taught enough to satisfy requirements, which basically means he had obtained enough names on the sign-in form, so he dismissed[448] the inmates early. Donald stayed back after class to talk to Houts about getting his approval to go on the shopping expedition.

With almost equal amounts of anger and sadness about this topic, Houts explained to Donald, "Getting my approval to go shopping isn't good enough. Apparently, you need to be a **<air quote>** *real doctor* **</air quote>** to give an approval." Then in a conspiratorial whisper, "But, if you can get the nurse on accompaniment duty to sneak you onto the bus, I won't tell anyone."

Donald wasn't sure where this spate of whispering had come from, but he liked it! He also liked his chances of going shopping because it was Nurse Jack who was on bus duty. Things were starting to look up.[449]

Putting aside all of his apprehensions about deliberately breaking a rule, Donald requested, "A plate of various sandwiches please." from Chef in his preparation for an illicit shopping expedition. Donald didn't know what excited him more, the thought of him breaking a rule on purpose, the anticipation of some overpriced coffee, or his lunch plate of various egg sandwiches.

Over the next couple of hours, Donald spent much of the time discussing, amongst himself, the pros and cons of willingly participating in a rule breach.

<u>PROs</u>

- Coffee!

<u>CONs</u>

- Breaking a rule on purpose
  (Which is nearly as bad as lying)
- Don't want to get Jack in trouble
  (Because he is one of the good guys)
- They might keep me here longer
- It will cost me more than $0.00
- I will stress about getting caught
- Someone might recognise me
- The bus[450] doesn't look too safe

---

[448] This was also in the good way. Dismissed is another of those strange words; *Dis* from Latin meaning not; and *Missed* from Cowboy meaning to not hit. So, Houts **didn't not hit** the inmates on their way out.

[449] He literally looked up at this point, and immediately regretted his action. In preparation for the McʌDavid's infiltration, someone had seen fit to pre-introduce some of the *Yes, they are real food!* pickles to the roof.

[450] Don't believe anything dopey Donald has to say, what would he know? Bertie the Bus has seen many years of faithful service.

Looking over his list, weighing up the one to seven ratio, then deliberately crumpling it up, Donald decided it was past time to "Cry 'Café!' and let slip the dogs of coffee purchasing!" and be damned with any of the consequences.

Donald found his own way back to the Nurse's Bowl and, with most of the subtlety he could muster, stood somewhat casually obvious near the doorway until someone noticed him. The *noticee*, in this instance, was one of the Greys. This distinctive Grey looked to be one of the female persuasion. Donald decided to address her as such, "Pray tell me please, my good madam, would you happen to know the current whereabouts of the esteemed Nurse Jack, at this present point in time?" completely failing in the art of subterfuge.

Grey, not wanting to miss an opportunity to perform her duty as a student nurse, asked Donald to sit down and said, "I'll be baaaaack." Disappointingly, when she returned, she didn't have Nurse Jack in tow, as Donald had naïvely expected. She instead had the morning ritual devices.

After taking his temperature, roughing it up a little and thrusting it back, Grey admitted to having no idea where Nurse Jack was, "But if you go to the waiting area near the front administration desk, and wait… I'm fairly sure he will be there in a few minutes to take people shopping. WINK. WINK."

Double takes aside, Donald went straight to the waiting area. There were already three groups of people milling around and waiting:

- Regulars - Those who came ready equipped with a shopping bag, half full of pre-emptied bottles of water;
- Newbies - Who had turned up equipped with only their wits, and even then, some of them had packed lightly; and
- Others - The always present, uncomfortable with just existing looking sort of people… Donald's people.

His wait wasn't too long. Zzzyxon Zzippy and Nurse Jack came swaggering along the corridor like the victorious saviours they were going to be. Donald could have sworn he saw a rainbow of shooting fireworks following them.

Nurse Jack, seeing Donald was one of the patients waiting to go shopping, took the clipboard away from Zzzyxon and instructed, "It's my turn to check their names off,[451] so I guess it's your turn to help them onto the bus."

---

[451] Get ready for your mind to be blown…

Checking people **off** a list, is done by checking they are **on** the list.

Boom!

Zzzyxon replied, in his own uniquely downtrodden style, "Again? All right, this way, people... You know the drill:
- ☒   Three steps up, then watch your head;
- ☒   Find a seat... No, not that one; that's the driver's seat;
- ☒   Put your bags under the seat... No, under your own seat;
- ☒   Thank you, now buckle up; and try to
- ☒   Look normal... *sigh* No... I meant *normal* normal, not your normal."

During this time, Nurse Jack's head was doing the:
- ☒   Drinking-duck dance... Checking all of the regulars off the list;
- ☒   My-glass-is-empty dance... Verifying the newbies signed authority; and then finally the
- ☒   What's-in-it-for-me dance... Sneaking the remainder onto the bus.

One promise for a real cup of coffee later, Donald was on the bus and on his way to go shopping. He was also on his way to intentionally breaking his first rule in possibly, ever.

And so, it was that:
- ☒   Seven (or eight WINK WINK) slightly irregular inmates;
- ☒   One pastoral care shopping assistant people supervisor; and
- ☒   One nurse Jack, the negotiable chaperone.
Headed off:
- ☒   In Bertie the Bus;
- ☒   Driven by the unknown bus driver of SaRS;
- ☒   On their journey to an undiscovered, as yet today, shopping centre.
And timidly went where many people have gone before.

The Bus trip story ends here, as whatever happens outside of SaRS stays outside of SaRS.[452]

---

[452] Except for: Remember those pre-emptied bottles of water, well they aren't empty anymore, and localised Vodka sales went through the roof.

Stay tuned to find out if they get caught; or get drunk, and then get caught.

Chapter 17:
Non-Brief Debrief
of his Brief-Less Debrief

As soon as Donald arrived back at SaRS, he was shuffled into the nearly empty room next to DD's office. A niggling sense asking, "Have I been in this room before?" escaped his tactile memory. He couldn't quite rationalise the thought away from the tip of his tongue, so he settled for placing a small off-white picket fence around it, determined to not let it escape and join with the wild bush-league thoughts tumbling around in his head before he could remember it completely.

With nothing much else to do, he sat down and contemplated stuff.

STUFF you should know...[453] was the informational acronym spelled out on a poster, blue-tacked to the wall, directly behind where the door would swing open. It was thus, always effectively hidden from everyone's view, except for those who were in the room when the door was closed...

STUFF you should know...

SaRS (Saint Rita's Sanatorium): Where you are right now. It is a safe place.

Treatment: What you are here seeking. Generally, of some mental variety.

Usual: What this situation definitely is. We usually seek the normal.

Freely: This is voluntary. But you can't leave until we say so...

Free: Nothing like what it will cost your medical insurance!

---

[453] One of my personal favourite five letter TLA misnomers.

Becoming just a little antsier in the *pantsy-errrrr* region than usual, Donald stood up and wandered anxiously around the confined space for a short while. After two laps of the interior perimeter, he felt he knew as much about this room as he was ever going to learn. He completed his obligatory third lap and returned to his seat to think up something else to think about.

The room was completely devoid of any standard measurement reference points, so when Donald's mind gave itself the order to start wandering around, only seconds after it had ordered his body to stop, it began thinking absolutely theoretically, hypothetically and literally about the room itself.[454]

Donald measured the width of the room using the international standard man **Baby Steps**. This was a heel to toe shuffle he had perfected in the physical form but had completely failed to exploit in the abstract. Each Donald BS pace was approximately 26.5cm long. With allowances made for any shoe and building inaccuracies, the distance Donald covered in 15 Donald BS paces was as close to four metres as makes no difference.

The visualisation of Donald's thinking looks a little something like this:

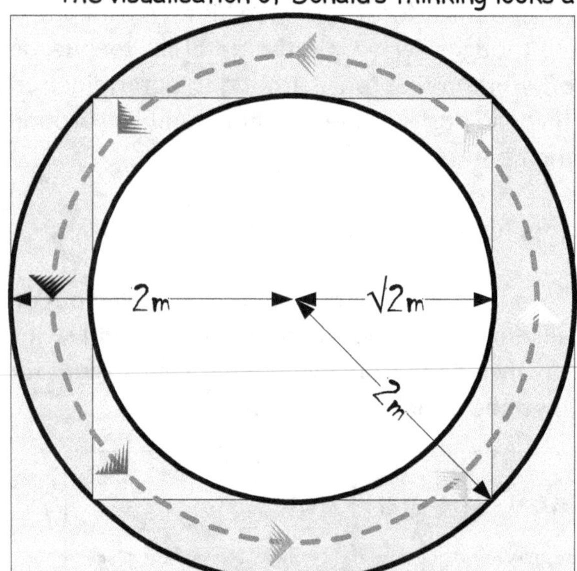

Donald Official 2 – Interrogation Room Won Wandering Wondering

The door to the room swung open before Donald got much further than the philosophical side of his thinking, thankfully avoiding most of the mentally exhausting practical thinking workout.

---

[454] Thought Process: Theoretical ⬅➡ Literal ⬅➡ Hypothetical

Dr Jay sat down opposite Donald and looked at him with a hint of sadness tinged with melancholic disappointment. After a few moments of this silence, she spoke, not so much condescendingly... It was more like she had expected more from him, mixed with some he should have known better. "Why would you think it was acceptable for you to go out shopping without me knowing? Houts informed me immediately after you sought his authorisation to go and that he had also already made Nurse Jack aware of the situation.[455]"

"When Nurse Jack was doing his shopping preparation, he rang to get my consent on the matter of you participating without securing my authorisation. He felt comfortable that you would be able to cope, and he could easily handle any situations, should any arise, if you weren't. I duly gave him, and therefore you, my consent. This is a process we go through every shopping day. Did you think you were the first person to try and go shopping in their first week?"

Dr Jay, unusually, gave Donald a mini-lecture: "Donald,
- We know all about the contraband smuggled back into the hospital, which has already been switched out for non-alcoholic substitutes;
- We know exactly who is enabling the Platypus ward shopaholics and have already either approved the purchased items or returned them;
- We know who has, and who does not have, the authority to go;
- We know everything... and
- You shouldn't blame Houts; he didn't tell just anyone... He told me."

Dr Jay continued with the debriefing, reading from Nurse Jack's report: "Shopping predilections - Donald Halfbrain...
- Supermarket: Up and down each aisle, concentrating on the bakery, lolly, chocolate and frozen dessert sections... But... No purchases;
- Department Store: singled out the entertainment section, specifically the DVDs, and after several promising false starts... No purchases;
- Historic DVD shop: perused all of the discount displays, a quick glance at the new releases, very dejected and... No purchases; finally
- Coffee shop: A coffee with one of everything (including extra hot), and one for me, 'thank you very much,' but no pastry accompaniment."

Dr Jay would have been well within her rights to say, "We knew you, baby, and we knew you good!" but being a spectacular professional, all she said was, "We had the situation well under control, Donald. You see, we are actually very good at what we do here at SaRS and won't let you make a mistake."

---

[455] Which is a simple, safe and practical example of a time anomaly, which you can practice in the safety and comfort of your own home.

Donald quietly hung his head, in a well-deserved shroud of shame, for the lacklustre trilogy of conspiring to break a rule on purpose, getting caught and most anti-importantly[456] , for disappointing Dr Jay.

Straightening the obscenely detailed and immaculately presented report, considering the insanely short amount of time Nurse Jack had to prepare it, the feat was escalated to just shy of incredible, with the assumption he had prepared one on each of the other inmates who participated in the shopping trip.[457] Dr Jay asked, "Is there anything else you would like to discuss?"

This had the sound of a loaded question to Donald, and he felt he should really have known the answer to it. But he didn't, and that concerned him.

Dr Jay lifted several pages of the report, read a few lines, thought, looked at Donald, thought a bit more, wrote a few comments on the page she was reading, read a bit more, added in a few "Hmmmmms," and finished with an official sounding... "Alright then, Mr Donald Halfbrain, having discussed all of the apparent pertinent details, of your recent clandestine shopping foray, into the wilderness outside SaRS, I will now sign the debriefing form, indicating to the relevant nursing staff you have just been successfully debriefed, vis-à-vis the aforementioned anomalies, and you may now be returned you to your regularly scheduled programming, as soon as possible.[458]"

Just before he left the room completely, Donald turned back to ask Dr Jay if he had ever been in this room before, but seventeen moments before this question was formalised and audible, Dr Jay preplied, "Yes... You were in here. On the afternoon of your admission to SaRS last Sunday. This is where we performed the necessary pre-admittance medical insurance held check and completed the intake questionnaire... Interrogation Room Won.[459]"

---

[456] This doesn't mean an antonym of important, which would be irrelevant, meaningless, or even insignificant; it is a significantly more important meaning than any of those words could ever convey, in the bad way, again.

[457] He hadn't... This was a specific report just for Donald, as he was the only patient who had participated without first obtaining their Doctor's authorisation. But Nurse Jack would have liked very much the thought that he was capable of performing such a feat.

[458] What Dr Jay was reading was Nurse Jack's observations of Donald on the bus trip itself. There was a comment about him not reacting to a funny joke some of the other patients shared with each other.

[459] Donald could even hear the incorrect spelling of the correct word.

Shaking his head, more in abject amazement than dismay, Donald left to go back to his still only temporary abode, with the comforting notion that his psychiatrist did indeed know what was going on in the deep, dark depths of his unique mind.

Arriving back at the shared common area, as soon as he stepped through the doorway into the view of the Kangaroo and Tasmanian-Tiger commoners, there was a kind of hush all over the-everyone there this afternoon. It was an incredibly pervasive silence, very much like the silence not heard from people in a church attending a funeral ceremony.

Donald was about to find out, this wasn't too far from the mark.[460]

The silence, and many of the in-patient eyes, followed Donald as he warily followed his nose to a destination. He didn't know where this destination was exactly, but he continued on regardless, using the strength of their silence to gauge his closeness in a very strange game of hot and cold.

When the silence indicated an extreme level of frozen hitherto unknown, Donald somehow just knew that he had arrived. The message on the nurse's whiteboard, "Donald Halfbrain, please see DD and Nurse Jack in the interview room at your earliest possible convenience,[461]" was also a good indication.

Suppressing the violent shudder building at the base of his spine, Donald ventured unhurriedly towards the Interrogation Room Too. He was imagining all manner of brutal metaphysical conclusions about to have his name entered into the usual place for all contracts signed at the crossroads.

Unsurprisingly, DD and Nurse Jack were both already in the room waiting for him before he tentatively opened the door. What was surprising, though, was DD's greeting, "Ah, good, Mr Halfbrain, please have a seat. Thank you."

Donald didn't like this demeanour change in DD.

He was getting used to and accepted it was easier to recognise when she was being the controlling bossy overlord. At least he knew what to expect and how to behave. This nice unfamiliar version of DD might go so far as to ask him for an opinion that he didn't, or want to, have.

---

[460] It would be a little more accurate to say: it wasn't far from *The DD*, or from *The Nurse Jack*, because *The Mark* wasn't there anymore. He had gone out flying kites with the Dave, after Norm had a fatal heart attack.

[461] Donald was expecting bad news, because DD was never this polite to anyone, let alone to a troublemaker. Donald could tell by the obscenely neat writing he was going to be made to pay for making some sort of trouble.

Facing a blatantly apparent imminent death, or worse, Donald's journey from his first memory through to this last thought didn't take nearly as long as he would have liked. What he also saw in this brief moment was death does not always have to wear a face, but if it did, it would look very much like what Donald would see looking back at him in a mirror right at this moment.

This disconcert didn't appeal to Donald in the slightest, and neither would his actual death. Commenting internally, "My own death doesn't concern me, as long as it happens a long time in the future."

Once Donald made himself uncomfortable on the remaining seat, Nurse Jack began reading from a clipboard affixed standard list, "Ahem... Discussion with one: Mr Donald Halfbrain - Today's date - Thursday afternoon - Interview Room Two.[462] Present are DD, Nurse Jack Call and Mr Donald Halfbrain.

Topics to be discussed are as follows:
- Medication increase, with the additional option of a PRN supplement;
- Overnight monitoring decrease;
- Daily permissions;
- Patient Nurse Relationships; and
- Impatient Nurse Relationships.

Sorry, I added that last one for some light humour, ha, ha, ha, hmmmmm."

"Yes, thank you, Nurse Jack. *That* will be enough of...humour, was it?"

DD didn't seem to understand the concept. And when she monotonically slowly added, "Ha, ha, ha, very droll." It was the second scariest sound Donald had ever heard uttered.

Speaking now directly towards Donald, "We are all gathered here today... Not to dredge over the alleged minor, inconsequential mistakes of your past... But to proactively influence the possibilities of what could be created out of what has already begun to become your manifest future destiny..."

Donald lost all hope of trying to follow DD's words after the "But" bit.

He was typically still all the way back when Nurse Jack had begun reading from the clipboard. It sounded more like a conversation you would have thrust upon you in a claustrophobic crowded interrogation room if you were in the process of being arrested before being arraigned for murder.

When DD continued, Donald took a small amount of comfort from the fact that her verbal tirade appeared to be now directed squarely at Nurse Jack instead of *trapezoidally* at him.

---

[462] Yes, they know, thank you for your observation... It is on their To-Do list, which unfortunately came from the same business as the room labels, and there is another large sub-set of issues entirely relating to their Do-Do lists.

"We do not create mental health because we cannot create anything. All we can do is provide the necessary tools and give direction to all those who choose to listen. The commitment we have made by working at SaRS is to try and make it just a little easier for others to meet their own commitments. We, therefore, discuss various items of importance with our valued clients."

Nurse Jack looked appropriately chastised, and Donald felt for him.[463]

"Now, to address the list of topics, shall we start at the beginning? I find the start is usually a good place to start…" DD confiscated the clipboard from Nurse Jack and gave him back a much-practised look. One which didn't need the words, "Dummkopf! Ziss is SaRZ, Vee Don't Humour Here![464]"

"Medication (increase/~~decrease~~) for Mr Halfbrain: Dr Jay has suggested - we increase the dosage of two of your medications, the antidepressant up to four happy pills,[465] and the liquid sunshine up to ten thousand thingamajigs, as, and I am quoting her here, 'This will surely be enough medication to quell most of Donald's negative thinking. But please don't tell him his positive thinking will most probably definitely be suppressed as well.' … Oops."

DD looked over to Donald for any confirmation of understanding and waited approximately three and a half seconds. When none was forthcoming, she kicked his leg under the table to discern if he was paying attention. This elicited an "Ow!" from Nurse Jack and a confused guffaw from Donald.

"OK, now that I have your attention, may I also have your understanding, appreciation, and acknowledgement, please?"

"Ermmmmm, Yeeeees?" Donald made a mental note to try and come up with a way for him to keep his thoughts to himself.

"PRN (option/~~withdrawal~~) for Mr Halfbrain: Dr Jay has also suggested - during your peak periods of stress, in all probability, you may like to avail yourself of one of several temporary *de-emotioning* medications in the future."

Donald was wondering why it had taken them so long to tell him of this ~~possibility, probability~~, whichever it was, and he could probably use some of it right now. "Hai, Moshi Moshi?[466]"

---

[463] Not much mind you, but just enough to be worthy of mentioning it here.

[464] Siegfried is very much alive, well and kicking within DD.

[465] DD has been told by the higher powers that be, to not call them Make Donald More Awesome pills anymore, so has reverted to using their generic brand pet name, which just isn't the same, even if it is still as effective.

[466] Donald was just showing off now. And failing. He thought this phrase meant, "Yes, Hello?" But it was really, thoroughly and sarcastically better aligned to, "Yes, and it's about freaking time, Hellooooo!"

Making a note in Donald's file, "Good. If you decide you want some PRN, and a Nurse agrees with you, and you haven't exceeded your daily limit, and there is stock available, and…"

This had already turned into "Blah… Blah… Blah…" for Donald.

"Next point, an overnight monitoring (~~increase~~/decrease) for Mr Halfbrain: Dr Jay has hesitantly indicated - we may lower the frequency of the overnight flight risk checks to only two interruptions per night at our discretion."

Back to the here and now, Donald had already mentally ticked *correct* his previous thoughts about what the *flashlight sorry* checks were all about and went, "OKaaaaay…"

If DD was wearing glasses, this is where she would have removed them and then cleaned for emphasis, "Daily permissions, including undocumented walks around the grounds; voluntary supervised attendance at the SaRS art classroom;[467] and fully supervised shopping trips." DD tilted her head so she could look over the top of her *emphasisery* glasses after this last item.

"Yeah. Sure.[468]"

"And finally, Patient Nurse Relationships: This is where you get to provide some anonymous feedback on our performance as your nurses. You may air out any possible grievances you may be harbouring."

DD handed the clipboard back to Nurse Jack, who removed the majority of the dangerously attached pieces of paper, leaving only a small post-it note and a safety-yellow crayon, and offered it to Donald to complete.

Donald was thinking, "I think we need to have a conversation about what you consider to be anonymous…" but the rest of his sceptical body realised there has never been, and there never will be, such a thing as *anonymous* on any managerial feedback form.

Embracing the smile he thought he might have been required to wear for the interview to end on a reasonably positive note, Donald relinquished all of his achievable expectations. Even if he was able to write something legible on the post-it note with the blunt pastel crayon supplied, these comments would neither stay confidential nor change anything in any way, anyway.

---

[467] Confusingly called the Beethoven art room. It was originally called the Picasso art room, but when they started to receive the ears, of a number of previous patients, decorum (and DD) dictated they change the name. It was a complete coincidence when they chose the name of a dead deaf person.

[468] Always an appropriate answer… As the question asker can decide for themselves if it means, "Yeah sure, absolutely," or, "Yeah sure, no way!"

The plausible definite, definitely inappropriate and bogglingly confusing response Donald came up with was, "I don't understand why understanding is not the opposite of overstanding, or why you are told to sit up straight after you sit down, or why filling in a form is the same as filling out the same form."

Twin incredulous looks[469] from DD and Nurse Jack signalled the interview had come to an end.[470] They took their clipboard, interview notes, blank post-it note and blunt yellow pastel crayon and stomped off home, leaving Donald in the interview room to fend for himself.

Steeling himself for the barrage of discomfort he was about to feel, Donald, exited the safety of seclusion. Two seconds later, just outside the door, Donald nearly bumped through Seth, who was floating in an obviously, trying hard to not look too, conspiratorial manner.

A most humorous conversation then occurred, except for Donald:
Donald "Did you see where they went?"
Seth   "Did I see where 'who' they went?"
Donald "Did you see where DD & Jack went?"
Seth   "Did I see where DD & Jack went what?"
Donald "Did you see where they went right now?"
Seth   *sigh*
Seth   "Why do you want to know where they went?"
Donald "Why do you want to know why I want to know?"
Seth   "I don't have a specific reason why I want to know!"
Donald *heroic frustration*
Donald "Well, I do. Did you see where DD & Jack went just now?"
Seth   "Do you mean did I see where they went ten minutes ago?"
Donald *confusion and acquiescence*

Donald slumped against the wall, disappointed things had started to go in the wrong direction, and he was right back to having to explain his every move. "What I wanted to do, was to ask them why I haven't made any appreciable improvement and why this doesn't seem to concern them."

---

[469] The look given was very nearly exactly the same as one produced by a pair of currently drunk partygoers, taking a romantic pause, to rest on a seat situated over a recently cracked septic tank, while trying to not throw up.

[470] Donald's mind is sometimes compared to a one-lane one-way dead-end street. This is an example of when it could be appropriately applied.

Seth was walking over a politically correct tightrope, "I wouldn't point out, to either of them, any of their perceived shortcomings. They blame each other for your lack of progress and have come to the tenuous point where they are agreeing to disagree. If you get yourself stuck in the middle, while they are like this, they are likely to join forces against you[471] until they defeat you."

Donald didn't know how Seth knew all of this, but it sounded feasible.

Seth continued, "What I suggest you do, is to start writing a diary. A lot of the other SaRS patients like to keep track of what goes on inside their heads while life goes on outside their heads. They document their every experience and any feelings about those experiences so they can remember and reflect on them at a later stage. All without the unsettling uncertainty that they might have forgotten something important."

Donald may not have been a smart man.
But... He knew a good idea when he was fish slapped by one.

Seth, seeing that his work here was almost done, finalised things by hitting a home run when he told Donald, "and I think there is a special dessert tonight for dinner... Coffee Toffee!"

"Coffee Toffee?" Donald's attention had been absolutely grabbed. These were two of his favourite words, flavours and food groups. He didn't need to be told twice to be told twice and broke into a fast amble as he headed off to dinner, with the intent to have lockjaw for the foreseeable future.

Caution: Contents may be hot after heating

Donald didn't know if Sven was referring to his last outburst; or if he was issuing a public service announcement regarding the ~~new old~~ different coffee machine that was recently installed in the dining room; but either way, he was glad to see things were getting back to a crazy kind of normal.

Another step in the crazy normal direction was Skit behaving his not quite predictable self, "Holy sticky situation, Batty-Man! The coffee toffee is making it impossible for the good people of SaRS to open their mouths and speak. This could spell the end of all civilisation as we know it!" Robin was standing there in his overacting profoundly wide stance, with his hands-on-hips at the ready and looking towards Donald for a calming speech...

Owedebt and Nota fell about laughing when they realised "Robin" was wearing his gold safety underpants on the outside and had drawn 
a large backwards "R" on his face, not understanding mirrors at all.

---

[471] Something to give definition to the concept of an Unholy Alliance.

Donald appreciated the humour but didn't laugh, as the deep sadness he felt for Robin was holding him back. Donning his superhero sidekick enabling persona, "Now, now, Boy-I-Really-Do-Wonder, there is no need to go jumping to such an extreme conclusion." Donald put his thinking fingers to his mouth in the overacting extended prayer-shhhhh position and paced in a small circle, "I think, if the people so afflicted, were to drink some Batty-coffee…"

Caution: Contents may be hot after heating.

"Yes, Sven, you are Batty-correct. They must sip some hot, but not Batty-*scaldingly* hot, coffee. The situation will then likely become less Batty-sticky. And of course, all those with Batty-dentures may simply remove and dunk."

"Holy Batty-proposition Batty-Man, you have just saved the entire Batty-universe from an unbelievably sticky peril with an equivalently unbelievably simple solution. How awkwardly Batty would it have been if we all had to learn how to read lips to hear what people were saying?[472]"

With everyone choosing to have coffee-toffee and coffee…

Caution: Contents may be hot after heating.[473]

…with their dinner, Donald's upcoming attempt to plan, a hatching of a Medication Avoidance scheme, was put on hold. Donald reasonably reasoned, "as the few people in the vicinity of the dining room who can still talk are: Skit (Robin), Owedebt, Nota and Sven; it probably isn't a spiffing jolly good idea to try and formulate a strategy, regarding the avoidance of any mind-altering medication, without at least, the sum total of, three whole minds present."

Owedebt and Nota left on their conjoined oblivious way, telling everyone (or, more correctly, anyone), who would listen to them about the "Bats in the Belfry" episode of the *Batty-Man and Robin* show, they had just witnessed.[474]

---

[472] He really was just a simple one-dimensional sidekick of a character.

[473] Yes, we get the picture, thanks. Sven has apparently contracted a case of scratched record. What do you mean, "What is a scratched record?"

[474] Justifying Donald's earlier People Bongo answer to, "2. Has a secret they have told everyone." with, "Owedebt Dear (She seems unable to help herself)" If Owedebt ever hears what Donald wrote, she will probably help herself to a half full schooner glass of slapping him upside the head.

Sven (taking on the stereotyped role of Alfredo, the Swedish Butler), Robin Boy-I-Really-Do-Wonder and Donald as Batty-Man, all retired to the "library" where Sven lit the fantasy open fireplace; poured Donald and Robin a helping of port flavoured jelly; and passed out some *"It's a Boy"* chocolate cigars.

They stayed there for several hours and discussed some most important and to them pressing worldwide issues, including:

- Why is "it" always found in the last place you look for anything?
- Is a frozen dog called a "pupsicle?"
- Is "Halo-ween," a programme to detoxify a computer game addict?
- Why is *infinitesimal* such a long word?
- Why is *tall* shorter than *short*, and *big* smaller than *small*?
- Why isn't coming down an escalator a "de-escalation?"

And, to round it out to a nice even seven, the most important question:

- When you put a DVD away in its DVD case, *upside down*, is the writing on it upside down, or is the silver side facing out?

Donald selected a random book from the shelf and sat back down to enjoy his jelly and chocolate while reading the book and expanding his mind. When he started to read the book, he discovered it was a story all about a fascinating old building and how it became a mental hospital...

Before long, but after short, probably somewhere around medium, Nurse Hatchet made her introductory appearance. Donald hadn't stayed up this late before and had missed all the times she had been on duty. He wasn't even aware there was a medication time available after 8pm.

Nurse Hatchet said, "There you are, Mr Halfbrain; I have been looking for you everywhere... Your room, here...literally everywhere!"

Donald didn't bother to correct her.

"The bell for last-ditch medication has tolled... And it told me you haven't had your medication yet tonight."

He didn't bother to correct her again.

"Please follow me to the medication nook, where I can dispense with you and the formal notification of the medicine delivery process in one of the big books of medication given, received and prescribed."

He didn't even bother trying to understand why she thought she was making sense this time. He knew what she was miserably failing to mean. He was tired, obviously feeling non-confrontational, not to mention he was now hearing voices in his head saying he should just get it over and done with, so he thought, "Why don't I just get it over and done with?"

The voices he was hearing were coming from Sven and Robin.

After exhausting their touched, less-than-full mental capacities, Sven and Robin took their leave of Donald, and by association of Nurse Hatchet, as they had both already taken their given, received and prescribed today's evening's medication. Somewhere between the pupsicle and the DVD conversations.

Sven parted with a final, for the day, extended cookie:

OCD/C - the band you simply must go and see.
With hits such as:[475]

- ♯ Autistic Re: Autistic (Inspired by TNT - AC/DC) p265.*
- ♯ Back in SaRS
- ♯ Brain Shake **
- ♯ C. O. D. (Cause of Depression)
- ♯ Dirty Deeds Done with Drugs
- ♯ For Those About to Crack (We Commit You)
- ♯ Gimme My Tablet
- ♯ Give the Man a Drug
- ♯ High Dosage
- ♯ Highway to SaRS
- ♯ Inject the Venom **
- ♯ It's a Long Way Through the Day (If You're Feeling Sad 'n' Blue)
- ♯ Let There Be Meds
- ♯ Meltdown **
- ♯ Nervous Breakdown
- ♯ Overdose **
- ♯ Rock 'n' Roll Is Medication
- ♯ Rock the Blues Away **
- ♯ Safe in SaRS Asylum
- ♯ SaRS-Break
- ♯ You Drugged Me All Night Long
- ♯ Who's Mad? Who?

---

[475] * Extract from The Donald Diaries.

** These are actual unmolested titles of Accadacca songs.

Do I have to do more than just indicate where I got the inspiration for things such as this? I guess an editor/publisher will tell me. This might also prove interesting (for me), to see if they actually read this and tell me the answer. (She said: No you don't and yes I read it hahahaha – Awesome job Kerry).

Two un-laden Swallows and a quick tooth Brush Cuckoo later...[476]
Donald, the dopey Galah, was in bed.

And I'm off too.
Night, Night...

---

[476] Ni, it doesn't come with wafers!
And "African or European" don't enter into it, you very naughty boy.
I think I'm mixing my *Montyphors* to come up with these euphemisms...

Chapter 18:
Friday on His Mind
(Inside/Outside SaRS)

"**A**nother day in the coal mines for me." was not a thought Donald traditionally had when he woke up first thing in the morning, or rousing in the late afternoon, or becoming conscious whenever. And in keeping with one of his most sacred of traditions, from long before he was ever born, he didn't have it on this fine Friday morning at SaRS either.

"You really think this is fine?" he rhetorically asked himself.

"Well, just take a look out the window... That's outside, that is!"

"And it can jolly well, just stay out there, for all I care."

"Do you really believe that is true? Underneath, I think you do care."

"I believe, only that I believe, I think it to be true."

"Oh, come on... It's an awesome day! The sun is a bright shade of shiny; the laughing kookaburras aren't laughing at us; and the next-door cows are all lined up alphabetically, by size, waiting to be milked. We should get up, all one of us, and go out there... To see what there is to be seen..."

"Can I have some of whatever it is that you are on?"

"Aren't we forgetting something...? Where did our manners go...?"

"Someone left my couth out in the rain."

Thunk......!

      Boing......!

            Splotch......![477]

---

[477] Donald came splashing down back to planet Earth. It was an inelegant journey... Via the wall of his room, his borrowed mattress and a, surprisingly unexplained, puddle of something on the floor, explaining the splashing.

All the medication Donald takes to make himself *better* is firstly going to play havoc with his, before and after waking up, dreams... apparently.[478]

Even though he was still in a partial stupor from his earlier *morningmare*, Donald's dressing, morning ablutions and devouring of breakfast all went off without a hitch. The recent memory of falling into an unidentified puddle on the floor, hopefully, left by a mundane wet uncouth, wasn't helping his sanity any. Rather than going back to his room to hibernate, to the common area to consternate, or even trying to alternate between the two, Donald made what might have, in fact, been the first decision he has ever made 100% on his own. The fact he suggested it to himself earlier made this fact slightly dubious.

Utilising his newly acquired ability of undocumented walking around the grounds, Donald set out to walk around the grounds of SaRS, with no specific goal in mind, except to go for a quiet walk around. But, as he was walking, he started to pay attention to his surroundings, appreciating the various colours, multitudes of sounds and assortment of smells. While at the same time letting go of all the noxious thoughts flowing through his mind. Donald hated to admit it to himself... This was actually becoming a very calming exercise.

In no apparent order,[479] Donald discovered many interesting things to look at, to listen to and even to have a smell of. He still wasn't prepared to touch or taste anything of nature in its natural habitat yet.

Carpark 1 - Donald deduced this was the senior staff's carpark. He could recognise the authority permeating the area, the quality of the vehicles parked in the individually assigned spaces and the sign posted at the entry said...

---

[478] Dreams spilling over into the semi-lucid time between asleep and awake is a less common, but marginally humorous to watch, side-effect, commonly attributed to a change in medication amount, timetable, or as in this case, both. I'm fairly sure I have told you this already... Do try to keep up please.

[479] Actually, it looks like it is somewhat alphabetic to me.

Walking alongside the short row of parked cars, Donald started mindfully allocating the various cars to the various senior staff. Naturally, this was a task his literal mind was adept at.

The standouts of the group:
"**DR MD**"   Black Mercedes Benz 600 Limousine - Dr Andy Coughed[480]
"**DR GJ**"   Pink Debonair Convertible BMW M3 - Dr Gee Jay
"**I AM MD**" Stink Pink Try Hard Convertible Mini - Houts Marted
Squeezed into a spot usually reserved for a motorcycle:
"**BNDOVR**" Svelte Suede Red Suzuki Cappuccino - Ma'am Cybill Flex
And parked, just to the side, attracting no undue attention or complaints:
"**DD 666**"   Desert Camouflaged Hummer H1   - Nurse Dolly Dix

Carpark 2 - Identified easily as the visitor/patient/rest of staff's car park:
- Cars parked under a layer of tree excrement, bird poo and bat guano probably belong to the long-term residents;[481]
- Vehicles parked randomly on the grassy knolls; in disabled person car spaces; or in the six six-minute-maximum-allowed-time drop off zone spaces are likely owned by outpatients attending a group session; and
- Any others who park their cars here are either visitors or are the left-over remaining non-senior non-Flex non-DD staff.

Donald included the long driveway as part of this area because the sides of the driveway are used much like a third overflow carpark. There is nothing of importance to mention here, except for the eight speed bumps. Each speed bump, from the Hospital to the out direction, increases in size, resulting in the last speed bump being referred to as the Stumpy Sumps Bump.[482] This is there to remove the possibility of a quick escape, and the amount of striped yellow paint that has been stripped off shows the effectiveness of this ploy.

---

[480] This is a real vehicle. It appears alternately with a 35-year-old two-door Rolls Royce Camargue that looks like an old brown Aston Martin Vantage.

[481] Any inmate who parks here has to relinquish a set of car keys, which are then locked up with their other confiscated dangerous items. This process works extremely well for first time admissions. However, once you become aware of this rule, it is easy to bring a second set of keys or just park outside the grounds. Neither of which is *technically* breaking any of the rules.

[482] This speed bump is sponsored by Stumpy Sumps, and they advertise a discount, on sump replacements, for any SaRS patient or visitor.

Cows - The cows next door made it onto this list by virtue of a countback. Initially tying with the church-like facility, the cows ultimately triumphed. Their brand of smelly excrement was more useful by being a good fertiliser for the sideways rose garden. Donald also likes the fact that you can count on a cow to always go, "Moo," no matter what its breed is, where it lives, who owns it, who is telling the story and even what language the story is being told in...

Donald didn't particularly approve of the field segregation based solely on hide colour. Still, when he asked one of the black and white ones, they weren't worried about colour discrimination. It may have been a poor choice, though, as it clarified: it couldn't understand the accent of the brown and white ones; the plain whities had an elitist attitude it didn't much care for; and mumbled something about the greater availability of its chocolate milk, over the caramel equivalent and a much higher profit margin product, over ordinary white milk. The cow ambled away to go and stand udder deep in the damn dam.

These cows, along with Seth's suggestion from a few pages ago for him to start writing a diary, and because he already writes most things down anyway, will eventually culminate in Donald expelling many pages of his own fertiliser... For example:

Re: Excuse Me Myth? (No inspiration required) p269.

⚥   Extract from The Donald Diaries.

Cubby House - Around the side of the SaRS mansion, hidden from all the places where a person might be able to see, is a track that disappears into the forest. If you follow this track, far into the forest, to a point where you think the path can't possibly go on any further, you will find a giant tree. When you look up and see that the lowest branches are closer to the sky than they are to the ground, with no possible way of reaching them unless you are equipped with claws, wings, or more than a vestigial tail, the presence of a cubby house up there is miraculous.

The tree is an old gum tree.
There is a laughing Kookaburra sitting in it.
But he doesn't eat gumdrops, and there aren't any monkeys.

Donald has no idea if any of this story is true. While he was out walking, he bumped into Nurse Jack, who was out following his own ritualistic morning mindfulness intake routine in the garden.[483]

---

[483] The gardens of SaRS are going to be atypically, amply and aptly, described in a minute or so, depending on your reading proficiency.

Nurse Jack asked Donald if he would like some company. When he said he did, they both sat in the garden, and Nurse Jack entertained Donald with some of the local legends. One of which was the story of *The House in the Sky*.

This story has been around for tens of thousands of years in various guises:
- About a place for the Bunnyip to hibernate during the dry season far above the reach of any predators;[484]
- A nesting home for the pre-flightless Emu before they were tricked into cutting their wings short and lost their ability to fly; or
- As the hideout for the despicably cunning Drop Bear, who needed to be high enough to escape the jumping reach of the Giant Kangaroo.

Gardens / Maze / Pavilion - Donald didn't see much more overall around here than he did several days or 75 years ago...there were lush green lawns throughout the garden; with many rose beds, of various colours, in differing states of being made, and either yes, or no, when considering their verticality attribute; and the centrepiece of the garden is a flourishing hedge maze.

Donald added to this complex description by recalling that at the maze's very centre is a spectacularly ornate pavilion which, if the not-a-memory scene details are to be believed, is situated above a Minotaur's dwelling.

Navigating his way through the hedge maze was a *geekingly* simple D&D task for Donald. He is an avid proponent of the left-hand-out method[485] and was able to utilise this to successfully negotiate himself to the middle of the maze without any sign of stress, either due, undue, or overdue.

When he promptly arrived at the pavilion, Donald shared another private chuckle with himself as he remembered the label given to the space inside the pavilion in the black and white aerial photo.

---

[484] Three predators who may have hunted the Bunnyip were: the rare and extinct Wellington Cave Cows (Heffalump sized carnivorous wombats); Tas-animated Antipodean Devils; and the Long-Legged Land Lizards (an eleven-meter-long relative of the Saltwater Crocodile).

[485] The left-hand-out method is where a person travelling through the maze, without a map or chainsaw, puts out their left hand until it touches a wall. The maze traveller then follows their nose, keeping their left-hand in contact with the wall at all times, until they reach the centre of the maze.

If you are deficient in left hands, the right-hand-out method will achieve the exact same result, only backwards.

He then went on to contradict himself about not seeing anything new by recalling all of the new information he discovered on his foray into the gardens of today. The gardening team utilises water from the adjacent river to keep up the lushness. This information was garnered (eventually) from a sign located at the end of the tunnels leading to the river...[486]

PSH... Garden Liquefication [487]

Riviera Water is in Usefulness

Wholly Mowly Hydrostatic Allowance #345-987

The Battle of Kingswood Hill memorial garden commemorates (it doesn't celebrate) the first recorded battle between Aboriginals and *The Settlers*:

- White settlers arrived and assumed the farming rights of the land;
- Local Darug people fought to defend their land from this invasion; and
- Colonial authorities sent in the troopers with the express instruction to destroy the whole local Aboriginal population of the area.

The sacred fire pit, forming a central part of the memorial, is now covered with mesh, overgrown with weeds and full of stagnant water.[488]

Smokers Hideouts - There are several of these dotted over the grounds of SaRS. Smokers are sent as far away from the civilised population as is humanly possible, both literally and figuratively. The major hideout is located where the staff carpark meets the mostly disused tennis court, a second one is where the driveway meets the little-used swimming pool, and the third is, conveniently, situated wherever the smokers hope they won't be seen and get caught.

---

[486] "Tunnels? What tunnels? We don't know about no stinking tunnels!" you say. Patience, all will be revealed as soon as I figure out what to write.

[487] Doesn't it annoy you? Because it annoys me! When people, especially commentators and reporters use big words instead of infinitesimally ones. They think it makes them sound edumacated, but when they don't know what the magnanimous word means, they can get it incredulously differential.

[488] This is sadly fitting; reflecting on what the settlers did, the depth of all ongoing ignorance and the lack of remediation said not to be required.

Donald kept his distance from all three hideouts. Treating the smokers like you would a tribe of monkeys in a zoo: interesting to look at, but if you get too close, they are liable to heap their poo onto you instead of onto each other.

Some tell-tale signs you are getting too close to them are:
- A cessation of all chatter and a flinching of looks towards you;
- Reactive hiding behind their backs of anything incriminating;[489] and
- Obviously, the omnipresent omnipotent smell!

It is a legendary undocumented fact; the worse a smoker smells, the less they are aware of their smell's pervasiveness, and the greater is their increase in the associated vehement denial of this fact.

Tunnels - Underneath the Head Shrink's office, inside the spectacularly ornate pavilion and in the middle of the lush hedge maze, lies a dated system of tunnels that ultimately take you right down to the river. Donald was able to grab one of the glossy tourist information pamphlets containing a detailed description of the under-the-hedge-maze maze in-amazing-completeness.

Entering the old tunnels, through the previously not hidden "Beware of the Minotaur!" signed trap door, and then following the detailed map on the back of the middle page of the standard tri-fold pamphlet,[490] Donald was able to negotiate the sanitised, illuminated and de-thrilled tunnels to their river end.

When Donald cautiously went through the trap door to begin his hunt, a great load of downright disappointing nothing happened:
- No ancient, potentially deadly traps were incongruously activated;
- No hidden angry foe was revealed, and there was defiantly
- No great feeling of triumphal success.

Donald was disappointed. It felt similar to walking through a forest on an artificial man-made elevated, ironically, wooden trail, so there is no damage to the natural surroundings. When it should have felt, exactly not.

What did create an interesting amount of interest for Donald, however, was the presence of several untouched, unmarked and unlit corridors leading off somewhere into the undocumented and unknown as yet underneath. It kept alive some hope he may, one day, be able to find the lair of the Minotaur, the hospital archives and finally, the solution to the *Clueless!* puzzle.

---

[489] This tell is related to their third hideout only. At the first and second, they proudly display their instruments of mass carcinogenic rejection.

[490] You know, the ones that have three pages and only two folds...

When Donald returned from these wanderings, he found Houts and DD[491] waiting for him. Houts had ventured into the Kangaroo ward looking for him and a reason for his morning group gathering lack of attendance. It wasn't so much Donald had missed group; it was Houts had missed Donald's input to the group, thereby saddling him with the responsibility he held in the first place.

DD was all set to start berating Donald about missing the not-mandatory but-you-still-need-to-go-to group session when he said he had been outside mindfully walking around, catching vitamin D and having some much-needed exercise. Any scolding of Donald now would have come across as being pretty petty. Instead, she turned to, and on, Houts... Saying something along the lines of, "Donald was right. You were wrong. Get over it."

Donald was left a little dumbstruck by this. He never expected to be on the right side of any conversation about him, held partially by or with DD. This is the excuse he will ultimately use for his own edification, as to one possible reason why he couldn't recall exactly what words she said.

Houts was also a little put off by what DD said. He hadn't come to scold Donald for missing the earlier morning's group session. He had only come to give him the pre-prepared handouts and a copy of the group's notes. All he could manage was a bewildered, "here are the notes..." After handing over the stack of paper, he turned to the left and left without further explanation.

Donald quickly flipped through the mountain of notes. Several question-conversation-statements instantly started to slowly manifest in his mind:[492]

- ✗   *"English Language Idiosyncrasies... No wonder the pile is so big;"*
- ✗   *"Surely this amount can't be the product of just one group session;"*
- ✗   *"Part 1 (Friday morning)... Ahhhhh;"* and
- ✗   *"Maybe it was a good thing I had missed it."*

Entirely obliviously, he had left DD hanging there, waiting for a respectful amount of thank you very much; Donald took the morning's notes and went eagerly to his room to have a good old read.

DD, sensing the requirement for her to be here was no more, also left.

---

[491] DD is very cunning, she will rarely fight a battle on her own, preferring to have someone else to blame if things go pear shaped.

[492] You have probably figured this out by now, but still...

Donald likes to do most of his thinking in bullet points when he is able:

- ✗   It makes it easier for him to understand what he is thinking;
- ✗   He likes everything to line up nice and neatly; and
- ✗   There might be more than a little OCD flowing through his veins.

English Language Idiosyncrasies

○ *Part 1 (Friday morning) – Regular English Language Concepts*

    Euphemisms

    Plurals

    Schoolyard Spelling Rules and Exceptions

    Sounds vs Spelling

    Real Words that should be Made Up

○ *Part 2 (Friday afternoon) – Irregular English Language Concepts*

    Usage of Words

    Foreign Languages (Today's choice is stereo-a-typical Russian)

    Made Up Words that should be Real (Selection)

○ Extra Credit – Scrabble Rules

SaRS Whiteboard 3 – English Language Idiosyncrasies

Part 1 - Regular English Language Concepts[493]

      Euphemisms

        ○ Abbreviations

           - "The big C" (Incorrect spelling of The big Kahuna)

           - "W.C."   (The original Euphemism)

        ○ Complete Phrase Replacement

           - "I'm on a career break" (Unemployed)

           - "Not with us anymore" (Dead, Bereft of Life)

        ○ Dropping the Word

           - "What the - is happening here?"

           - "Who the - do you think you are?"

        ○ Basic Word Replacement

           - "Let's get the heck out of here!"

           - "Lick off, Chunky"

           - "What the flock?"

        ○ Technical Word Replacement

           - "English language idiosyncrasies"

           - "He's a gluteus maximus"

           - "I am going to use the facilities"

---

[493] Acknowledging the top page of the most-unhelpful-standard-sideways-layout-that-always-makes-stapling-a-minor-disaster style, Donald mentally removed the formatting for the following pages.

- ¤   Plurals
  - ○   Plurals that don't have a single
    - Arms   (as in gun, knife, etc.)
    - Jeans   (except in the case of Billy)
  - ○   Singles that may/or may not also act as a plural
    - Fun
    - Poetry

- ¤   Schoolyard Spelling Rules and Exceptions
  - ○   "A" before consonants; "An" before vowels[494]
    - Donald is a unique person
    - Donald wrote this in an hour
  - ○   I before E except after C[495]
    - Science
    - Weigh

- ¤   Sounds vs Spelling
  - ○   Different spelling, same pronunciation
    - Red / Read
    - Sense / Cents / Scents (Is the S or the C silent in scents?)
  - ○   Same spelling, different pronunciation
    - Advertisement / Advertise
    - Plait / Trait
    - Rhetoric / Rhetorical

- ¤   Real Words that Should Be Made Up
  - ○   Abluted
    - Washed clean
  - ○   Acronymised
    - Past tense of turning a phrase into an acronym in Britain
  - ○   Oxymoronicity
    - Having the quality of being oxymoronic

Lunch was another non-event. Donald managed to avoid all verbal, visual and physical contact. So much so that we now find ourselves jumping forward a few hours to the outcome of Part 2.

---

[494] This is a rookie mistake… An accurate rule is: An *a* before a consonant sound, and an *an* immediately preceding a vowel sound.

[495] There are approximately 6,496 exceptions to this rule.

Part 2 - Irregular English Language Concepts[496]

- ¤ Usage of Words
  - ○ Acronyms
    - BOGOF   - **Buy One Get One Free**
    - BotM!   - Beware of the Minotaur!
    - DOGoN   - **Donald-Oh-Goody-Not scale**
    - PSH... for Men   - Private Psychiatric Hospital for Men
    - SPLAT   - **Select, Practice, Leave, Always, Tell**
    - STUFF   - **SaRS, Treatment, Usual, Freely, Free**
    - TftPoO   - **Two for the Price of One**
  - ○ Alternate Meanings
    - Hippocampus   - Where hippopotamuses go to study
    - Unison   - What Cane (of Cane and Abel) became
    - Universe   - A very short song
    - Wonderful   - Full of I wonder and questions
  - ○ Misuse
    - Decimate   - Is NOT an extreme word for Devastate
    - Petrified   - Is NOT an extreme word for Terrified
  - ○ Negative Questions (Where there is no short positive answer)
    - "When did you stop beating your wife?"
    - "You don't like me, do you?"
  - ○ Oxymoronic
    - Monosyllabic
    - Infinitesimal
  - ○ Rhetorical Rhetoric
    - If you answer a rhetorical question, are you wrong?
    - Is a rhetorical question just a statement in disguise?
    - What do you get when you cross a rhetorical question with a bad joke?

- ¤ Foreign Languages
  - ○ How to write stereo-a-typical TV Russian
    - No "a"
    - Rolling "r"
    - Use "ee" instead of "i"
    - Use "khkhkhkhkh" instead of "h"
    - Use "ye" instead of "e"
    - Use "ze" instead of "the"
  - ○ Donald would like computer languages recognised here, please

---

[496] Otherwise known as *Donaldisms*.

Made Up Words that Should Be Real (with Donald Meanings)

- ahalf — the fraction portion before *behalf*
- ahockphlegm — a juicier *ahphlegm*
- ahphlegm — the sound of saying *ahem*
- Alanis-type — coincidences, good/bad luck; not irony
- a-mental-ican — misinformed, mistaken, misnomer
- banananana — can start spelling *banana*, but can't stop
- blurtation — a sudden spraying excitement
- browny — could be mistaken for *brown*
- chidlets — baby children (an all-offspring group)
- clumless — clumsy and helpless to prevent it
- coinsidious — insidiously coincidental
- Confuciusectomy — procedure to remove mindless thoughts
- convenientness — having a convenient quality
- cookied — recited a fortune cookie saying
- déjà vu-dar — ability to detect occurrences of déjà vu
- déjà vu-dar — ability to detect occurrences of déjà vu
- disacquired — negative past tense of *acquire*
- Donald — Hero
- edumacated — uneducated way of saying *educated*
- emphasisery — used for the purpose of emphasising
- ~~exclamestion mark~~ ½ — replaced by an interabang ‽
- faultfully — thoughtfully at fault
- forernal — a very, very, very long time
- gredisess — a great disaster with great distress
- hink — to think hopefully
- inconspiratorial — trying to avoid looking like a conspirator
- inershated — 2:1 mix of inundated and overshadowed
- institutionalisable — worthy of being institutionalised
- interprebriefing — concurrent interviewing and debriefing
- ism — generic term for all discrimination
- ist — it is, but it isn't
- laughlargic — too tired to laugh (esp. at bad jokes)
- lemminged — behaved as one of a group
- literalation — providing a literal definition, literally
- lyring — rhyming lyrics (esp. poet, don't know it)
- malproficient — performing a proficient task badly
- mastress — a genderless androgynous boss
- monomage — a self-painted homage of self
- Montyphors — Monty Python quotes (esp. Ni)
- moreology — more than three books in a sequence
- morningmare — a bad dream during the morning hours

- muttbled — muttered mumblings
- outroduction — closing remarks at the end of something
- outternal — emotions you emit but don't experience
- pantsy — relating to the region of your pants
- patty-man — a subordinate who pats on demand
- pleeeeease — a desperate request
- plottens, the thick — spoonerism of *the plot thickens*
- polite-ish — verging on the *polite*
- preplied — replying to a question before it is asked
- pupsicle — a frozen dog
- purpley — could be mistaken for the colour *purple*
- realisationalist — one who helps uncover artistic talent
- rectangularprismicle — a cubicle with uneven edge lengths
- scaredest — the person most scared
- schnozdinger — a punch in the nose (or not)
- screwdrivering — using a metaphorical screwdriver
- sest — sitting and resting
- shmancy — looks fancy and expensive, even if it isn't
- sphygmopersonometer — non-sexist *sphygmomanometer*
- spoilerification — revealing some facts, but not the ending
- strae — disturbed air flow (esp. behind a walker)
- tantrumed — past tense of *tantrum*
- teenagerish — teenage like (esp. immature responses)
- tenish — ten, or nearly thereabouts, give or take
- thats — plural of *that*
- twangy — the sound of the first pluck of a banjo
- un-manage-a-trios — an uncontrollable group of three
- untrovert — overt avoidance (esp. of people)
- weirdios — exercising using both weights and cardio

Donald came up with this list, and the correlated definitions, all by himself. Focussing on a selection of the thoughts to have gone through his mind during the past week has assisted Donald to stay sane while he has been in SaRS. He will also go on to complete the optional extra credit topic, as usually required, even though he didn't know what he was earning credit towards.[497]

---

[497] The ward award system at SaRS hasn't been in use for a long time and they haven't updated the documentation. At one stage, it was used to pit each ward against the three others, vying for a perpetual trophy. While this might sound like it is a normal thing to do, when it was introduced the staff observed a considerable decline in the cooperative attitudes of the patients.

Scrabble Rules
- ✗ Word Meaning
  - ○ You may only play a word if you know roughly what it means.
  - ○ If you play a word and are challenged successfully on the meaning (i.e. you don't know the meaning), all the tiles you played this turn are removed from the board and placed back in your hand, points are scored negatively to your score, and your turn is complete.
  - ○ If any[498] challenge is unsuccessful (i.e. you do know the meaning), points for the challenged word only are scored negatively to the challenger's score, and play continues as normal.
  - ○ A challenge must be made as soon as a word is played.
  - ○ These rules apply to all words played or extended in this turn.

- ✗ Bonuses
  - ○ Offensive words earn a double word score multiplier bonus.
  - ○ This bonus only applies to the offensive word and only when the player of the word designates it to be offensive.
  - ○ If the played word extends an existing word, where the word was not previously designated as offensive, if it is appropriate to do so now, then you may choose to designate it as such.
  - ○ If a challenger can use the designated offensive word in a correct non-offensive manner, the bonus does not apply.

- ✗ Blank tiles
  - ○ You may replace a played blank tile with a letter tile it represents.
  - ○ You may replace any played letter tile with a blank tile.
  - ○ These actions are permitted at any stage during the game.
  - ○ Points scored for any words affected by the addition, or removal, of a blank tile, are not altered from the initially played score.
  - ○ You may not reverse this action once it is fingers off complete until the next turn.

After Donald diligently completed this extra credit task, he went to Houts to hand in his work. He was hoping to get some sort of well-done-pat-on-the-back, but when Houts referred him to Sven, all he got in response was a brain full of surprising disbelief and astonishment.

---

[498] Any number of players may challenge any number of words played or extended (even though it doesn't make sense) this turn. In challenges where there is more than one challenger, they equally share the negative points scored (rounded up to the nearest whole number) if unsuccessful.

Donald's disbelieving reaction changed to be just surprising astonishment when Sven cookied...

Why does resign not mean to sign again?
Why is dismember not the opposite of remember?
Why isn't palindrome a palindrome?

Three questions that Donald has in his *to be asked* pile.

Gobsmacked with discombobulation, he barely watched as everyone else packed up and left. He firmly resolved to play a game of scrabble, with Sven, before too much longer.

But the game was going to have to wait for another day because today, Donald was focused on just getting through. His full amount of physical and mental exertion had been exhausted for today, except for the small amount of both he expected would get him through dinner, medication and into bed.

And it did.

Re: The Poet p270.
x   Extract from The Donald Diaries.

Chapter 19:
Weekend Artists
(and Amateurs)

Waking up today would have been like any other day for Donald if today had been any other day, but it wasn't. Donald liked the days that bookended the working week because it evened out the platform for his train of thought. He had trained himself to think everyone else was sad on the weekends because they didn't get to go to work. Donald didn't realise most normal people didn't like missing, not having to go to work on the weekend.[499] He twisted himself into knots just thinking about it.

A weekend at SaRS means there are no group sessions to fill in the bulk of the day, and there are no Greys to perform the Daily Health Check. On the flip side of this dejection, it also means there are no psychiatrists or psychologists chasing after you, so there are no becoming normal hoops to jump through.

What was available on the weekend was the Beethoven art room.

There are many types of art available for the inmates, each with its own individual benefits and drawbacks. Donald will find out the major drawbacks for him are his lack of physical art talent, his lackadaisical attitude to this lack and his incorrect expectation of the typical condescending nature of some of the well-meaning volunteer artistic talent extractors.

---

[499] Most commonly, the *calendar* week goes from Sunday to Saturday. Saturday, therefore, is the end of the week and the start of the weekend (the week-end-weekend-start), while Sunday, is the start of the week and the end of the weekend (the week-start-weekend-end). Seems legit.

But before any of this could be discovered, there was the small matter of discovering what would be for breakfast. Donald failed to get up moments before his alarm went off, an unusual occurrence because his alarm had failed its purpose, as wasn't its usual practice. He was conveniently forgetting he had left his alarm clock at home and was relying on his paddle to wake him.

Donald instinctively gathered he had missed breakfast. This unimportant event made his greeting of the day about as enthusiastic as his answering the phone manner during normal dinner time, when he knew it would most likely be a telemarketer from a different time zone calling about a big investment opportunity in something he didn't want, but most definitely needed.

Forcing himself to get dressed in a left-over ensemble of whatever looked to be the cleanest,[500] clearly indicating, to all and sundry, he had a desperate need for a trip to the laundry. Putting this thought on the backburner, with all of his other neglected outward appearance thoughts, Donald went out in search of food. He checked his pockets for two $2 coins on his way.

When Donald arrived at the common area, he became aware of the shock and awe goings-on in the TK kitchen area. Apparently, Mindy had the culinary skills to cook up a gastronomic feast out of the slim pickings available from the dual fridges, corner cupboard and her personal collection of at least thirteen assorted, unmarked and non-sequential secret herbs and spices.

Perusing the captivated crowd, this is what Donald found:

- Owedebt was over the moon, devouring a large plate of Arnold's Milk Cardboard biscuits,[501] buttered with margarine and salt 'n' peppered with sultanas. They sounded lip-smacking good;[502]
- Nota, as usual, was right next to Owedebt and making nearly as much noise slurping her two-minute instant porridge noodles. It did sound like an odd juicy breakfast to Donald, but who was he to judge?
- Nelo was hoeing into a breakfast black pudding. These are made using the same recipe as normal black pudding, but with extra oatmeal; and
- Got's empty bowl showed evidence of once holding some sauerkraut laced with lashings of fruit-flavoured vodka. Her *sableish* grin was also displaying evidence of being laced with lashings of the same vodka.

---

[500] And therefore, it probably also smelled and tasted the cleanest.

[501] Only the quintessential, original, historical flagship product would do. Sadly, the largest producer of biscuits in Australia is being passed around the coffee table of international big business, like so many biscuits.

[502] Not the concept, the actual sound she was making while eating them.

Shock and *awe* are two words that Donald rarely finds reason to use in the same sentence, except in a sentence trying to explain that *shock* and *awe* are two words he rarely finds reason to use in the same sentence, recursive. This particular Saturday morning, Mindy had unwittingly facilitated Donald in their use; both of them have now been written three times in two sentences.

Mindy proactively grilled Donald about his desires, "What delectable, non-leftover food would you like me to prepare for your breakfast today?" which was almost as surprising as the actual food she was preparing.

Donald hesitantly replied, "Coffee… With one of everything, please." and soon he was just as content as everyone else. While he was calmly sitting, drinking and thinking, he also made the discovery of the availability of the art room. Once he had a chance to digest the recent strange occurrences, he went on to explore what options were available to him, artsy-fartsy wise…[503]

Art Therapy at SaRS

Traditional Painting – Up to five colours may be used at once

Plaster Mould Painting – Large selection of gnomes available

Paper Mâché – Various colour gloss publications for inspiration

Bead Bracelet – Limit of one band and 19 beads per customer

* Canvases may be purchased from the Administration Desk

** Only soft solid, hollow, or liquid media is allowed at SaRS

*** Copper Embossing and Wood Carving no longer available

SaRS Official 8 – Art Therapy at SaRS

Donald investigated the art facilities at SaRS, using his paddle, and found: "Here at SaRS, we offer a wide variety of art styles for selection in conjunction with our *Art as Therapy* programme. This gives all of our patients a personal, often unique, outlet to express their innermost emotions in a non-destructive creative way. They are all given the opportunity to imagine their own journey of deliverance to a specific time and place, providing them with a well-being synergy and holistic health in a way only they can understand.[504]"

---

[503] The existence of the Beethoven art room is an example of when Donald doesn't remember he has forgotten something, as DD had mentioned it to him, during the non-brief debrief of his brief-less debrief, after shopping.

[504] Donald didn't even try to understand what the author meant by this. As long as no one was going to force him to start playing the banjo, he was fine and dandy. Twangy, twang, twang, twang, twang, twang, twang, twang…

When he navigated down the SaRS art page to find out what "wide variety of art styles" were available, he was much more than a teensy bit disappointed to find all of the information available was obviously far out of date:

Copper Embossing - A sheet of flat copper is used as a base, and a design is drawn on it with a soft pencil. The image is then teased out of the copper by hammering various shaped tools with a light hammer, wooden mallet, or shoe until the image is clear or the artist is too tired to continue. The copper art can then be scratched by and with a sharp tool to create various shades. Etching with a caustic solution can also be made available upon special request.

Wood Carving - Donald didn't even bother reading this description, as his attention was hooked, caught and released to the next entry.

Leather Working - SaRS is proud to announce, for a strictly limited season, that Ma'am Cybill Flex will be *hostessing* a class on creating wearable gym art from vegetarian pleather. If you are interested in participating in this class or just want to be involved as a test mannequin, please leave your name with the administration desk no later than 1.11pm on the 14th of January 2019.[505]

Not knowing what else he could do, Donald started down the path of his own personal (unique?) creative deliverance journey to wellbeing synergy and holistic health. Once he arrives there, he hopes to be able to understand it.

Throwing caution to the wind, Donald navigated his way to the art room by himself, using only the thirteen signs posted at random intervals along the least indirect route. These signs were remarkably similar to the signs showing him the way to the dining room… As a guide… (Apologies if this is in B&W)

---

[505] Donald moved from being completely attention released, through most of attention disappointed, to arrive at "Attention! Dismissed!" in the blink of an eye. He wasn't even the slightest bit interested, anym⊗re, as to why copper embossing and wood carving were no longer available.

"You maniacs! You uploaded it! Ah, damn you! God damn you all to Hell!"

When he arrived at the art room, Donald found it was guarded by an anti-ferocious feline of the *I'm not fat, I'm just big furred* variety. The sign around its neck read, "Meow. My name is Picatso, Don't feed Me." This made Donald groan a lot and think a little about how Picatso and Chunky would be able to provide absolutely no entertainment if put together in a confined space.

Picatso da Kitty is a permanent resident of SaRS. She arrived one day as a vagrant, following Willy at ten paces and decided to stay. Apart from *probably* being feline, not much else is known about her lineage. If she was able to talk, there is little doubt she would tell you of her mother, who is the queen cat and her father, who is the top mouser, at some fancy dining establishment. Content with eating choice leftovers from Chef's kitchen, and a converted dog kennel as her sleeping chamber, there isn't much else a cat of leisure could desire. She has also consented to being the subject of an inmate's painting on occasion. The most famous piece from her subjectivity, *Cat Having a Nap*, is a cubist rendering homage to her namesake.

Stepping inside the art room was like stepping barefoot into a deep warm puddle of peculiar and not being able to wipe it off fast enough. The amount of art on the walls made it hard to distinguish between what was being called art and what would be complimented by being called a grimy window.[506]

Of the options available, Donald was leaning toward painting to be his vehicle of self-discovery. It looked to be the least messy, least gauche and least girly proposition. Plaster moulding, followed by painting, an Irish garden gnome didn't appeal in the slightest; papier mâché wasn't spelled correctly, and you don't want to know what Donald thought about them trying to limit his one bracelet beading to just 19 beads.

But… If painting was going to be Donald's chosen path to recovery, he was going to need much more information. The whole painting of something, not basically wall-related concept, was daunting. Not only because his most recent exposure to his own art, since high school 35 years ago, was walking down the street correcting the spelling and grammar of the graffiti artists.

He thought he knew the basic painting process:
- Start by painting the background;   No, that was wrong…
- Start by finding a space on the table to put your canvas so it doesn't interfere with any of the drying artwork;   No, that was wrong too…
- Start by obtaining a canvas.   Bingo…

---

[506] Even some of the grimy frosted windows had inmate art covering them. This was in the form of coloured-plastic-decoupage-stained-glass displays.

Not being one to be stymied by the third first step of the painting process, Donald went looking for one of the volunteers undoubtedly floating around.[507] Fairly quickly, he found Sue Rhea Liszt, the Art Therapist. Although she didn't like that term, she preferred to be thought of as the SaRS Art *Realisationalist*: One who helps people therapeutically uncover a repressed artistic talent...

Art Therapist – SaRS
Sue Rhea Liszt (no relation)
Who can paint a RAINBOW?
Sue Rhea Liszt 'Realisationalist'

Sue and Donald had an unusually long conversation about what they both considered to be art. Freely discussing ideas, including a bit of back-and-forth banter, with none of the condescension Donald had expected.

Sue Rhea Liszt is an artist of spectacular talent. Who, being an artist, has already had to deal with her own mental issues and came through unscathed with shining colours...literally! She donates her time and talent to the SaRS art room and has no expectation of any reward except for the satisfaction of knowing she is helping someone else.

She is also in the process of organising a fundraising art exhibition for the art room. Putting on display, and hopefully selling, some of the art produced by the many SaRS inhibited budding artists. Any proceeds from the sale of their artwork will be equally shared, 60:40, between the artists and the art room. This will ensure the stock of excessively prohibitively expensive non-donated art supplies will not run out in the near future.

Sue doesn't like the "Oh, never mind..." blasé attitude towards any of her artists by some of the people she has had the displeasure of meeting at SaRS. If someone produces a piece of art; expressing their innermost emotions and personal journey of deliverance, they shouldn't have to deal with anything like those condescending, "your life doesn't matter" comments.

This is exactly what Donald is fearing, "What if I paint (or write) something which is representative of *my* personal emotional journey to deliverance, and *they* don't like, or even understand, it? I mean, I sure as Hell don't like, or even understand, the subject matter I would be basing the artwork on..."

---

[507] Metaphorically only. Donald didn't have the capacity to be able to deal with any extra ghosts. Two was too many. He has trouble enough dealing with the eccentricities of the few living artists he knows. (Hi Griff☺.)

In Donald's mind, the results of his artistic efforts would elicit only positive comments, by saying he has produced a beautiful piece of art, as opposed to a disastrous piece of never mind... Because, as in group, he will be incorrectly told, "There are no wrong answers,[508] just wrong questions."

Sue could see the desire for understanding in Donald's eyes; she heard all of the trepidation in his thoughts and could smell the faint scent of fear in his heart. Taking his hand and feeling the trembling unknown, she took him for a tour of the art room, starting with the sign-in sheet.

The next while was spent in a mindful, mindless, mind-boggling blur.[509]

Sue retrieved, for Donald, two small pristine canvasses she had secretly stashed behind the storage room door. These were left behind by a previous patient who had fallen behind in his art as a cure study. She selected a couple of clean paint brushes, including a paint sponge on a stick. Finally, she asked Donald what his favourite colour was.

Donald was about to say, "I generally like me a bit of Prussian Blue," but had a second, pre-vocalised, thought this might have sounded a bit penthouse apartment pretentious. Instead, he went with, "Artists' Pigment Purple is my favourite," thus avoiding a humorous trip off the bridge of death.

Loaded up[510] with all of the painting instruments he could carry, a pair of soon to be not blank canvasses and enough purple paint to paint two purple paintings of the inside of his head, Donald found an empty space and set himself up in the perfect painting manner and set to work painting his purple mentality in progress. *Sucking in a breath after this long-winded sentence*

---

[508] Donald is feeling there are indeed wrong answers, very wrong answers and answers so very wrong they will turn a complete 360 degrees, which will leave them in exactly the same state of wrongness as they were in before.

[509] Which, I think, is partially the whole idea. As long as you notice, and then dismiss, the thought that there are no thoughts requiring notice or dismissal.

[510] Or, loaded down; whichever is your preferred choice of load direction. But do choose carefully... The first giant step is looking to be quite a doozy.

Doozy: noun, informal: Something that is outstanding or *unique of its kind*. Kind: noun: A group of people, or things, that have similar characteristics. I'll let you ponder these two doozies of dictionary meanings for a while...

Reviewing the previous painting process points:

- ☒   Start by obtaining a canvas.   Check.
- ☒   Start by finding a space on the table.   Check.
- ☒   Start by painting the background.   Bingo…

<Insert here> Some, just under three-and-a-half lines should be enough, timely time-lapse verbiage, caramel flavoured waffle or long-winded blather about Donald painting his two small blank donated-but-still-must-be-replaced canvasses completely purple. **</Insert here>**

Standing back to admire his thoughts of art, there were several arguments already forming in Donald's mind as he prepared himself for the onslaught of, "Oh well… Never mind. Art isn't for everyone." comments:

- ☒   "Was Whistler deterred when his mother: threw up on his canvas for the third time; sent him to bed without his supper; sat there wistfully looking out the covered, closed window, wondering where she had gone wrong; and if moving to Russia, during the cold war, might be a good way to set things right?"
- ☒   "Was Picasso deterred, even in the slightest, when he was ridiculed for using inspiration from a post-non-metaphorical metamorphosised adult flounder that his best friend, Rubik, had happened to catch one afternoon off the coast of Hungary when all he was at the time was just a starving escargot delivery boy?"
- ☒   "Was Michelangelo deterred when David took him aside and quietly told him that size really did matter sometimes? Or when Pope Julius II exclaimed, 'stop laying down on the job,' and, 'a three-year over-run on a one-year commission was wholly unacceptable.' Never mind the, 'What the place-down-there-that-doesn't-exist-yet-for-us-Catholics is your fixation on male nudity all about?[511]'"

Leaving his unfinished-but-with-no-idea-what-comes-next artwork on the table to dry for another time, Donald said goodbye to Sue, signed out on the sign-in sheet and headed back to the common area; artistically musing about another concept[512] to have gotten him riled up in the past… After this effort, he was undoubtedly, going to be labelled an *amateur* artist.

---

[511] Mr II had obviously not read any of Michelangelo's "poetry." He also may not have understood what irony was, even after it had slapped him about the face with an uncooked flounder his mother had stolen for dinner.

[512] Or to be more accurate, "one of the other thousands of concepts…"

Donald felt this was another widely misunderstood word due to its gross misuse and abuse over time and space by misinformed people… And it has had its meaning thoroughly mistakenly changed and adopted by the masses. "The definition of amateur should NOT mean: someone who is untalented or doing something in an incompetent way!" is always his pre-argumentative reply to anyone who spoke out or to him otherwise.

Donald was often heard imploring: "I feel this is a gross bastardisation. The correct meaning of amateur is quite the opposite of what a person using it, in a negative fashion, generally assumes. Amateurs are doing whatever it is they do because they enjoy it and not just because they are being paid to do it."

He usually goes on to explain: "Amateur is not the opposite of professional in terms of quality, is it only opposite in terms of payment. Professionals will perform only as well as their payment might suggest, whereas every amateur will always perform as well as they possibly can because admiration received for their efforts is the only reward they will ever desire."

Getting technical: "The term *amateur* comes from a French derivation of a Latin word meaning *lover*. Amateurs are lovers of what they do. In practice, it means someone who does something because they love it, not because they are being paid to do it."

Progressing to factual examples: "Some famous artists, writers, musicians, scientists etc… were *technically* amateurs, as they didn't earn any money from their efforts. Edgar Allan Poe, Vincent van Gogh, Emily Dickinson, John Keats, Johann Sebastian Bach, Galileo Galilei, Gregor Johann Mendel, Franz Schubert, William Blake and Jeff Buckley. Even Olympic regulations used to call for the best athletes in the world to remain as amateurs to be eligible."

Finishing with his personal opinion: "Feel free to call me an amateur. But remember, EVERY professional started out as an amateur who didn't give up. So, call me an amateur… It is the best compliment you can possibly give."

Arriving back at the common area to a welcome from Sven…

Quality goods. Are they *good* quality or *bad* quality?

…caused Donald to review his previous mental ramblings and to virtually exclaim, "Yes! Exactly!" Donald had just eaten a Sven cookie and liked it. But being more of an *untrovert*,[513] he kept quiet, preferring to not stand out like a non-struggling artist, poet, or writer in a bread line.

------

[513] Donald is most definitely not an extrovert, but neither is he an introvert. This might imply that he enjoys his own company, instead of the reality of, preferring to overtly avoid all people, including himself.

Then something weird happened.[514]

Time did the exact opposite of time standing still.[515]

No more than one instant passed through Donald's brain until he became aware that he didn't know what was going on, what had just happened here, or when for both. Because they both seemed to have happened together.

Donald considered himself well acquainted, even au-fait (sounds like trait and tray), with most of SaRS' customs and idiosyncrasies:
- Knowing to ask for medication: Just before you realise it is too late;
- Being woken up to see if you were fast asleep;
- Mostly unreasonable complaining about the food;
- General recalcitrance when it came to attending group sessions; and
- The belief that "You can fly" if only you try just a little bit harder than anyone else has ever tried before…

But he didn't know what to make of what he could see happening at the moment because he could also see what was happening in the thousands of moments just before what was happening now. It was like he was watching himself, watching his own past, pass right before his other self's eyes.

He had experienced time escaping before. Blank sections in his memory were a frustratingly common occurrence. He knew there were memories he had forgotten, just not what the forgotten memories were.

There had been time gaps before as well. But they had always been before and after food, before and after group, or before and after sleep. Never before had there been such a large amount of missing authentic-time condensed into such a small amount of perceived time.

As far as Donald could figure, otherwise known as guessing… A whole day, 24 hours and most dreadfully, three meals had been missed in the previously mentioned less than one instant passing through his brain.

––––––––––––––

[514] Yeah, like nothing else here has been weird? Do me a favour…

[515] Well, it didn't really, not so much at all, for two reasons:
- Firstly, isn't this what time normally didn't not do all by itself?
- Secondly, even if it didn't not, not do what it normally did, isn't all of this just conjecture and hyperbole?

Donald is fairly sure he understands what the meaning of hyperbole is; and it doesn't mean: a container full of red coloured lollies. (Take your time.)

Donald thrived on food, literally, and was more unwilling to forgo a meal than he was to forgo a chance at being normal… So, the missing of three meals deeply disturbed, angered and hungered him.

Oh, never mind… Do not look back to the past; look forward to the future.

Sven had nicely bookended Donald's anti-time travelling experience.

Grabbing a couple of pieces of cold white toast, which were actually lightly brownish, from the toaster in the TK kitchen for his trip back to the art room, Donald continued down the path of his deliverance journey.

The art room was, generally, much the same as he had left it yesterday, except that neither Picatso nor Sue were there to greet him this time. Donald continued on inside, unperturbed.

Remembering his way around the art room, Donald fully loaded his plastic plate pallet with the maximum allowance of five colours:[516]

- Vantablack;[517]
- Artists' Pigment Purple (for re-touching);
- Melancholic Blue;
- Prussian Blue; and
- Blue-Earl-Grey.

Using this monochromatic array of drab colours, matching his monolithic array of dreary thoughts, Donald started completing his inner *monomage*. And after another few hours, he was nearly finished, then he was mostly finished, and finally, he was finished with being finished and was completely finished.

Standing back to admire his two masterpieces, Donald didn't know what to think. As usual. The images certainly astounded him, partially because they were as unidentical as was possible when using the same variety of colours, brushes and talent. Yet, to an untrained observer, they would look exactly the same. It was like trying to tell the difference between a line drawn from left to right and one drawn from right to left.

The only thing left for Donald to do while he was still in the Beethoven art room was to leave… And so, he did. Leaving his **<air quote>** art **</air quote>** behind to dry.

---

[516] Wikipedia entry… *sigh*

Color (American English) or **colour** (Commonwealth English)

[517] A black blacker than the blackest black previously known. Truly.

At some stage, probably far outside the purview of this book, Donald will return to the BAR to retrieve his two paintings. At which point, there might be an understanding[518] of what the paintings represent to and about him.

Until then, life for Donald within SaRS will...
- Continue on its own merry way accepting only minor guidance;
- Be tentatively trying to get back on track, as much as possible, without any training; and
- Hopefully, be returned to approaching a comfortable abnormal.

...with Donald...
- Enjoying a meal, or many, in the dining room;
- Being left to his own devices to do as he pleases; and
- Be completely unnoticed by anyone and everyone.[519]

The only hiccup to Donald's routine was when his medication time came around, and there was a distinctly not DD nurse type person inside the nook trying to handle both windows by herself at the same time. She was obviously new and hadn't been briefed about the alternating nature of the windows on the weekend. Donald guessed[520] this is why he wasn't missed at medication time last night during his 24-hour time blip.

Approaching the West medication window, also for a change, with some newly-found apprehension mingled in with his normally occurring trepidation, Donald looked in hesitantly and was then suitably rewarded with another one of his own pet annoyances, "Hello there, I am the token weekend nurse, Nurse Wendy Swirl, *and who might you be*?"

Donald has a prepared response to this question, "Who might I be...
- I might be Sir Donald Bradman,   but I'm not out;
- I might be Sir Donald Knotts,   but I'm not;
- Would you believe I might be Don Adams?   I didn't think so."

But what he actually said was, "Hi, I am Donald Halfbrain, most lately from Kangaroo ward, room number 41."

---

[518] Up to 33% chance.

[519] As everyone else (inmate wise) was being fed a weeks-worth of shock and awe leftovers by Mindy in the common-area.

[520] Correctly, for a change.

Then continuing on silently, "Poet, Author and The Hero of this comedic, semi-autobiographical and semi-fantastical but oh-so-very-close-to-reality semi-whimsical yarn...
And don't you forget it...
Missy Swirl!"

Donald then obediently took the medication being offered by Nurse Swirl, commenting further to himself, "and I am an easy, really low maintenance, no trouble at all and patient patient..."

"Ha!" was his own final word.

Outroduction

This is where I have to leave ***Donald Halfbrain***, the quiet, unassuming and intelligent character, who was simply perfect for the narrative of this comedic, semi-autobiographical and semi-fantastical but oh-so-very-close-to-reality semi-whimsical yarn.

He is sitting on the bed he is borrowing at SaRS, with pillows propping him up, recently showered and dressed, ready for contemplation. Reaching over to turn the reading light off, he picks up his paddle on the way back and settles down for a lengthy download of his first week of SaRS activity.

By now, you have realised Donald is exactly where he should be.

In the very long week, Donald has been at SaRS, he has come so far:
- Meeting and being befriended by several characters;
- Understanding himself a little bit better and even
- Participating in some of life's normal activities.

Donald's previously ordinary life has been indelibly, incontrovertibly and incredibly changed. And although he mightn't be a legend quite yet, he is well on his way to thinking it might happen one day, if he is very lucky, now that he has recorded and retold some of his story.

He has become exceptional.
He has become creative.
He has become just a little bit more normal.

The everyday struggles of life now have little handles. He is able to get a better grip and even direct some of the flow of the outside world looking in. He will still struggle with many things, but some of the struggles will now have a little pinprick of light at the end of the tunnel.

He still doesn't really think his life has been going so badly. But now, he at least acknowledges it might have been drifting a little bit wrong when he did think about it.

And so...
We bid farewell to Saint Rita's Sanatorium for the Clinically Mental.

Donald may not have all the answers:
- Is there really a Minotaur's lair?
- Where are the hospital archives?
- What is the solution to the *Clueless!* puzzle?
- Who will Skit be tomorrow?
- Will Houts Marted ever publish his dissertation on Ghosts?
- Will he ever find the perfect cup of coffee?
  (i.e. One with one of everything, including its freedom)

But cruising along at the moment, with a comfortable six DOGoNs showing on his Donald-Oh-Goody-Not meter, Donald has decided to accept one of the suggestions saying he should write a book about his experiences at SaRS.[521]

And so, so...
Donald started writing his book, changing names, places and reality, all to protect the innocent...

Enter the protagonist, the hero,[522] the star... David.

---

[521] Dr Jay (the real one) said, if I ever run out of ideas, I could always use the outpatient inmate sessions as a continued supply of inspiration and/or audience. I don't really know if she was joking or not, but probably not *not*.

If I do have this published one day, and I'm forced to write (right?) another instalment of my alter ego's life, I think a year-long commitment to DBT might be useful; it may even be required.

Hands up all those who think I should continue the saga...
Bueller... Bueller... Bueller...

[522] If you could be convinced to call one of the green exit lights in the movie theatre of life a *Hero*.

Appendix 1:
Read and Sing-Along
(Without the Sing)

Autistic (Inspired by *TNT* - AC/DC)

Watch me scared in the hospital
I have no idea what I am
Feeling... I will lose the battle
And no one else could give a damn

Death to the left of me, solitary to the right
Just you make sure that my sheets continue to be white

Cos I'm Autistic, I'm Asperger's
Autistic... With words like daggers
Autistic... I am HFA
Autistic... With nothing to say

I'm silent, mean, often unseen, a superior man
I'm lonely, antisocial, and you don't understand

I am here now, so teach me how to live
Show me feelings, and teach me how to give
Hide me away from sight
My future is very slight

Cos I'm Autistic, I'm Asperger's
Autistic... With words like daggers
Autistic... I am HFA
Autistic... With nothing to say

David Halpin

Mulligan's Tyres (Inspired by *Mull of Kintyre - Paul McCartney*)

Mulligan's Tyres
The best rolling stock to be found
Blacker than black and rounder than round
Those Mulligan's Tyres

From great behemoth down to the minute
Mulligan's Tyres have the tyres that'll suit
Down among the mud, up over the spires
Everything's for sale… Here at Mulligan's Tyres

Mulligan's Tyres
The best rolling stock to be found
Blacker than black and rounder than round
Those Mulligan's Tyres

Open wheeled race car to humble golf cart
Mulligan's Tyres is the right place to start
Floating on water or driving through fires
You can't go past us… Here at Mulligan's Tyres

Mulligan's Tyres
The best rolling stock to be found
Blacker than black and rounder than round
Those Mulligan's Tyres

Nuts to hold them on and gas to inflate
Mulligan's Tyres, always open 'till late
Everything's in stock, whatever you require
It all can be found… Here at Mulligan's Tyres

Mulligan's Tyres
The best rolling stock to be found
Blacker than black and rounder than round
Those Mulligan's Tyres

Mulligan's Tyres
The best rolling stock to be found
Blacker than black and rounder than round
Those Mulligan's Tyres

Life on Meds? (Inspired by *Life on Mars? - David Bowie*)

Depression's a terrible pain
On resources, it is a drain
When answers are often unknown
Inflicted respond, just a groan

    Psychologists know what to do
    Eliminate some of your blue
    You worry on what you control
    And then SMARTing all of your goals

        The answers don't please anyone
        Your friends still continue to shun
        Community's not there for you
        Denying what you're going through

[Chorus]   Mental?   Hide them away from sight
                Voices?   Don't put them in control
                Depression is body and soul
                When you pity the inflicted
                You take away their self-esteem
                Visions?   Depression takes its toll
                Nothing you can do but console...
                Is there life on meds?

        Medication is not a cure
        Depression is an evil... Pure
        Makes your family pushed away
        There is nothing that they can say

            There is a dwindling in the wards
            Cos many people can't afford
            The money that they're asked to pay
            You must go home; you cannot stay

            These answers don't please anyone
            Your madness continues to run
            The people do not believe you
            Denying what you're going through

            [Chorus]

David Halpin

SJOG (*Inspired by the St. John of God, North Richmond legends*)
St. John of God, peeps, you really saved me
By making sure I was always well-fed
Checking when I was hiding in my room
Or telling me I should have been in bed

You were there at each medication time
And you were willing to take me shopping
While never thinking to try and lose me
Even one of you... He got me to sing!

Always caring and bringing me right back
Trying to arrange my destinations
Urging me often to participate
Alas, there weren't any magic potions

I can't remember any of your names
Indeed, I can't remember anyone
To the lady who was my favourite
Your smile was nearly brilliant as the sun

Cos you got me to try out some painting
You made a point to bid me fond farewell
And even though you always called me Dave
I forgive you; you made it not like Hell

Now, looking back, you all looked after me
And to all of you, sincerely... THANK YOU!
With my lost cause, you did a sterling job
By helping me to fend off feeling blue

To the kitchen staff, to the reception
To all the nurses, to pastoral care
To the bus driver, the maintenance team
To counsellors and psychiatrists, there

To the psychologists and to their boss
To all the doctors, to the fitness crew
To the dietitian and the cleaners
You're all fantastic! Past time that you knew!

Excuse Me Myth? *(No inspiration required)*

Yodel, chant, or whisper tales to anyone who wants to hear
Forgetting all your sadness, try not to give into the fear
Put pencil to your story, for your children, write your memoir
Telling good along with bad, not lamenting your au revoir

Easy in, and hard way out, this is how all your friendships go
Starting out, always with truth, needing to learn to take it slow
Wear a mask upon your face, do not let in a grain of sand
Hiding out behind a veil is how you can come into land

Words excuse a sorry myth, delusional diagnosis
Dreaming without a nightmare, dysfunctional the prognosis
Cock and bull, as stories go, there is nothing here that is new
Call for the Psych Doctor stat, listen for your cow, going moo

He Became Late Too Early *(Inspired by BLT)*

Not knowing the diff'rence, tween a shit and a fart
Or thinking, "It's a Doodle," when really, "It's Art"
Expecting the pain when you are trying to rise
And seeing the hurt you put in some other's eyes

I don't even know
if I'm coming or going
Or the speed and direction
the wind is blowing
Is it right? Is it wrong?
Is it left? Is it right?
Does the sun rise in the morning
and set at night?

What is it that I want
my memory to be?
Or am I to leave nothing
as my legacy?
Can I see my future,
stop reliving the past?
And am I too late
for my memory to last?

The Poet (Inspired by the mirror)

The poet shirks a loathsome rhyme
And neither keeps to metred time
Alliteration and allude
Are almost always aptitude

The poet chooses to be bold
Though stagnant lay the forms of old
It's true; the limerick fits that mould
But no Nantucket will be told

The poet writes his English words
American is too absurd
When colour misses out, the "u"
It's not a word describing hue

The poet tackled meter pre
By switching both the "r" and "e"
And trying to romanticise
Replaced a zed, but not in size

The poet has a funny bone
But will not laugh into a fone
Phonetic is a stupid word
With "ph" where an "f" is heard

The poet uses simile
Like Bunyan uses axe on tree
A metaphor will not be wrote
It's already a bigger boat

The poet's licence gives him reign
To cut a word that is too hein
He changes "f" into an "s"
Look, hey presto, no sucking mess

The poet's finished for today
But he won't go too far away
Until the next instalment comes
Sit right down and twiddle your thumbs

Author Bio

David was born on Valentine's Day, 1968, in Fairfield, NSW, Australia. He grew up or at least grew older in Taree. Educated without much effort on his part... Culminating with a Bachelor of Computer Science from Newcastle University.

He worked as a drone in various Banking and Insurance systems for too many years. Then, escaping the mundane, he went to work in the Australian Defence industry. Finally, he worked in the Immigration and Security world of the Middle East.

During this time: he met various people; got married to one of them; had two very beautiful children; became divorced; and then had several failed relationships. Always making sure everything was done in the *correct* order.

Following his last relationship, too much stress from his last job and a general air of unhappiness, he found himself inside a facility. *One Flew Over the Cuckoo's Nest* is an accurate documentary of these places, and this one was a good one. It was there he took to writing all about himself.

Dredging up his previous attempts at poetry, documenting his downfall and making many errors along the way to recovery, he found writing was to become another avenue for failure... Thus, was born the *Nobody* described in his first book. But he didn't give up...

Then, for his second book, he turned his imagination outward at all of the Numpties of the world. Combining the best aspects of...

- Mother Goose;
- Doctor Seuss; and
- The Brothers Grimm.

...in the concrete mixer of his mind. Applying a modicum of *numptyism*, he produced ~~some~~ many anti-nursery rhymes, anti-songs, anti-lullabies and just lots of anti in general. But still, he didn't give up...

And you may find these... (I suggest you buy one, just to prove him wrong)

Shameless Plugs[523]

The Nobody Saga (7 eBook series):
https://www.amazon.com/gp/product/B08BZTSD2G

Poetry and Random Thoughts from a Depressed Mind
(Autobiography of a Nobody)
https://www.amazon.com.au/gp/product/1795787457

More of the Same
(Continued Saga of a Nobody)
https://www.amazon.com.au/gp/product/B08579P9GH

Some More of the Same but Better
(Episode Three of the Nobody Saga)
https://www.amazon.com.au/gp/product/B08BDDP32Q

Even More of the Same and Even Better
(Chapter 4 of the Nobody Saga)
https://www.amazon.com.au/gp/product/B08CP9DLGB

Yet More of the Same ... Still Better
(Book V of the Nobody Saga)
https://www.amazon.com.au/gp/product/B08GTL737V

Much More of the Same... Gratuitously Better
(Volume (////\ /) of the Nobody Saga)
https://www.amazon.com.au/gp/product/B08MMZ73PX

Bigger and Better ... Sameness
(Lucky #7 of the Nobody Saga)
https://www.amazon.com.au/gp/product/B096TJLG8Q

Numpty-Rhymes, Numpty-Bys and Numpty-Songs
(Poetry from Numpty's Doctor's Brother's Goose)
https://www.amazon.com.au/gp/product/B098H61Q8X

---

[523] Finally, have I mentioned Coffee? One with "one of everything" please.

www.ingramcontent.com/pod-product-compliance
Lightning Source LLC
Chambersburg PA
CBHW071139180726
48291CB00007B/2248